I0724984

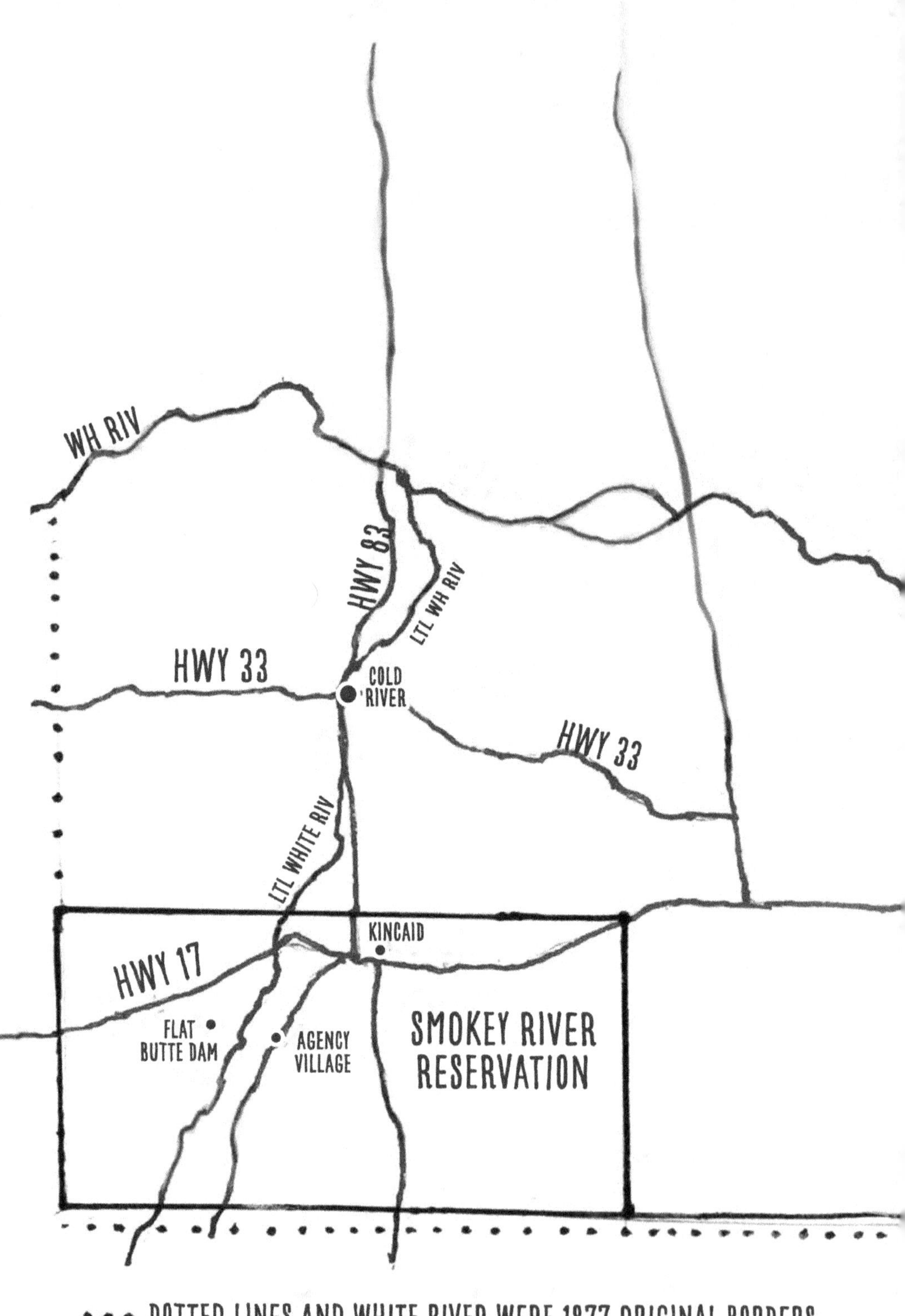

WH RIV
HWY 83
LTL WH RIV
HWY 33
COLD RIVER
HWY 33
LTL WHITE RIV
KINCAID
HWY 17
FLAT BUTTE DAM
AGENCY VILLAGE
SMOKEY RIVER RESERVATION
DOTTED LINES AND WHITE RIVER WERE 1877 ORIGINAL BORDERS
SOLID LINES CURRENT BORDERS

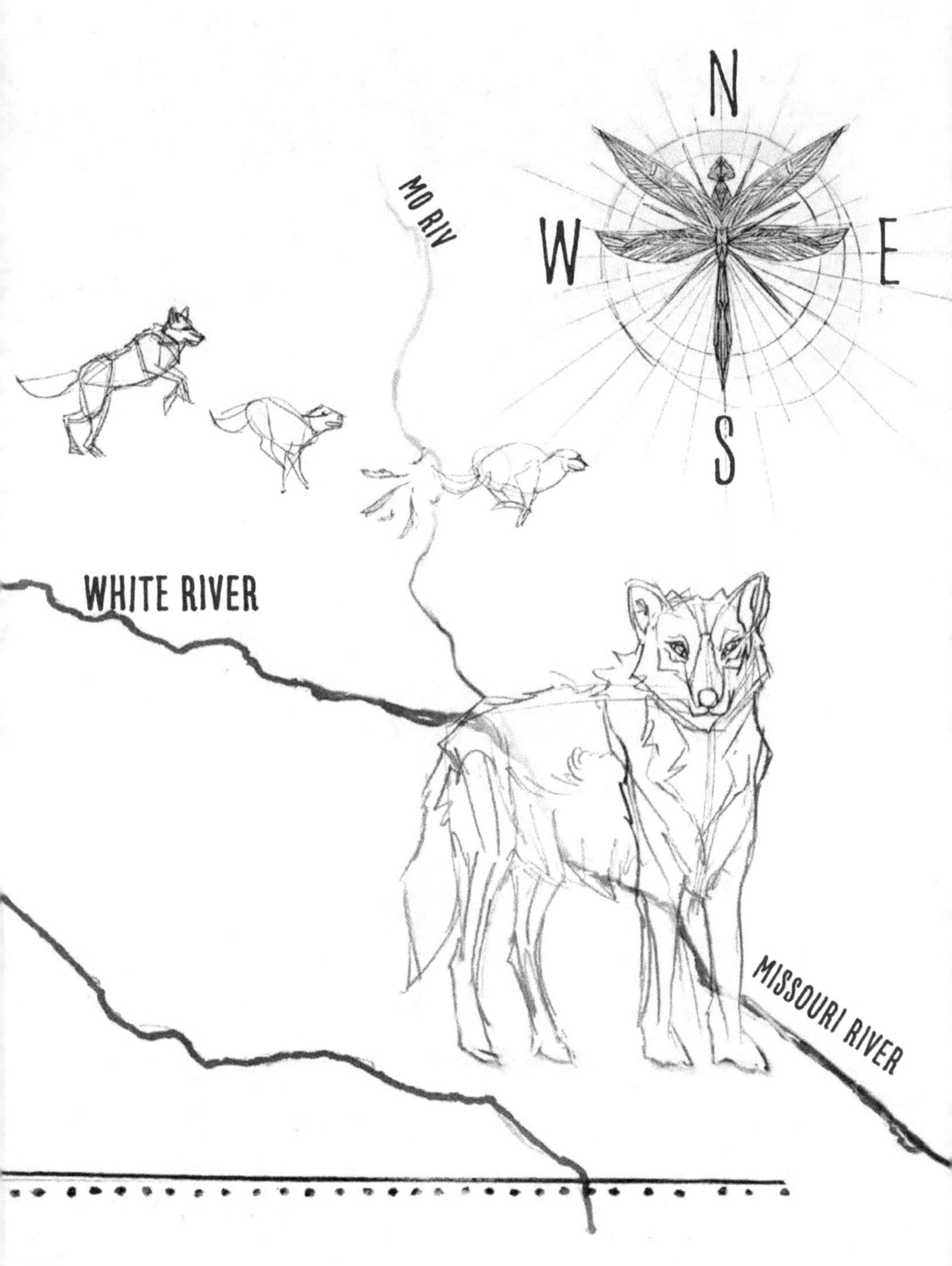

MO RIV
N
W
E
S
WHITE RIVER
MISSOURI RIVER

THE WOLF AND THE CROW

Smokey River Suspense Series

By Joseph M. Marshall III

LUCID
HOUSE
PUBLISHING

Published in Marietta, Georgia, United States of America by Lucid House Publishing, LLC
www.LucidHousePublishing.com.

Cover design: Troy King
Author photos: Kevin Garrett
Interior layout: Jan Sharrow, The Design Lab Atlanta, Inc.
Map Illustration: Beebe Hargrove

This novel is based on the author's heritage and knowledge as one of the leading Native historians and writers in the United States. Lakota is his first language, and he was born into a traditional Lakota household on the Rosebud Reservation in South Dakota. The characters and events in this novel spring from the author's imagination, and any resemblance to a person living or dead is coincidental. Names of some places are fictionalized.

Library of Congress Cataloging-in-Publication Data:
Marshall III, Joseph M., 1946-
The wolf and the crow: Smokey River suspense series/ by Joseph M. Marshall III–1st ed.
Library of Congress Control Number: TK
Print ISBN: 9781950495528
E-book ISBN: 9781950495610
1. Lakota 2. Kidnapping 3. South Dakota 4. Argentina 5. Drug cartel 6. Family drama
7. Indigenous 8. Leukemia 9. Teton Sioux, 10. Cowboys and Indians
FIC030000
FIC059000
FIC022080

Lucid House Publishing books are available for special promotions and bulk purchase discounts. For details, contact info@LucidHousePublishing.com

PROLOGUE

Long ago, all the inhabitants of Turtle Island could speak each other's languages, including the two-legged. Everyone led a more harmonious existence because they understood each other's strengths and weaknesses. Still, that did not mean that life was less contentious.

All the beings of the land, air, and water knew that the wolves were the greatest of all hunters, not because they were the most powerful or the swiftest, but because they never gave up even though they failed more than they succeeded. Other creatures envied them, but one—the crow—did not let his envy cloud his good judgment.

The crow was wise enough to see that, like his own people, the wolves mated for life and were fiercely loyal to their families. But the one virtue the crow admired most about the wolves was their steadfast perseverance. So, the crow found a way to take advantage of the wolves' dogged determination.

The crow listened to the wolves as they spoke to each other with their barks and howls and knew when they were hunting and when they had been successful in bringing down an elk or a deer. The crow would follow the wolves and wait, patiently. After the wolves had eaten their fill, the crow and his family would swoop in to finish what was left. It was a good arrangement for the crow, who was wise, and for the wolf, who was powerful.

ONE

On a mild summer afternoon on the Smokey River Sioux Indian Reservation, in what is now south-central South Dakota, a white woman sat amidst a clump of bristly soapweed on a high plateau just west of the Little White River. An attractive brunette with a pair of expensive sunglasses on top of her head, she was looking into the eyepiece of a powerful spotting scope. By outward appearances, she was probably a shade beyond forty years old. Her attention was fixated on three people who were leisurely dismantling their camp along the banks of the river below her, a quarter of a mile to the east. One was a tall Lakota man, one was a girl about twelve, and the other was a blond, white woman. The woman on the hill knew for a fact they were a family. She knew because she had been stalking them for nearly a week and was overjoyed when the family had gone camping for a day and a night—an unexpected piece of luck that fit with her plans.

She stretched out one leg, reached into the pocket of her cargo pants and pulled out a phone. "Hey," she said, in a low, husky voice when a man answered on the other end. "I think they're breaking camp, and there's only one road out, the one they came in on. Get the pickup and the other things ready by the time they leave."

"Everything is ready," the man on the other end assured her.

"Good. If it all goes according to plan, we'll be leaving in two days." She took one last quick look through the scope, nervous anticipation building in her stomach.

TWO

Nearly fifty miles away, on the southwestern corner of the reservation, the parking lot of the Smokey River Sioux Tribal Council Building was filled to overflowing. Cars and pickup trucks were parked all along streets near Agency Village. The Council Room itself was filled to standing room only and people overflowed into the adjacent hallways.

There was an important reason that so many members of the Smokey River Sioux Tribe, or Sicangu, the third largest group of the Lakota, showed up on this day: the matter of white theft of Lakota lands—a lightning rod issue from the early days of the reservation through the present—was being examined at a field hearing by two United States Senators. The senators were two of several co-sponsors to investigate and rectify that century-old injustice.

A United States Senator, even one from South Dakota, visiting an Indian reservation in the state was a rarity. Two such visitors coming to the same reservation on the same day and sitting at the same table was on the order of seeing a two-headed snake.

At the end of the crowded room, on a raised stage, the two senators sat at a covered table, with aides to either side. The man running the hearing was Senator Dennis Grant of South Dakota, a third-generation farmer and former governor beginning a second term in the Senate. Grant was a hardline conservative Republican. Though he was one of the Sioux Land Restoration Bill's many sponsors, he was not sponsoring the bill because he agreed with its core purpose. Senator Grant had signed on to—as he put it—"Ensure that the rights of the good people of South Dakota are not trampled," unabashedly implying that the state's one hundred thousand plus tribally enrolled Native population was not "good people." His attitude was not new to the Lakota people who had occupied the land area that became South Dakota long before statehood crashed down on them in 1889; and it assured a continuation of the simmering feud over land and its ancillary issues, such as civil and criminal jurisdiction, between whites and the Lakota. Many Lakota people who were aware of his statement regarding the Sioux Land Restoration Bill were surprised he would show himself anywhere near any reservation, much less chair a hearing in a tribal council hall. To them, he was either very brave or very stupid. Of course, the fact that he had two armed deputy U.S. Marshals standing behind him demonstrated he was neither.

Senator Grant looked out over the heads of the two witnesses at the table toward the room full of Lakota people. Though born and raised in the state, the fifty-year-old had never in his life been in the physical presence of so many Lakota people at one time. He hid his nervousness by affecting a scowl.

Also sitting at the table was Senator Charles May, a Democrat from New York and the bill's co-author and strongest supporter. A third-term senator, he was a liberal and champion of tough issues such as abortion rights, gun control, racial equality, climate change, and minority voting rights.

In front, below the senators and facing the stage was another long table for anyone making comments or submitting testimony. Two men sat side by side, neither acknowledging the presence of the other.

The man on the left facing the politicians was tall and broad in the shoulders and dressed in an expensive western cut suit, his white Stetson sitting brim up on the table next to his left elbow. Harold "Hal" Lamar was sixty and a prominent rancher in Redoubt County. With salt and pepper hair and blue eyes, he was the Hollywood image of *cowboy*. Sitting to his right was a man equally broad in the shoulders but a bit taller. William Black Spotted Horse, who might well have stepped out of a late 1800s historic photograph, was waiting patiently after finishing his prepared statement. At sixty-one his hair was still black and hung down his back to his belt in one long braid. His eyes were dark and his nose long, slender, and Romanesque. He had only recently retired from thirty years with the Bureau of Indian Affairs (BIA), the last ten as superintendent of the Smokey River Bureau of Indian Affairs Agency. He was dressed in a dark business suit, without a tie.

"Mr. Black Spotted Horse," Senator May said, nodding, "thank you for your statement. The Senate Select Committee on Indian Affairs would be interested in any documentation you can provide relative to the issue of illegal taking of Indian lands, which is part of the basis for this bill. Can you provide such documentation?"

Senator Grant leaned forward toward the microphone in front of him. "Ah, may I remind my esteemed colleague that, at this point, the so-called 'illegal' taking of Indian lands is only allegation. It remains to be seen if allegation can be proven as fact."

"Thank you, Senator," May replied, maintaining a cool courtesy. "Mr. Black Spotted Horse, is there documentation to suggest or credibly allege that, in some instances, title to Indian lands was obtained by non-Indian individuals outside of the regulations promulgated by the Department of the Interior and the Bureau of Indian Affairs?"

"Yes, Senator, there is such documentation," William affirmed.

"Thank you, and can you provide that documentation?"

"Senator, I no longer personally have access to that documentation since I have recently retired from the Bureau of Indian Affairs. However, your committee can, as you know, subpoena that documentation."

"Of course. One last question, sir. How long has this alleged questionable acquisition of Indian lands by non-Indian individuals been going on, as far as you know?"

"It started shortly after the allotment period began, after 1910, after certain provisions of the Dawes Severalty Act were implemented, one of which enabled white people to homestead land within the exterior boundaries of the reservation."

"Thank you, sir," the senator concluded. He turned to Hal Lamar but said nothing further.

"Mr. Black Spotted Horse," Senator Grant began, affecting his most paternalistic tone, "when did the Smokey River Sioux Tribe establish and implement its own land buy-back program?"

"In the late 1930s."

"I see. And is it true that the program itself, which was administered by the tribe, might have been involved in some questionable land sales and title transfers, starting in the early 1940s?"

William stifled a smile and nodded. "That's true, Senator Grant, but any land sale was to have been overseen by the Bureau of Indian Affairs. The process is known as a 'supervised sale' and it was, and still is, intended to protect the rights of the individual Indian landowners. Yet, I must point out, until the 1970s all the superintendents of the local BIA agencies were non-Indians, as were most of the administrative staff."

William locked eyes with the senator until Grant dropped his, making a point of studying one of the papers on the table in front of him. "Ah, I see. That sounds like a serious accusation to me, Mr. Black Spotted Horse. I assume there is sufficient documentation to support it."

"There is, Senator."

"And how, pray tell, will the land restoration bill that we are here to discuss, settle the issue of how Indian lands were lost?"

"I've read the bill, Senator, and as I see it, the main thrust of it is to enable us to re-acquire or buy back any lands that were sold to or otherwise acquired by non-Indians, from 1910 forward, if and when such land comes up for sale. I saw no stipulation or language anywhere in the bill, as it is written, that such land had to have been acquired illegally."

Senator Grant nodded and attempted a flanking maneuver, turning to William's seatmate "Mr. Lamar, is there anything you would like to say in closing?"

Hal lifted his hands briefly. "Sir," he said, "my main concern personally, and as a member of the Northern Plains Cattlemen's Association, is that the issue of questionable land acquisition was ever included in the language of this bill. There is an implication that I resent. I can assure you, Senator, that members of our association who bought Indian lands, and that includes previous generations, did so quite legally."

William resisted the urge to glance sideways at the man next to him. He had seen transaction reports dating back to the 1940s that clearly indicated that Hal's grandfather, Alfred James Lamar, had paid 11 cents an acre for 640 acres. He bought four separate quarters of land (160 acres each) through a series of sales for a grand total of $70.40. In each case, the white

BIA Indian Agent at the time approved the sales over the objections of the Lakota landowners. Today that land was worth $360 an acre, which means that the four quarters purchased have a current value of $362,000.00.

William had seen those documents, and too many others like it, for the first time 13 years ago, a month after his only child, Jarod, had married Jennifer Lamar, Harold Lamar's only child. A year later, their daughter Annie Erica Black Spotted Horse, named for Jarod's paternal grandmother Annie and Jennifer's maternal grandmother Erica, had been born. Frequently during those thirteen years William wrestled with a dilemma: did Hal Lamar know about his grandfather's probable illegal—and certainly unethical—land purchases?

William had never broached the subject to any of his family, much less his son and daughter-in-law. Furthermore, BIA and tribal officials were uncertain as to how to proceed with what was at the very least evidence of mismanagement by BIA officials 70 to 80 years ago. Now that he was no longer the Superintendent at the Smokey River Agency, he had no role in the decision to take legal action. But that didn't prevent him from knowing what he knew, how utterly corrupt or inept the early BIA agency was. And if the tribe or the BIA took any action to rectify the illegal land acquisitions, William knew it might well inflame the racial divide on the reservations.

"I share your sentiment, Mr. Lamar," Grant replied. The senator paused, deciding to say nothing further, owing mainly to the cold stares from the nearly one hundred pairs of eyes focused on him. He turned to his colleague, "Senator, unless you wish to recall any witnesses, I believe we can conclude this hearing."

Senator May looked down at the two men at the witness table. "I have just one final question for these two gentlemen. Do either of you plan to be in Washington, D.C., for the final hearing on this bill? I believe it is scheduled for the end of July."

"Yes, Senator," Hal said. "I will be testifying on behalf of the ranchers' association."

William nodded politely. "I will be there," he stated.

"Thank you, gentlemen, for your statements here today and we look forward to seeing you in two months."

Of the over one hundred or so people in the tribal council chambers and hallways, just over a dozen were not Lakota. Most of that number were either tribal or BIA employees, and of course the two senators and their aides, and Hal Lamar. The rancher quickly approached the senators for handshakes and a brief word, then was quick to leave the building. Though he had been to Agency Village where the Smokey River Sioux Tribal and BIA administrative offices were located several times, he had never been inside the tribe's office building. William watched his son's father-in-law exit out the side door to the parking lot with a mix of emotions. A hand touched his arm and drew his attention back to the moment.

Dr. Clayton Lone Hawk, the new President of the Smokey River Sioux Tribe, extended a hand. "I liked your statement a lot," he said to William.

William shook his friend's hand. "Thanks, Clay. This legislation's been a long time coming. I sure hope it makes it out of committee this time."

"Me, too. Thanks for bringing me up to speed on it." Lone Hawk had been the first witness of the day, presenting the tribe's official position regarding the bill. "I'm surprised Dennis Grant actually came," he admitted.

William nodded toward two men in business suits who were standing behind the senator on the stage. "Yeah, but he brought U.S. Marshals with him."

Lone Hawk chuckled. "Stop by when you have time. By the way, I hear you're into Spanish Barbs."

"Yeah, I am. I've always liked them. As a matter of fact, Marie and I are heading for the Black Hills tomorrow to look at two mares. I already have a stud."

"Sounds like fun; let me know how it goes."

"I will. How's it going for you so far, after a month in office?"

Lone Hawk smiled. "It's about what I expected. I keep thinking of what the father of a friend of mine said: 'There's nothing wrong with running; the trouble starts if you win.'"

William grinned. "Well, if you decide to run after you finish out this term, I'll help you all I can."

"I appreciate that. See you later. I'm going to see if I can't reclaim my office."

With that Lone Hawk was gone, but just as quickly another familiar face appeared.

Julie Sacroix, a tall, slender Lakota woman with sparkling eyes, and the deputy realty officer from the BIA, held a letter in her hand. "Hey, good afternoon, boss."

"You mean ex-boss, right?" William said good-naturedly, shaking her hand.

"Of course, but old habits are hard to break, and a lot of us sure miss seeing you around." She held up the letter. "I have some good news for you."

"Does that mean I have pasture for all the horses I don't have yet?"

"It sure does. Congratulations, an entire section of good pastureland. I'm sure the current leaser won't be pleased, but preference for Indian lessors works. By the way, he sure didn't give you the time of day, did he? Even though he sat right next to you. I was surprised when he made that comment about all the legal land purchases. Either he doesn't know what his grandfather did, or he doesn't care."

William shook his head. "I'm hoping he doesn't know."

Sacroix shrugged. "Anyway, good to see you. Tell Marie I said 'hello.'"

After Sacroix was gone, William stared at the letter in his hand without opening it. Six hundred and forty acres, much of them prime bottomland. He could almost see Spanish Barb colts playfully galloping through tall grass. For certain, he could hear the expletives when Hal Lamar learned he had just lost the lease on those acres.

THREE

As it turned out, Hal Lamar expressed his opinion about losing the lease on the 640 acres of prime grazing land later that very afternoon when he saw William Black Spotted Horse's half-ton Chevy pickup in front of Dora's Café on Main Street in Cold River. His copy of the BIA lease office's letter in hand, he pushed through the front door, startling nearly a dozen patrons, and stomped to the rear where William sat in a booth with his wife Marie. Hal had changed from the expensive suit to his usual faded denim jeans and shirt.

William had seen Hal the second the front door had flown open, immediately noticing the angry snarl on the rancher's face. He figured it would be best to meet the man standing, so he stood to face him.

"Good afternoon, Hal. Something on your mind?"

"Goddamn right! You stole my land, you son-of-a-bitch!" he growled, waving the letter under William's chin.

William clasped his left hand over his right, ready to ward off any blow that might come. He noticed that the other diners, all white, were staring warily at the brewing confrontation. Marie was getting over her initial shock and sat staring hard at her son's father-in-law.

"If you're referring to the section of pastureland I'll be leasing, I didn't see your name on the title deed to that acreage," he said calmly, but loud enough for everyone in the café to hear. "That land is owned by the tribe. Just because you've leased it for several years does not make it your property."

"You know damn well what I mean, William. My cattle grazing on it now need it more than the goddamn horses you don't have! You can't do this to me! It isn't fair, you thief!" Hal's face was red, his eyes nearly bulging from their sockets.

William looked into the angry eyes, wondering how this Indian-hating rancher could be the father of his daughter-in-law, a young woman who didn't have a mean or prejudiced bone in her body. "What are you really pissed about, Hal? That you're now going to have to lease non-Indian land and actually pay a fair-market lease? Sixty dollars an acre as opposed to the sixteen dollars per acre you were paying the tribe?"

Hal continued to glare, taking a step closer. "Listen, chief, I'm going to appeal this one-sided deal. I'll get that land back!"

"You're welcome to try, but Indian preference has never been overturned on appeal. Indian people have first consideration, by law, when leasing Indian land. Imagine that."

The veins on his neck were bulging as Hal continued to glare up at the slightly taller William. He crumpled up the letter and tossed it. The paper bounced off William's chest then fell to the floor. Hal turned and then stopped, squaring up to face William once again.

"This isn't over, chief!" he hissed, turning and stomping across the café and out the front door, nearly tearing the screen door off its hinges.

William sighed and slid back into the booth.

"Well," Marie said, eyebrows raised. "That was interesting."

"If I never set eyes on that man again, it would be too soon," William said under his breath.

"You know that's not possible," Marie reminded him.

Dora Caruthers came and refilled their coffee cups. "That's the most excitement I've had here in years. Just for that, dessert is on me. Amy's outdone herself with the apple pie if you're interested."

"That sounds lovely," Marie said.

"I'll have a slice, too," William agreed.

Marie Black Spotted Horse looked across the table at her husband. They met in high school and after graduation he enlisted in the U.S. Army, ending up in the 173rd Airborne. After a year in Vietnam, William stayed in six more years, becoming—among other things—a certified hand-to-hand combat instructor. He was discharged at the age of 25 with the rank of staff sergeant. With 14 ribbons above his left breast pocket, among them a combat infantry badge, a purple heart with cluster, and a bronze star with V device. If Hal Lamar had thrown a punch, Marie was confident he wouldn't have won the fight.

"I forgot to tell you," William said to her. "Julie Sacroix said to tell you hello. I saw her after the hearing."

"Oh, how nice," she replied. "You think the regional office will take your recommendation and appoint her assistant superintendent of the Smokey River Agency?"

"I sure hope so," he said. "She's more than qualified."

Dora returned with their dessert and a bonus. "I've decided that little escapade should have a bright side. So, dinner and dessert are on me."

William chuckled. "That's not – ."

The café's owner waved aside his protest. "I'm serious. It's on me. Despicable behavior shouldn't be rewarded but enduring it gracefully should."

"Thanks, Dora."

The woman waved a hand and walked away to attend to her other customers. Marie turned to her husband. "So, what do you think will come of this, ah, 'little escapade,' as Dora put it?"

"It's over," he said, "as far as I'm concerned. If he does file an appeal, it'll be denied. It's not losing the acreage he's angry about, it's just losing, period. At the most, he'll have to find pasture for 30 head, but that's not a lot. So, he might cry hardship to the leasing board, but it isn't adequate grounds."

"Does he actually think he has exclusive rights to that land?" Marie wondered.

"His father leased that land before he did, so maybe he does think that way. I do know Hal is every bit like his father was. Same attitudes toward Indians. Did I ever tell you what Anson Lamar did when Hal was a sophomore in high school?"

"I don't think so."

"Well, I had a bad cut from a rusty barbed wire fence, and I ended up in the IHS hospital, blood poisoning. I shared a room with Elijah White Bear, who had been run over by Hal Lamar, on the highway just a block from here. It was the talk of the town. Broke both legs, a couple of ribs, he was hurt badly and had been in the hospital before I got there."

"The second night I was there," William continued, "Anson Lamar walked in, although it was past visiting hours. He went over to Elijah's bed and was talking to him. I couldn't hear because he was talking low. He left after about ten minutes. The next afternoon Elijah showed me the $500 in cash Anson had given him, not to press charges against Hal."

"Oh, my," Marie was incredulous. "So did Elijah ever press charges?"

William shook his head. "No. Five hundred dollars was a lot of money in 1962, and who knows what else Anson promised, or threatened."

"My, my! Is that why Elijah walks with that limp?"

"Yeah, since he was nineteen."

Marie continued to shake her head. "I'm sure Jennifer, and maybe Virginia, don't know about that."

"I'm guessing they don't."

"Right. I'm wondering about how Jarod and Jennifer will react to the little episode that just transpired. I'm sure Hal will have something to say to Jennifer."

"I don't know, but I think it'll be okay. It'll blow over."

"Speaking of Jarod and Jennifer, I think they will be home this evening," she told him. "They were only going to camp the one night, unless Annie talks them into staying another night."

"Which could very well happen," William pointed out. "That is one precocious and strong-willed little girl."

Marie glanced at her watch. "I did get a text a couple of hours ago. They were packing up then. I invited them to stop by."

After finishing their dessert, they left the café and drove north out of Cold River. Eight miles later they turned off a gravel road onto a plateau above the Smokey River. At the end of a narrow trail, they turned into a grove of trees, in the middle of which stood a one-story log house. Nearly 30 yards to the east was the barn with four stalls and a hayloft. In the adjacent paddock was a dark gray roan horse, a five-year-old Spanish Barb stallion with the registered name of Black Mountain Lancer. William simply called him Lance. He had an extraordinarily calm disposition for a stallion in addition to being nimble and intelligent. All were traits that William hoped he would pass on to the colts and fillies he would sire. Furthermore, Lance was a superbly trained reining horse.

Marie, whose maiden name was Mareschault, was a few years from retirement. For the past 15 years she had taught in the history department at Smokey River University, one of the first two Native-controlled reservation colleges anywhere in the country. For two of those years, she had also been the associate academic dean for the university.

Jarod had followed in his mother's footsteps, getting his master's degree in communications technology from the School of Mines after a bachelor's from SRU. He was, according to William, the only computer geek William liked. He taught computer science at the university.

William hurried inside to change out of his suit. He had picked Marie up from her office after the field hearing and before stopping for supper at Dora's Café. He contemplated a quick ride on Lance before sundown but put the idea aside. The field hearings stuck in his craw, owing to Senator Grant's attitude. But mostly because the issues raised in the hearing reminded him of what he already knew. He had seen documents that at least strongly suggested that Lakota lands had been illegally and unethically sold and purchased. He hadn't thought about them for months. Nonetheless they represented an ugly chapter in the reservation's history. William knew much about that tough history because of his tenure as superintendent of the Smokey River Agency but was enough of a realist to know that history cannot be changed. It was a sad fact that some of the white people in charge of the early agency cared not a whit for the rules, and consequently Lakota lands had illegally ended up in the hands of white homesteaders, the first generation of farmers and ranchers to come to the reservation. Not all of them had stayed and not all of them had been dishonest, but there were those who put their names illegally on the deeds to thousands and thousands of acres of Lakota land, often for less than five cents on the dollar. That practice had continued until the 1950s.

Just about every white farmer or rancher who operated on the reservation, on any of the reservations in the state for that matter, had at some point leased Lakota land for pasture or farmland. Leases paid to individual Lakota landowners were often below the going lease rates for non-Indian land. Because he grew up on the reservation, William knew which farmers and ranchers had done shady deals to buy Lakota land for far less than fair market value, shady deals sanctioned by corrupt BIA officials. But the ugliest reality was that they had gotten away with it.

William took a quick shower, washing away the vestiges of an unsettling day. Dressed in blue jeans, a sweatshirt, and sneakers he joined Marie in the kitchen. The expression on her face was between worry and puzzlement.

"What's going on?" he asked.

She shrugged. "Oh, I don't know, probably nothing, but I called and texted Jarod and Jennifer's cell phones, and still haven't gotten any kind of reply."

"Well," he suggested, "sometimes the coverage is spotty along the river. Isn't that where they went camping?"

"Yeah," Marie replied. "They're kind of off the beaten path, literally. Jarod found information on an old village site, and he wanted to check it out. And you're right, cell phone coverage may be a bit sketchy there. But the funny thing is, I did get a text from Jenny earlier."

William shrugged. "I'm sure we'll be hearing from them soon."

FOUR

The objects of Marie Black Spotted Horse's concern were driving on a back road in northeast Redoubt County in an area with only a few remote ranches. Jennifer Lamar Black Spotted Horse was 32, trim and athletic, a beautiful blue-eyed blond. Her long hair was in a ponytail this day as she drove down a gravel road with her family. In the passenger seat was Jarod Black Spotted Horse, two years older than his wife, six feet two inches, tall and wiry, nearly an exact copy of his father, except for his hair, which was short and neatly trimmed due to his status as a captain in the Army National Guard. He was the executive officer for a transportation company based just east of the reservation. As a newly minted second lieutenant he had done a tour in Afghanistan.

"You want to go camping again? Is that what you said?" Jennifer asked her daughter in the backseat.

"Yeah, Mom. It's fun." Annie was an exact cross between her parents, not as dark as her father and not as light as her mother. Auburn hair and hazel eyes completed the unique blend of characteristics, along with her father's high cheekbones and her mother's eyebrows.

From a cord around her neck hung an elaborately quilled medallion. Made from dyed and plaited porcupine quills, it depicted a dragonfly, a symbol of endurance and adaptation for the Lakota. The medallion was a birthday gift from both of her grandmothers.

"We have the rest of the summer to do more camping, hon. Your dad has summer camp, remember, with the National Guard? So, we should look at the calendar and pick a time after that."

"Yeah, I know. He's got to go play soldier. Right, Dad?"

"That's right. And maybe the next time we camp we can pitch our *tipi*."

Annie brightened at that idea. "That would be so cool!"

"Hey," Jennifer called out. "What's going on here?" She pointed to a vehicle on their side of the road, pulled off on the narrow shoulder with its hood up.

"It's an old pickup truck," Jarod said. "Someone might need help. Pull over."

Jennifer slowed the SUV and pulled up behind the truck. "Stay in the car," she said to Annie. "Your dad and I will see what's going on here. Looks like someone's stalled."

The couple stepped down from the car and walked to the front of the truck. Bent over and looking down into the old truck's engine compartment was an elderly gray-haired woman.

"Something go wrong?" Jarod asked. He glanced briefly at her face but didn't recognize her. He noticed that the license plate was from one of the northern counties in the state.

The woman straightened up slowly. "Yeah, something did," the woman said, pointing at the bottom of the engine. "It sputtered and stopped, and I haven't been able to start it. I don't know a thing about cars. I'm just looking because it seemed like the thing to do."

Jarod chuckled.

"But I did notice a bit of smoke from down there," the woman said, pointing down.

Jarod leaned in. "Okay, let's take a look."

Jennifer looked down as well as the woman pulled out a wicked looking object, known in police circles as a *sap*, from the side pocket of her cargo pants. About a foot long, shaped like an elongated teardrop, and made of hard black leather, at its thickest end it was loaded with lead balls.

In a split second she swung and hit Jarod behind the right ear. He immediately slumped down. A second and harder blow jellied his legs and he fell next to the truck's front tire.

Before Jennifer could comprehend what had happened, the woman pulled a can of mace from another pocket and sprayed it at her. Instinctively Jennifer reached up to wipe the stinging wetness from her eyes, unable to see. In that split second the woman bashed the sap against the Jennifer's left temple. She fell in a heap beneath the trunk's front bumper. Neither she nor Jarod had the opportunity to scream or yell.

The woman looked down, making sure both of her victims were unconscious before pulling off the gray wig, then walked toward the SUV and the girl sitting in the back seat.

When Jennifer awoke, her head throbbing and eyes stinging, it was nighttime. She pulled herself to a sitting position, confused and disoriented as she spat out the dirt in her mouth. Grabbing the hem of her t-shirt, she dabbed at her eyes, trying to wipe away the stinging and blurriness. The old truck was gone.

Seeing Jarod's inert form a few feet away, she scrambled to him. Alarmed by the blood caked behind his right ear, she cradled his head gently, kneeling over him.

"Honey! Oh, honey, please, wake up!"

A slight moan encouraged her.

Jennifer wiped the dirt off his face. "Jarod! Jarod, please, wake up!"

An even more horrifying reality assaulted her when she saw their SUV.

"Annie!" she cried out. Gently lowering Jarod's head, she stumbled to the car. The rear passenger window had been shattered, the door was open, all the tires had been slashed—and the rear seat was empty.

Annie was gone.

Hoping against hope, Jennifer looked inside, then circled the outside of the car on still rubbery legs.

Annie was gone.

Out of the corner of her eye she saw a bit of movement from Jarod and ran to him.

"Honey, oh, honey, please wake up! Annie's gone!"

"My head hurts," he mumbled, his eyes blinking as he slowly came to consciousness. "What the hell happened?" He reached up to grab his head.

"That—that woman attacked us," Jennifer told him, cradling his head. "She's gone, and she took Annie!"

Jarod squinted up at Jennifer and tried to sit up, struggling with his balance.

"What did you say?"

"Annie's gone! Annie's gone!"

FIVE

Nearly an hour later, Jarod and Jennifer stumbled up the porch steps of an old farmhouse and knocked on the front door. Lights were on inside and a sedan was parked in the driveway.

A tall brunette woman opened the door and immediately reacted to the disheveled and obviously injured couple.

"Oh, my!" she said. "What happened?"

"Our daughter was taken," Jennifer told her. "My husband and I were attacked. Can we use your phone?"

"Of course, of course." After they stepped inside, she guided them to a sofa in the living room and grabbed a cell phone from a nearby table and handed it to Jennifer. "While you're doing that, let me take a look at you."

"Thank you," Jarod said. "Thanks for helping. I'm Jarod Black Spotted Horse, and this is my wife, Jennifer."

The woman looked closely at the bloody cut behind his ear. "I'm Eunice Stearns," she said. "I've got a first aid kit. I'll be right back."

An hour later the living room was full of people. An emergency medical technician carefully finished the basic first aid Eunice Stearns had started. "You're going to need stitches," she told Jarod.

Behind the EMT was Sheriff Mel Triplett and hovering around the couple were Hal and Virginia Lamar and William and Marie Black Spotted Horse. An ambulance was waiting outside in the driveway.

Hal Lamar was incredulous as he listened to Jennifer recount the incident. "Wait," he said, "are you saying that a woman did this to both of you and took Annie?"

Jennifer nodded. "Dad, please, I told you. She looked like she was having trouble with her truck."

The EMT looked into Jarod's eyes. "I think you should go to the IHS Emergency Room. Have a doc take a look at you. You have a cut and two really nasty bruises, not to mention that bump that seems to be growing. We can take you in the ambulance."

Jarod shook his head. "No, we have to go look for Annie!"

Sheriff Triplett stepped up. "I think you should take Ellie's advice. Go to the hospital. I've got men combing the area around your car. We'll work through the night." Triplett looked toward William and Marie. "Seriously, folks, we're doing all we can right now. Take him to see the doctor. Those injuries aren't small things."

Marie agreed. "I'll ride in the ambulance with you, Son, and there'll be no argument."

She looked at Jennifer. "And I think you should come along as well, to see a doctor."

Virginia Lamar spoke up. "In that case I'm riding with you all in the ambulance, if you don't mind."

Hal had been staring at Jarod, a hint of anger in his eyes. "I'll stay here with the sheriff," he said to Virginia. "We've got a lot of ground to cover in the dark."

Marie looked at William, who nodded. "I'll see you later, more likely sometime in the morning."

Twenty minutes later the ambulance had left and the last two people at the farmhouse were Sheriff Triplett and William Black Spotted Horse. William spoke to Eunice Stearns.

"Thank you for helping my son and daughter-in-law," he said, shaking her hand.

Triplett echoed the sentiment. "We appreciate your help," he told her. "Did you happen to notice any traffic on the road out there?"

The woman shook her head. "I got back from Pierre around sundown," she said. "I was the only car coming my direction. I really didn't notice anything else once I was in the house."

"Okay. Have you noticed an old pickup truck around?"

"A few, I guess."

"Yeah," Triplett admitted. "Lots of folks have old trucks. I thought this place was boarded up, years ago. Are you related to Josh Stearns? I think he used to own the place."

She smiled and nodded. "Yes, he was my grandpa. I've been living out of state, but I'm thinking of moving back here after I retire. So, I'm trying to get the place back up and running, the house at least."

A minute later she watched the men climb into their respective vehicles and drive away, both turning west out of her driveway. She waited until the taillights were out of sight.

She turned and walked across the front room into a corner bedroom. From the drawer of an old nightstand, she took out a cell phone and an elaborately decorated medallion made from dyed porcupine quills. She had seen many like it when she was a girl. Her dad had even bought a few from the local Indians.

Accessing the phone's camera function, she took several close-ups of the medallion. Then she walked back through the front room to the small kitchen in the corner of the house. Opening a door next to the refrigerator she stepped carefully down narrow wooden steps with no railing.

The basement was dark except for the light showing from the bottom of a closed door in the far corner. Crossing to it, she slid open the heavy gravity latch and stepped inside. The room was brightly painted and furnished with a bed, a dresser, a nightstand, and a stuffed chair in the corner. It was a girl's room. Atop the dresser, which was against the wall opposite the bed, was a flat screen TV connected to a DVD player.

Sitting where she had left her, on top of the bed with her back against the wall, was Annie Black Spotted Horse. Her hands and feet were tied, and a strip of gray duct tape covered her mouth.

Stearns sat at the end of the bed and held up the medallion.

"Now, since you cooperated and were quiet, I'll give you back your medallion."

Annie stared at the woman, frightened, but with a spark of defiance as well.

The woman untied the cords around Annie's ankles and wrists, and then gently peeled off the tape.

"I'm going upstairs and fix us some dinner," she said. "You have a choice. I can bring you a plate or you can join me upstairs at the table. Which will it be?"

Annie's face was a mask, but her lips trembled. "Upstairs," she said, barely above a whisper.

"Wonderful!" The woman stood and pointed to a composting camping toilet in the far corner. "Remember, if you feel the need to use the restroom, that is there for you." She pointed to a pitcher of water and a large ceramic bowl on the small table next to the dresser. "Water, soap, and towels."

With a motherly smile, she turned and stepped out the door. Annie heard the gravity latch fall into place. She sat staring at the door as a tear slid down her face.

By the time Jarod had been admitted and assigned a room at the IHS hospital it was 4 a.m., and Marie had asked a co-worker to drive her and Virginia Lamar back to Cold River. Jarod was not pleased at being admitted, but according to the doctor he needed to refrain from strenuous physical exertion and needed further tests. Jennifer decided to stay with her husband.

Marie's co-worker took them to her and William's house along the river, since it was closer to the abduction site and Hal and William were still there, according to William's last text message. They took Marie's car there, riding in silence for a few minutes. It was the first time the two women had been alone since the ambulance ride, and they had never—in their children's twelve-year marriage—had a prolonged conversation. At least nothing more than obligatory exchanges in Jarod and Jennifer's presence. Neither had heard anything further from their husbands.

"I don't understand why this happened," Virginia said, finally breaking the ice.

"It's beyond comprehension," Marie responded. "I'm still having a hard time believing it. But the bruises on Jenny's face and Jarod's skull fracture are real enough. And where is our precious granddaughter?"

"I hope the sheriff, or someone, knows something by now," Virginia said, distraught.

Marie concentrated on the road in the early morning light. "I'm sure they've been searching the area," she said.

"Who would do such a thing?" Virginia blurted out.

""I can't imagine who would be so cruel," Marie replied as she clutched the steering wheel tightly.

Sometime after sunrise the second group of searchers, this time on horseback, rode out from the spot of the abduction. Jarod and Jennifer's SUV was as they had left it—its tires flat and the rear passenger door open. Camping gear was still in the back cargo compartment.

Sheriff Triplett took a delivery of hot coffee and shared it with Hal and William.

"I'm thinking I'll run home and get one of my horses," Hal said. "I can't stand sitting around and doing nothing."

Triplett shrugged. "Well, far be it from me to tell you what to do, Hal. But I think we got this covered. Most of those riders I sent out are trained in search and rescue."

Hal paced along the narrow shoulder of the dirt road. "Okay, okay. But what are they looking for?"

"Any kind of sign," Triplett said patiently. "But my guess is that woman, if it was a woman, didn't go cross country. According to Jenny, it was around six when they stopped here. We got the call around 9:30 and we were out here after 10. That's four hours more or less. Even at 30 miles an hour that's 120 miles. My guess is that pickup truck is long gone."

"I was thinking the same thing," William admitted. "Whoever it is, she's long gone."

Hal spun on his heel and stepped in front of them. "Then why are we wasting time looking? Maybe we should be doing something else!"

"To eliminate one possibility," Triplett replied. "In the meantime, there's a technician from the state on his way to get fingerprints off the car. They've offered investigators as well. But there is one question we need to consider."

"Why?" William said. "Why would someone take Annie?"

"The usual motive is money," Triplett responded.

"So, what are you saying, Mel?" Hal said irritably.

"At this point, we can only make that assumption and do what makes sense in these situations. However, I wouldn't be surprised if you get a call, Hal."

"Me? Why me?"

"Money, Hal," William said. "You're the biggest rancher in Redoubt County."

Hal moved and stopped in front of William. "On the other hand, you can't say that in your illustrious 30 years in government service, you didn't make enemies here and there. How do we know this isn't someone taking revenge?"

"We don't!" Triplett raised his voice. "The point is, I wouldn't be surprised if there is a call to make a demand or ask for ransom."

The sound of Marie's car approaching diverted their attention momentarily. Marie and Virginia wore grim expressions as they stepped down and approached the tight group of men.

"Where's your son?" Hal turned an angry glare at William. "Why isn't he here? He couldn't protect his family and now he's slacking off? That's damn cowardly!"

William's sudden move took both Hal and the sheriff totally by surprise. First the dull *thud* of his clenched fist hitting Hal's jawbone, then Hal flopping on his back into the grass. Seconds later Hal scrambled to his feet, only to be met by Triplett who stepped in between the two men.

"Boys," he said evenly. "There'll be none of that! If you want to push it, either of you, I've got jail cells waiting for you."

Hal's vitriol went down a notch, tempered by surprise at the swiftness of William's response. He stared past Triplett at William, though his expression was mostly confusion.

Virginia stepped in front of her husband. "I'm disappointed in you, Hal. You want to know where Jarod is? He's been admitted to the hospital because he's got a hairline crack in his skull. That's why he's not here!"

Hal wilted under his wife's withering stare, and nodded slowly, lowering his gaze. "Okay, okay," he said, in a low voice. He lifted his hands and turned away.

"Hal! Hal!" Virginia pulled on his sleeve. "Aren't you going to apologize?"

Hal stopped but didn't turn around. "Not today," he said. "Not today." The rancher walked away to his truck and climbed in.

Virginia turned toward William.

"Virginia, I shouldn't have done that."

She shook her head, exasperated, and reached up to wipe away a tear. "I don't understand what's going on here, William. What are we going to do?"

"The sheriff and his people are doing their jobs," he pointed out. "All we can do is wait and pray for our little girl."

Marie stepped forward and touched Virginia's arm. "Why don't you take your husband home?" she said. "Rest, if you can. You were up all night with us."

"Yes, I suppose you're right." She turned to the sheriff. "You will call us if you hear anything?"

"Of course, Virginia. I will."

The sheriff caught William's attention. "You might as well go with them," he suggested. "We're doing what we can here. If we don't find anything, we'll get together, maybe later tonight or tomorrow, and figure out what our next move is. In the meantime, do me a favor and come up with a list of people you think might even remotely have a grudge against you."

William nodded and watched as Hal made a U-turn in the pasture and drove off to the west.

"Yeah," he said. "I'll do that. Mel, do you have any thoughts or hunches about this? Anything at all?"

The sheriff somberly shook his head. "No, sure wish I did. But I don't think it was a random thing, you know? Whoever did it planned it out. He, or she or they, knew your boy and his family would be using this remote road, probably even knew they had gone camping. They faked a stalled pickup truck. And from what your son and daughter-in-law said, the attack was fast and hard. Whoever it was knew what they were doing."

"So, a phone call or some kind of contact is not out of the question?"

Triplett shook his head. "I'd bank on it, Will."

"I'd rather not," said William. "I'm going to see about my son."

He stopped at Marie's car and leaned down. "I'll follow you," he told her.

The expression in his wife's eyes alarmed him. Marie was a strong woman, the brave heart of his family. But she was hurting. Her loved ones were under attack, and she hadn't seen it coming.

"Okay," she said, summoning a smile.

SIX

The next day, Eunice Stearns drove a late model mini-motorhome out of the old barn on the farmstead, then stopped as a dour-faced man in his late thirties put a false wall back into place at one end of the barn, concealing an old pickup truck.

Deke Smith painstakingly swept away all the tire tracks inside the barn with an old broom, then closed and locked the barn's double doors, taking pains to wipe the metal latch clean of fingerprints. He finished his task with the broom outside, erasing the tracks leading to and from the barn.

Not quite half an hour later, Eunice Stearns boarded the motorhome with Annie Black Spotted Horse in tow. Deke Smith followed with luggage in hand. After Stearns drove the motorhome onto the road, Deke Smith turned on a garden hose and sprayed the loose ground in the driveway until he obscured all the tire tracks. Carefully coiling the hose, he placed it near the porch. Then, staying on the grass, he hurried to the motorhome and got in. A sedan was left in the driveway.

Deke Smith had spent the day wiping away all vestiges of fingerprints in the house and then double-checking the timers connected to the house lights and front porch. Any casual observer passing by would assume that the place was still occupied. And anyone who happened to enter the premises would find a cozy old farmhouse furnished much like all farmhouses, with a few canned goods in the pantry, a fridge stocked with what appeared to be perishables and leftovers but were really containers of fake food, and dishes on the drying rack by the sink. It was all to give the impression that the resident of the farmhouse had just stepped out the door.

After traveling down the dirt road, the motorhome turned southwest onto a graveled county road. A few miles later it pulled to the side of the road and idled while Smith jumped down. Within two minutes he exchanged the fake South Dakota license plates for real Florida plates. A mile later they turned south onto a major highway that would eventually connect to Interstate 80 in Nebraska, nearly 180 miles away.

The motorhome had all the amenities a traveling family needed, a well-stocked galley, beds for four people, a bathroom, a shower, and even satellite television. Eunice Stearns and Deke Smith would share the driving and stop only for fuel. In the back Annie Black Spotted Horse had the freedom to move from a bottom bunk in the back to the main area in the middle. All her food and entertainment needs were at hand and her movements were tracked with two overhead cameras and displayed on a monitor above the windshield on the driver's side. In four days, they would be in Naples, Florida.

In a twist of irony that life now and then spins, the motorhome passed by the town of Cold River just as a meeting was getting started in the sheriff's office in the Redoubt County Courthouse, three blocks from the highway. Sheriff Mel Triplett sat on the end of his desk, a deputy stood against a wall, and seated near him were Hal and a fingerprint expert from the state's department of criminal investigation. To his left sat William Black Spotted Horse.

"Jerry," the sheriff said to the man from the state. "I read your report but maybe you can fill us all in."

The man cleared his throat and nodded. "It's simple and direct really. I found no fingerprints other than those of the owners of the vehicle. We covered every inch of the car, but it's safe to assume that whoever broke out the window and took the little girl wore gloves and laid hands only on the rear passenger door latch, inside or out."

"So, no trace at all, of any kind," the sheriff said.

"No, and my partner noticed something peculiar. It's a dirt road but the only foot tracks around were those of the young couple leaving the site."

"Damn," muttered the sheriff. "Someone was very thorough. Ah, thanks Jerry, for stopping by." He glanced at Hal and William. "We should talk about what we need to do next." He waited while the technician closed his briefcase and exited the room. "We can call the state DCI to help and there's the option of involving the FBI. This is a kidnapping, and our concern is Annie's safety."

Hal shifted in his chair and was about to speak when his cell phone rang.

"Go ahead," the sheriff said. "It could be Virginia."

Hal pulled the phone and tapped a green icon that appeared on the screen. "Hello," he said tentatively. Astonishment and confusion washed over his unshaven face. After listening for a moment, he lumbered to his feet and stepped out the door, leaving it open behind him.

From the hallway came Hal's muffled voice. "Hollister McGiven?"

Sheriff Triplett turned to William. "Did he say 'Hollister McGiven?'"

William nodded. "I think so."

Hal's voice trailed off and faded until they could no longer hear it.

"McGiven? Is this really you?" Hal was incredulous, standing in the parking lot of the courthouse.

"It is, old buddy. A blast from the past, don't you know? How the hell are you?" The voice on the other end was low and a bit raspy, but very familiar.

"Ah, well, I'm kind of having a tough day, Hollister. Why are you calling me?"

Hollister McGiven chuckled. "Well, I'll tell you, I'm not calling just to catch up on old times. So let me get straight to what this is about. Hal, old buddy, I have your granddaughter."

Hal stood in shocked silence for few seconds.

"You son-of-a-bitch!" he finally hissed. "You better not be jerking me around! I haven't seen hide nor hair of you in over 20 damn years! How can you possibly have my granddaughter?"

"You bet your hairy ass I do, Hal, old buddy. Listen to me with both ears now. I do have your granddaughter. Pretty little thing she is, too. What's more, I can prove that I have her. Now, here's the thing. Do not, and I mean *do not*, bring any law into this, you hear? Especially the FBI! This here thing is between you and me, $750,000 worth. Remember them numbers, old buddy? It's what you didn't pay me when you forced me out of our partnership. But you're going to come across now, if you want to see this little girl ever again."

Hal's legs felt shaky. He grabbed a Handicap Parking Only signpost to steady himself.

"I'm listening, Hollister."

"Good. I'm about to give you instructions, so follow them to a T. You stray a bit, just a tiny bit, and the deal is off and you will not see your granddaughter again. So put your remembering cap on, old buddy. But, you know, just in case you forget some details, check your mail today. Now, as soon as I'm done issuing instructions, I'm sending you proof on the phone in your hands."

After hearing the instructions, Hal stared at the photograph that popped up on his phone. It was a photograph of a medallion with a blue dragonfly in the middle. Woodenly, he turned and walked toward the front doors of the courthouse.

Inside the motorhome Deke Smith disconnected the call. On his face was a slight, smug smile of satisfaction. He glanced at the woman who was driving. "So, did I sound convincing enough?"

Bernadette McGiven, who had told the young couple she was "Eunice Stearns," nodded her approval. "You sure did."

"So, when do I call him again?"

"In a day or two." She glanced up at the monitor screen above the visor. Framed in the screen was Annie, sitting in the same spot she had been for an hour, on the couch in the center area of the motorhome.

Slow footsteps approached his door as the sheriff waited expectantly. Hal peeked in, clearly agitated, his face an ashen gray. "Ah, William?" he said. "Can I have a word with you, outside?"

"Sure."

Five minutes later William Black Spotted Horse could only stare in disbelief at Hal Lamar. Hal's shocked and hollow-eyed expression was a certain indication that he was telling the truth, backed up by the photograph of Annie's medallion on the cell phone screen.

"Hollister McGiven? Weren't you partners once?" he asked.

Hal nodded, still dumbstruck. "Yeah, over 20 years ago."

"So that's the call the sheriff was telling us to expect."

Hal nodded again, his expression unchanging. "Yeah, yeah, but we can't tell him. McGiven warned we wouldn't see Annie if we told any cops or the FBI."

"You believe him?"

"We can't afford not to, William. It's Annie we're talking about."

"I got nothing against the sheriff, Hal, and he would be the first to tell you he's not trained to handle this sort of thing. The FBI does handle this sort of thing. They know what to do."

"Yeah, I got that, but what if McGiven knows what *he's* doing, and he gets word that the FBI is involved? If he's crazy enough to kidnap Annie, he might be crazy enough to do something even worse."

William watched a woman exit the courthouse and get into her car before he spoke again. "Okay, okay, listen, I don't know Hollister McGiven. But what I'm wondering, Hal, is *why*. Why would he do this?"

Hal sighed deeply, staring at the sidewalk before he looked up at William, and then only for a second. "I forced him out of our partnership," he said. "Twenty some years ago. I bought him out because he sold cattle without telling me."

William nodded. "That sounds straightforward, but there must be more to it than that."

"Yeah, well, I paid him back what he initially invested. He took me to court demanding I pay what his half of the business was worth when I forced him out. The court sided with me and that was that. Or so I thought."

William threw up his hands. "So now the other shoe has fallen, squarely on top of Annie."

"Please, William, this is our granddaughter we're talking about. We can't take any sort of chance!"

William noted two things. First, he never thought he would hear Hal Lamar say "please" to him, and second, the look on the man's face was pure anguish.

"Okay, okay, but I think we need to be square with Virginia and Marie and Jennifer and Jarod. We have to tell them about this, Hal."

Hal stared vaguely at the sidewalk. "Yeah, okay. I think Virginia is home, now."

William nodded. "Yeah, Marie is at the hospital with Jarod and Jennifer. I'll go see them. I don't know when Jarod will be discharged."

"Yeah, yeah, okay."

"Is there anything else you need to tell me?"

Hal glanced up, his eyes full of confusion. "Ah, yeah. I'm supposed to wire a shitload of money to a bank in Buenos Aires, Argentina, two days from now."

"Damn! How much money?"

"$750,000."

William's jaw dropped. "That is a shitload. Can you do that?"

Hal nodded. "Yeah, but there's more. I'm supposed to wait for instructions after they get the money."

"Argentina? Why Argentina? That doesn't sound good."

As Annie's grandfathers stood in the courthouse parking lot, immobilized by confusion and indecision, Virginia Lamar answered the landline telephone in her house southeast of Cold River.

"Hello."

"Virginia? This is Dennis Cline."

"Oh, yes, Dr. Cline." Virginia's voice quavered slightly. "I'm assuming you're calling about Annie's diagnosis."

"Yes, yes. But I would be seriously violating some laws if I were to tell you first. I'm calling because I couldn't reach Jarod and Jennifer. I need to deliver the news to them first. Do you know where they are?"

"Yes, yes, I do know where they are, and later on we will all be together, meaning Annie's parents and her other grandparents as well. Would you be able to call later? Perhaps in about two hours?"

"Of course. I would be happy to."

"Thank you, Dr. Cline—Dennis. I appreciate that. And judging by your tone, I assume the news is not good."

Dr. Cline sighed. "I'll talk to you all later, Virginia."

She didn't want to reveal to Dr. Cline the circumstances of the moment but changed her mind.

"Before you call Jennifer and Jarod later, you should know that Jarod has suffered a serious head injury, so I don't know how this will affect him or them."

"Oh, hardly a good time to deliver sobering news."

"No, it isn't. As I said, give us a couple of hours, that way everyone can be there with them."

"Right, of course. And how's Annie doing right now?"

Celia closed her eyes for a moment and then looked toward the sound of Hal's truck in the driveway. "I think she's doing okay, Dennis. I haven't seen her for a couple of days."

Hal had seen his wife shed tears now and then, but mostly tears of joy, such as for Jennifer's high school graduation, college graduation, and wedding. During hard times her emotional toughness emerged, which he envied and wished he had. So, when he walked in and saw her sobbing, he didn't know how to react. Hal felt like crying himself.

SEVEN

The drive to the Agency Village Indian Health Service Hospital with Hal was, Virginia reflected, what purgatory must be. Not only was she carrying the anguish of anticipation about Annie's diagnosis, but also of Hal sharing the phone call from Hollister McGiven with their daughter and her husband.

"And to think," Virginia said, "a few days ago my biggest worry was your attitude toward Jarod and his family. Now circumstances are worse than I could possibly have imagined. What are we going to do?"

Now Hal was beginning to feel responsible for what was happening, or what seemed to be happening. There was still an unreal tinge to it all. But the gut-wrenching reality was that Annie was gone and seriously ill. He sensed that the worst thing to say to his wife would be 'I don't know.'"

"We will figure it out," he told her, hoping he sounded confident. "Nothing else matters but Annie. We'll get her back."

Virginia reached and grabbed his right hand, putting her slender fingers inside the curve of his, as if they were looking for a place to hide. They rode that way until he turned into the hospital parking lot.

Jennifer, Marie, and William were already with Jarod in his room. Hal was taken aback at his son-in-law's appearance. Some of the hair behind his ear had been shaved for two rows of stitches. He looked haggard and barely acknowledged them as they walked in. Jennifer was sitting in a chair next to him. His parents were seated on the opposite side of the bed.

Virginia immediately hugged her daughter and then her son-in-law. Hal followed her and leaned down to hug Jennifer and then awkwardly reached out his hand to Jarod, who immediately reached up to take it.

"I'm glad you're okay," Hal told the younger man.

Jarod nodded slowly and smiled with his eyes. "Thanks."

Hal took a seat in one of the two empty chairs, but Virginia remained standing by the bed. She looked over at Marie and William and then at the young couple. William, Hal had told her, was going to inform Marie, and only Marie for now, about the McGiven phone call. By the strained expression on her in-laws' faces, Virginia assumed he had done so.

She took hold of Jarod's hand and reached out for Jennifer's. "My dears," she said gently, fighting to keep her own emotions in check, "Dr. Cline is planning to call you. He has some news. I'm sure he wouldn't mind if I were to call him and give you the phone."

Apprehension immediately filled the young couple's eyes as they nodded. They reached for each other's hands as Virginia took out her cell phone and placed the call. In a moment the doctor answered.

"Dr. Cline, this is Virginia Lamar…yes, we're all together, and I'm going to put you on speaker." She pressed a button and held the phone in her upturned palm.

"Hello," the doctor began. "I'm sorry I can't deliver this news in person, but, in any case, I've reviewed all the testing we did on Annie, including the biopsy, and the diagnosis is a form of childhood leukemia."

Jennifer laid her head on Jarod's shoulder while Marie looked at her husband and rose to stand on the other side of the bed, reaching out to the young couple.

"That's the difficult news," the doctor continued. "The very hopeful aspect of this is that this form of the disease has a very, very high rate of cure. I will be consulting with two colleagues of mine, oncologists, and we will form a treatment plan for Annie. I am confident that we have an excellent chance of taking this into remission, and then eradicating it altogether. Do any of you have any questions?"

After a moment of silence, Jarod cleared his throat, and despite his injuries and the situation the doctor did not know about, he spoke with a strong voice, the voice of a man and a father.

"Thank you, Doctor Cline. I'm sure you'll tell us the kind and method of treatment when you know, but how soon do you plan on initiating the treatments and how frequently will they be administered?"

"Excellent question, Jarod. Yes, when my colleagues and I have reviewed all the tests, then we'll decide on the method of treatment. And that can range from oral medication to chemotherapy to a stem cell transplant. We can talk about these specific approaches later. At the moment, I just want you to be aware of the diagnosis. As for frequency of treatment, it will likely start at once a week, and, depending on progress made, be gradually reduced."

"Thank you, Doctor," Jarod replied, after a moment of silence in the room. "What's the immediate next step?"

"I will consult with my colleagues, and I have scheduled an appointment with them for Annie in about a month from now. That will probably be when treatment begins."

After another moment of silence, during which Jarod lifted his wife's hand to kiss it, Virginia spoke.

"I think that's all the questions we have, Doctor. Is there anything else?"

"No," he replied. "Not now, but I'm available any time if anyone wants to call and talk. How's Annie doing? I'm assuming she's not there with you."

His question was a silent hammer crashing down. Jennifer leaned over to bury her head in Jarod's embrace.

Virginia spoke again. "Ah, no, Annie is not here, but she's a very strong little girl and we all love her very much."

"And that's what will get her through this," the doctor pointed out. "I wish you all well. We can talk again soon, and I'll see you all in a month."

William watched his daughter-in-law throw herself on top of her husband, and heard her sobs erupt from the depths of a wounded soul. Jarod held her tight as she wept, as his own tears slid silently down his face. Marie and Virginia moved closer, trying to protect their children from pain and heartache. William felt the despair of powerlessness. There was nothing he could do but watch and feel the crushing weight of helplessness. Not once did he glance up at the man standing across the room. The man who was responsible for part of this chaos and heartache.

In a few minutes, after comforting words and gentle touches from their mothers, the two young people regained their composures. But it was his son's words that cut through William's heart.

Jarod took his wife's face tenderly in his hands. "Listen, my love," he said. "I'm going to stop being a weakling and get up out of this bed, and I'm going to go find our daughter. I don't care what it takes. I will find her."

As resolute and brave as those words were, William knew his son was in no condition to follow through on them. Jarod's doctor had told him of the plans for further evaluation in Sioux Falls. Jarod would be flown there the next day. There were concerns over lingering effects from the skull fracture and the only way to ascertain the extent of the injuries was with tests the IHS (Indian Health Service) hospital could not perform.

Jarod and Jennifer did not know of the phone call from Hollister McGiven, and William felt that—for the time being—that news should be withheld.

An hour later he was walking with Jennifer toward the coffee kiosk in the waiting area on the ground floor. "Listen," he said to her, "yesterday I did something I'm ashamed of, and I want to apologize to you."

"You mean when you hit my dad?"

"Yeah. I shouldn't have done that."

"He deserved it. Mom told me what he said about Jarod. Don't worry about it, okay?"

William pulled her into a hug. "We're going to find Annie," he said. "I don't know how we're going to do it, but we're going to find her. Meanwhile, we have to make sure you and Jarod are okay."

"Yeah, I know. I'm going to fly with him to Sioux Falls."

"He's a lucky man, to have you." William stepped back and looked down into her blue eyes. Whether she knew it or not, she was tough as nails, and even without make-up and after a lot of tears, a beautiful young woman.

"We're lucky to have each other," she said. "We just want our daughter back."

Two hours later William made what he would later see was a fateful decision, at least for him. He invited Hal to small café inside a convenience store a couple of miles from the hospital. To William's surprise, Hal accepted the invitation, albeit hesitantly, and drove his own truck.

"What's on your mind?" Hal asked warily after the waitress brought their coffees.

"McGiven," William replied. "And Argentina."

"What do you mean?"

"He told you to wire money there. Maybe he's going there since that's where the money is going."

"That's possible, I guess, but there are ways of accessing funds without going to the bank. You know that."

"Okay, but don't you have to be physically at a bank to open an account? You know, to sign forms and prove your identity?"

Hal stared into his coffee, suddenly not wanting it. "Yeah, you're probably right."

"Okay," William nodded. "And maybe because he's a foreigner, there are different, more stringent requirements for a non-citizen to open a bank account."

"Yeah, you're probably right about that, too. But what's your point, William? Where you going with this?"

William shrugged. "I'm not sure, but I can't shake the thought—and it's scaring the hell out of me—that McGiven is taking Annie to Argentina or plans to."

"Shit!" Hal hissed. "I hadn't thought of that."

William sipped his coffee and looked around. Not many people were here at this hour. He leaned forward. "I've been thinking, too, that it might be wise to err on the side of caution, you know, and not bring the cops into this. He expressly warned us not to do that."

Hal nodded slowly. "Just what I been thinking. But we're greenhorns at this sort of thing, William. What are we going to do? Where do we start?"

William took a deep breath and exhaled. "We have to start somewhere. I have a friend, the tribal chief of police. He's educated and experienced, nearly 30 years as a cop. I like him as a person. Maybe I should talk to him, throw some hypothetical questions at him."

"Yeah, okay. But what if he figures out this isn't hypothetical?"

"Well, maybe I swear him to secrecy and put the cards on the table."

Hal leaned back. He looked tired. "Makes sense, I think. But I want to be there, too."

"Okay, I'll set up a meeting as quick as I can."

Hal rubbed his face nervously and put his elbows on the table. "This is a fucking nightmare," he said.

Later at the hospital, sometime after eleven, Virginia and Hal left for home.

Hal caught a glimpse of their mailbox in the headlight's beam. He stopped and backed to it and stepped out of the truck to grab the mail. It wasn't until he was in the house that he sifted through the bundle. One plain envelope addressed by hand caught his attention. It did not have a postage stamp. In the upper left corner there was a partial return address:

Hollister McGiven

750K Revenge Rd.

On the plain folded white sheet inside were typewritten instructions for wiring the money to the Banco Nuevo Rio in Buenos Aires, Argentina, including an account number and an international routing number.

Hal stared at the account number, labeled Holding.

At the bottom of the page were more instructions.

Expect a phone call. The incoming number will be outside your area code. Be prepared for a long trip. If you follow all instructions, like not involving the police or FBI, you will be told where to go to retrieve your granddaughter.

Two thoughts immediately popped into Hal's head. One, William Black Spotted Horse's assumption was correct. Hollister McGiven was somehow connected to Argentina. Two, who the hell had put that letter in his mailbox? Someone had put the envelope in his mailbox. And that someone knew where he lived. He immediately thought of the woman Jennifer and Jarod had described as their assailant.

Hollister McGiven was not acting alone. But who was the woman?

EIGHT

True to his word, William arranged a meeting for himself and Hal with Smokey River Sioux Tribal Police Chief Ben Avery. Avery was a Choctaw from Oklahoma, a big man, six feet five inches and every bit of 240 pounds. He was not as dark-skinned as William Black Spotted Horse, but his short hair was just as black and his features were definitely Native. Though dressed in civilian clothes, he still wore his 9mm Glock sidearm. He was a downright imposing figure of a man in Hal's estimation. There was a no-nonsense air about him, rather like William Black Spotted Horse. It was something Hal didn't usually feel about Indians.

They met at a little used roadside park southwest of Cold River, on one of the reservation roads. The place was no more than a picnic table, a trash bin, and his and hers outdoor privies. William had the foresight to bring a large thermos of coffee, which he opened and poured into paper cups.

After he introduced Hal to the chief, William got right to the point.

"We have a serious problem, Ben," he said. "But we need to keep it close to the vest and I think you'll see why."

"Well," Avery said, nodding. "I'll keep your secret. Lay it on me."

Ten minutes later William finished telling the story and turned to Hal. "Did I leave anything out?"

"Nope," Hal said.

Avery looked out over the prairie. "Argentina, huh? Well, remind me later to tell you something about Argentina. Might be helpful." He poured himself more coffee from the thermos and glanced in turn at the two men sitting across from him at the picnic table. "First question that pops in my mind is this: Who is the woman? Or was it really a woman who assaulted your kids? From what you've told me it might have been this McGiven guy in disguise."

Hal shook his head. "Hollister McGiven would now be pushing 60, maybe 65. And he was near as tall as you guys. From what Jennifer and Jarod said, it was a woman, and she hit them with something in her hand, some kind of weapon."

Avery nodded. "Tell me about McGiven. Was he married, did he have a family?"

"Yeah, when we got into business together, he had a wife, a daughter, and two sons. His wife's name was Mary Lee, her maiden name was Cronin. The youngest boy was born while they were here. He died before he was three. The daughter was Bernadette and the older boy was Gary. I don't remember the younger boy's name. Bernadette would be almost forty now, or thereabouts. After we broke up our partnership, they moved away."

"Any idea where they went to?" Avery wondered.

"Ah, somewhere in the northwest part of the state, last I heard."

"Did he ever contact you, or try to, over the years?"

Hal shook his head. "Not really. After he lost the lawsuit against me it was like he fell off the earth."

"I don't know about you, gentlemen, but I think it's damn critical that we find out where McGiven's been these past 20 years, and what we can learn about his wife and children. Anything we turn up might give us some idea about what's up his butt. Does he still have relatives in the area?"

"No," Hal answered quickly. "He came up from Texas. His wife was from North Dakota, she was a teacher at the grade school. He was a rodeo cowboy, a bulldogger, entered up in the local rodeo and that's how he met Mary Lee."

"That was before I moved back here," William volunteered.

"Did you work for the BIA the entire time?" Avery asked.

William nodded. "Yeah, started out in Anadarko, then Albuquerque, Billings, and even Alaska. Finally ended up at home."

"Yeah, well," Avery sighed, "maybe your man McGiven went home, too, to Texas I mean."

"How can we find out?" Hal asked.

"I got a couple guys that can do some checking. I won't give them all the details. It just amounts to shaking the trees and seeing what falls out." He looked at Hal. "In the meantime, might be a good idea for you not to go anywhere without your phone, or just hang close to your land line phone."

Hal nodded.

"Everything you've told me indicates planning," Avery pointed out. "Your kids were not randomly ambushed. Someone was after your granddaughter and had a plan. They sent the instructions for wiring money out of the country and left that letter in your mailbox. So, here's my suggestion to you, gentlemen. Don't dismiss the idea of bringing in the FBI. They have ways of gathering information. For the moment, I—and my department—can lend a hand unofficially and basically off the record. We can play this out step by step, depending on what McGiven says each time he makes contact."

Hal and William nodded simultaneously.

"You think he's taking Annie to Argentina?" Hal wondered.

"At this point it's 50-50. It's either a bluff or he does have more of a connection than the bank. In any situation people tend to stick with things that are familiar. It's easier to function that way and there's more familiarity. Big or small, there's a reason Argentina is part of this."

"One thing that scares me," Hal admitted. "How do we know Annie's okay? Especially now because she's sick."

William nodded at the unspoken question in Avery's eyes. "Yeah," he said. "She's very ill and McGiven doesn't know that."

"Oh, crap. Well, ask for proof of life, but don't use those words. Ask for a photograph to be texted. That's the quickest way."

William finished his coffee. "You said to remind you of something regarding Argentina."

"Yeah, yeah. I have a friend who recently made an extended trip there. Quite an adventure he had. If this situation takes a turn in that direction, he might be a good resource."

"That's good to know," William said. "Who's your friend, if I may ask?"

"You sure may. He's none other than Dr. Clayton Lone Hawk, your new tribal president. I believe he's a friend of yours as well."

The call came in on the Lamars' landline at two o'clock in the morning. Startled out of a troubled sleep, Hal squinted at the tiny caller ID screen and didn't recognize the number. A split second later the reality of the moment swept in. He grabbed the phone and hit Talk. On the other side of the bed Virginia awoke and sat up.

"This is Hal Lamar," he said, not quite awake.

"Well, top of the morning to you, Hal, old buddy. How the hell are you?"

"Just grand, Hollister, just grand."

"Good to know. Did you get my letter?"

"Yeah, I got it."

"Peachy keen, old friend. Now, tomorrow you saddle up and go to the main branch of your bank in Rapid City and wire the money. Do it by one in the afternoon Mountain Time."

"Okay, I will."

"That'll be good. When I know the wire is in the pipeline, I'll ring you up again."

Hal's hand shook. "Ah, could I ask a favor. I want to be sure Annie's okay. Lots of people here worried about her. Can you, ah, text me a photo? Just so we can see she's okay?"

"Yeah, I suppose I can do that, just for old time's sake. I'll text it to your cell phone."

Before Hal could say another word, the call disconnected. He looked at his cell phone on the nightstand. There was nothing to do but wait.

Thirty seconds passed, then a minute. Virginia came around and sat down next to Hal. Just as his heart started pounding, his cell phone chirped an incoming text and a photo of Annie appeared on the screen. Virginia gasped and started to sob.

"Oh, my god! She looks sleepy, but she looks okay."

They sat together staring at the photo. Virginia reached out with a finger and caressed the screen. "Be strong, honey. Be strong."

Hal wiped a tear out of his eye. "I'm not very good with texts, so you should send this to, ah, Marie and William."

Five hours later Hal was on Interstate 90 West toward Rapid City. He wanted to arrive at the bank in plenty of time. Virginia left the same time he did, heading for the IHS hospital to be with Jennifer and Jarod before they were flown to Sioux Falls. She was stopping at their house in town for fresh clothes and other personal items.

Driving long distances always had one inherent problem, a lot of time to think, especially during times of stress. Hal was not given to listening to music or anything on the radio, so silence was his only companion. A scary thought popped into his head and would not go away. If they—meaning Annie's family—had any kind of leverage in this situation, it would be gone once he wired the money. With $750,000 in hand, Hollister McGiven would have what he wanted. He wouldn't need Annie. A knot began to form in Hal's gut.

He slowed and pulled over onto the next exit ramp and stopped, then hit Virginia's name on the contact list in his phone. She answered after one ring.

"Hi, dear. Are you there already?"

"No, I just stopped for a minute. I have a question for William. Is he there?"

"Yes, of course, he's here. Shall I give him my phone?"

A few seconds later William came on the line. "What's up, Hal?"

"Ah, I just thought of something, and it's bothering me. Maybe you can step out of the room so we can talk."

"Right, okay, the doc's in here so I'll step out into the hallway." After a few seconds he spoke again. "Did you get another call from McGiven?"

"No, not since last night. But there's something I'm wondering about, maybe it's nothing, but I wanted to hear what you think."

"What is it?"

Hal rolled down the window to get fresh air. "McGiven has Annie and that's powerful leverage, you know, the threat to hurt her if he doesn't get the money. But what about after he has the money? Does he need her after that?"

"I don't like the gist of that, Hal. What are you leading up to?"

Hal sighed deeply. "What's he going to do with Annie after he doesn't need her? That's what's scaring me."

"I see what you mean. But I don't know what we do about it." William paused for several seconds. "I'll talk to Ben Avery."

Hal glanced at his watch. "I wanted to initiate the wire at noon mountain time. You got a little over two hours. Get back to me before then if you can."

William returned Virginia's phone to her.

"Can you write down Hal's number for me?" he asked, somewhat detached.

The two older women looked at him curiously.

"Anything wrong, honey?" Marie asked.

"No, I just need to make a call and give Hal some information."

Virginia handed him a small slip of paper. The doctor had left the room and a nurse was helping with last minute details before Jarod and Jennifer's ride to the airstrip.

"I'll go to the lobby and make the call, then I'll be back."

Marie smiled nervously at him as he walked out of the room.

Jarod caught his mother's attention. "Mom, did I just hear Dad say he was going to call Hal?"

Marie nodded. "That's what he said."

Jarod looked up at his wife. "Maybe that woman hit me harder than I thought, or I'm dreaming."

Virginia smiled at her son-in-law. "Will wonders never cease?"

The lobby was nearly empty when William placed the call to Ben Avery. Hal's question weighed heavily on him and he hoped the police chief would have an answer that was reassuring.

NINE

"I understand Hal's concern, but a bigger one is what would happen if the money was not wired," said Avery. "In that scenario your granddaughter would damn sure be in jeopardy. In principle, I'm not in favor of paying a ransom. But, how do you know McGiven isn't going to demand more money?"

That was a new one. William had not considered that, and in a way it was a glimmer of hope. "I guess it's possible. He apparently has a hell of grudge against Hal."

"Yeah, and that may be in Annie's favor," Avery pointed out. "Maybe McGiven's plan is to bleed Hal dry. I'm sure Hal is worth more than three quarters of a million dollars."

"Yeah, he's worth several million."

"Realistically, William, we don't know what will happen. But it's a matter of considering the possibilities and probabilities. To me there's a strong possibility that McGiven is going to use the leverage he has for more money or some other kind of demand."

"Makes sense. At the moment, all we can do is wait to see how it unfolds."

"That's the hard part, William, waiting."

William thanked the chief and immediately dialed Hal's number to recount the conversation.

"Yeah, you know," Hal said, "a lot of what the chief says makes sense. Bottom line is at this point we don't want to piss McGiven off. I'll wire the money."

Immediately after he finished the call to Hal, he returned to Jarod's room. He along with Jennifer and the mothers were looking at the photograph of Annie from last night. One of the floor nurses was kind enough, and had the technological skill, to print several copies. Virginia handed one to William.

"Dad," Jarod called out. "Any news?"

William shook his head. "Nothing new, except that Hal and I talked to the tribal police chief. I guess you can say he's our case consultant."

"Let us know if anything comes up," Jarod said, a bit wistfully.

Jennifer turned and hugged her father-in-law. "Thanks, Dad. Thanks for being here for us, and for everything you're doing, all of you. Jarod and I know we can't do this alone."

"You won't have to," William reassured her.

Marie on one side of the bed, and Virginia on the other, quietly wiped away tears and dabbed at their noses with handkerchiefs. In a moment a nurse rolled in a wheelchair.

They walked along as Jarod was wheeled to a waiting patient transport van that would take him and Jennifer to the airstrip. In a little less than two hours they would be in Sioux Falls. The plan was for Virginia to ride there with Marie and William, and Hal would join them in the evening.

At 12:30 p.m. Mountain Time Hal walked out of Cattlemen's Bank with a folder in his hand containing receipts and copies of forms indicating that a hefty sum of money had been wired into a holding account at the Banco Nuevo Rio in Buenos Aires, Argentina.

"You should check with that bank to see how long they will hold those funds," was the banker's advice as she watched her computer screen.

A little over three hours later he was exiting the Interstate at Mitchell to gas up his truck when the call came from Hollister McGivens.

"You did good. The bank just verified that the funds are pending and will be credited within 48 hours."

Hal went weak with relief as he pulled up to a line of gas pumps at a truck stop. "Glad to hear that. How's my granddaughter, and when can we get her back?"

"She's doing fine, old salt. Don't you worry. Now, listen with both ears. I'll be sending a text with more instructions. Read 'em carefully and then text back to me that you got the instructions. Do that and I'll send you another picture of your granddaughter. You with me?"

"Yeah, I am."

"Good on you, Hal. Talk at you later."

Hal sat for a few seconds staring at the top of the sedan in front of him. Rubbing his face, he stepped down and followed the steps to refuel his truck. He remembered the days when you handed cash to the owner of the gas station, or an attendant, and they pumped the gas. Everything changed, and sometimes not for the best.

Who would have thought that my only daughter, the apple of my eye, Miss Rodeo South Dakota and a college graduate, would marry a Lakota boy? And who would have thought that my granddaughter would be half Lakota? Hal sighed sharply. There were moments when Annie looked like her mother and there were moments when she looked like her father.

Just as Hal hung up the nozzle, his cell phone chirped with an incoming text. He started the truck and pulled off to the side, away from the flow of traffic.

He read the text twice to make sure he was seeing it correctly.

Travel is in your future. Dust off your passport and book a flight to Ministro Piatro International Airport in Buenos Aires, Argentina, to arrive 1 week from today, and reserve a room at Hotel Conquistador. Once there you will get further instructions, including where to make the necessary retrieval.

Hal was so distraught he could barely manage to send the reply. The return text was one word—*Aces*—which was McGiven's expression when he was pleased with anything, and the promised photograph of Annie. She was looking into the camera, dressed in a dark blue sweatshirt with the dragonfly medallion around her neck. Her hair was neatly combed and braided. Hal felt like crying.

He debated whether to call Virginia but decided against it. He was an hour out from Sioux Falls and his news could wait. Besides, he didn't know how to forward the text.

Deke Smith shut off the cell phone, slid it into his shirt pocket, and looked up into the monitor above the driver's side visor. Bernadette and the girl were seated at the small table having lunch. In all their years of working together, he had rarely seen Bernadette so soft and tender toward anyone but her own family. Her marriage to Ernesto Govena had often been volatile, and after he and their daughter were killed, she had gone into a funk.

When she looked his way he nodded, letting her know that the task had been completed.

"Are you ladies ready to go?" he asked.

"We're ready," she said.

As Smith reached for the key to start the motor, Bernadette turned and smiled at Annie. "Hey, buckle your seat belt."

Annie nodded and did as she was told.

Half an hour later they crossed from Georgia into Florida.

Hal stopped at the Help Desk in the main lobby of the hospital to ask if someone could print out copies of the photograph from his phone. He was a hero when he handed out the photographs.

During the dinner hour, while Jennifer stayed in the room to eat with Jarod, Hal maneuvered the other adults to the cafeteria. After they were seated with their trays, he pulled up the text and showed them.

"Well," Virginia said, "that's somewhat reassuring and scary at the same time."

"Ben Avery had a thought," William said, mainly to Virginia and Marie. "He thought McGiven might have a longer scheme up his sleeve, more than a one-time ransom payment."

"That doesn't sound good," Marie said.

"Maybe, but Avery's point was if that's the case, Annie isn't in danger since he needs her to keep collecting money. I say that because I know we're all afraid of that."

"I hope you're right," Virginia said.

"Let's see if Avery's people can think of a way to determine where McGiven is or where he might be taking Annie," William commented.

"That's kind of a long shot. Why do we want to do that?" Hal asked.

"Because McGiven won't be expecting me to go there. Maybe we can think of a way to outflank him, take him by surprise."

"And rescue Annie?" Marie asked, a bit incredulous.

William nodded.

Virginia shook her head. "I don't know. Frankly, I'm in favor of asking the FBI for help. They have considerable resources. Annie must start treatments in a month. What's going to happen if she can't? And even if she weren't so sick, we need to get her back as fast as possible! I mean, every minute of every day, her parents are hurting over this."

"That makes sense," Hal said. "But McGiven warned us not to bring in the FBI, or any cops, for that matter."

"Well, tell me this," Virginia persisted, "how is he going to know if, for instance, I call the FBI?"

"I don't know, I really don't know," Hal admitted. "But do we want to take a chance? I mean, someone put that letter in our mailbox. I don't know about you, but that scared the hell out of me."

"It did me, too," Virginia said. "But how do we know, how will we know without a doubt, that he's taking Annie to Argentina? And where in Argentina? That's a big damn country."

An uneasy silence settled for a few moments, until Hal softly cleared his throat. "Bottom line is I'm willing to do what it takes to get our little girl back. Maybe we should just tell Jennifer and Jarod what the hell's going on and let them decide. Annie is their daughter."

"That's the best idea I've heard so far," Marie said. "Jarod is scheduled for an MRI tomorrow morning. His doctor's name is Michael Jennings. He stopped in briefly after Jarod was admitted. I would like to talk to Dr. Jennings and ask how added stress might affect Jarod. Then, depending on the answer he gives, we tell our kids the rest of the story."

Virginia nodded. "I agree with you, but on the other hand, I think they deserve to know everything we know. Let's tell them. They may be our kids, but they're adults, strong adults."

TEN

Though he agreed that Jarod and Jennifer had a right to know, William was bothered by one not so small detail. Hollister McGiven was fully expecting Hal to travel to Buenos Aires. If Hal did not show up in Buenos Aires, there could be dire consequences. McGiven had set a hard deadline and William didn't think giving McGiven any reason to be upset would be wise.

William expressed his concern to the others.

"Then we cover all the bases," Virginia insisted. "We tell Jarod and Jennifer. In the meantime, you, Hal, should book a flight."

"And if circumstances warrant, Hal can always step aside," Marie declared.

Just after eight the next morning, while the MRI was happening, Marie and Virginia found Jarod's doctor and explained the situation.

"Well," Dr. Jennings said, "Jarod's physical functioning is not impaired. His hand-eye coordination is normal, his vision seems to be normal, and his speech is not impaired. In fact, all the factors we check, as far as physical and mental abilities after such a head injury seem to be normal. I emphasize 'seem to be.' I'm confident that the MRI will bear that out, but we do it to determine the extent of the physical injury and what that might mean.

As far as emotional stress, I think he'll be able to handle it as he would if the injury had not occurred."

While Marie and Virginia were speaking with the doctor, Hal was talking to an eager young travel agent at one of the few travel agencies still in business in Sioux Falls.

"Since you'll be leaving in a few days," she told him, "I was worried about domestic connections. But luckily I'm seeing a few flights with seats still available departing from here, FSD, Sioux Falls. Most of them have only one stop, and then arrival in Miami. From Miami I think we can get you directly to Buenos Aires. Sound good?"

"Anything, as long as I get to Buenos Aires, a week from yesterday."

"Okay. What about a return flight?"

Hal thought for a moment. "I'm not sure about that, as far as when, exactly."

"Okay. Most countries require a scheduled return flight for foreign travelers. You can schedule one and change it, if necessary."

"Let's do that for two weeks out."

An hour later Hal walked out of the travel agency with airline confirmation codes, a printed itinerary, and a truckload of apprehension as he headed home.

Late that evening, almost at bedtime, Dr. Jennings stopped in during his rounds to deliver good news to Jarod.

"Although there are significant exterior contusions, there is no indication of bruising inside the skull," he reported. "But you do have two hairline fractures, one slightly longer than the other. The longer of the two is nearly two centimeters. I'm prescribing a mild antibiotic as well as a topical ointment. And I'm strongly advising no strenuous exertion, such as chopping wood, running, and heavy lifting. We should start to see healing, meaning bone fusion, in about a week."

"When can I go home?" was Jarod's immediate question.

"Tomorrow, after I have a look at you one more time."

William, Marie, and Virginia decided to let the young couple enjoy the good news and get a good night's rest. After breakfast the next morning, they gathered and gently broke the rest of the story.

Surprisingly, Jennifer and Jarod took it well, under the circumstances. Jarod opened his laptop and accessed a web site while he listened.

"So is Dad flying to Argentina?" Jennifer asked.

Virginia nodded. "He's already bought a round trip ticket."

"What we'd like to know from you two," William told the couple, "is how you feel about involving the FBI, or any other law enforcement, considering McGiven's warning."

"We're against it," Jennifer replied.

"That was a very quick answer," Virginia fretted. "Maybe we should all talk about it."

Jennifer smiled and gestured toward her husband. "Well, let me put it this way. I married a computer nerd, and we've been on the Internet doing research about what the FBI does in kidnapping cases, when you all were not around. Domestically, they can do a lot, but outside of the country, not so much."

The older adults exchanged puzzled glances.

"Maybe you can enlighten us," Marie suggested.

"Okay, Mom," Jarod replied. "First of all, there are any number of web sites that focus on people searches, background checks, and the like. I just got on one to find Hollister McGiven." He studied the screen. "This one says his trail ends in Bison, South Dakota 22 years ago, 1995, to be exact.

There is a Mary Lee McGiven, his wife, I think. Here it says she lives in Garrison, North Dakota. We can check other web sites and see if anything we find is corroborated to any extent. I'm guessing most of it will."

William was astonished. Marie looked his way and simply shook her head in wonder. Virginia could only stare at the young couple.

"Okay," William said, after a moment. "So, what you're saying is that you just dug up the same kind of information that a law enforcement agency would have."

"Pretty much," Jarod allowed. "And most of it was not encouraging. For instance, We looked up information on the Hague Convention on Protection of Children. It's an international treaty, of sorts. Its purpose is to protect children when they're adopted by families from a different country against corruption, abuses, and child laundering. We were probably grabbing at straws, but our hopes were dashed when we learned that, although Argentina is a signatory, they've been non-compliant."

"So, okay," William asked. "What about how helpful the FBI could be in Argentina?"

Jennifer replied, "The FBI does have a presence in most foreign countries and usually they're attached to our embassies, as legal attachés, or LEGATS. But as far as criminal cases, they do little more than assist local agencies."

Marie sighed. "My word, you two have been busy."

"Of course," Jarod said, his voice nearly strident. "Jen and I, our nerves are frayed, to put it mildly. Taking any kind of proactive role helps us, and, who knows, it might help Annie, too. I'd go crazy sitting on my hands waiting for someone else to do something."

"That's fine," William said. "But what do you think of us involving Ben Avery, the tribal police chief?"

"That's good, Dad," Jarod assured him. "Maybe he can somehow help track down Mary Lee McGiven. It's not enough to know where she is. Someone should talk to her. She's got to know something."

It was William's turn to sigh. "Hell, why didn't I think of that? I'll give Ben Avery a call. Can you find anything more about Mary Lee McGiven?"

Jarod looked away from the computer screen and leveled his gaze at his father. "Working on it, Dad. Call the chief, the sooner the better."

By midmorning Chief Avery returned William's phone call. William passed on the information Jarod and Jennifer had uncovered regarding Mary Lee McGiven.

"I have an idea," Avery said. "A good friend of mine is a captain with the BIA police up at Fort Berthold. Garrison is southeast of there. I probably can talk him into making some inquiries, maybe send someone to talk to her, if she's still in the area."

Two days later everyone was back home. Jarod was able to opt out of teaching his summer course, and he and Jennifer set up their little study as a "command and control center."

Hal met with his top hand, Adrian Kidder, a wiry 40-year-old who had worked for him for 20 years. To the man's credit he had not asked why his boss would be gone for at least two weeks.

"I'll be completely out of touch phone-wise, starting three days from now," Hal said. "If you have any questions or if anything comes up, talk to Virginia."

Kidder nodded and glanced down at his notes, written in a thin journal.

"I know you can take care of things. I appreciate you taking the load when I'm gone."

"Sure thing, Mr. Lamar. We'll get it done."

Special Investigator NoHand Hillenbrand considered himself something of a cultural anomaly. After sixteen years in law enforcement, most of it with the BIA, he was accustomed to the strange and unexpected, especially since his name fit in that category. At first, he had used only his initials, even printed on his business card, but after a lot of teasing he decided to use his first name and let the chips fall where they may. NoHand was an ancestral name given by his Hidatsa mother. NoHand was eternally grateful he wasn't named for his German father, Prodwatter Christian Hillenbrand. He couldn't imagine the amount of teasing that would have garnered.

Hillenbrand rechecked the address for Mary Lee McGiven provided to him by his captain. His task was to learn what he could about a man named Hollister McGiven. As far as the captain was told, the man was Mary Lee's current or former husband, and he was connected to a likely child abduction case on or near the Smokey River Sioux Reservation in South Dakota.

Hillenbrand, dressed in civilian clothes, stepped down from his unmarked car, fully aware that he was outside his jurisdiction. Mary Lee McGiven was not Native and lived off the Fort Berthold Reservation in west central North Dakota. Whatever she was willing to divulge needed to be entirely voluntary.

A petite, white-haired woman answered the door of the small frame house on the quiet street. With a curious but friendly look on her face, the woman said "Yes?" tentatively. Hillenbrand decided to lay all his cards on the table.

"Good morning, ma'am," he said, pleasantly. "I'm Officer Hillenbrand with the Bureau of Indian Affairs police," he explained, showing his badge. "I'm trying to find a lady by the name of Mary Lee."

She nodded. "I'm Mary Lee."

"Good, I'm pleased to meet you. If you're willing to give me a couple of minutes, I have some questions regarding a man named Hollister McGiven. But it's totally up to you. I don't have jurisdiction here."

"I'm pretty sure he's dead," she said matter-of-factly. "He left the country, oh, 'bout 20 years ago, I s'pose, after I divorced him. He and my daughter."

"Left the country?"

"Yeah, they went to Argentina."

"And you think he died?"

"Yeah, if Bernadette, my daughter, wasn't lyin' about that. She sent me a letter telling me her dad died. It came from Argentina. I still have it."

An hour and a half later Hillenbrand handed the letter to his captain, after making his report. "Some people just have stories," he said, "and now and then some people back it up with evidence." He pointed to the letter. "That letter verifies Mary Lee Cronin—she took back her maiden name— was being truthful. It's from a Bernadette, who Mary Lee said is her daughter. It's short and implies a lot about the people involved."

The captain picked up the envelope with the letter inside. He didn't bother to open it. "What do you mean?"

"Well, to me it's what's between the lines. For instance, Bernadette doesn't say 'Mom' or 'Dear Mother.' It just starts out 'Mary Lee.' She doesn't sign off like a daughter who has any affection for her mother. Nothing like 'Love, Bernadette.' She just signed her name at the bottom. There's a sad story there, with that family. Mary Lee is a nice old lady, lives by herself."

"The world is full of sad stories," the captain said, still staring at the postmark on the envelope. "Thanks for doing this. I'll give Chief Avery a call down at the Smokey River Tribal P. D."

Ben Avery asked for the letter to be faxed, as well as both sides of the envelope. He knew now that they were dealing with an imposter, someone posing as Hollister McGiven. Furthermore, he would bet a week's pay that the woman who attacked Annie's parents was Bernadette McGiven. He read the letter again:

Mary Lee,
Dad died a week ago. His heart finally gave out, but it was broken a long time ago. Before he died, he asked me to tell you after he passed. I buried him here. He liked this little place we bought. There was no place back there for him. He had no land, and I was his only family. He was a good man.
Bernadette

He had the same thought as the special investigator. This was a letter written by someone who didn't like the person to whom she was writing. But beyond that, an unavoidable fact was staring him in the face—someone was pretending to be Hollister McGiven. Furthermore, the postmark on the envelope verified the connection to Argentina. Ben Avery was certain Annie was being taken there, and he guessed not by any kind of public transportation. There were two ways to travel to Argentina from the United States, by air and by ship. In this day and age, cameras were everywhere and Annie's abductor—probably Bernadette—was smart enough to know that. So, what did that leave? With a heavy heart Chief Avery reached for the phone to call William Black Spotted Horse.

ELEVEN

In Annie's twelve years, she had experienced a variety of adventures: a ride on the Amtrak Sunset Limited to Los Angeles, a two-day excursion to Disneyland, followed by a drive up the Pacific Coast Highway to San Francisco to cross the Golden Gate Bridge, and then a plane ride home, a trip east to New York City and Boston. Though she had seen them in the harbor in San Francisco, the only major mode of transportation she had yet to experience was a ship. And that, she was thinking, was about to happen.

At dusk, the harbor was ethereal in the fading light. Bernadette held firmly to Annie's hand as they walked across a wharf to a long, low, white yacht, though to Annie it was just a big boat. She didn't want to get on it, because she knew it would take her farther from her mom and dad. Everything that had been happening meant more and more distance from them. She had seen the sign that said *Welcome to Florida*, and she knew where Florida was relative to where she lived in South Dakota. In the last hour she heard the name of the place they had driven to—Naples. She knew nothing about Naples, but she assumed the endless stretch of water she was looking at was the ocean. She wanted to cry, but she held it in.

Four luxurious staterooms were below deck, two aft and one on each side. Bernadette and Annie followed the steward who showed them to theirs on the starboard side. Deke Smith had the suite across on the port side. He would be along with their luggage and a check for the motorhome, which Bernadette had arranged to sell.

Bernadette opened the folded note on the dresser with her name on the outside and smiled at the message: *Everything is arranged.*

Forty minutes later, the yacht cast off from her moorings and slipped into the calm waters of the harbor. At that hour the coastal and harbor lights reflected off the water, a picture postcard scene. Dinner was served in the small dining room just off the galley. Broiled sea bass was the main course. Annie liked the aroma but only picked at her plate. She perked up when the server brought her a grilled burger and cottage fries.

Sometime in the night the yacht would round Key West and set a southeasterly course for the eastern tip of Puerto Rico. With calm seas favoring her, the captain would let her run at 21 knots, once they were past the 12-mile limit.

Two hours after dinner, Annie quietly sobbed herself to sleep, once again, as she held her medallion tightly in her hands.

For Jennifer and Jarod, the proactive approach only went so far when it came to mitigating anxiety and apprehension. Uncertainty was a constant. Every time any phone buzzed, chirped, or rang, anxiety reared its head, along with a generous dose of plain old fear. Both were only sleeping in snatches. And there was no way to ignore the empty room at the end of the hall.

"I guess it's times like this that people seriously consider going to church," Jennifer said.

"Yeah. We all hope there is a benevolent power that watches over us," agreed Jarod.

"Yeah, and I hope that he, she, or it is watching over our little girl every second, and that she's warm and is eating properly."

"Some people would say that you just prayed. But that's what I think about, too, constantly."

She wrapped her arms around him and put her head against his chest. "What are we going to do, honey?"

"We're going to think of our little girl all the time, put good thoughts out there, and do everything we can to find her and bring her home," he declared.

"You think it's the right thing that Dad is going to Argentina?"

"I do. There's no choice at this point. Actually, if my head wasn't split open, I'd be going with him."

She stepped back and looked up into his face. "I know you're that kind of a man." She paused for a moment. "I've been meaning to ask you something, or at last bring something up that's been sort of on my mind."

"Okay, go ahead." He led her to the stools at the breakfast bar and they both took a seat. "What is it?"

She shrugged. "I barely remember Dad's business partner, Hollister, and I kind of remember his daughter, Bernadette. She was older than me. For some reason I don't think Dad and Mom ever had them, you know, the family, over for supper, or anything. Then, Dad told me that he and Hollister weren't working together anymore. So, if he's the one who took Annie, why did he do that?"

"I've thought about that, too. Your dad was the one that dissolved the partnership, I think, and there was a reason he did that. It must have been a reason McGiven didn't like."

Jarod's phone rang. "Hey, Dad, what's up?"

"They're here," he said to Jennifer. "My mom and dad just pulled up. They have some news."

While they waited for the coffee pot to finish brewing, William delivered the news from Chief Ben Avery.

"Hang onto your socks," he warned. "This news is hard to get my mind around. An investigator up in North Dakota found Mary Lee, who divorced Hollister McGiven about 20 years ago. But the kicker is this that she revealed that he died in Argentina."

He pulled a copy of the faxed letter from his pocket and handed it to Jarod. Jennifer read it with him.

"Damn!" Jarod said. "So, who's been calling Hal?"

"And who took Annie?" was Jennifer's question.

"My money is on the person who wrote that letter to Mary Lee," William said.

"Whosever idea it was, they—Hollister and his daughter—moved to Argentina. Given what she said in that letter, they might have bought some property, at least a house, maybe."

Jarod was deep in thought for a few moments. "If that's the case, we can probably find where they lived, at least find a starting point. If we do, that might give us an advantage. This Bernadette won't be expecting that. If we locate her in Argentina, chances are that's where Annie will be!"

"Hal is leaving tomorrow," William pointed out. "The more he knows about Bernadette McGiven, the better."

Jarod stared at the kitchen island countertop as Marie and Jennifer poured coffee and set out cookies, croissants, and napkins. William watched his son, knowing that thoughts were whirling a thousand miles an hour in his head.

"What are you thinking, Son?"

"Ah, well, just this. Let's assume that Bernadette is the person in control. She is expecting Hal to do what she instructed. She'll likely make him jump through hoops. Anyway, I'm thinking her focus will be on Hal, and she won't be expecting anyone else to be involved."

"Interesting thought," William agreed. "So, what are you saying?"

"We locate Bernadette. The odds are that's where Annie will be. I go there and get Annie while Hal sort of keeps Bernadette's attention elsewhere."

Marie protested immediately. "You're seriously injured, Son. I'd almost guarantee that your doctor would advise against air travel."

"She's right, hon," Jennifer seconded.

William held up a hand. "They're right, Son. Here's my thought. You and Jennifer have uncovered a lot of information, very quickly. That's a valuable ability and you won't be able to do that as well if you're traveling. So I'll go, and you and Jennifer coordinate things from here. You can guide us, Hal and me."

Jarod was about to launch a protest on his own, then decided against it. "Great idea, Dad."

"Hal leaves in two days," William said. "We need to do some planning."

The wheels were turning in Jarod's head. "You can't travel together. You, Dad, have to get to Bernadette from a different direction, literally. Once we locate her, then we'll figure out a way for you to get there. Bernadette will dictate Hal's moves. She won't be expecting anyone else to be part of it."

"What about the police or the FBI?" Marie asked.

"Well," Jarod said, "the threat of harm to Annie if police or the FBI are brought in is one we shouldn't take lightly. Bernadette, or someone, did a lot of planning to pull this off and carry it through, to whatever end she has in mind. We should assume she has skills and abilities and has access to information, like we do. She might have a way of knowing if any law enforcement becomes involved. I don't want to take the chance."

"Me neither," Jennifer confirmed.

Marie looked toward William. "In other words, we put our hopes squarely on Annie's grandfathers."

Jennifer looked at her father-in-law, hope and respect written on her face. "Who better to fight for our little girl than her grandpas who love her so much?"

At that moment, William couldn't say which he felt more, the love and trust of his daughter-in-law or the sudden crushing weight of responsibility.

A little less than two hours later he was sitting in an old friend's backyard, some 15 miles west of Cold River. A fire burned in a circular pit, its sides scorched black by years of use. An old man with his life trails etched on his brown face poked at the embers and added two more pieces of dry wood. His eyes lifted in a quick probing peek at his visitor and then looked into another place, not of this earth. His face was browned by the sun, his hair, though thinning, hung in two braids, and his long nose and wide mouth added to the air of mysticism that he projected. He was 82, and his name was Henry Two Crow, a traditional healer and spiritual interpreter, known to white people as a medicine man.

He spoke in a voice low and strong. "Tomorrow we'll do a sweat and a ceremony," he said, "and a *lowanpi* (a singing). Bring your wife and your granddaughter's parents."

"Thanks, Uncle," William said, using the title of respect for an older man, though he was not related by blood. "The doctor wants to start her treatments a month from now. We need to get her back by then. I was wondering if you could give her some medicine, too."

The medicine man nodded. "We will do that," he said.

For the first time since he had heard the gut-wrenching and astounding news that his granddaughter was missing, William began to feel hope.

Some 20 miles away, Mel Triplett sat in the Lamar living room, sipped the last of his coffee and set his cup down, nodding slowly as he considered what Hal Lamar had just told him. Some of it he understood and some of it he didn't like.

"Yeah, I remember Hollister and his family," he said, "Mary Lee and Bernadette. I believe they had two sons and one died. So, he passed away 15 years ago, and you just found out?"

"Just today," Hal told him.

"And Mary Lee is living in North Dakota?"

Hal nodded.

"So, what's your take on this? If Hollister is dead, who took your granddaughter? Could it be Bernadette herself?"

"Looks that way to me," Hal said.

"Maybe she waylaid your daughter and her husband," Triplett suggested.

"I'm convinced it was her."

"I get your reasons for not bringing in the FBI, but I don't like it. The state DCI might have helped, somehow. They still might."

"Our guess is that they're taking Annie to Argentina. Law enforcement from here won't be much help there. Besides, we don't want to take the chance of Annie being hurt, or us never seeing her again if whoever has Annie finds out we involved them. You can understand that, can't you?"

Triplett nodded. "Yeah, I do." He looked at the empty cup on the coffee table. "Well, if there's any way I can help, let me know."

"Thanks, Mel."

"But, you know, I might just go talk to that woman who helped them kids. She said her name was Stearns, I think. Maybe she saw something."

TWELVE

William Black Spotted Horse stared at the stuffed animal heads hanging from the walls of Hal Lamar's den. Roosevelt elk, pronghorn antelope, Dall sheep, Rocky Mountain sheep, mule deer, white-tail deer, black bear, and New Mexico peccary were the ones he could identify. There were a few he couldn't and assumed they had to be African game, especially the one with thin wicked horns about three-feet long. But he wasn't here to talk about Hal's hunting adventures.

He turned down the offer of a draft beer and waited while Hal finished mixing a drink for himself and took a seat on the high stool at the end of the bar. William decided not to explain that he was going to a ceremony later in the evening and that one of Henry Two Crow's unbending rules was no alcohol prior to it.

"Here's my thought," Hal said, picking up the conversation. "Jenny told me she and Jarod are tracking Bernadette and they think they can find where she or her dad bought property and take up their trail from there. It amazes me they can do that. I'm leaving tomorrow. You could follow once we know where Bernadette lives. I'm betting that's where Annie will be."

To his own surprise, William agreed with every word Hal spoke. "Yup," he said. "One thing bothers me, though. Once we're both in country, how do we keep in touch? I think we need to know where each other is. If we don't, we'll both be operating blind and then we're bound to make a serious mistake."

"Yeah, yeah, you're right. Hey, why don't we ask them whiz kids of ours? They're into that stuff."

William placed a call to Jarod and posed the question, raising his eyebrows as he got the answer.

"Satellite telephones," William said. "He said there's a shop in Sioux Falls where you can stop on the way to the airport. Works like a cell phone, except he said to get the one that has the broadest coverage. I'll get one, too. Have them set it up for you and give us the number."

"Damn," was Hal's reaction. "Why didn't we think of that?"

"Anyway, the kids will know where you'll be staying in Buenos Aires so that's another way to be in touch. Then there's the Internet. You do email, right?"

Hal chuckled. "Yeah, of course, Jenny taught me."

Just then Jarod rang.

"Hello, again," William answered.

"Hey, Dad, put me on speaker so Hal can hear, too."

"Okay," William said, "you're on."

"Great," Jarod said. "Jennifer came up with a great system. We'll find out where public internet is available down there and you both need to buy as many international calling cards as you can. That way if the satellite phones don't cut it, you can use a public phone or a phone from a hotel room or any landline with the credits on the card. If you can't contact each other, you call us and we'll be your message board."

"That's brilliant," William said. "I knew there was a reason I liked that girl the day you brought her home. Anything else?"

"I have the address for the store with the satellite phones. We can give it to Hal later. Jennifer just called them and they're setting aside two phones, with extra batteries."

Virginia came into the den and heard the last part of Jarod's comments.

"Okay, thanks, you two," Hal said. "I guess we'll call if we have any other questions." He turned to Virginia. "Those two are smarter than all get out."

She glanced at her husband. "So, what have you two decided?"

Hal summarized what had transpired.

She listened, a worried look on her face. "You're going to be—both of you—half a world away," she fretted. "But I guess there's no other choice, is there?"

Both men shook their heads. "We got to do it this way," Hal told her. "I heard someone say once that no matter how short or long a road is, there's an end to it. But to get to the end you got to walk the road."

As William and Hal finished their meeting, Sheriff Mel Triplett was pulling into the driveway of the Stearns place. He had checked records at the courthouse earlier in the day. Stephan Stearns was the original owner, dating back to the 1940s. His wife Melinda had lived there after he had died, leasing out the farmland to a couple of the neighbors. There was a daughter named Eunice, but according to what he had dug up, the farmhouse itself had been empty for a lot of years. The Stearns women had moved away some time ago.

An older Buick sedan was parked near the house. As he got out of his truck, Triplett noticed that there were no other tracks. It looked like the Buick had not gone anywhere for a while. He knocked on the front door and waited. Everything was quiet. There were birds in the few trees nearby and somewhere from a pasture he heard a bull bellowing. He knocked again, harder this time. His impression was that no one was around. Walking to the end of the porch, he shaded his eyes and looked in through a window. He saw the couch, with a tall stuffed chair near it. Triplett stayed at the window but saw nothing and heard nothing. No radio, no television, no voices.

Stepping to the door, he tried the handle and was not surprised to find it locked. Hurrying to his truck he grabbed the L-shaped tire wrench he used to force open doors. It didn't take much force to pry open the old lock and the door swung open.

Standing in the living room, he listened for a minute. There was no art on the walls and no photographs of family or friends on credenzas or end tables. Walking into the southwest bedroom, he visually searched the room without touching anything. He did the same in the northwest bedroom. It was an older house with small rooms and bare floors. His footsteps were loud.

The kitchen was clean, but he noticed the thin veneer of dust on the table's surface. He opened a drawer and saw utensils. Pots and a couple of skillets hung from hooks, and china plates, bowls, and cups were in the cupboards. He assumed the narrow door next to the refrigerator led to the basement and when he opened it, he was correct. He carefully went down the steps to the bare wood floor and was surprised to find the power still on when he flipped a light switch. A bare bulb from somewhere in the basement came on.

An old fuel oil furnace stood in one corner and a hot water heater near the other corner. There was no washer or dryer. He walked across to the small room at one end. In it he found a fully furnished bedroom. The bed was made. Triplett lifted the spread and found a blanket and sheets beneath it. He couldn't help but wonder who had slept in it, since it was smaller than a double bed. In fact, it was more like a child's bed.

With a sigh he turned and started back for the stairs. He had left open the kitchen door leading to the basement. As his eyes came level with the kitchen floor, he noticed something small and dark near the leg of the table. Stepping up into the kitchen, he closed the basement door, bent down to look at the object, and knew immediately what it was: a flash drive.

Digging into his pocket, he brought out his pocketknife, opened a small blade and picked up the flash drive by inserting the blade into the slot on the end. Holding it carefully upright, he walked out of the house, stopping to close the front door, and headed for his truck. In the glove box he found a small plastic bag, from a container he carried for just such occasions, and carefully dropped the flash drive in. He wanted fingerprints off it but also to see what was on it. He was going to need someone who knew about computers. He thought he knew just the person.

He was about to get into the driver's seat when he saw the barn. Without hesitating he shut the truck's door and headed for the old building, trusty L-wrench in hand. The old hasp on the double doors was locked. Triplett inserted his wrench and broke it open then pulled on the doors to let light into the interior.

His first impression was just an empty barn. A few boards in the stalls had fallen loose. It felt empty. No old tools or old hay, just an empty barn. He stood and cast an appraising eye around the interior. Something didn't seem right, and then he realized what it was. The wall he was looking at was not an exterior wall. Its boards were vertical, not horizontal. He walked to it and pushed. It wasn't solid and felt more like a door than a wall. Triplett pushed again, harder this time, and saw two boards separate. He pushed again, forcing a wider separation and stuck the tip of the L-wrench in the space. With a grunt he forced it in farther and pulled.

Triplett heard old wood groaning, then a crack and a squeak. He cussed and jumped sideways as half the wall toppled toward him. It landed with a crash and the sound of breaking wood. He waved at the small cloud of dust as it billowed around him and stepped through the space where the wall had been. There was plenty of light in the room behind the section of the wall still standing. Triplett grinned broadly. He saw the old pickup truck.

A minute or two later he returned to the barn with a digital camera and snapped several shots of the truck, from as many angles as he could. He wasn't surprised when the South Dakota license plates turned out to be cardboard. At first glance they looked real enough, but hardly anyone took more than a passing glance at license plates.

Two hours later he was knocking on the front door of a neat little frame house on the east edge of Cold River.

"Afternoon, Sheriff," Jennifer said, though her tone was tentative.

"I just have a favor to ask," he said, wanting her to know he was not bringing bad news or trouble of any kind. He nodded at Jarod as he walked into the room. Two minutes later he was describing to the young couple how he had found the flash drive.

"Your dad swears by your skills with all kinds of electrical and digital stuff," he said to Jarod. He held up the flash drive, holding it on the sides with a small needle nose plier. "So, I'm guessing you can show me what's on this little gadget."

"Yeah," Jarod said, "easy as falling off a log."

"Good, but don't touch it, use this plier, it might have fingerprints."

Jarod opened his laptop and showed Triplett where to insert the flash drive. A couple of seconds later a name popped up on the screen, causing the young couple to gasp. There on the screen in capital letters was ANNIE.

"What does that mean?" the sheriff asked.

"Someone gave a name to the flash drive," Jarod said.

His hand shaking slightly, Jarod clicked on the name, the screen became bright and three small square icons appeared, all resembling pages of a book. Beneath each was the name of the file. The first was GROUND, the second was WATER, and the third was AIR.

"Damn," the sheriff muttered. "Looks like a dead end."

"Maybe," Jarod said quietly. "There's one way to find out."

He moved the cursor to the word GROUND and clicked it.

All the wood in the large fire pit behind Henry Two Crow's house had burned down to embers. It was dusk, the fire had been burning since late afternoon, and all the rocks—some larger than a man's fist—were glowing red. A small crowd of Lakota people was waiting near the sweat lodge, a dome shaped structure, 12 feet in diameter and 4 feet high. Heavy canvas snugly covered the frame of two-inch willows. A part of the covering over the doorway was pulled open and faced west. Inside in the center was a circular pit where the hot stones would be placed whenever Henry Two Crow decided the *inipi*, the renewal or rebirth ceremony (referred to as "sweat" in English), would begin. After the stones were placed in the pit and the door was closed, the ceremony of prayer and song would formally begin with Two Crow pouring water on the hot stones, generating steam. The resulting intense heat would cause the participants to sweat profusely.

Physiologically sweating expelled toxins; spiritually and symbolically it purged the participants of illness and difficulties.

After the *inipi*, the *lowanpi*, or "the singing" ceremony, would happen next. That would be conducted inside the ceremony house, a small frame building just east of the sweat lodge. Tonight, the *lowanpi* was at the request of Annie's Lakota grandparents, to ask for healing and protection for their seriously ill granddaughter.

As the crowd waited, William and Marie Black Spotted Horse among them, an older sedan arrived south of the Two Crow residence, parking alongside the other vehicles already there. Two figures emerged from the half-light of dusk. Jarod and Jennifer hurried toward William and Marie, their expressions a mixture of excitement and anxiety.

"Dad," Jarod said, stopping and leaning in close to his father. "Do you remember the woman who helped us at that farmhouse? She said her name was Eunice Stearns."

William nodded. "Yeah, I do. Why do you ask?"

"We think she's the woman who attacked us and took Annie. We think she might be Bernadette McGiven."

William and Marie looked at their children with unconcealed surprise. "Why do you think that?" William asked.

Jarod smiled. "Well, Sheriff Triplett went to check out the place. No one was there. But he found a couple of pieces of evidence that, as far as I'm concerned, confirms the woman who took Annie is Hollister McGiven's daughter Bernadette."

"Well, tell us, Son!"

"The sheriff found a flash drive and a 1972 Ford half-ton pickup, the one that we thought was disabled by the side of the road."

William and Marie could only shake their heads in astonishment.

Jarod delivered his other news. "We opened the flash drive. It didn't reveal Bernadette's plan in so many words, but based on what we saw, it's a good bet that she took Annie and drove to Florida, took a yacht to the eastern end of Puerto Rico, and from there caught an amphibian seaplane to Bahia Blanca in Argentina. They're probably flying there now. As we speak, Annie may be on a plane to Argentina. That sort of proves that Bernadette McGiven is the mastermind behind all this. I'm certain the flash drive belonged to her. That house was not occupied when we drove by it on an earlier camping trip. She was the only one to occupy since."

THIRTEEN

The sweat lodge ceremony began just after dark and concluded about an hour later. The nearly 20 or so participants had dressed casually. Women had worn specially designed loose-fitting cotton dresses and men usually wore tank tops or T-shirts and gym shorts, which was always the case when women and men participated together. After the sweat ceremony concluded everyone changed back into street cloths After they all gathered in the ceremony house the *lowanpi* began. No one cared about time or if the ceremonies started or ended at a given hour, only that they happened.

Jennifer had accompanied her husband to ceremonies since before they were married, so she was an experienced participant and a firm believer. Likewise, Jarod had accompanied his wife to Methodist services, though they didn't attend every Sunday. Although Virginia was aware of her daughter's participation in the traditional Lakota spiritual ceremonies, she divulged nothing to her husband. Hal blindly assumed that his daughter was "true" to all things white and Christian.

Jennifer was the only non-Lakota in this night's ceremonies. It was not unusual for non-Lakota people to be included in Lakota spiritual rituals and ceremonies due to generations of mixed marriages. Their presence was allowed by some Lakota medicine men, but not always.

When Jennifer, like many non-Lakota participants, first attended a Lakota spiritual ceremony, she was afraid, primarily due to misinformation, misinterpretation, and plain misrepresentation. Many white people, especially Christians, are quick to believe that Lakota spirituality is "heathen," or at least unconventional, archaic, and not genuine, and therefore something to be suspicious of or avoided.

In the early days of the reservations, after the end of the so-called Indian Wars, many Christian denominations—Catholicism foremost among them—did everything in their power to convert Lakota people to Christianity. Of course, in carrying out what they believed was their "sacred duty," they managed to seriously diminish the practice of Lakota beliefs. But not entirely. Ceremonies and rituals, such as the Sun Dance, went underground for several decades, conducted and performed far from the prying eyes and ears of Catholic priests, government officials, and their enforcers—the Indian police, Lakota men who essentially turned their backs on their culture to help stamp out Lakota "religion."

As destructive as the government and their religious cohorts were, they were not entirely successful. Lakota men, and some women, answered the calling to be healers and spiritual interpreters, ensuring that—despite persecution and prosecution—Lakota spiritual beliefs and practices did not entirely die. That night it was fortunate for little Annie Black Spotted Horse that these had survived.

At the same hour that Jennifer was joining her husband and her mother- and father-in-law and the other participants in Henry Two Crow's ceremony house, Hal Lamar was at the bar in his den, nursing his second whiskey and water. He sighed and glanced over as Virginia walked in.

"What time do you think we should leave for Sioux Falls in the morning?" she asked.

"Early, probably seven. We need to stop at that electronics store and pick up the phone. I guess you can bring the other one back for William."

Virginia wrapped her robe tighter and took a seat on the stool next to her husband. "You look worried," she commented.

"Yeah," he snorted. "Just a bit. I've never taken a trip like this before. It's like walking into a whiteout blizzard. Maybe we should have called in the FBI, I don't know."

"We've been over that, my dear man."

"I know, I know. It's just that there's a lot of hope riding on two old men."

"Two old men who love their granddaughter very much," Virginia said, trying to reassure her husband.

"Of course, but what does that guarantee? William, well, maybe he doesn't hate me, but he sure doesn't like me. Hell, we never liked each other going back a long way before our kids married each other. And now, irony of ironies, my granddaughter is half-Lakota, she's seriously ill, and half a damn world away, and it's my job to get her back."

"To William, his granddaughter is half-white, and it's not just your job, it's his, too. And my prayer is that the two of you are grown up enough to put aside your dislike of one another. Because this is about Annie."

Hal took a sip of whiskey and glanced sideways at his wife. "You sound like you're talking to a kid."

"Am I?"

A split second before he almost lost his temper, Hal took a deep breath, expelled it slowly, and put the glass down on the bar. After a moment, he shook his head. "No, no, you're not. You're talking to Annie's grandpa."

"Good," she said gently, sliding off the stool and wrapping her arms around him. "Because that's what we need. The best of what Annie's grandpas are. Come on, you need to sleep, you have promises to keep."

Henry Two Crow was instructed by his helper Spirits to prepare a medicine from a common prairie plant, its root and its leaves to be thoroughly ground and placed in a special container for a long journey, to be delivered by her Lakota grandfather.

Sometime after two in the morning, all the participants had left after sharing a meal. Only the Black Spotted Horse family remained. Henry Two Crow's helper Spirits had come into the ceremony after the songs of invitation were sung and he prayed, and many of the participants added their prayers as well. The Spirits told Henry to prepare a special herbal tea for Annie. Its leaves had to be thoroughly ground and then placed in a small soft leather bag.

"I'll have the medicine ready in four days, it will take that long to dry," Henry Two Crow told William. "Your grandmother Ollie will make the bag to put it in, to hide it from ignorance and prying eyes."

"Thank you, Uncle," William said.

"There's one other thing," Henry said. "The Spirits said that someone was taking revenge against Annie's blue-eyed grandfather."

"That explains a lot," Marie commented. Jarod and Jennifer nodded in agreement.

Two Crow nodded slowly "A woman who is using money to hurt the blue-eyed grandfather," he added.

"What does that mean, 'using money'?" William asked.

"She is angry because of something that the blue-eyed grandfather did many years ago. She is angry and full of hate."

"Grandpa," Jennifer said, "what does that have to do with Annie?"

Two Crow looked sympathetically at Jennifer. "The woman knows that taking the blue-eyed grandfather's granddaughter will hurt him badly."

"Will we see her again?" Jennifer asked timidly.

Two Crow nodded and waved a hand toward the open door. "Tonight is the full moon. By the next full moon, you will see your daughter again, my girl. In the days and nights in between, all of you must be strong because you will be tested by the things that will happen. You must stay strong and use your minds. That is what the Spirits say will bring your little girl home. And one other thing."

The medicine man paused and smiled gently, trying to reassure the circle of worried faces. His gaze settled on Jennifer once again. "The Spirits say the angry woman made one mistake. They say she has forgotten your daughter's brown-eyed grandfather."

Nearly an hour later, after helping Ollie Two Crow clean up and put away food, Marie, William, Jennifer, and Jarod walked out to their vehicles. Jarod paused and touched his father's arm.

"I think I know what Grandpa Henry meant," he said. He looked thoughtfully at his wife and parents. "When we opened the flash drive the sheriff found, there were three files. Grandpa Henry said that this was happening 'because of money,' and that the woman is 'using money.'"

He paused again to look at his parents. "The files on the flash drive were part of a plan. The first one was titled Ground, and it was about driving a motorhome from here to Naples, Florida. There was a map, a driving map. The second said Water, and it had the name of a dock in Naples and a yacht club in eastern Puerto Rico. The third was Air, and it had the name of a person and a photograph of an amphibian airplane, you know, the kind that can take off and land on water. The plane's destination was off the eastern coast of Argentina, near a place called Bahia."

William nodded, grim realization on his face. "Of course, all of that isn't cheap. Maybe it was financed by the money Hal wired to Argentina."

"There seems to be a lot of layers here," Jarod pointed out. "If that is Bernadette's methodology, using Hal's money to finance a kidnapping, why is she doing that and what's the real motive? I mean, if she's spending all that money on using a motorhome, a yacht, and an airplane, she's not profiting financially. Isn't a kidnapper's motive to get money because they need it? Maybe that's not the case here. And if so, what is she really after?"

Jennifer looked frightened. "But Grandpa Henry said we would get Annie back, right?"

Jarod took her hand. "Yeah, and I believe that, with all my heart. But he also said that we would be tested, and we have to use our minds. I'm just thinking that the more we know, the more we figure this out, the easier it'll be for your dad and mine."

"We shouldn't overlook anything, not even things that seem inconsequential," William warned. "In that light, I think I'll go see a friend of mine tomorrow. Someone who's been to Argentina recently."

Jennifer and Jarod were awake early to go see Hal and Virginia off. A 15-minute drive brought them to the ranch southeast of Cold River. Hal was nervous and on the verge of irritable, until he laid eyes on his daughter. He knew he needed to be strong for her.

Jarod carried his father-in-law's bag out to the truck and loaded it. Stepping back, he reached his hand out to Hal.

"I can't thank you enough, Hal," he said, looking the man square in the eye.

Hal took the younger man's hand and held it firmly. "We're in this together," he said, huskily. "We'll get it done."

After a long hug from Jennifer, Hal reluctantly let go. In her tear-filled eyes he saw fear, hope, and love.

"I love you, Daddy. Thank you."

He wiped the tears from her check. "Don't you worry too much," he said. "Cause the next time we see you, Annie will be with us."

"I believe you, Dad."

When he and Virginia reached the end of the driveway, he saw the young couple in the rear view mirror, standing hand-in-hand. There was only one thing wrong with that picture—Annie was not with them.

Hal stepped on the accelerator pedal and coaxed the truck onto the gravel road that led to the main highway. All he could see in his mind were the images of his daughter minutes after she had given birth to Annie. She had the same look her mother did when the nurses finished weighing and measuring Jennifer and then laid the tiny blanket-wrapped bundle in her arms—pure love. After the pain of childbirth, so much love. It was something to marvel at and protect. Hal was determined to bring his granddaughter home, if for no reason other than to see that look on his daughter's face again. He didn't know how he and William Black Spotted Horse would do it, but there had to be a way.

FOURTEEN

William sat in the Smokey River Sioux tribal president's outer office with four other people also waiting to see President Clayton Lone Hawk. A receptionist emerged from the president's office and smiled at him.

"Go right on in," she told him.

Clayton Lone Hawk came around his desk to greet him as the receptionist closed the door. "Hey, William, thanks for stopping by. I've been meaning to call you." He gestured toward a pair of chairs behind a coffee table.

"Not at all, thank you," William replied, taking a seat. "If I would have known six months ago that you would be sitting here, I might have pushed back my retirement."

Lone Hawk laughed and took the remaining chair. "Funny you should say that. The reason I wanted to call you is to ask you to be an advisor."

"I'd be happy and honored to help you in any way I can. By the way, I hear you got married, so, congratulations! All the women in the tribal office are talking about your beautiful wife."

"Yes, thanks, on both counts. I've told Veronica about you and your family, and we'd both love to have you all over one evening, perhaps on a weekend."

"We'd love it."

"Anyway, you said you wanted to talk to me about Argentina. Not many people know I was there recently."

"Well, there's a situation my family and I are facing, and it involves Argentina. A mutual friend, Chief Ben Avery, suggested I talk to you."

Lone Hawk heard the somber tone in William Black Spotted Horse's voice.

In the next few minutes, William took Clayton Lone Hawk into his confidence and told the story from the day of Annie's abduction up to Hal Lamar leaving for Sioux Falls that very morning. Lone Hawk listened, his sympathy growing as the story unfolded.

"Damn, William," he said, shaking his head. "What can I do to help?"

"Well, I'll be leaving in a few days. We have a plan in place, basically to find and rescue my granddaughter. So, anything you can tell me about your experience in Argentina, getting around there, the people, and just what it's like would really help."

Lone Hawk nodded. "Certainly. Ah, just give me a minute," he said, reaching for the phone.

William hesitated. "Listen, Clayton, your time is precious. I know that you face really tough issues every day, an epidemic of meth abuse, all the factions on the tribal council fighting each other, the state trying to take away our sovereignty, and all the issues related to land. There are people waiting out there who need your help. I just want information."

Lone Hawk nodded. "I appreciate what you're saying, and you know as well as I do those problems will be here tomorrow." He picked up the phone on the desk and buzzed his receptionist. "Cora, could you step in for a minute? Thanks."

The young woman entered a few seconds later, notepad in hand.

Lone Hawk glanced at his watch. "Cora," he said, "I'm going to visit with Mr. Black Spotted Horse for a bit, so I'm going to ask you to use your considerable skills of diplomacy and persuasion and explain to the people in the outer office that we'll need to push things back at least fifteen minutes, maybe more. If any one of them has an emergency situation, please send them to George Whirlwind Horse."

Cora finished writing and looked up. "Certainly. Anything else?"

"No, I'll let you know when we're done. Thank you."

A few seconds later President Lone Hawk pulled a small cylindrical object from a desk drawer, placed it atop his writing pad, and pushed a button. "This is my wife's idea," he explained, "a scrambler, of sorts. Just in case there are listening devices, it emits a range of sound waves that interfere so no one can hear what we're saying."

"Very James Bond," observed William, smiling, "and probably necessary in this day and age."

"Right. So, let me tell you about my trip to Argentina."

William and his family had attended the funeral of Lone Hawk's only daughter, though they hadn't known all the circumstances that had led to her death. As he listened to Clayton Lone Hawk tell the story, he was aghast.

A white pheasant hunter from Ohio had raped Autumn Lone Hawk, after luring her into a motel in Cold River. She had become pregnant and died when she hemorrhaged during an abortion. From the beginning the then sheriff of Redoubt County, Trent Cole, had refused to investigate, astoundingly allowing the rapist to go free.

Consequently, Clayton Lone Hawk pursued the rapist to Argentina, where the perpetrator was on a big game hunt. The story of Lone Hawk's lonely revenge odyssey to southern Patagonia astonished William. Because the FBI could not ignore the DNA evidence from the strand of hair Clayton had taken from the hunter's hairbrush, the rapist was finally charged. Amazingly, the man had come after Clayton, trying to exact his own revenge. Fortunately, the Smokey River Tribal Police and the FBI were on hand to apprehend him. The man was tried in federal court and was now serving a 25-year sentence. Sadly, this was an unusual outcome for a perpetrator of a white on Indian crime.

"Though I was clearly out of my element, the one advantage I had in Argentina was to be able to sort of blend in, thanks to being brown-skinned," Lone Hawk said. "It's a damn big country, and it doesn't seem as though you know where the Hollister woman is."

"We're shooting in the dark a bit," William agreed. "But I'm confident in my son and daughter-in-law's ability to dig up information. We know Bernadette bought some property down there. They're working now to find out where."

"Once you narrow the search area, I'd advise you to buy clothes like the locals and carry Argentinian pesos. I'll give you the names of two friends. They were a big help. You may not need them, but it might be worthwhile to have that ace up your sleeve. I'll call and give them your name, just in case, and I'll give you their phone numbers and addresses."

"Thanks, I appreciate that."

"You've got Uncle Henry Two Crow on your side. That's powerful help." Lone Hawk wrote names and numbers on the back of his business card and added his own personal cell phone number. "If there's anything I can help with, or if you get into a bind, give me a call. Good luck, my friend."

After he stepped out of Dr. Lone Hawk's back-office door, William's phone rang. It was Marie.

"Hal is on his way," she told him. "Virginia has a satellite phone for you. She'll be back tonight."

A buzz sounded in his ear and a quick glance revealed Jarod's name flashing on the screen. "Hey, hon, Jarod's calling. I'll talk to him and call you back."

"Hello, Son. I'm just leaving Agency Village. What's up?"

The excitement in Jarod's voice was obvious. "Dad! We found Hollister McGiven—I mean, his house. He bought a house and some acreage in the Pampas, the grasslands, east of a town called Santa Rosa. And according to their probate laws, the property went to his only surviving relative. It was inherited by Bernadette McGiven."

"You continue to amaze me, Son. Does she still own it?"

"We couldn't find anything to the contrary. Now we're trying to see if she still lives there. If we can locate her whereabouts, that will be your destination."

"Okay, I'll see you in about forty-five minutes."

Six thousand miles to the south in a land where the curve of the earth was downward, Annie Black Spotted Horse stared out of one of only two small windows on the right side of the airplane as it landed on water. Eight hours ago, they had taken off from water and now they had landed the same way. She saw another airplane floating on the water, but it was smaller and wasn't moving. It was simply floating next to what she knew were sailboats. All that mattered to her, and the reason for the lump in her throat, was that she was so far from home she couldn't begin to imagine where she was.

She and Bernadette and the chubby man were the only other people in the airplane, besides the two men she knew were pilots. The seats were comfortable and hers folded down into a bed, so she had slept part of the way. There was plenty of food and Bernadette had heated a delicious smelling chicken dish in the microwave and later there had been snacks. Annie had eaten a bit, but mostly sipped water and juice and used the bathroom three times.

Food and the obvious comforts were lost on Annie. Every passing minute away from Mom and Dad and home became nearly unbearable. The thought that she might never see them again was prodding her, like someone poking her in the back. She tried to ignore it, but like the growing sadness that hung like a dark cloud, it was harder and harder to push it away.

In a little while, the airplane slowed to a stop and the whine of the engines faded. She heard voices from outside, and then a door opened behind where the pilots sat. Light poured in along with the smell of the water, just like before they had taken off from a place called Caya Obispo, and she had heard someone say Puerto Rico. She had recognized that name from a geography class. She remembered the last time she had seen her mom and dad, walking toward an old truck stalled on the road, back home. She wished she could go back to that minute, so she could tell them not to go, because that's when things had changed.

FIFTEEN

By the time Virginia Lamar walked into her daughter and son-in-law's house in Cold River, her husband was in line in the international terminal at Miami International Airport. Having twice hunted in Africa and toured the European continent with Virginia, he was no stranger to the rigors and idiosyncrasies of international travel. For those trips, there was a discernible start and end, and an itinerary to show the way. Such was not the case now. He didn't know when he would be going home. Hal felt strangely disconnected as he moved in line a step or two at a time. He would land in Buenos Aires and had a return ticket from there as well. What would happen in between the arrival and departure dates was an unknown, a total blank. He hoped that in two weeks, or less, he would be arriving at this very terminal holding Annie by the hand. Hal was not a praying man, but in this moment, that was his prayer.

Meanwhile, Virginia walked in on her daughter huddled over a map at the kitchen table with Marie and William. Jennifer greeted her mother with a long hug.

"Dad called me from Miami about fifteen minutes ago," she said.

Virginia smiled wanly. "Yes, I just talked to him, too. He was complaining about the 'endless lines.'"

"How did he seem to you?"

"Tired, and anxious." Virginia moved toward the table. "How are you two?" she said to Marie and William. "And where's Jarod?"

"We talked him into resting for a bit," Marie answered. "He's been trying to ignore a headache. We older folks are trying to hang in. Has Jenny told you the latest she and Jarod have uncovered?"

"No," Virginia replied, sitting down at the table. "You've got some good news to cheer up a tired old lady?"

"We located property deeded to Hollister McGiven," Jennifer announced. "Near a city called Santa Rosa, in the central part of the country."

Virginia nodded wearily. "I guess the obvious assumption is that's where Annie is—or will be. Or maybe I'm just hoping it'll be that simple."

"You and me both," William admitted.

Virginia glanced toward the map and Jennifer put her finger on the name Santa Rosa. "So, how far is that from Buenos Aires?"

"About 300 miles," Jennifer told her. "Rapid City to Sioux Falls, essentially."

Virginia looked toward William. "Knowing this about Santa Rosa, what are your plans?"

"Well," he said, "I'll follow as soon as I can, depending on what Hal tells us after he gets further word from Bernadette. We have no choice but to make this up as we go along."

Marie moved to sit next to Virginia, reaching out and touching the other woman's arm. "I miss her, too," she said. "And I believe, with all my heart, we'll see our little girl again. Alive and well."

Gazing at her own hands silently for a moment, Virginia sighed. "Thank you, Marie. I've always been thankful for the blessings in my life. Now, I'm asking for one for all of us."

Hal tilted his seat back and tried not to feel guilty about upgrading to first class. But it was a long flight, and he didn't want to sit for hours with virtually no legroom and arrive stiff and sore from just sitting. He refused the champagne and asked for coffee.

There was no guarantee, of course, that Annie would be anywhere in Argentina. Fear and assumption were driving everything. Annie's family was afraid that ignoring Bernadette McGiven's instructions would result in Annie being hurt or killed. But Bernadette McGiven had yet to say, "Come to such-and-such a place in Argentina and get your granddaughter." Therefore, Hal was in an airliner 35,000 feet above the Atlantic Ocean, heading to the other side of the equator because he, and all of Annie's family, had been forced to take a leap of faith.

Hal peeked at his watch. Six hours to Buenos Aires. He sighed and leaned his head back against the cushion. The seat was comfortable, but he was not. In his gut was a feeling that he was responsible. Whether Virginia or Jennifer held him responsible, he didn't know, but he felt responsible.

Truth be told, he knew he had been heavy-handed in his response to Hollister McGiven in their business dealing. McGiven had sold 20 head of registered Shorthorns without his permission, clearly violating two conditions of their limited partnership agreement. He had made the sale without Hal's approval, and he had then deposited the money in his own account. Hal lost his temper and threw McGiven out of his den when he came clean.

Anger made him deaf to McGiven's pleading. His reasons didn't matter. McGiven's youngest son was ill, and McGiven explained he had thousands of dollars in hospital bills. His son had died not quite a year later.

The partnership had been a limited one, and it was dissolved after only ten years, in 1987. Hal had exercised his right to dissolve the partnership in writing, an action upheld in court, and had refunded McGiven's original investment. A lawsuit filed by McGiven sought payment for what he estimated his share of the partnership was worth at the time of the dissolution—just over $250,000. Hal had won in that instance as well. The court had ruled that the figure was based on an estimate rather than on verifiable evidence.

Thirty years was a long time to carry a grudge, but clearly McGiven had wanted retribution for the wrong he deemed he had suffered. Since the wire transfer was for $750,000, Hal hoped that it was the atonement McGiven, or his daughter, was seeking. Somewhere in his gut Hal had an ugly feeling there was more he might have to pay, and it would require more than just money.

Annie looked stoically out of one of the large windows in the room Bernadette said was now her bedroom. One window faced east and the other north. The endless expanse of grass on the rolling hills seemed to go on and on. Annie knew what prairie was since she had grown up with open spaces, but here the grass looked different. Seeing the yellow and brown grass stretching away in the distance brought a lump to her throat. The bars on the windows told her she might never go home. They made her sick to her stomach. Total confinement had never been part of her world. She tried to hold back a sob but couldn't.

She quickly wiped the tears that slid from her eyes. On the way to her room, they had passed another room with a desk and a computer. Annie wondered if the computer needed a password to turn it on. She would wait and see. Bernadette had to use that computer sooner or later. First, though, Annie had to figure out where this place was. If that computer had map search software, her dad had shown her how to find GPS coordinates.

One thing she knew for sure. If they—Dad, Grandpa William, and Grandpa Hal—knew where she was, they would come get her. Suddenly, the bars on the windows looked thinner.

At the other end of the house Bernadette McGiven Covena had just closed the small journal in her hand when she heard heavy footsteps approaching. She put it in the middle drawer of her desk and slid it closed quickly. A soft knock came at the door.

"Come in," she said.

Smith entered and took a seat in a large, overstuffed chair, looking expectantly at her. "When do you want me to leave for Buenos Aires?" he asked.

"As soon as you can if you're not too tired. I'm guessing Hal will be arriving late this evening."

"No, I feel fine. Is there anything else you want me to check on, besides making sure Hal gets where he needs to go?"

She shook her head, her eyes full of anticipation. "No, everything else is under control. Marta will be here later to help me with the girl. I've got phone calls to make. There's a shipment I've got to square away."

"Okay, good. Sounds like things are back to normal," Smith said.

Bernadette nodded slowly. Her eyes shifted and settled on a framed image standing on her desk. It was a black and white photograph of a man on a horse. She stared at it with a mixture of love and sadness, as she always did. "Dad loved being a ranch hand and a rodeo cowboy. He grew up working cattle with his dad. That's all they knew. They rode for the biggest ranches in two states. Grandpa McGiven died before he was 50 from some kind of rare sickness. Mom and Dad met when he was 37 and mom was 10 years younger, well, you know the story. She was a teacher. They got married and made a plan. Dad had been saving his money for years. They lived mostly on her paycheck. When he was nearly 40, he took his savings and bought into a limited partnership with Harold Lamar, using every cent. Lamar wanted to add a line of Shorthorn cattle and my dad knew all about Shorthorns. So, he managed the Shorthorn part of the operation. Then Tommy got sick, inherited grandpa's rare disease. It cost a lot of money. Dad sold twenty Shorthorns to pay the doctors and hospitals. He always believed a man paid his way."

Bernadette paused and loosed a melancholy sigh. "Lamar said Dad violated the partnership agreement by selling the cattle without his permission. So, he forced Dad out. He gave him back his original investment, but the hospital bills took most of it. After Tommy died, we moved so Dad could get work, but Lamar blackballed him. None of the big ranchers would hire him. He never finished high school. All he knew was being a cowboy. He got discouraged and started drinking. It got bad enough that Mom left him. He lost himself in the bottle and all he could ever find were dead end jobs for minimum wage."

"He gave me $100 he had saved so I could go on a trip to Colorado my senior year in high school. I bought a scratch lottery ticket for a dollar and gave it to him. Turned out to be a winner—$10,000. That's how we came here. He read an old magazine article about the Pampas, but he also read where the dollar was worth a heck of a lot more than the peso. So that's how we bought this place, though it was run down. We fixed it up and bought a few head of cattle, but he didn't live long enough for us to buy any more."

Bernadette tenderly placed the photograph down on the desk and lifted her face to Smith.

"Damn," he said. "I don't understand why Lamar got pissed over money to pay hospital bills."

"Yeah, he could have overlooked it. It didn't hurt him. It didn't take food off his table. Last time I checked that son-of-a-bitch was worth $20 million, when you add up the land, cattle, equipment, and all the property, as well as cash on hand."

"Oh, hell, he can afford a bit of ransom money."

Bernadette shook her head. "Yeah, but what hurt Dad the most was that he couldn't find good paying jobs. So, I want from Lamar what he can't pay in gold, silver, pesos, or dollars. For what he did to Dad, he's got to pay back in the same currency."

Deke Smith was about to ask what that meant until he saw the look on her face. It was a look that almost made him feel sorry for Harold Lamar. He had never seen so much hate ever on the face of a human being.

Hal turned his watch ahead to match the local time after he heard the flight attendant's announcement upon landing—11:32 p.m. By the time he retrieved his bag and cleared customs, it was one in the morning. At 1:30 a.m. his taxi dropped him in front of Hotel Conquistador. Twenty minutes after that he was on a bed in single room staring up at the ceiling. When he felt himself drifting off to sleep, he remembered the satellite telephone. Using the adaptor plug the desk clerk had given him, he plugged in the phone to charge it.

For the first time in weeks, he slept through the night. A red light blinking on the room phone was the first thing he noticed when he awoke, other than gray light seeping through the curtains. Sleepily he punched zero for the front desk.

"Good morning, Señor Lamar," said a woman's voice.

"Morning, my message light was on," he said.

"Of course, there is an envelope for you here at the desk. You may pick it up at your convenience."

"Thank you."

Well, he thought, *that didn't take long. And so it begins.*

Apprehension settled between his shoulder blades, and even a good hot shower couldn't make it go away.

SIXTEEN

After taking the envelope from the front desk, Hal walked as nonchalantly as he could to the middle of the lobby. He picked an upholstered chair next to a small table. His heart pounding, he opened the envelope and read the typewritten note:

> *Go to Banco Nuevo Rio two blocks south of the hotel, ask for Ricardo Guiermo. Show proof you wired the funds from your bank. Have a cashier's check for entire amount issued to The Children's Trust. Then check out of your hotel and check into Hotel Menaul at 767 Cristobal Avenue. Instructions will be delivered. Talk to no one, here or at home.*

Precise instructions, he thought, no room for misunderstanding or mistakes. Lamar folded the message and slid it back into its envelope. He looked out a large front window, using his peripheral vision to see who else was in the lobby. Those last eight words of the message indicated to him he was likely being watched. Resisting the urge to look around, he decided to test that possibility.

Returning to the desk, he asked for the nearest restaurant.

"Ah," said the young man in a sport coat. "We do have one on the premises. Go past the elevators." He pointed at the corridor at the end of the counter. "Or there's a very nice café on the other side of the street at the end of the block. Go out the front doors and turn right and turn left at the street corner."

Lamar gave the young man his friendliest smile. "Thank you," he said, pleasantly. His affected cheerfulness belied the resentment and anger roiling in his stomach. Back in his room, he gathered his overcoat, turned on the satellite phone, silenced the ring, and placed it in the overcoat's inside buttoned pocket. He wasn't exactly hungry, but he thought it might be a good idea to get something in his stomach. Besides, if the little clandestine episode he was planning were to appear genuine, he would have to eat. Lastly, he grabbed his zippered leather folder, checking to see that all the necessary papers for the bank were inside.

Following the desk clerk's directions, he was able to find the restaurant—Claudine's. It didn't seem like a Spanish name, he thought. The hostess led him to a narrow booth against the wall halfway into the room. He took the seat facing the front door. The lovely young, dark-haired girl asked him a question in Spanish. Trying not to be obvious, he peripherally saw several people already in the restaurant: two older men at the counter and a few in the larger part of the room where he sat.

"Ah, sorry," he told her. "I don't speak Spanish."

"No problem. What would you like to drink?"

"Coffee, just black. Thank you."

Nodding, she reached into a metal holder against the wall at the end of the table, pulled out a menu in English and handed it to him with a smile.

Lamar slid from the seat and removed his overcoat, draping it neatly over the back of the booth, and sat back down. The front door opened and a slender woman entered and paused for a moment, seeming to look about for someone. In a few seconds the hostess met the woman and gave her a large envelope.

"Gracias," the slender woman said softly. The hostess returned to the back of the restaurant.

The slender woman left just as a man in dark clothes entered, holding the door open for her. He took a seat at the counter after a quick glance around the room.

A server appeared with a small carafe of coffee and stopped at Lamar's table. "Señor," she said. "What may I get for you?"

"Ah," he said, "a small breakfast steak and scrambled eggs. Well done for the steak."

"Of course," she said and placed the carafe on the table.

A man and a woman, presumably a couple, entered and were guided to the back of the restaurant. Hal glanced at them as they passed. They were not elderly but were definitely past middle age and well dressed. He crossed them off the list of people who might be keeping him under surveillance.

The man at the counter placed an order and focused his attention on a cell phone, seeming to text. Other people began arriving, some alone, some in pairs, and some in groups. Truthfully, any of them could be watching him—or none of them.

His food came and the steak turned out to be tender and delicious; instead of toast there was a sort of hard tack cracker. He took his time. The note in the envelope had not indicated deadlines. As he finished his coffee, a man entered the restaurant and pointed to one of the narrow booths when the hostess arrived to seat him. Hal looked at him closely, noticing his dark trench coat, which he kept on after he sat. The man had a round face and short brown hair, basically an average non-descript, slightly over-weight appearance, perhaps 40-years-old. He didn't look local to Lamar, too pale.

A moment of sudden panic struck him when his server brought the ticket. He had not yet converted any of his cash to pesos. Fortunately, the cashier took his credit card. He took quick glances at the man at the counter and the chubby newcomer in the booth. Neither looked his way.

The Banco Nuevo Rio was half a block down on the opposite side of the street. Hal walked through a revolving door into the bank's main lobby. He immediately saw a long reception desk, with two young women sitting behind it.

"Good morning," the young woman to his left said. "How may I help you?"

"My name is Harold Lamar and I would like to talk to Mr. Ricardo Guiermo. I'm sorry I don't have an appointment."

"Not a problem, Señor Lamar. What can we do for you?"

"A few days ago, I wired money to your bank from the United States. Now I need to collect the funds in the form of a cashier's check and deliver it to the recipient."

As he spoke, the woman wrote on a pad, then placed a call in Spanish.

"Señor Lamar, come with me, please," she said.

She led him down a hallway past two sumptuously furnished floor-to-ceiling enclosed glass cubicles and opened the door to a third cubicle. "Please, have a seat. Señor Guiermo will be here momentarily."

"Thank you."

"Not at all, Señor. Is there anything else you need?"

A thought struck him. "Ah, yes, actually. I need to exchange dollars for pesos. Where do I go to do that?"

She dazzled him with a smile. "If you have American dollars or a credit card, I would be happy to do that for you."

He pulled out his wallet and slid out a credit card and passed it to her.

"How much would you like?"

"Ah, perhaps $2000 worth. How much is that roughly?"

"32,000 pesos," she told him. "Approximately."

"Thank you, that will be fine."

"I will return in a few minutes."

A young man in a dark blue three-piece suit arrived not two seconds after the young woman left. He looked like he wasn't quite old enough to shave.

"Good morning, Mr. Lamar," he said. "I'm Ricardo Guiermo. I understand we are processing funds for you this morning." His handshake was firm as he took in Hal's face and appearance.

"Yes, that's right." Hal slipped the papers out of the leather folder. "I have a copy of the wire transfer here."

"Thank you. Please, have a seat."

Guiermo took a seat and typed in his password on the desktop computer, and then a number from Hal's copy. He took several seconds to read the information on the screen, nodded and turned to Hal.

"The transfer was into a holding account. For your information we can hold your funds up to 30 calendar days. What would you like to do, Mr. Lamar?"

"I would like a cashier's check drawn for the entire amount, to The Children's Trust."

"Of course," the banker said, writing the name on a small pad. "May I see your passport, please?"

Guiermo studied the document before handing it back and began typing on the keyboard. "There is a 1 percent fee," he said. "We can deduct it from your wire or you can pay separately."

Hal took out his wallet and extracted another credit card, passing it to the banker.

As Hal sat back and waited, a thought popped into his head, like a coyote peeking over a hill. The instructions in the envelope had specifically said to contact Ricardo Guiermo. Why? Was Guiermo somehow involved with Annie's abduction, or simply someone known to Bernadette McGiven in the course of doing business? And what kind of business was Bernadette McGiven involved in?

Guiermo unlocked a desk drawer and took out a sheet of watermarked paper, placing it in a printer on a credenza. With one tap of his finger on the keyboard, the paper moved silently through the printer and emerged from a top tray. Meanwhile he processed the credit card payment and handed the invoice to Hal for his signature, took the cashier's check from the printer, signed it and slid it into a fitted envelope with the bank's logo, then handed it to Hal, along with the wiring papers and his credit card.

"Is there anything else I may help you with today, Mr. Lamar?" he asked courteously.

Hal was about to mention his pesos when the young woman entered and gave him his credit card and a small bank bag,

"Your cash is in the bag," she said. "Along with your receipt."

"Thank you," Hal said, shaking their hands. "That's everything I need today."

The young woman smiled and left. Ricardo Guiermo turned back to the computer and logged off. "You know, Mr. Lamar, The Children's Trust is a fine charitable foundation," he commented. "It was set up to help children in the poor rural areas of our country, especially children who have lost one or both parents or a sibling. But I'm certain you knew that, since you are a donor."

Hal paused for a second, trying to mask his surprise. "Any organization that helps children is doing good work," he said quietly.

A few steps down the hallway he pushed open the door to a restroom. Since it was empty, he took off his overcoat, grabbed the satellite phone, powered it on, and dialed Jennifer's cell phone. She answered in two rings.

"Hello?"

"Jenny, it's Dad. We have to make this quick. Is there any way you can record this call?"

"Hi, Daddy! Yeah. Hold on a sec, don't hang up!"

Hal waited while Jennifer conferred with Jarod. Something clicked and she was back. "Okay, Dad. Jarod connected my phone to a digital recorder. That should work. Are you okay?"

"Yeah, yeah, I'm good. I didn't want to use the hotel phone or the business center because Bernadette knows I'm here. She may have a way of checking. I'm checking out of the hotel and into another, and there's to be more instructions."

"Okay, you can use your tablet, too, remember? It's like a small laptop and no one can trace that to you. Jarod programmed it with an IP address in New York."

"What does that mean?"

"Just don't worry, okay? And if there's a place, you know, like a coffee shop that has Internet, you can send emails that way. Justin also created an email account for you, so if you have something to write with, I'll give you the account name and password."

"Just a second." He slipped out the receipt from the bank and took out the pen from his pocket. "Okay, I'm ready."

"The account name is canberra@platitudes.com. It's a server in New York. The password is 'kangaroocourtyesterday.' Got it?"

"Yeah. I'll email after I get the next set of instructions. In the meantime, check out a foundation here called The Children's Trust."

"The Children's Trust. Okay, will do. Anything else?"

"When is William leaving?"

"He should be landing in Buenos Aires right about now. He knows about your new email account, so use it to contact him, or his satellite phone. We found him a hotel in another part of the city. He'll wait there until we all decide where he should go next."

Hal sighed. "Okay. I'll contact you in a couple of hours."

"Okay, Dad. Love you. Be careful, okay?"

He emerged from the bank with his thoughts in turmoil. Crossing the street at the light, he walked back to the hotel, trying to clear his head and remind himself why he was here—to get Annie back.

Back in his room he worked quickly. He began repacking to make room for the pesos because he didn't want to carry a bank bag. A quick look revealed both 5 and 10 peso denominations in neatly wrapped bundles. In order to carry what he could without his pockets bulging, he had to put some in the roller bag.

At the desk he settled his bill and walked out to the taxi stand. Settling into the car, he gave the address of the next hotel to the driver and leaned back. As it turned the corner, he recognized two men standing together at the light. One was the man from the counter in Claudine's and the other was the chubby one in the black trench coat who sat in a booth.

They were standing together, talking. In the restaurant they had not acknowledged one another. A shiver went up Hal's back. As the taxi rolled past, Hal turned in his seat and looked back. When the light changed the two men stepped into the crosswalk, still talking.

SEVENTEEN

The Hotel Menaul was definitely a step down from the Conquistador. Though clean, it was a bit worn around the edges, having seen its heyday. Hal was not surprised when the desk clerk handed him an actual door key on a chain. He was glad the room was on the first floor because there was no elevator. There was a small café on one end of the property.

"Señor," the wiry desk clerk with coal black hair and intense dark eyes said. "Your first meal is complimentary. They stop serving at two."

The room he let himself into was small, with a double bed, two nightstands with large lamps, and a long dresser against the opposite wall. A new flat screen television stood on one end of the dresser and a tall mirror hung on the wall next to it. There was no art on the walls.

Not knowing how long he would be staying in the hotel, Hal decided not to unpack.

Suddenly wanting a good cup of coffee, he decided he would partake of the free lunch offer. He removed the leather folder from his bag. The tablet was inside and he was hesitant to leave it in the room. He also wished there was a way to carry all his cash with him. He had to worry about the cashier's check as well. He decided to take the bank bag along with him.

He realized he was obviously an American to most of the people here and that everything about him screamed money. He wondered if he should visit a clothing store and find something that would blend in more with the locals. He couldn't very well shrink himself, however, since he was a good head taller than most of the men and bigger overall as well.

He kept his overcoat on because the satellite phone was in the inner pocket. In the small, nearly full restaurant he stood out like the proverbial sore thumb. He sat at a smaller table against the back wall. A very young server appeared with a menu and a pitcher of water. Filling a water glass already on the table, he handed the menu to Hal with a toothy smile.

"We have a bar," he announced, "with many choices."

"Coffee would be just fine," he said. "And what is the specialty of the house for lunch?"

"Yes," he said. "Very many people like the quail and wild rice soup. Also, I bring fresh bread. It is baked in stone oven."

"Well, add me to that list of very many people," Hal said. "I'll have the quail soup."

After he finished his meal, instead of a ticket the server brought a small, sealed envelope. He opened it with the edge of the butter knife. The font was the same as the first note.

Do not leave your room after dark. Order room service. Check out of hotel at 11 a.m. Wait outside front door for a white van. Your ride to Annie.

His heart pounded a bit as elation and disbelief swirled in equal parts through his head. Folding the note, he slipped it back into the envelope and slid it into his shirt pocket. Suddenly he lost his appetite. Giving in to nervousness he gathered his bag and case and left.

Hoping he was like anyone else going about their business, he strolled through the small lobby and out the front. No one was at the front desk.

He moved down the sidewalk until he was half a block from the hotel, then he stood at the curb. As he had hoped, a taxi pulled up and Hal quickly ducked into the back seat.

"Do you speak English?" were his first words.

"Un poco—a little," the driver replied, an older man.

"Good. I need to go to a clothing store."

The man looked in his rear view mirror at his big passenger, nodding after a moment. "Si, si. I take you."

A right turn and two blocks later, the taxi pulled over and the driver pointed to a store front window. "Good clothes in there," he said brightly.

Through the window Hal saw what appeared to be long racks of clothes and a few people browsing. "What's the fare?" he asked.

"10 pesos, Señor."

Hal gave him 20 pesos and climbed out. Two steps inside the store, he realized the cab had brought him to a used clothing store. For a moment he wondered if he would find clothing large enough for him as he was easily the largest person in the place, but he did find a Large and X-tra Large section and began to look in earnest.

Hal took the satellite phone from the overcoat pocket and pushed the power button, holding it in his palm as he looked at shirts. He touched Jennifer's name on the contacts screen. She answered almost immediately.

"Dad?"

"Hi, hon. How's everything?"

"We're good, Dad. I'm about to take Jarod in for a checkup, and his dad is in Buenos Aires and has a room at the El Centro Hotel. Mom's doing fine. How is it with you?"

"I'm okay. The second set of instructions came this morning. I'm to check out of the hotel tomorrow and wait for a ride.

"And then what?"

"Not sure. Someone is picking me up."

"That was it?"

He sighed. "Yeah, brief and to the point."

"Any idea where you'll be going?"

"No, not geographically, but hopefully to Annie since I have the money."

"Oh, I hope so! Anything else? We should keep this short to save your battery."

"You're right, Hon. I'll call later, maybe tonight. I'll give William a call as well. Give my love to your mom for me."

"I will, Dad. Hug my daughter for me when you see her. Love you."

Hal stood for a moment after he disconnected the call, staring at the rack of shirts. Just for a second, it seemed, Jennifer had sounded like a little girl herself. There were moments when the realities of life seemed incomprehensible. This was one of them. His little girl had a little girl of her own, but that little girl was missing.

In a moment he returned to the task at hand. He held up the garments to check the sizes because he couldn't always read the labels in the shirts and trousers. Twenty minutes later he was paying for three shirts, two faded denim jeans, a well-worn brown leather jacket, a sturdy pair of leather and canvas hiking boots, and a black canvas military-type backpack. The female salesclerk threw in a new cap with the logo of the Argentinian national soccer team on the front. For good measure, he also picked out a pair of sunglasses.

"Is there a dressing room or a fitting room?" he asked.

"Un momento," she replied, and turned and called out a name. "Consuelo?"

A teenaged girl appeared and the clerk pointed to Hal and said something under her breath. The girl stepped up to the counter. "My mother speaks very little English. May I help you, Señor?"

"I was just asking if there was a dressing room. I'd like to change."

"Si, yes, in the back. Use the one that says 'Hombre' on the door."

Fifteen minutes later Hal emerged from the fitting room practically a different person, at least outwardly. Between the dark blue cap, faded brown leather jacket, and even more faded blue denims he was unrecognizable. In the black backpack hanging from one shoulder was his bank bag full of pesos, the tablet, various chargers, and the zippered leather case. Rolled up under one arm were the clothes he arrived in. Only the black Luchese boots were left over from his rancher ensemble. They were a birthday gift from Virginia and he would not part with them. He dropped the rolled up bundle into what he hoped was the donations bin and headed for the front door.

But he stopped and turned to approach the young girl who spoke English. "Excuse me," he said. "May I ask a favor?"

"Yes?"

He pointed to the old phone on the glass counter. "Could you call a taxi for me?"

"Yes, I will call."

While he was waiting on the curb for the taxi, he placed a call to William.

"Good afternoon," came a strong voice. "Are you still in this fair city?"

"Good afternoon. I am here until tomorrow. I think we should get together and talk."

"Where are you?"

"At the El Centro Hotel. I checked in about half an hour ago."

William stopped at the front desk and left a message for Hal to go to the back courtyard. Stepping into the covered open-air café attached to the hotel, he found a corner table.

"Que te gustaria?" the server asked.

"Sorry, I don't speak Spanish."

"Si. What would you like?"

"I'm waiting for someone. He should be here in a few minutes."

"Si. I be back."

The surrealism of the situation would be almost laughable if the overall circumstances were not so grim. Here he was in a foreign country, anxiously waiting for someone he had despised as a boy and man. Now that person was the only "friend" he had in a friendless land. Likewise for Hal.

A quick survey revealed the courtyard to be a pleasant setting. All the tables were wooden and round, some larger than others. All chairs were wooden with flat seats and tall, straight backs. A breeze rustled the flat leaves on the branches woven into the overhead trellis. At this hour there were only half a dozen patrons, all of them were various shades of brown with black hair. He almost felt at home. Taking out his wallet, he slipped out Annie's photo and stared at it fondly.

Hal put on the sunglasses when the taxi arrived and gave the address of William's hotel to the cabbie. Twenty minutes later, he stepped out of the cab in front of the double doors of the El Centro Hotel located in the eastern part of the city. At the front desk he asked for the directions to the back courtyard.

Seated at a table in a corner was William Black Spotted Horse. The incongruity of them both being here at this place and in this moment was not lost on Hal. He never expected to be glad to see this man. William looked tired.

"Don't take this the wrong way," he said, taking a seat. "this is one of the strangest moments ever."

William nodded, gazing at Hal with a look of mild surprise. "I know what you mean. You look like you went to a rummage sale."

Hal chuckled as he dropped his pack on the floor. "You aren't wrong there," he said. "I got tired of sticking out like a sore thumb." He noticed William slip a small school photograph of Annie back into his wallet. He had the same photo in his own wallet.

"You and me both," William admitted. "I haven't seen anyone here taller than five-eight."

"Ain't that the truth? Long trip, huh?"

"Damn straight. I just talked to Jarod, he told me about the latest instructions." William waved at the server who walked into the area. "Want something? Might be a good idea to look normal or casual. Whatever that is around here."

Hal looked at the server. "Coffee, maybe, cake, or pie. Something sweet."

The girl nodded. "Si. we have berry cakes."

"Good, for both of us," he told her, motioning to include William.

The girl smiled pleasantly and turned on her heel. Hal waited until she was through the doorway and leaned over the table. "It just dawned on me that we're taking a chance meeting here. They know I'm here and someone could be following me."

William glanced sideways without moving his head. "Well, there is street access to this courtyard, I think, and the only other one is from the lobby. We just keep an eye out. And maybe when you leave you go out the street entrance."

Hal nodded and leaned back in his chair. He reached for his wallet and pulled out Annie's picture. On the back she had written: *To Grandpa Hal, world's best grandpa.* "I noticed you have this picture, too," he said, showing it to William. "I'm just curious. What does it say on the back of yours?"

William's brow knotted in confusion as he pulled the photo out of his wallet and handed it to Hal. On the back of it Annie had written: *To Grandpa William, world's best grandpa.*

Hal showed William the back of his copy of the photo. They shared a quiet chuckle.

William was dressed much the same as Hal now was, though his blue jeans were not as faded and his leather jacket was black suede. Except for his height and long single braid, he resembled many of the local Indians.

"My instructions are to stay in my room after dark," Hal told William. "I am to check out at eleven in the morning and wait for a white van. The note said it would take me to Annie."

"Do you believe it?"

"I want to, but I have a feeling there may be another hoop or two to jump through."

William nodded, deep in thought.

"Don't be surprised if somewhere along the line someone searches you. You might think of finding a way to hide your phone. It's our only connection."

"Yeah, I'm sure you're right, about a search. What are your plans?"

William removed a small, folded map from a pocket. "Jenny and Jarod are damn sure that Annie is at the Hollister place near Santa Rosa. They're guessing that's where they'll take you. So, I'll follow if that happens."

"Yeah, sounds good," Hal agreed. "How will you follow?"

William leaned back and nodded toward the door as the server returned with coffee, cups, and two small plates with desert on a tray.

"Thank you," they told her, and waited until the door to the restaurant closed behind her.

"I have a friend who was down here, believe it or not," William said, sliding one of the plates over. "Quite an adventure he had. One of the things he did was buy an old vehicle. Gave him mobility and helped him blend in. Thought I'd do that. Maybe a four-wheel-drive."

"That's a great idea. I'll go one better. How about we rent a truck?" Hal glanced at his watch. "We got a few hours. A cabbie can take us to a car rental place. If I'm back at my hotel before dark, hopefully I'll stay under the radar. We'll put it on my card. What do you say?"

William was hesitant.

"We should have that kind of mobility," Hal insisted, "just in case we need it, and a newer vehicle would be more dependable."

William nodded "Okay, let's do it. But let's finish desert first, you know, to look normal."

An hour and a half later they drove out of a car dealership that also rented vehicles. They had selected a mid-size four-door Japanese made four-wheel-drive truck with less than 5000 miles. Best of all, it was equipped with the latest GPS system platted specifically to Argentina. Because Hal's credit card was virtually unlimited, it was an open rental with maximum insurance coverage. William was listed as the second driver.

On the way back to Hal's hotel they found a tiny restaurant on a street corner and decided to have coffee and a final strategy session. Traffic in Buenos Aires, they decided, was about the same as Denver. It didn't take them long to figure out the usual road and street signs, especially those using universal symbols and shapes.

"I don't know where this is headed. We're all living from one set of instructions to the next," Hal pointed out. "If I was damn sure our little girl was at Hollister's place, I'd be tempted to storm the place."

"I know how you feel," William agreed. "But first we need to find the place on a map. As soon as we know that we tell Jenny and Jarod. Then maybe I can move in close. We just figure this out as we go along. But the critical thing is to know exactly where Hollister's place is."

"That about sums it up," Hal said. Pausing for a moment, he nervously swirled the coffee in his cup. "We're still shooting in the dark. And we should stay in touch as much as possible."

"Yeah, makes sense. You uncomfortable with that, for some reason?"

"No, no, of course not. I'm just not sure what's going to happen from one minute to the next. What happens if they take me there?"

William studied Hal's face for a few seconds. "I don't know. I think we're doing the best we can. Or are you having second thoughts?"

"No, no, not that. Just hoping me and you are up to getting this done."

"We're in it, Hal. We've come this far. We have to get it done."

Hal rubbed his eyes. "Yeah, yeah. Let's start with getting me back to my hotel."

"Unless I hear otherwise from you, I'll assume they're taking you to Hollister's place near Santa Rosa. Or let the kids know if you can. They can tell me and I'll head that way."

"Okay."

"And I just had a thought. If you can't call for some reason, turn your phone on at five minutes to the hour for ten minutes and shut it off at five after. That way Jenny and Jarod can ping your phone to get a location for where it is. I'm sure they know some software that can do that."

"That's amazing, isn't it? Yeah, that's a great idea."

Hal gave half the pesos to William, mainly to reduce his load, before he caught a taxi back to his hotel. He was in his room by six-thirty. Halfway into repacking everything into the used backpack, he stopped and ordered room service. He decided on a pulled pork sandwich with cottage fries, a carafe of coffee, and two bottles of water. Thirty minutes later his order was delivered, along with a small loaf of the stone baked bread and a pot of peppermint tea. A house specialty on the house, the man who delivered the food told him.

While slipping off his boots, Hal realized how he could hide the satellite phone in the seam in the middle of each boot sleeve. The intricate stitching on the outer leather would help conceal the bump. He found his pocketknife in his Dopp kit and began carefully slicing through the thin thread at the top edge, until he had an opening wide enough for the width of the phone, just behind the seam. Hal slipped the phone in to make sure the opening was wide and deep enough. He slipped the boot on and walked around. He could feel the slight bulge just behind the ball of his left ankle, but it was tolerable, and more importantly, it wasn't noticeable at all.

He did the same to the other boot to conceal the two phone batteries. His food and coffee had cooled off, but he didn't care. Whatever effect hiding the satellite phone would have on this entire surreal situation, Hal didn't know. But he felt as though he had won a small victory.

In a different part of the city, William Black Spotted Horse had a different slant on the same situation. After leaving the rental truck in a parking garage half a block from the hotel, he placed a call to Marie on his own satellite phone and asked her to call him back on the hotel line.

"What's up?" she asked.

He quickly filled her in on the latest developments

"What's bothering you, then?" she asked.

"Well, Hal seems to be, ah, a bit hesitant," he told her. "Not that either of us were overwhelmingly confident to begin with."

"Pardon me if I don't share this bit of information with anyone," she replied. "Frankly it's not good if either one of you is less than 100 percent committed to doing this. Honey, I'm not asking for a guaranteed outcome, but I do need you to go into it feeling confident."

"I know, hon, I know. I see your point. But being here, being one step away from actually getting Annie back is not the time to hesitate. I need to be able to trust Hal to do everything he can to follow our plan. What if he hesitates during a critical moment?"

"I don't know if there was ever a moment in your life when you actually liked Hal. You've never said too much, but from what I've heard over the years, the two of you have been at each other since you were in high school. So, here's my message: this isn't about him or you. It's about our granddaughter, Jarod and Jennifer's daughter. It's time, at this of all moments, for you two old billy goats to put aside your animosity. Stand on what you feel for your granddaughter and not on what you think of each other."

William sighed. "You're right. This old billy goat hears you."

EIGHTEEN

Hal tried hard to hide his reaction to the men in the van when it pulled up to the curb outside the Hotel Menaul. The driver was the chubby man in the dark overcoat from Claudine's Restaurant. His companion in the passenger seat was the younger man from the counter, who had come into the restaurant first.

It was real now. They had been watching him. They were the hands, the worker bees, the doers. That meant Bernadette McGiven was higher up the food chain. She gave the orders and these men carried them out. She had power over them and him.

The younger man was dressed in the dark jacket and dark trousers he had worn the day before. He stepped out and opened the sliding door. It was like the mouth of a giant creature opening up to swallow him.

"Put your backpack on the middle seat," the man ordered, speaking with an obvious accent. "You get in the far back seat."

Hal shoved the backpack onto the middle seat and squeezed past the opening on the end. It was tight in the midsize van, so he had to turn sideways to have room for his knees.

"Make yourself comfortable, Mr. Lamar," the driver said, looking into the rearview mirror. Something about the man's voice seemed familiar. Hal nodded and settled back for what he assumed would be a long ride.

After numerous direction changes and traffic lights, they entered what appeared to be an industrialized area with heavy traffic. Gradually, the traffic thinned and they were on what seemed like the outskirts of the city. The traffic became sparse. Finally, they merged onto a major westbound highway.

After half an hour they slowed and pulled over onto what appeared to be a wide, graveled parking area and stopped at the end of it. The younger man, who Hal thought of as Black Jacket, stepped out and quickly opened the sliding door. Before Hal could protest, he grabbed the backpack and unzipped it. Here was the search William had warned him about. He sat back and watched, realizing there was nothing he could do to stop it. He silently congratulated himself for creatively hiding the phone and batteries.

Black Jacket was thorough, even poking through the Dopp kit and reaching his hand into the hiking boots tied to the side of the pack. From a side pocket he pulled out the tablet, which he tossed onto the seat. From the other side pocket, he took out the coiled cords and chargers, one for the tablet and the other for the satellite phone. Hal held his breath. He had forgotten to hide the chargers, though he didn't know where he could have hidden them. Black Jacket tossed them on the seat as well.

Black Jacket put everything back but the charger, the cords, and the tablet, handing the bag to the driver. He motioned for Hal to climb out and extend his arms out to the sides, then executed a thorough search and pat down and stepped back.

"Empty your pockets on the seat, please, sir," the man said, pointing to the middle seat.

Hal had nothing in his pockets but a bit of loose change, the pocketknife, a white handkerchief, and his wallet. Black Jacket looked in the wallet and gave it back. Hal could suddenly feel the satellite phone and the batteries against his ankles and wondered if Black Jacket would search his boots. His heart sank when Black Jacket kept the pocketknife.

"Please get back in, Mr. Lamar," the man said.

Hal complied, his heart pounding. For the time being, his satellite phone was safe, but a shiver went through him when he saw the handle of a semi-automatic pistol protruding from a black holster at Black Jacket's right hip.

The van pulled back onto the road. The driver called someone on his cell phone and uttered four words, "We're on our way." A short time later, Black Jacket tossed back a bottle of water. That was the only acknowledgement of Hal's presence until the next stop, a bathroom break two hours later.

During the stop, Black Jacket had a long phone conversation in Spanish, not a word of which Hal understood.

A road sign indicated Highway 113 and a speed limit of 75 kilometers an hour, or 60 miles an hour. Hal glanced down at his watch. Four hours had passed, and he estimated they had covered about 250 miles. He knew that Santa Rosa was southwest of Buenos Aires, according to a map he had looked at earlier. But as far as he could determine, they had been heading west, not in the direction of Santa Rosa, and Annie.

Forty-five minutes later, the van suddenly slowed and made a left turn onto a gravel road. Only a few yards in, it was evident it was not well-maintained. There were numerous potholes and small ruts from rain run-off. Hal surveyed the surrounding landscape of high hills and deep gullies and patches of forest. There were no buildings or any of the usual signs of human habitation, such as power lines or fences. It was a slow, jostling ride up a long slope with the road switching back now and then. Eventually the road turned into nothing more than a rutted trail.

At the top of a hill, the trail entered a forest and meandered with gradual turns left and right. Looking back, Hal no longer saw the road they came in on. After nearly an hour of slow, bumpy progress, they came to a small, square, log house in the middle of small clearing surrounded by dense forest and stopped.

Chubby glanced back over his shoulder at Hal. "Your accommodations for the night. Grab your pack and follow me."

Black Jacket opened the sliding door, then closed it after Hal stepped down from the van. He followed Chubby up a barely discernible path to the door on the northwest corner of the cabin. From the luggage area of the van, Black Jacket unloaded a large blue cooler. He put it by the door and walked around to the back of the house. Chubby unlocked the door, entered, and motioned for Hal to step inside.

Hal suddenly heard a small engine that he immediately recognized as a generator. He wasn't liking this unexpected turn of bad luck. In a few seconds, a lamp on a table by the bed blinked on. Black Jacket walked in with the cooler and put it on the table.

On the east wall was a refrigerator and small propane cook stove, bordered by a long, narrow table that served as a counter. Above it hung a cast iron skillet, a pot, and several large utensils. At the far end of the table were two dishes, two cups, and two shallow bowls.

The bed was against the south wall and on top of the bare mattress were folded blankets and a bare pillow. A small, square table and two chairs stood against the row of three windows on the north wall. The windows and the lamp next to the bed were the only sources of light. Against the east wall was a small cast iron wood stove.

Chubby pointed to the cooler. "There's water in there and food and coffee. You have enough of everything until tomorrow. The outhouse is outside in the back. Your next ride will be here tomorrow around mid-morning. Now, I'll take the cashier's check."

"What?" Hal muttered in surprise.

"The check," Chubby said firmly. "Give me the check."

Hal gazed as passively as he could manage at the man. "I, ah, I would prefer to give that to Hollister myself," he said.

The man shot a glance at Black Jacket and turned his attention back to Hal. Black Jacket pushed aside his coat and put his hand on the handle of the pistol,.

"I'll say it again, Lamar," said Chubby. "Give me the check."

Hal reached inside his leather jacket and pulled out the folded envelope with the bank logo on it. His hand shook as he opened it and pulled out the check.

Black Jacket approached and held out his left hand. Hal passed the check to him, his heart thudding against his chest.

He watched Black Jacket step back and give the check to Chubby, who quickly looked it over.

"You've done well, Mr. Lamar," the man said.

"Who's going to find me way out here?" Hal asked.

Chubby smiled. "Someone who knows the way," he said.

Chubby was the first out the door. Black Jacket waited, keeping a cold stare affixed to Hal, and then he was out the door as well. Hal stood in the silence.

"What the fuck just happened?" he asked.

He didn't have the answer. There was only silence until he heard the van start up. He moved to the windows and watched it reverse to an open area, then turn and drive away.

Soon it was out of sight.

Hal burst out through the door and then remembered that Black Jacket had a gun. He stopped, breathing as though he had run a mile. How long he stood, staring at the spot where the van's tracks disappeared into the trees, he didn't know. Finally, he looked at his watch. It was past six.

He had to do something. For a minute he looked at the forest around him, which was growing dark with long shadows. Retracing his steps to the house, he walked in and closed the door. For the first time, he felt a chill in the air and there was no thermostat to turn up the heat in this room. A quick inspection of the wood stove showed the last occupant had cleared away the ashes, and there was an armload of wood on the floor. Next to it was a small bin of kindling with a box of matches.

"I may be lost and confused as hell," he said, "but at least I'll be warm."

He hurried out the door to the edge of the trees, suddenly aware that the generator was steadily, softly puttering away. Working quickly, he gathered an armload of dry wood and carried it inside. After the third load, he guessed he had enough for the night. Next, he inspected the generator and found the gauge on the fuel tank, which looked to be at about two gallons. The gauge indicated three-quarters full. He saw the motor started with a pull cord, a simple enough system with a choke.

Back inside he prepared a pile of kindling in the stove, using the smallest twigs and an old newspaper he had found. The date on the banner said 17 Avril 2016, over a year earlier. He decided he would light the fire later.

Sitting down on the edge of the bed, he considered what to do next. His eyes fell on the cooler and he went to it. As Chubby had said, there were bottles of water, a loaf of bread, a package of luncheon meat, a can of coffee, and a block of cheese wrapped in plastic.

"What? No steak and eggs?"

His voice was loud in the cabin. On the propane stove was a smoke blackened coffee pot. He moved the pot, lifted the top of the stove, and found the pilot light holes. He went out and circled the house until he found a small propane tank on the east side, opposite where the stove was inside. He turned the release valve on the top and heard a slight hiss. Pausing, he sniffed for a leak, but it seemed to be working smoothly. Back inside, he grabbed a match and lit the pilot light. Coffee was a definite possibility. But it could wait.

Now he had to make a phone call. A sudden thought stopped him for a second or two. *What if this is the end of the line? What if their plan is to let me just sit here and rot?* He shrugged, trying to shake off the thought and sat on a chair.

Taking off his boots, he slid out the phone and its batteries. Inserting one of the batteries he powered up the satellite phone. When it was on and ready, he found William's name and tapped his number. There was no answer, so he called Jarod.

"Hal, is it you?"

"It's me, it's me. Listen, are you alone?"

"Yeah, Jenny went to the store with Virginia and my mom is on her way here."

"Okay, good! We have to do this quickly to save my batteries."

"Sure, go ahead. What's happening?"

Taking a deep breath, Hal recounted the day's events as fast as he could.

"I get the feeling they're not coming back for me," Hal concluded.

"Okay," Justin said, "If Dad didn't answer then he doesn't have his phone on. So here's what we do. It's 20 to the hour. When we hang up, shut off your phone to save the battery and turn it back on again on the hour at 6. By then I should have gotten a hold of Dad, so that when the two of you do talk, he'll know your situation. In the meantime, I'll get my gear ready so I can find your position with GPS. And if you're right about no one coming back for you, the best plan is for Dad to find you, but that will have to be tomorrow. Does that make sense, Hal?"

"Yeah, it does. And one more thing, don't tell Virginia and Marie about this glitch. Just let them know that you heard from me and things are, ah, moving along."

"Okay, right I'll talk to you in about 20 minutes."

Hal hated to disconnect the call, but battery life was critical now.

Silence surrounded him. He was alone. Utterly, fucking alone in a place he knew nothing about. Chubby and Black Jacket had left him miles from nowhere. There was a bright side, however. He had shelter and a bit of food and water, which was better than being alone in the forest. When they asked for the cashier's check Hal knew there was no next ride. But why had they left him? Worse yet, what did this mean for Annie? Was she safe? Her captors didn't know about her illness, and that scared him the most. What he thought was his bargaining chip, the check, was gone. Why had they instructed him to come here, to Argentina, if they weren't going to let him bring Annie home?

A grain of hope materialized, perhaps a bit like a pebble in an avalanche, but it was something. Maybe, just maybe, they would demand more money. He had not objected to making the payment or to the amount. In their minds—or hers—might be the simple expectation that he had paid once and would pay again. Or perhaps multiple payments had been the plan all along. They had placed him in a vulnerable position. He was alone in a remote area in a land he didn't know, where he didn't speak the language and didn't know anyone. They would probably exploit that vulnerability. They would leave him here to soften him, isolate him, and make him hungry and thirsty. Then come back friendly and concerned and demand more money. If this was the case, then perhaps Annie was safe. On the other hand, maybe the cold hard reality was they didn't need him anymore. Therefore, maybe the next person coming up the road would be armed and loaded for bear, coming to end his life.

In the end, all that mattered was that Annie had to be rescued, somehow. If he could find out where she was, he was in favor of storming the place. But first things first, the boy he didn't want his daughter to marry had to use GPS to get his location so the man he'd despised all his life could rescue him. Maybe.

Hal glanced at his watch. He had time to put on coffee. He opened the can of coffee, filled the pot with water, put grounds in the basket, and lit the burner. Grabbing one of the chairs, he wedged it under the doorknob. Futile perhaps, but since he had no weapon it was all he could think of to do.

Just as the coffee started to boil, the phone rang. It was Jennifer.

"Dad," she said, anxiously. "How are you?"

"Doing well. How are you, Hon? How's your mother?"

"We're good, Dad. Listen, we have a plan to figure out what your map coordinates are and pass them on to William. So, here's what we need to do. We're going to hang up and call William and then call you back and hook us all up on a conference call. Then hopefully we can use our GPS software to find you. Follow me?"

"Got it. So, we hang up now and I wait for William?"

"That's it, Dad. And then we'll hook back up with you. If it all works Jarod should be able to tell his dad where you are. Okay, bye for now."

Hal disconnected the call and waited. Phone in hand he went to the stove to adjust the flame under the pot. The smell of coffee filling the room was strangely reassuring. Staying near the stove, he looked out the three windows on the north wall but saw nothing moving outside. The phone rang.

"William," he answered. "Where are you?"

"Coming up on a town called Tres Arroyos. Hey, Jarod and Jennifer filled me in on your situation, so I'll turn around and head your way. Once they locate you, they can give me directions. That won't be until tomorrow though."

"Yeah, okay. I wasn't counting on what happened," he said, chagrinned. "They threw me a curve."

"Not surprising," William replied. "They led us to believe Hollister McGiven was alive. We can't trust them, or whoever's calling the shots."

"I'm thinking they're going to ask for more money, but I hate not knowing how Annie is."

"My gut says she's safe," William said. "I think we have to assume she's at the McGiven place. We have to go there. They won't be expecting us."

Hal checked the time, just as he heard another call beeping in. Nervously, he touched Accept. "Hello," he said tentatively.

"It's me, Dad," Jennifer said. "Just stay on the line, both of you, Jarod's doing some kind of magic with his gadgets."

After nearly a minute Jennifer spoke again. "Okay, great! Jarod just gave me a thumbs up. I think that means it worked. Maybe you should both disconnect to save your batteries and we'll call you back and tell you what he was able to find."

Hal reluctantly disconnected, poured himself some coffee and took a seat at the table to watch out the window. Jennifer called three minutes later. They had indeed managed to locate Hal. He was a few miles west of the Salado River in the foothills of the Andes Mountains. That was the good news. The bad news was it was over four hundred miles from William, at least an eight-hour drive. They left it up to William and Hal to figure out a plan.

"I hate to state the obvious," Hal said, after he reconnected with William. "That's a hell of a long drive. Maybe get a room and start out early in the morning. I don't know about you, but I don't like driving through strange country at night."

"Well, that's for sure," William agreed. "But according to my map, I'm about two hundred miles from Santa Rosa. If I keep going now, I'll get there about ten or eleven. Then I can start out early and have a look at the area in daylight. Might give us an edge."

"That's a great idea."

"It gets light around 6:30. I'll be on the road by then and let's agree to talk at nine. Did you notice any highway numbers?"

"Yeah, Highway 113 out of Buenos Aires. We stayed on it for about five hours, then turned onto something like a section road, not maintained at all, rough and in bad shape. We were on that for about an hour, I think, and it turns into a pasture road, essentially. This cabin is up in some rough country, foothills."

Hal could hear a passing truck through William's phone and heavy paper rustling.

"I found the highway on the map," William said. "A major road. Did that turnoff road have a number?"

"No," Hal recalled. "Nothing. It's a left turn, to the south."

"Okay. Do you suppose you could walk to the highway?"

"Yeah, I could. They told me the next driver would be here at mid-morning to get me. Either no one is coming or someone is coming for no good reason. So, I figure I want to be out of here. I can leave at dawn and follow the road back to the main highway."

"Good. I'll call Jarod. He said he would plot a course for me. I'll call you at nine in the morning. You should call Jenny now."

Hal called Jenny. "My next ride is supposedly coming to pick me up tomorrow," he said. "Jarod is going to plot a course for William so he can get here before that arrives."

"Okay, Dad. Hang up and save your battery. We'll talk tomorrow. Love you."

Hal powered off the phone and sat in the silence, half a world from home.

NINETEEN

Annie realized that Marta Manzanares, the person watching her while Bernadette was gone, liked to talk on the phone. Annie sat at the dining table in the place designated for her by Bernadette. This evening she ate alone. Bernadette would be back by 10.

Marta was a kind person, Annie thought, someone who smiled easily. She did the cooking and cleaning for Bernadette. A thin woman with quick movements, even her dark eyes darted about quickly. But what Annie liked most was that Marta was on the phone a lot and paid little attention to anything else when she was. When she spoke in English it was sometimes hard to understand her.

Nothing seemed real to Annie. This was a real house, a real place, but she was a long way from home, and she didn't know why she had been taken from her Mom and Dad and brought here. She wished this were a dream she would wake up from.

Annie ate her food slowly, mainly because she was not all that hungry but also because she didn't want to attract Marta's attention if she ate fast and hurried away from the table. The meal was baked chicken and yams. Marta was a good cook.

"Miss Annie, do you want more?" she asked.

Annie shook her head. "No, I'm full. I want to go to my room and watch a movie," she said.

"Yes, yes, okay." Marta smiled graciously. "I take your dishes. You go to your room. I check on you later."

Annie knew that the outside doors to the house were always locked. They were big heavy doors. She knew by looking out the windows that men were outside keeping watch. They were not like Grandpa Hal's ranch hands. They were different than the men who took care of the horses she had seen in the corrals. If she managed to sneak out, those men keeping watch would probably see her.

Upstairs there was a short hallway with Bernadette's bedroom, a bathroom next to Annie's room, and the office. Bernadette's office and the room Annie slept in were side by side She knew the office door was locked at night because she had snuck out of her room the first night and tried it. Still, whenever she was alone in the short hallway she checked the door as she passed. She reached out and turned the knob as she passed. It turned! It was not locked!

Ducking quickly into the office she found the tape dispenser on the desk and tore off two strips about three inches long. Carefully, placing them just so, she taped over the latch hold inside the door jam, pressing one strip over the other.

Marta would come up to check on her before Bernadette came home and if she noticed the office door was ajar, she would likely close it. Annie slowly and carefully pulled the office door closed, stopping just short of depressing the door latch. She waited a second, but the door stayed in place. Hurrying into her room, she put a movie in the DVD player, turned on the flat screen, and pressed Play. She put on pajamas, pulled back the covers, and got into bed, hoping that Marta would come soon.

The movie was almost over when Marta finally came. Hearing the footsteps on the stairs, Annie turned over and feigned sleep. The woman carefully pushed the bedroom door open and stepped in. Seeing Annie apparently asleep, she turned off the movie, turned off the lamp on the nightstand, and pulled the covers higher over her.

Annie heard Marta's faint footsteps going down the stairs and waited another few seconds before she pushed aside the bed covers and slipped out of her room. Wasting no time, she stepped into the office, and closed the door behind her. Walking to the desk, she found the power button to the computer screen. Before she pushed it, she pulled the window curtains closed so the guards wouldn't see a light from the window. Annie clicked the mouse and held her breath.

The screen lit up in a second. She quickly perused the headings and icons. This was a very basic set-up and had no GPS program. But she did find the icon for internet access in the lower left corner and moved the mouse to it and clicked. The screen changed and she saw it open to a browser. Not exactly sure what to do, Annie typed in her parents' internet server and was surprised and relieved when it appeared on the screen. She moved the cursor to Compose for email and wrote MESSAGE FROM THE HALF-PINT in the subject line. It was the name her dad still called her. Taking a deep breath, she typed as fast as she could, conscious of the risk of being discovered.

Dear Dad: I'm in Argentina close to a town called Santa Rosa at a house with a woman named Bernadette. Don't have address. It's a ranch with black horses that have long manes and tails. She drives a big black Dodge pickup license EN24178T and a black Durango too. There is a big white barn and corrals and men who guard outside. I sleep in a room in the upstairs that has bars on the windows. I will delete this cuz it's her computer. I really love all you guys. Come get me. See you soon. Half-Pint. xxxooo

Annie read it over quickly and then moved the cursor to Send. Next, she deleted it from Sent Mail, logged off the server, and shut off the monitor.

A minute after taking off the tape she had put on the latch earlier and carefully shutting the office door, she was back in her bed. Tears rolled down her cheeks as she imagined her family's faces—Mom, Dad, Grandma Marie, Grandma Virginia, Grandpa William, and Grandpa Hal—finally drifting away to sleep.

Jennifer's persistence yielded the telephone numbers of hotels in Santa Rosa. Jarod gave them to William then ended the call. His headache still banged away, forcing him to reach for the pain pills in the bottle next to his keyboard. He didn't like taking them because they affected his ability to concentrate, but the hammering in his head would not subside. It reminded him not only of the injury but that Annie was half a world away.

A message blinked on his computer screen, a new email.

He quickly took the pills with a mouthful of water, but nearly choked when he saw the subject, MESSAGE FROM THE HALF-PINT. He immediately forgot about the headache and called out to Jenny, who looked out from the door of the laundry room.

"Come here, honey. There's something you need to see."

Jennifer couldn't gauge the expression on his face. His eyes were opened wide, but she couldn't tell if he was excited or scared. "What is it, hon?"

He motioned faster and then guided her to the computer screen. "Read it, honey!"

Halfway through the note Jennifer started sobbing. "Oh, my God! This means she's okay, right? I know it's her, she's the only one who would know you call her Half-Pint!"

Jarod picked her up in an enthusiastic hug. "It's her! It's her! She somehow got onto a computer! Forward this to our moms, then call them." He glanced at his watch. "Then we have to call Hal and my dad in about ten minutes. They need to know this."

Nearly an hour later everyone's emotions finally began to calm a bit. Virginia and Marie decided to spend the night at their children's house. Hal would not hear the good news until he turned his phone on in the morning.

William estimated he was an hour out of Santa Rosa. Since he could plug his phone into the rental truck's charging ports, he had an extended conversation with Jarod.

"There's a certain logic to Sheriff Triplett's theory that the woman at the farmhouse was Bernadette McGiven," Jarod said to his father. "That being the case, she saw you there as well. Obviously, Dad, she doesn't know you're in country. Her focus is on Hal."

"I know where you're going with this. We want to keep the element of surprise. So I'll gas up the truck before I check into the hotel and stay in once I get there. It'll be around eleven anyway. On the other hand, there's got to be another town with a hotel. It wouldn't be good if she saw me inadvertently. We can't take a chance."

"You need the rest, Dad. You have a rental with local plates."

William had to agree. "Yeah. I'll get Hal and then we can do some nosing around. At the most it'll be two days from now. The only worry is if they move her elsewhere. You think someone will figure out she sent that email?"

"I'm keeping my fingers crossed. From what we've been able to find out, the area around Santa Rosa is pretty rural and I'll bet the McGiven place is kind of isolated. You might be able to get close on foot, like at night."

"Yeah. Well, I think I'm getting close, I see some city lights in the distance. I'll let you know when I'm checked in."

Some 400 miles away, Hal Lamar reclined against the pillows and blankets propped on the bed. The cabin was dark and a fire crackled inside the stove. He had shut down the generator. The only light was the red glow from the stove's air intake holes. Outside was even darker if the blackness of the three windows was any indication.

Hal was nervous. He was alone in a cabin at least 10 miles from the nearest road, in a foreign country. If William Black Spotted Horse were not coming for him tomorrow, he would be up the creek without a paddle. But tomorrow wasn't the only problem. Tonight could be a problem, mainly because he didn't know if someone was out there right now, waiting for him to fall asleep.

Why had they brought him out here miles from nowhere? He was convinced it wasn't because the next ride was coming to pick him up.

The only thing he knew for sure was that this would be a sleepless night. He sat up suddenly and tossed the blankets and pillows onto the floor. Grabbing the feather tick mattress, he carried it to the north wall and laid it there beneath the windows. If anyone came through the door, they would likely expect him to be on the bed. He went back for blankets and pillows and arranged them on the mattress.

Jennifer told him he was in the foothills of the Andes Mountains, nearly 500 miles west of Buenos Aires. On Highway 113, they had driven by or through small towns and stopped for gas twice. He didn't see anything near the main road that looked like ranches or farms. After they had turned off the highway, there was nothing. The only hint of civilization was the rough road that dwindled to a trail, and the cabin at the end of it.

Hal knew nothing about what sort of wild animals were out there, night or day, in the wilderness surrounding the cabin. He had read about a red stag, when he had researched hunting in Patagonia years ago, but he wondered about predators such as bears and mountain lions. Hunting in bear or lion country in Montana or the Yukon, one was always on the alert for possible encounters. Of course, a hunter was armed with both a rifle and a backup pistol, as well as bear spray. Here he had none of those things. He had no way to defend himself, not even from an angry squirrel.

He decided to let the fire burn down. He rearranged the pillows and pulled both blankets over himself. Turning to lay on his left side, he kept his eyes on the door.

Tomorrow was another day. In the daylight he could at least see what was out there.

# TWENTY

William used the small window scraper he found in the glove box to scrape the frost from the truck windows while the engine was warming. It was definitely autumn here. Yielding to caution, he wore sunglasses and tucked his braid beneath his jacket. The sun was just over the eastern horizon. Not many people or vehicles were moving yet. The hotel was a block east of the highway.

Jarod had told him he was nearly 400 miles from Hal's position. Ironically, he was likely within 20 miles of where Annie was, maybe less. But in which direction? Jarod and Jennifer were working to solve that puzzle. He finished his task and drove away from the hotel with a heavy heart.

"We'll be back, my girl," he said out loud. "You hang in there."

After he turned onto Route 7, the truck's onboard compass indicated he was driving north. Santa Rosa was a city with a population of 100,000, according to the brochure he found in his room. The main industry was agriculture. Soon he was past the city limits and into low rolling hills and grasslands. He was surprised not to see numerous herds of cattle, though he did see what he assumed were ranches and farms, and a few that were likely no more than rural residences. Maybe one of those was where Annie was, a place with a large white barn and black horses.

He set the cruise control at the speed limit and settled back for a long haul. Soon he would call Hal. He glanced occasionally at the spectacular landscape and the wide-open spaces. If he were here for any other reason than finding Annie, he would be enthralled and excited about seeing new places and experiencing the local culture firsthand. But none of that mattered. He and Hal were here for one reason only—find Annie and take her home. First, however, he had to rescue the other greatest grandpa in the world.

Two weeks ago they were bitter enemies. This hellish predicament had not stopped them from being enemies, it had simply put it on hold. The Northern Plains Cattlemen's Association had fought hard to keep the Smokey River Sioux Tribe, and other tribes on the plains, from recovering tribal lands formerly owned by tribal members, even to the point of bribing tribal council members. William knew that a few mixed-blood Lakota ranchers, members of the Association, had been talked into running for election to the council.

Just about every enrolled tribal member was mixed blood to a point. There were hardly any bona fide full-bloods who could prove they had no European or Euro-American ancestors in the family tree. William's mother was three-quarters Smokey River Sioux, or Sicangu Lakota, and one-fourth French. His father was enrolled as full-blood. So that made him seven-eighths Lakota. Marie was also seven-eighths, which meant that Jarod was also.

An individual had to be at least one-quarter Smokey River Sioux to be enrolled in the tribe. Many such individuals were from families whose bloodlines were so thinned out that they had lost all cultural connection to being Lakota. Those individuals and families were culturally white. They certainly didn't speak the language and sometimes denied they were in any way Native. They did, however, take advantage of their tribal enrollment when it came to BIA scholarships for college, or for other entitlements, such as Indian preference for leasing tribal or individually Indian-owned land. It wasn't unusual for such individuals to be fronted by white ranchers to lease Indian lands at low lease rates. White ranchers and farmers in the state took 80 percent of the income generated from those lands, from crops and cattle, and according to a report he had seen from the BIA, that was just over 70 million dollars.

The sum total of reality on any Lakota reservation in the state was that the tribes or their members were not in control of their own lives—not by any stretch. A large part of that reality existed because of the federal government's paternalistic attitudes and indifference, and a state full of avowed "Indian fighters" such as the governor and two U.S. senators. But the tribes' own lack of leadership and corruption within the tribal governments were also contributing factors.

William had spent the last 10 years of his career in the BIA deeply frustrated because he could do little, even as a BIA agency superintendent—the most powerful BIA official on the reservation—to right those wrongs. He didn't retire because of a long and satisfying career. He retired because he was powerless to affect change and was tired of banging his head against a brick wall. That brick wall was his bosses—some of them Native—at the regional and national levels who thwarted his efforts at every turn.

William sighed and refocused his thoughts to the present. Annie and her parents were at the forefront. Jennifer Heather Lamar was nothing like her father, thankfully. It was the height of irony that his only son would fall in love with the only daughter of the richest rancher and leading Indian fighter in Redoubt County. The result of that union was a granddaughter who was nearly half Lakota.

There was one comforting reality. He knew that Hal Lamar loved Annie more than his own life, just as he did. And if that wasn't enough to find and rescue that little girl, nothing was.

The satellite phone rang.

"Hey, good morning, Dad," Jarod said. "How's the weather there?"

"Bright and sunny and a bit chilly. Why? How is it there?"

"Thunder, lightning, and rain," Jarod said. "Sometimes storms interfere with satellite phones. Anyway, I have fantastic news. A computer geek friend of mine in D.C. found Bernadette's place."

"Damn! How did he do that?"

"The place is 12 miles northwest of Santa Rosa. He found the internet server for that area and that led him to the username Dancing Horse. He checked it out since Annie said there were horses. There's a ranch by that name owned by Bernadette McGiven Covena. If you bunk down tonight in a hotel, make sure it has internet. I'll send you a map you can print out."

"Outstanding! Thanks, Son. I probably drove by the road to it earlier when I left."

"That's possible," Jarod said wistfully. "I wish we could find the road where Hal's cabin is, but I know you two will figure it out if we can't. We'll keep trying."

Twenty minutes later William pulled off and stopped at the local version of a rest stop—an outdoor privy, a large trash receptacle, and a picnic table. The privy was one structure with a door on each end for Men and Women. Surprisingly, the area was neat and tidy and the privy was clean.

Back in the truck, he decided to take a break and wait since it was seven minutes to nine. Distance was critical and seven minutes was seven miles, but he was less apt to draw attention parked at a rest stop.

Hal answered William's 9 a.m. call. "Good morning," he said in a hoarse voice.

"Good morning, Hal. How is it with you?"

"Good, considering. I've been hiking since about 6:30 and I'm making progress. Terrain is uneven, you know, intervening hills and such so I can't see the highway yet. But I'm back on the wider part of the road. That's the good news."

"Ok. What's the bad news?"

"Well, some wild pig, a peccary, was bothering me a couple miles back. But it's gone now. Where are you?"

William glanced at the road atlas he had open. "I think about 40 to 50 miles south of Route 113. About another hour and I'll turn west. That'll put me about 200 miles from the Salado River. Jarod figures you're southwest of there. So, I'm about five hours away."

"Hell, that's more than enough time for me to get to the highway. I'll probably get there in about two hours or so, if that damn pig don't get me."

"That's still about a three hour wait. I have some news that should cheer you up. Annie, our brave little Annie, sent an email to her dad."

"Damn! Did she say where she is?"

"As much as she could. And using the email screen name and the IP address, a friend of Jarod's was able to find the place. It's about 12 miles northwest of Santa Rosa."

"Oh, hell! Now we really have to make a plan."

"Yeah, oh, yeah. But first, I have to find you. Jenny and Jarod know generally where you are and gave me directions. So, after I get past the Salado

River, I'll turn in at every road and trail that turns south and go in about 100 yards. So, if you want, just wait somewhere near the road within 100 yards, where you can see me coming."

"Great idea. That way I won't be near the highway. People around here might get suspicious if they see a big-ass white man standing on the highway."

William couldn't help but chuckle at that image. "How's your battery holding up?"

"Ah, I think I got about 20 percent left in this one. I haven't used the other one yet. So, I'm good."

"Okay, how about I give you a ring at 10 o'clock?"

"I'll be here, watching out for that damn pig. Sure was a ferocious little sucker."

William found Route 113, and crossed the Salado River at about 2 p.m. At the top of each hour he had checked in with Hal.

The first three roads that went south off Route 113 were well-maintained gravel roads that led to houses or other structures. Fortunately, there were not many roads that connected to the highway from the south. At about 3:30, he turned onto the seventh. It had all the indicators Hal had described: it was not maintained and cut by rain runoff. But the best indicator was two sets of tire tracks.

It was a rough road and William began to look for thickets and shrubs. He saw Hal rise up out of a wide thicket and wave. William pulled the truck into the grass. Hal looked bone tired and wrung out.

"I wonder if this qualifies as finding a needle in a haystack," he said by way of greeting. Opening the back door, he tossed in his backpack. "It's damn good to see you, Will."

"You look like you been rode hard and put up wet," William observed.

"Damn sure feels like it, too," Hal admitted.

"No fresh pig meat, I see."

"No, but I'm damn sure there's other kind of wild critters in that forest. It just looks like that kind of country. Speaking of fresh meat, did you happen to pass by any restaurants or any place to get food?"

William put the truck in gear and backed out to the dirt road. "Yeah, as a matter of fact I think there's one in a place called San Luis, about 80 miles back."

"Works for me."

At William's urging, Hal connected his phone to the charger and then called Jennifer. After he finished the call, they talked for the next hour and 20 minutes about Annie, primarily where she was, how to get to her, and how to get her out.

"Seems to me there's two basic options," Hal concluded. "We go in bold and in the open and get her, or we go stealth. Trouble is, we don't know the setup exactly. We know there's a house and a big barn and corrals."

"One thing bothers me," William said. "Annie said in her email there are guards. If we take that information at face value, we have to ask why. Why guards? If it's just a horse ranch, why are there guards?"

"I don't know. Damn expensive horses, maybe?"

William shrugged. "But, you know, why doesn't matter."

"Yeah, you're right. But if they are guarding something expensive or important, we have to assume they're armed. That makes me nervous."

"Damn nervous," William agreed. "So, okay, let's back up a step. We need to check the place out. For that we might need to go stealth. Best way is to observe unseen, with binoculars. Would be good to have a spotting scope."

"Yeah, where can we get one here? Do they have sporting goods stores?"

"Maybe the kids can find that out for us."

San Luis was a large town. William turned onto what looked like a business district and in a couple blocks they saw a Cantina sign and pulled in.

"What do you think?" William asked. "This might be easier than trying to find a grocery store. I don't know if they have fast food joints."

"Well," Hal said, after a few seconds. "Maybe get something to go and get back on the road."

William nodded, a worried look on his face. "Yeah, but we're kind of conspicuous. We're not locals and we're taller than anyone here. Together we stick out. How about I go in alone? What do you want, to eat?"

"This is cattle country. Maybe they have cold beef sandwiches."

The place was small and about half full. A young man pointed William to an empty table in the corner.

"Sir," William said. "Do you speak English?"

"Si—yes, I do."

"Good! Thanks. Can I place a take-out order? You know, get the food to go?"

"Yes, we can do that."

William nodded.

The young man brought a menu in Spanish. In a moment a thin, middle-aged woman appeared, an interested smile on her face. "What may I get for you?" she asked in heavily accented English,.

"Two cold beef sandwiches," he said. "And two coffees."

"Two?" she asked.

"Yes. I'm—I'm hungry. Didn't have breakfast."

She took the menu. "I come back with coffee," she told him, and pointed to an empty table nearby. "You can wait there, if you wish," she said as she walked away.

William took a quick glance around the room. The conversation had died down when he walked into the restaurant. *They all know I'm not from these parts*, he thought to himself. He had a feeling the waitress was especially curious.

The woman returned shortly with a ceramic carafe and a cup, and as she was pouring the question came forth. "Something for you as you are waiting. My thought is you, ah, from United States. Correct?"

He nodded. No use denying it and arouse any kind of suspicion. "Yes, that's correct."

She smiled a satisfied smile. "Ah, good. You are different. Same skin as us, but you are tall."

He nodded politely, not knowing what to say.

"Yes, very much tall." She looked toward the kitchen. "I go get food."

William loosed a small sigh of relief. He waited, trying to hide his nervousness as he noticed the curious glances cast in his direction. Mainly to settle his nerves he sipped his coffee. Five minutes passed before the woman appeared with a large paper bag.

"I put potatoes in for you with the sandwiches. Plastic forks and knives. Please enjoy," she advised.

Stopping for only a few minutes to eat their sandwiches and drink the coffee, they also gassed up the truck. A few seconds after they pulled away from the gas station, a white van pulled up to the pumps and two men stepped out. The driver handed a wad of pesos to the attendant. "Llenarlo," he said in Spanish. Then he walked across the lot to join his companion wearing a black jacket. Black Jacket lit a cigarette. They conversed in Spanish. Their casual tone belied the grim topic they discussed.

"So why did Señora Covena change her mind?" asked Black Jacket.

Deke Smith lit his own cigarette. "She decided on a different place," he said, "wilder country, more desolate."

"I think you are talking about Patagonia?"

"Yes. And she decided to starve him first before she dumps him in the middle of nowhere."

Estancio Andujar shook his head. "Are you joking?"

"No and give him only booze to drink."

"That doesn't make sense."

"It does to her. It has something to do with avenging her father."

Andujar continued to shake his head. "She is one tough woman. I hope she never gets angry at me," he said.

"Then don't do anything stupid. She doesn't cut anyone any slack, except for that little girl."

"Is that really the gringo's granddaughter?"

"Sure is. The señora has plans for her."

Andujar dropped his cigarette and stamped out the butt. "I had plans, too, for today, my day off. Now we are here again. Are you sure she won't change her mind again?"

Smith finished his cigarette and flipped it into the ditch. "No, she won't. I feel sorry for Señor Harold Lamar. He's going to die drunk and alone."

TWENTY-ONE

William drove as Hal described his time in the remote cabin up to the minute he saw William in the truck. Both men were puzzled about why Bernadette would leave him at the cabin. The next ride promised by Chubby the driver had not showed.

"I knew there was no next ride," Hal said, "as soon as they took the check. Maybe they were going to let me sit there and rot. Those guys mean business, one of them had what looked like a Glock nine-millimeter."

"Oh, shit. Bernadette must have had a reason for the cabin. I wonder what will happen when someone goes to check and you're gone. They'll probably assume you headed for the road and the nearest town."

"If you're right, that means they'll be watching for me."

"Maybe, but as far as they know you're on foot and you don't know anyone here that can help you. They don't know that you know where they are. That is a definite advantage for us. We just have to have a plan."

"Yeah, yeah, good point." Hal stared thoughtfully out the window. "As long as Bernadette doesn't get antsy and move Annie somewhere else."

"Maybe not. Annie's email said there were men guarding her. I have a feeling Bernadette feels secure. On the other hand, she knows you have money and can acquire resources. And if she has those two guys working for her, and guards at her ranch, she's not just some middle-aged woman marking time in life. She's got resources, too. Maybe she raises those horses she has, or something along those lines. So, I think if someone goes out to the cabin and you're not there, she's going to cast a net far and wide. If she wants more money, she's not going to let the golden goose get away."

"Or she's going to want to make sure I don't talk to the cops, here or anywhere." Hal finished his meal and motioned to the side of the road. "Pull over. I'll drive."

"I think you could be right," William said as he pulled off to the shoulder and exchanged places. "Okay," William said, after they were back in the cab, "she might be worried that you will talk to the cops. And if she's worried and nervous, we don't want that to come down on Annie."

"Crap, you might be right. Maybe I should go back to the cabin, maybe—"

"No, no. Somebody might have been there, by now. Maybe you should call her. You're worried and scared for Annie, and so am I. So maybe you act like the worried grandpa you are and call her. She'll buy that."

Hal checked for traffic. "Hmm," he said, quietly. "But we don't have her phone number, though."

"Yeah, Jarod and Jennifer could likely find it, but if you call her, she'll damn sure wonder how you got her number, not to mention how you got a phone."

"Ah, shit! There's got to be a—just a second." Hal reached back awkwardly and grabbed his backpack. From it he took out the receipt and transaction records from Banco Nuevo Rio. He held up the papers. "I think there's a way."

William kept his curiosity in check and waited while Hal looked through the papers.

"Yeah, there might be a way," Hal reiterated. "Hollister, or Bernadette, told me to wire money to this bank and talk to a specific person when I got there. That person was Ricardo Guiermo. He handled the transaction and made a comment about The Children's Trust, said it did good things." He paused for a few seconds, staring intently, thinking. "What if I call Mr. Guiermo and ask him to contact the people at Children's Trust and give him my phone number? It might be a long shot, but a safe one."

"Yeah, that sounds feasible, except for the phone number part. She can't know you have a satellite phone. You know what we need to do? We need to turn around and hightail it back to San Luis and get into a hotel. Then you call from the hotel, local number. You can tell Guiermo where you are and he can pass that on. Bernadette will assume—and it would be logical for anyone to assume—that you made it somehow as far as San Luis."

Hal nodded. "Yeah, if I call from Santa Rosa, that's too much of a give-away. Okay, l guess that means we turn around and go back to that town."

Within the hour they were checked into a hotel on the edge of town. The owner verified that they had long distance calling. They were able to get separate rooms across the hall from one another.

It was well past the bank's closing time so Hal would place the call in the morning. In the meantime, reasoning they should stay low and out of sight, William asked for and got directions to a grocery store where he stocked up on food, snacks, and water.

Using William's international calling card, they placed a call to Jarod and Jennifer and caught them up on the latest. A general plan was outlined. If Bernadette responded as they all hoped she would, and if anyone came for Hal, William would tail them. It would be the only option they would likely have. They spent the rest of the evening in their rooms, alone with their thoughts and worries, trying to calm their jitters and find their courage.

After a breakfast of coffee in William's room, they made notes for Hal's call, which he made from his room.

"Good morning, Mr. Guiermo," Hal began. "This is Harold Lamar. I was in your bank two days ago. I have a question regarding the transaction we did, with the cashier's check."

"Ah, yes, of course," Guiermo said evenly, using his best customer service tone. "I recall. What is your question?"

As he and William had decided, Hal took a matter-of-fact, businesslike approach. "I need to contact the people in charge of that foundation, The Children's Trust, especially a gentleman by the name of Hollister McGiven. Would it be possible for you to contact him for me? I don't have direct contact information, otherwise I would call them without having to bother you."

There was a pause. "I see. Is there a problem with the check?"

"No, not at all. I simply want to talk to Mr. McGiven. Since I was advised to contact you regarding the transaction, I thought you might know how to connect with him."

Another pause. "Señor Lamar, I would have to locate that file and see what restrictions might be on it. Sometimes our account holders want to remain anonymous. May I have your contact conformation, Señor?"

"Of course. I'm at the Arroyo Hotel in San Luis. The number here is 5555-2812, and my room number is 12."

"Thank you, Señor. I will access that account file and call you."

"Thank you, sir. I appreciate your willingness to help."

"My pleasure, Señor Lamar."

Hal sighed heavily after he hung up the phone. "The man was being non-committal, maybe even cautious," he told William. "I'm to expect his call back. Said he would look at the file.

"Well," William said, "it wasn't an outright 'no.'"

"Yeah, true. Now we wait."

Hal's room phone rang 35 minutes later. "Harold Lamar," he answered. In the next instant his jaw dropped in shock and he looked at William.

"Well, well, mornin' ole buddy," said a voice that sounded like Hollister McGiven. "We was wonderin' where you got yourself off to. You okay?"

It took a second for Hal to gather himself.

Meanwhile, William threw up his hands and mouthed "What?"

"Ah, yeah," Hal managed to reply. "I'm okay, Hollister. Thanks for calling."

It was William's turn to be shocked.

"Well, sure," the voice went on. "We thought maybe you went and got yourself lost."

"It was scary in them woods, Hollister," Hal replied, recovering his nerve. "When my ride didn't show, I hiked out. That place is in the middle of nowhere."

The voice chuckled. "Glad you made it out. Now here's the deal. You sit tight and them two fellas what took you to that cabin will be along. Where the heck are you?"

"Arroyo Hotel in San Luis, room 12."

"Okay. Check out of the room and be out front in about two hours. Them fellas know who you are. They'll be along."

"How's my granddaughter? When am I going to see her?"

"Just you be patient, ole buddy. We're getting to that. Be patient."

The call disconnected before Hal could reply, leaving him staring blankly at the receiver in his hand. "Damn, that took me by surprise."

"William shook his head. "That's damn spooky. For some reason they want you to think he's still alive. You got a ride coming?"

"Whoever it was told me to check out and wait out front. They'll be here in two hours. It's probably the same two guys. Goddamn, it's about to get hairy."

William stood up and looked out the window. "I think we should get our stuff and check out now, but separately. I'll wait in the lobby to get a good look at them and their vehicle. Then I'll follow."

"Right. Ah, what about my phone?"

"Hide it in your boot again."

"Okay, might work a second time. I guess all we can do is play this as it goes." Hal began packing his backpack. "Just stay close."

"I will. There's more than a good chance they'll take you to the ranch. I'll find a place I can watch from. First chance you have, call me."

Hal's nervousness was obvious as he finished packing. "Yeah, okay." He fumbled a bit as he put the satellite phone and batteries in their makeshift hiding place in his boots.

"One other thing," William said. "Maybe you should take only cash. We can store your credit cards, hide them somewhere, along with your passport and driver's license. If anyone asks, you can say you lost them."

"I think that's a hell of a good idea."

There was nothing more to be done, for the moment. "I'm not sure how this will turn out," he admitted. "I know how I want it to happen. Whatever happens, it's for Annie."

William held out his hand. "You're right. This is for Annie." He shook Hal's hand. "I'll wait until you check out, then I'll be along."

Hal nodded grimly and followed William out the door.

Chances were good that Hal was going straight into the lion's den, thought William as he packed his few things. William tried to come up with all the possibilities after that. Once at the horse ranch, Hal for all intents and purposes was as much a captive as Annie was. Bernadette was in control, with the odds probably in her favor. For a second William wondered if they shouldn't have involved the FBI. Maybe it wasn't too late. Maybe a call to Jarod and the rest of the family would be in order to talk about it. Annie needed to start her treatments in two and a half weeks, and here he was in a hotel room in boondock Argentina feeling totally inadequate. Perhaps there was a way to get advice from the FBI without involving them.

Four people were waiting at home, nervous, anxious, and sick with worry day after day, hour after hour. They were depending on him and Hal to bring Annie home. At the moment, he didn't know how that was going to happen. This was not the time to express doubts to Jarod, Jennifer, Virginia, and Marie. But maybe he should talk to Jarod.

He reached into his bag and grabbed the small cylindrical case with the medicine Henry Two Crow had given him for Annie. The instructions were to open it only in Annie's presence and brew a tea from the dried leaves. Inside the six-inch long and two-inch wide wood vial was a bag Ollie Two Crow had made for the medicine. Miraculously the container had made it through the TSA inspectors at Sioux Falls, not to mention Argentinian Customs without it being opened and inspected.

In this technological, industrialized, Christianized world people stood on what was considered accepted—conventional thinking, conventional wisdom, and conventional medicine. Anything thing outside of "conventional" was outside the comfort zone of most people in industrialized countries. Yet, that bag of medicine made it past the paranoia of TSA and Customs inspectors. Was it fortunate coincidence, twice?

Ollie will make a special bag to put it in, to hide it from ignorance and prying eyes.

The decolonized part of his intellect and psyche knew it was not just coincidence.

William waited another 10 minutes before he left the room. A woman at the front desk took the room key and wrote out a receipt. He nodded at her and said a polite, "Gracias" and went to a wicker chair in a corner of the small lobby. From there he had a clear view of Hal standing near the front doors. The room was empty so he decided to place a call to Jarod since it was just after 8 in Cold River.

"Good morning, Dad," he answered. He was up and having coffee.

"Hey, Son. Are you alone?"

"Yeah. What's up?" Jarod's tone turned cautious.

"I need to talk about a couple of things, but just you and me. Are you okay with that?"

"Sure, Dad. What's going on?"

"We're headed to Santa Rosa. Hal is probably going to meet with Bernadette face-to-face. We don't know how that's going to turn out. We're several hours away yet, so I have a feeling there won't be any new developments until later today."

"Damn, what do you think will happen?"

"Don't know. We think maybe she'll ask for more money. But here's the sticky thing. Hal talked to someone posing as Hollister McGiven again. We know he's dead, right?"

William heard a door open and close. "I'm stepping outside, Dad. Just in case. Mom and Virginia are both here. Yeah, I mean, we have Mary Lee's letter from Bernadette. We can check, I think. If they were near Santa Rosa at the time, we can see about looking into records. But why would Bernadette lie?"

"If McGiven is dead, that puts a spin on this that worries me."

"Dad, I agree with Sheriff Triplett. I think the woman that attacked us is Bernadette McGiven. She's gone now, no one's at that farmhouse. This has had all the earmarks of a well-organized, well-planned operation. She got Annie out of the country without a passport. I'm sure she's behind this and she's smart, probably has connections."

"Hal will go to her place. I'm hanging back out of sight. He'll contact me as soon as he can. After that we do what comes next. But I'm wondering about something. Do you think it's too late, or even a good idea, to contact the FBI?"

"Yeah, I don't think we go there, and for the reasons I just gave about Bernadette, Dad. She's shrewd and smart. I don't want to take a chance because she might have a way of finding out. You know what I think? I think she's after Hal. Annie was the way to get him down there."

"Why do you say that Son?"

"Well, a few things Virginia told us about the partnership between Hal and McGiven. She thinks Hal didn't have to force him out. After Hal blew his top, McGiven put the rest of the money from the sale of the cattle into the business account. He didn't abscond with thousands and thousands of dollars. At the most, he used $1500 to pay hospital bills. Virginia told us she pleaded with Hal, but he was hell bent on ending the partnership."

William looked out the window. Hal was still standing, pacing a bit. He was very obviously nervous. "Oh, damn," he said, under his breath. "So, it's probably not a good idea for Hal to go to her place."

"At this point, what choice is there? And Bernadette doesn't know you're there."

William sighed. "Okay, I just wanted to run that question by you. I'll keep you posted. Oh, and one more thing. Call Henry Two Crow and let him know I'll be calling him."

"Yeah, I will, Dad. Be careful, please, both of you."

"We are, Son. We are. Give my love to all the ladies."

William looked through the window at his son's father-in-law. Hal Lamar was a hard man, a tough customer, as the whites liked to say. To the Lakota who knew him, he was a racist like many of the white farmers and ranchers on or near the reservation. They made their living, and in some cases their fortunes, using Lakota land—for which they paid rock bottom leases—but had no use for the Lakota people.

Hal Lamar had learned the value of hard work, but he also led a privileged life, and had the attitude that went with it. A domineering father had taught him to look down on Indians and poor whites. Hal had been involved in several fights with Lakota boys in high school, William among them. He had learned to be hard and unbending, and maybe it was coming back to bite him. The trouble was, Annie was the pawn.

William was mulling over the conversation he just had with Jarod when he saw a white van stop in front of Hal. A Hispanic male in a dark jacket stepped out and opened a sliding door. Hal stooped to get inside and the door closed behind him. William wondered when he would next see or hear from Annie's other grandfather. In the next few seconds, the van was on the street and into the traffic.

Grabbing his bag, William hurried out the door to the rental truck. He saw the van turn east on Highway 113.

TWENTY-TWO

Bernadette saw the slender, elegantly dressed man walking down the middle aisle of the barn between the stalls. Esteban Palomino exuded authority no matter the setting or situation. Bernadette felt it was his way of compensating for his short stature. Today he had arrived at her place unannounced, which was unusual. It was not easy to assess what his mood might be because his intense black eyes were hidden behind the dark Gucci sunglasses. They were as much a power statement as his tailored gray slacks with razor-like creases, fitted black linen shirt, and black leather jacket.

She finished latching the stall door and gave the Andalusian stallion a final scratch behind the ears. This was her way of showing she was not flustered by Palomino's sudden appearance, although she was. When he was finally less than 10 feet from her, she turned to greet him.

"Esteban," she called out cheerfully, "how good of you to stop by."

"Gracias," he replied. "That is a very beautiful animal. I've always admired the Andalusian. They are elegant."

"They are," she agreed. "What brings you to this neck of the woods, my friend?"

"I love those cowboy sayings of yours," he said, chuckling lightly. "Well, as you might also say, I was just passing through. The builder has nearly finished my house on the coast, and I am to select tile for the flooring on the patios. So, I decided to drive to Punta Alta, and take a seaplane to Carnarones."

"Ah, I see. A pleasant trip so far, I trust?" She guessed he was driving one of his Porsche Carreras, or perhaps one of the fully restored 1973 Ford Mustangs in his stable of sports cars. Of course, following closely behind would be his entourage of bodyguards in a white Chevrolet Suburban. From Punta Alta, he would fly the seaplane and the security detail would be his passengers. Palomino had been an accomplished Formula One driver in his younger days but decided to devote himself entirely to his business interests. He was also a fixed wing and rotor pilot.

"It has been, thank you," he said.

"Wonderful," she said, maintaining her poise. "I hope you have time for a bit of refreshment."

Palomino waved a manicured hand and removed his sunglasses, slipping them into the slot on his jacket. "No, thank you, I am afraid not. I simply have a question, then I must be back on the road." His eyes probed her face. "I trust your trip to the United States went as planned?"

"It did, as a matter of fact."

"I am happy to hear that. This trip was the first time you returned to your home since you and your father moved here?"

"That's right."

"There has been much change, since you lived there, I imagine."

"That's true, as well. I hardly recognized the place. In a way it was very much a final goodbye. My home and my life are here, as they have been for decades."

He smiled a friendly smile, the kind he gave to cover small doubts. "I am pleased to hear that, *mi amiga*. Well, as I said, I must be back on the road." He took her by the shoulders and kissed her on both cheeks. She detected the subtle scent of Brut. "Be well."

"The same to you," she replied.

With a nod and a smile, he put on his sunglasses, waved a hand, and turned on his heels. His Italian loafers made hardly a sound as he walked out of the barn.

Bernadette stepped to the gate of an empty stall and leaned back against it. Her legs felt rubbery. She took a deep breath and gathered herself.

Although Palomino was not given to micromanaging his business, he insisted on knowing everything he could about his people. She had known him for 20 years and had risen through the ranks with him, though not side-by-side. He had operated in the cities and she in the rural areas. But now he was at the top because he was ruthless and decisive. At the bottom rungs of the organizational ladder as rookies, she and Esteban Palomino together had done the grunt work, some of it not pleasant, to say the least. But she was capable because her experience in several rough and tumble jobs in South Dakota had hardened her. Working alongside men, she had taken her share of licks and learned to be physically and mentally tough. Now that she was second in command, she handpicked a small core of trusted subordinates who carried out the tough tasks. She was the only woman to have ever risen so high in this organization. If the situation called for it, she wasn't afraid to get her hands dirty.

Being second-in-command, however, meant that she still answered to the boss, and Esteban Palomino expected nothing less than loyalty without hesitation. His biggest fear was someone infiltrating the organization. A friend had whispered to Bernadette that there were those that were suspicious of her, still to this day, simply because she was an American. Many had forgotten or overlooked the fact that it was Palomino who had befriended her while Bernadette was working as a cleaning maid in a hotel. She was a foreigner down on her luck when they had met and had no inkling what she was signing up for when she had become a runner for the organization.

Loyalty worked both ways and Palomino trusted Bernadette implicitly and had her back. Nonetheless, she knew he had doubts about her trip back to the United States. When she had first mentioned her plans, he had said nothing, because he trusted her. But he also was not above giving people enough rope to hang themselves with.

Bernadette had not shared her reason for the trip with Esteban, a decision she was beginning to regret. Kidnapping an American child was an offense that could bring unwanted attention to her. And if she were suspected in such a crime, then the unwanted attention would spread beyond her. Undue attention was the last thing the organization wanted. Of course, if her plan for Harold Lamar went off without a hitch, then she could inform Palomino that she had simply found a child to adopt. Anything less, and any deviation, would be disaster. So far, except for one minor slip, everything was proceeding according to plan. And now Hal was unknowingly furthering his own demise by coming to Santa Rosa. Once the next phase of the plan was carried out and he was out of the way, there would be no reason for anyone to be suspicious. Then she was home free.

Bernadette waited until she was certain Palomino was off the property before she walked back to the house. She was expecting a delivery from a children's boutique in Santa Rosa with a few items of clothing for Annie. She went out the west doors of the barn and paused to look toward the three white marble headstones at the top of a grassy rise 50 yards away— her father, her daughter, and her husband. Hollister Earnest McGiven, Aleta Marisol Covena, and Aurelio Cristian Covena.

The headstones were visible from her bedroom window and every morning she gazed out the window before she left the room. They were at once her reason to stay and her reason to leave, a bitter-sweet dilemma. Memories instantly rushed to the front of her awareness the second she laid eyes on them, warm memories that turned into painful memories. It was a daily ritual of figuratively and emotionally running to and from.

Bernadette was a realist. No matter how far she physically distanced herself from the graves, there was no way to outdistance the pain. Those graves were a constant reminder of how lonely life was. First it was her father, 15 years ago. Ten years later a car crash claimed her husband and daughter. Aleta was only two when that happened.

Two years after that awful moment, she had considered moving back to the United States with the intent of exacting revenge against Hal. In the process of some research, she had learned of Hal Lamar's granddaughter Annie, born the same year as Aleta. Years of careful planning followed, and she added a new wrinkle. A few weeks ago, Bernadette had followed the girl and her parents to Dora's Restaurant in Cold River and was utterly astonished by Annie's resemblance to Aleta. It was then that she knew what Hal Lamar's weak spot was.

Now she had a new worry. Esteban Palomino was obviously concerned about her trip to the United States. Bernadette understood that he didn't want any kind of scrutiny, no matter how small or seemingly inconsequential, about his second in command. So, for the time being, it would not be wise to reveal to Palomino that she had just kidnapped the granddaughter of a rich, white American cattle rancher. And that meant the next steps in her plan needed to be expedited in a hurry. First, Harold Lamar had to disappear and the adoption papers for Annie had to be processed immediately. She expected to have the papers in hand within a matter of days, since she had made large cash gifts to two provincial officials. Once Hal fell off the face of the earth and the adoption was in place, she would have a talk with her boss.

Bernadette glanced at her watch. In about two hours Hal would be checked into a small hotel in Santa Rosa. Tomorrow he would be her captive. She sighed, looking forward to spending some time with Annie.

Hal watched the grassy landscape roll by, thinking mostly of Annie and hoping he would see her before too long. Neither the chubby driver nor his black-jacketed companion had spoken to him, though they occasionally conversed with each other; they made no phone calls nor took any. William had told him the drive to Santa Rosa was about five hours from San Luis, and they had been on the road nearly three hours. Chubby and Black Jacket seemed unconcerned and it was clear to Hal they each had a specific job. One was the driver and the other his guard. Somewhere behind them was William Black Spotted Horse. Ahead of them was an unknown end to the day.

A mile behind them, William kept the white van in sight. He varied the distance hoping the two men who had Hal would think he was just another vehicle going in the same direction. The van was careful to not exceed the speed limit, even slowing a bit to let other vehicles pass.

Two hours later they reached the north edge of Santa Rosa and William recognized a few buildings and businesses. Ahead he saw the van turn left at a major intersection and go east. William followed for several blocks until they turned in to the driveway of a small hotel. He drove past and found a small café and parked. Inside he ordered a meal and waited. Twenty minutes later, Hal called.

"They bought me a room here, at Hotel Estonzo," he said. "Later this evening they will pick me up and take me to meet Hollister McGiven."

"Really? McGiven himself?"

"That's what they said. They don't know that we know about him."

"That would be my guess," William said. "I'll find a hotel and get a room. When are you expecting them to come for you?"

"Nine, on the dot. I'm to be outside on the curb."

"Okay. I've got a call to make and I'll check with you later."

"Right."

William finished his meal and was relieved to notice he attracted no attention from the other patrons in the small restaurant. He paid and left, driving another block farther to a hotel. As soon as he checked in, he called Henry Two Crow.

"Hau," the old man answered. "Your boy told me you would call. How are things?"

William summarized the goings on since he had entered the country, up to the present moment, and told him of Hal's anticipated visit to the Dancing Horse Ranch.

"You still have the medicine?" the old man asked.

"Yeah, still in the case you gave me."

"Good. You need to put it in a safe place, where you can get it later," Two Crow said.

"Okay. Is there a reason for that, Uncle?"

"Yeah, there is. The Spirits said that you will be bringing your granddaughter home at the next full moon. That's nine days from now, but in between some tough things are going to happen. So, it's important to protect the medicine."

"Okay. What kind of tough things?"

"They didn't say, but you and your granddaughter's other grandpa will need to work together to get through it."

"Yeah, well, whatever the next nine days bring, we'll do what it takes to bring our little girl home. Thank you, Uncle. I'm going to call my son and ask him to offer you tobacco to put up a ceremony for us."

The medicine man chuckled softly. "He already did. We're doing one in two nights."

As comforting as it was to talk to Henry Two Crow, William was worried about the "tough things" the medicine man mentioned. He sat for a few seconds after he disconnected the call. There would be time to worry later, he decided. Now he had to find a safe place for the medicine. He called the front desk and asked if someone spoke English. A woman came on the line a few seconds later.

"Yes, Señor, how is it I can help you?" she asked.

"I need to find a place to store something for a few days," he told her. "Are there businesses that do that?"

"Yes," she replied to his relief. "What do you need to store? Is it papers, or something large?"

"Small. A case, a small tube. I don't need a storage room, just a locked case."

"I see. There is a safe in our office."

He considered that for a few seconds. "Thanks, but I need something for several days, not just while I'm here."

"We can do that for you, Señor," she assured him. "It's a service we provide for travelers. There is a fee."

"That might be what I need. May I have a look at the safe?"

"Yes. My name is Martina and I will be here until midnight."

There were actually three safes and each had different size compartments complete with keys, similar to a bank safe deposit box. He picked the smallest compartment, signed a contract, and placed the medicine tube in it, and at the last minute he included the extra ignition key for the truck and Hal's credit cards and passport.

At quarter to nine he called Hal.

"Your guess is as good as mine as to what's going to happen," Hal said. "If you don't hear from me, use your best judgment. If I can, I'll call. Where are you, by the way?"

"El Gaucho Inn. Good luck."

William watched the clock hit nine and then move past the hour. He estimated the drive time from the city to the Dancing Horse Ranch at about 20 minutes, but he knew Hal wouldn't call while in anyone's presence. He decided to make himself comfortable and changed into a T-shirt and sweatpants. At 10, he brushed his teeth and called Jarod's number.

"I'm waiting," he told Jarod.

"Do you have any idea what's going to happen?"

"No, I'm afraid not," William admitted. "I'm worried."

"Yeah, well, check with me when you can. We're all holding together, but barely."

William paced the room after he disconnected the call, filled with anxiety, and suddenly feeling wholly inadequate. A glance at the power level on the phone indicated it to be at 50 percent. Finding the charger and wall plug adaptor, he plugged it in to charge. Finally, yielding to a bit of fatigue, he propped the pillows on the bed and laid down to rest.

He realized he had drifted off when he heard the satellite phone chirping. Rubbing his eyes, he saw the number on the caller ID. It was Hal. The time was 10:27 p.m.

TWENTY-THREE

Hal took the initiative and sat on the middle seat when Black Jacket opened the door to the van. The man's jacket was open and the handle to the automatic pistol was plainly visible. Though he was not surprised to see it, it still sent a jolt up his spine.

The route to Bernadette's ranch was easy to remember if he needed to. After several blocks westward the van turned north onto the main road into town. Five minutes later they made a left turn onto a secondary road, then right onto a graveled turnoff, stopping at a pair of iron gates. The gates were unobtrusive, rather modest. Chubby pushed a remote switch clipped to the visor and the gates swung open. Beyond the gates was a narrow gravel road. In the van's headlights Hal could see only the road and tall grass on either side. After about three miles they climbed a gradual slope, and as they descended the other side, two security lights and the dark outline of a house and a long, low building appeared.

At a fork near the house the van turned right and followed the road to the end of the long building and stopped in front of large, double sliding doors. A man in dark clothes appeared out of the shadows and pressed a button on the wall of the barn. He was clearly one of the guards Annie had mentioned. In a second, the barn doors slid open and the van entered the wide middle aisle of the barn. Interior lights came on automatically. Behind them Hal heard the barn doors closing. The van stopped at the far end of the barn and Chubby switched off the lights and shut down the motor. Hal was impressed with the interior of the building. It was a large, well-designed, clean barn for horses.

Black Jacket pulled open the side door and motioned for Hal to step out.

"Feet apart and extend your arms, Señor," the man ordered.

Hal complied and was subjected to a thorough body search. His cash was taken. The man next pointed down.

"Take off your boots," he said, "and your belt."

Hal slid off the belt and held it out for the man, and at the man's nod he slid off his boots. Black Jacket inspected the belt and gave it back, then picked up the boots one at a time. First, he felt inside. Hal willed himself to stay calm as the man next touched the sleeves.

"Que es esto?" he said, glancing up at Hal. Black Jacket rubbed the leather side of the sleeve. A glint of amusement flashed in his dark eyes. Turning the boot upside down he shook it until the satellite phone batteries slid out, first one and then the other.

"Baterias?"

Chubby, meanwhile, had opened a door and turned on the lights of a small room, and turned a curious look at Black Jacket.

"Que dijiste?" he said. "Batteries?"

"Si," said Black Jacket, triumphantly. He dropped the boot and grabbed the other and quickly felt the soft leather sleeves until he found the hard spot. He turned the boot up and shook it until the phone slid out part way.

"Ah, un telefono!"

Chubby grinned. "I'll be damned. That's a satellite phone. How clever."

He motioned for Hal to enter. Hal grabbed his belt and boots and walked in. It was an office with a desk against a corner, a leather couch, and two high-backed leather chairs on either side of a coffee table made from the cross-section of a large cedar tree. Beneath them was a large cowhide rug. In the corner opposite the desk was a small refrigerator. Above the desk on the wall was a flat television screen.

Chubby pointed to one of the chairs. "Have a seat," he said. Black Jacket, with batteries and phone in hand, took the other chair, while Chubby sat in the chair behind the desk. Hal fixed his eyes on the top of the coffee table. He guessed they were waiting for Bernadette to make an appearance. Several minutes later he heard a man's muffled voice, a door opening, and a tall woman walked in.

Hal recognized her immediately as the woman at the ranch house, but he also saw in her face the vestiges of a young Bernadette McGiven. Chubby and Black Jacket stood and nodded. Hal remained seated.

"Señora Covena," Black Jacket said.

Bernadette nodded affably at the two men. "Sit, please," she said, in a low, strong voice. She moved to the end of the couch and looked down at Hal.

She was dressed as though she had just come from a sit-down dinner, Hal noted. An attractive woman, he thought, but her eyes were hard and unyielding. Black Jacket dropped the cash on the table and held up the phone and the batteries.

"He hid them in his boots," Chubby explained.

"Well, well," she said, an amused smile on her face. "Harold Lamar, welcome to Dancing Horse Ranch. You and I have a bit of business to talk over."

"Thank you," he said. "What about Hollister?"

Bernadette glanced toward Chubby sitting at the desk.

"Well, Hal, it's like this," came Hollister McGiven's voice from the man. "I'm afraid, ole buddy, you'll just have to cowboy on without me."

Hal was not totally surprised, but nonetheless glanced at the man, shocked at the exact mimicry of McGiven's voice and inflections. He turned to Bernadette. "I'm sorry," he said, "when did he die?"

Her reply was quick and clipped. "I hardly think you're sorry, but if you must know, my father died 15 years ago."

Hal shook his head and watched Bernadette take a seat on the end of the couch. "I *am* sorry," he said. "It's not an easy thing, losing a parent. But I'm not here to convince you of my sincerity. I'm here to talk about my granddaughter."

"Ah, yes, the hard-driving businessman," she countered. "Well, you've come to the right place." She looked past Hal and nodded at Chubby. "Deke, if you please. Hal—you don't mind if I call you Hal, do you—look at the flat screen."

Hal shifted to look as the screen lit up, and nearly gasped as he saw Annie seated at a table, eating. His attention was riveted and he stifled the emotion building in his chest. She was eating spaghetti and was wearing dark jeans and a pale blue blouse. Her hair was neatly fixed in a long ponytail, and the quilled medallion hung around her neck. After a couple minutes the screen froze to a still shot.

"Note the time stamp," Bernadette told him. "That was taken earlier this evening. Your granddaughter is well."

Hal continued to stare at the screen. The time stamp indicated 7:14 p.m. and today's date. "Thank you," he said, hoarsely. "When can I take her home?"

Bernadette chuckled, low in her throat, almost like a slow growl. "Before I answer that question, let's talk about my father," she said.

Hal nodded, unable to take his eyes away from the screen. At a nod from Bernadette the screen went dark. "Okay," he said, "I'm listening."

"My father was a good man," she declared. "He never had more than two beers any time he drank, which was maybe once a month. He worked for every cent he had and most of what he earned went to support my mother, my brothers, and me. Mom had to talk him into buying anything new for himself, be it clothes, a fishing pole, or a straw hat. After you forced him out of the partnership, he couldn't find work as a ranch hand. Do you know why, Mr. Harold "Hal" Lamar? Of course you do. He couldn't find work doing what he loved because you blackballed him. You put out the word that he wasn't to be trusted. You took away the largest part of what helped him think of himself as a man. So, he started drinking heavily. And it wasn't just beer, no, sir, it was whiskey. Oh, he found work as a janitor, a cook's helper, a dishwasher, a ditch digger, anything but being a cowboy. And two years after my brother died, he and I went up to Washington state and got work gutting fish."

Hal dropped his head, looking down at the top of the coffee table. He could feel her stare boring into him and threw up his hands. "I don't know what to say."

"Hey, I'm not looking for an apology, Mr. Hal Lamar," she snapped. "Even if you offered one, it wouldn't be sincere. Do you have any idea what kind of hardship you caused my dad? My mother and I tried to keep him sober. We couldn't. There was nothing we could say or do. No matter how hard we tried or how much we loved him, nothing worked. Finally, she gave up and divorced him."

Hal kept his head down, his cheeks burning.

"Well, one day he gave me money for my senior trip in high school. He'd been saving it because he wanted to make sure I had enough so I wouldn't be shamed in front of my classmates. On that trip, I bought a lottery ticket and brought it back to him. It was a winner. He won $10,000. So, he decided to make a new start. We came here and bought this place. It was just 40 acres and a small house, but it was ours. Here he could get on his own horse and chase around a few cows that were his own. But the booze still had a hold of him, so did the shame of failing back home. Losing my brother and having my mother divorce him was too much for him to get over. You want to know what his last words to me were, Mr. Hal Lamar? 'Don't be a loser like me,' he said. Those were the last words he ever spoke to me."

After a few seconds of silence Hal looked up to see Bernadette wiping her eyes. "He wasn't a loser to me, Mr. Hal Lamar. He was a good man and his soul was too gentle to deal with the cruelties of life. My father died a broken man, thinking he was a failure, thinking that he was flawed. He never got to build a house for my mother, the way he always wanted. I'm not going to ask you why you blackballed him. An arrogant son-of-a-bitch like you never second guesses his own actions. But you will pay for doing that to him."

"If it's money you want—"

"No, I don't want your money. I've got enough of my own. It's your pain I want."

Hal looked up into her eyes and was astonished at the cold detachment in her expression. "What do you mean?"

"I want you to feel inadequate. I want you to feel like a loser that knows he will fail. And I've got news for you, Mr. Hal Lamar. I'm going to make that happen."

Dumbfounded, after a few seconds he finally spoke. "What about my granddaughter?"

"Oh, don't worry about your granddaughter. She is safe with me; no harm will come to her."

"There is one thing you should know," he stammered. "About Annie."

"Do tell."

"She's seriously ill," he said. "She has leukemia, a form of childhood leukemia. She needs to be in a hospital to begin treatment."

"That's a pathetic ploy," she snorted.

He shook his head. "No, please, it isn't. We got the diagnosis the same day you took her."

Bernadette stared hard at the worry and concern in Hal's eyes. If it was an act, it was a good one. "I hope you're kidding," she warned.

"I wish I was. We need to get her to a doctor, her doctor."

She turned from Hal and glanced at Deke Smith, who could only shrug.

"Please," Hal insisted. "You've got to believe me. She needs to start treatments in less than two weeks. The longer she waits, the harder it will be to stop the progression of the disease."

"My instinct tells me it's a ploy on your part. But—just for Annie's sake, I'll take her to a doctor."

"A pediatric oncologist," Hal told her. "If there are any in this country. Better yet, let me take her home to the doctor who is waiting to treat her."

"Part of that will happen," she replied. "The other part, not so much."

"What do you mean?"

"I will make an appointment right away," she told him. "There are pediatricians here, and oncologists. That part will happen. You, on the other hand, are never going home."

Bernadette pointed to the screen. "That was the very last time, Mr. Hal Lamar, you will ever lay eyes on your granddaughter. No ifs, ands, or buts, no debate, no plea deals. That was it for you. I have judged you the ultimate shitbird for what you did to my dad, and for that you will pay."

Hal didn't move, figuring that anything sudden would bring a swift reaction from Mr. Black Jacket, with that automatic pistol at his belt. If she wanted him to feel inadequate, he was experiencing it now. He simply didn't know what to do.

Bernadette stood slowly, her eyes boring into him. "This concludes our little chat for tonight. Tomorrow is another day, sort of a new beginning for you, or maybe the beginning of the end. Mr. Smith and Mr. Andujar will take you to your accommodations for the night. We'll talk again tomorrow."

She walked out of the room without looking back.

Hal was surprised that, at least for a moment, he felt nothing. Or perhaps numbness was a logical reaction to everything he had just heard. In the next instant, he remembered the last time he had talked to Annie. She and her mother had come to say they were going camping along the Smokey River, two days before she was kidnapped.

"Watch out for snakes," he had warned her.

"That's Daddy's job," she had replied. "He protects us from spiders and snakes."

"Oh, and what's your job?"

"To be sugar and spice and everything nice," she had said, impishly.

"Well, darlin', you're very good at it."

He was suddenly aware that a figure stepped into his field of vision. It was the man with the voice of Hollister McGiven, whom Bernadette referred to as Mr. Smith.

"Mister Lamar," Smith said, in his own voice. "Follow me."

Hal slipped on his boots, rose stiffly and followed the man out the door, aware that Andujar was a few steps behind them. They walked past the van, toward the other end of the barn and past the stalls, some with horses gazing curiously through the mesh top of the gates. Smith opened a sliding stall door to reveal a second door that opened inward, and pointed in.

Hal walked into an enclosed room with a concrete floor. There was a military style cot and a composting toilet in one corner. The only other objects in the room were a case of bottled water on the floor and two folded blankets and a bare pillow atop the cot. There was only one overhead light with a single bulb and a small square window high on the wall in one corner.

Without a word, Smith closed both doors and Hal heard a metal bar sliding into place on the stall door. Fighting a rising panic he stood in the middle of the floor for a moment, assessing the bare bones room. Luckily the switch for the overhead light was next to the door. He had control over something. He moved to the door and placed his ear against it for several seconds but heard nothing. He was in deep trouble and the only thing he could hold onto was that Annie seemed to be ok.

His mouth was dry, and his heart pounded heavily. Slowly he walked to the cot and sat, staring at the case of bottled water. The image of Bernadette McGiven and the sound of her angry, accusing words swirled in his mind, like angry bees, and he was strangely inclined to swat at them. Hollister McGiven had become a drunk, a broken man, and she blamed him. *And for that you will pay*, she had said.

The harshest reality of the moment was that there was nothing he could do to help Annie. He felt totally useless and inadequate. Bernadette was getting her wish. There was nothing he could do. He stared at the opposite wall, trying to control his rising panic. He rose on shaky legs and walked to the opposite wall and tapped on it. It was thick and heavy plywood and he would need an axe or a sledgehammer to break it. Even if he could, there was the outside wall of the barn. The window was too small for him squeeze through. For the first time he noticed that the room was not painted. He looked up at the ceiling. It was the same material as the walls and he had nothing to poke, scratch, cut, or carve with.

Hal went back to the cot and sat. *We'll talk again tomorrow,* she had said. That would be his chance, maybe his last chance, to make something happen. He had to try.

In a minute he stood and shoved the cot into the corner, tight against the wall. Then he propped the pillows up as a backrest. Sighing, he reclined against them, stretching his legs out on the cot, and covered himself with a blanket.

It was all he could do. That, and wait, and hope that William Black Spotted Horse was as smart as he took him to be.

TWENTY-FOUR

An insistent chirping prodded William awake.

"Hello?" he said, anxiously, as he sat up and swung his feet down to the floor.

"This is Hal. Hello?"

"Yeah, Hal. So, what happened?"

"Ah, not much, please listen carefully."

There was something in Hal's voice that was different, but William said, "Okay, I'm listening."

"Where are you?"

"Ah, at the El Gaucho Inn, don't you remember?"

A pause, and dead silence that continued for nearly 10 seconds. He began to wonder if the call had dropped.

Deke Smith put the phone against his trouser leg and looked at Bernadette. They were in her office in the house. She saw the shock on Smith's face.

"Whoever he is, he's at the El Gaucho Inn," he whispered. "In Santa Rosa!"

When they first powered up Hal's phone, they saw only two names on the contacts list: Jennifer and William. Bernadette knew immediately who they were, Annie's mother and other grandfather. She told Deke to call the number for William, imitating Hal's voice. She had to confirm it was William Black Spotted Horse. But why were they the only two names on Hal's satellite phone? They were shocked that he said he was at the El Gaucho Inn in Santa Rosa.

"What do you want me to do?" Smith asked Bernadette in a whisper.

"It has to be William Black Spotted Horse. Tell him there is someone on the way to pick him up, in 30 minutes. Say that you're with Annie and he can see her, too. Keep it short."

Deke nodded and brought the phone to his ear.

"William, are you still there?"

"Yeah, thought I lost you."

"Listen, William. Two men will be there in 30 minutes. Wait out front and look out for a white van. I'm with Annie and they will bring you so you can see her, too."

"How is she, Hal?"

"She's good. You'll see. Got to ring off. Be outside the hotel."

Deke disconnected the call and shut off the phone as Bernadette frantically looked for and found the number to the El Gaucho Inn, then and called the front desk.

"Mostrador," said a female voice. "Como puedo ayudarte?"

"Habla usted Ingles?"

"Si, yes, I do."

"Good. Can you put me through to William Black Spotted Horse, please?"

"One moment, please."

After a couple of clicks, a phone started ringing. Bernadette disconnected. It was very likely William Black Spotted Horse was at the hotel.

The desk clerk had not hesitated to place the call. And who could mistake a name like that?

William watched the phone's screen turn from green to red, indicating the call had disconnected. Something nagged at him. He looked at his watch—10:29. He thought for a moment. *Got to ring off.* That was it. Hal Lamar probably never said that in his life. Was he nervous, or simply overjoyed at seeing Annie?

The room phone rang, but he hesitated to answer. As if sensing his caution, it didn't ring a second time. He waited but it didn't ring again.

He looked at his bag, wondering if he should take anything with him. No, he wouldn't. Tough things were coming, Henry Two Crow had told him. Maybe he should be cautious. On impulse he took up the thin writing pad and pen on the nightstand and paused to mentally compose the note. Then he carefully printed his message, starting with today's date:

> *To Whomever finds this: if you found this more than 10 days after the date above, please contact Jarod Black Spotted Horse at 605-555-4084 in the United States, Cold River, South Dakota and inform him that his father and father-in- law are likely in dire need of assistance. Their last known location was Dancing Horse Ranch near Santa Rosa.*

He read it over twice, then grabbed his phone and touched Jarod's number on the screen. It rang twice.

"Come on, Son, be there please!"

Three rings, then four.

"Hello, Dad?"

"Yeah, hello, Son. Listen, there's been a development and I don't have much time, so listen carefully. Maybe take notes."

"Go ahead," Jarod replied.

"Hal is at Bernadette's ranch. He just called, or at least I think he did. A car is coming to take me there as well. I sure as hell don't know what to expect. I'll call you later if the opportunity comes up. But listen, don't answer, let it ring if it's either my number or Hal's. Then call back. We'll let it ring three times, and disconnect, and then call you back. Okay?"

"Sure, okay. So, you're saying that if that doesn't happen, it isn't you calling?"

"Yeah."

Worry was evident in Jarod's voice. "So, if it isn't you, what should I do?"

"Don't answer."

"You're scaring me, Dad."

"I'm sorry, I'm just being cautious. I don't want to let Bernadette think we've contacted the authorities."

"Okay, yeah, I got it. Anything else?"

"Well, if you don't hear anything from us in a few days, by email or phone, use your best judgment as far as calling the police or the FBI. If I have to use a phone other than mine or Hal's, I'll say Half-Pint calling."

"Now you're really scaring me."

"Just being cautious. Got all that?"

"Yeah. Be careful, Dad."

William reluctantly disconnected the call and sat for a few seconds before he mentally assessed the situation. He was already dressed and hadn't unpacked his bag. He grabbed it and the note he had placed in an envelope and headed for the door, and then out the back way to the parking lot behind the hotel.

He had parked the truck in the last row against a high wooden fence. Unlocking the door he laid his bag, which contained all his documents and cards and spare cell phone, on the floor on the passenger side. Opening the glove box, he carefully placed his note in the envelope with the rental contract. Anyone opening the folded sleeve inside would see it first.

William paused a moment, trying to calm himself and think of anything else he should do, or that he might have overlooked. He felt the ignition key in his palm. Walking to the back of the truck he slid the key and the remote into the tow bar sleeve below the back bumper until it was out of sight. After a few seconds, he locked the doors and walked slowly to the back door and exited out the front of the hotel.

A glance at his watch indicated he had a few minutes to wait. Staking out a spot by the front door where he could easily watch traffic both ways, he sighed deeply, trying to calm his jittery nerves. The moment brought to mind the way he felt waiting to go out on his first combat patrol in 1973, wondering if he were up to it. He quickly reminded himself that he had survived that, and all the fire fights after that in the ensuing year of his tour with Delta Company, 2nd Battalion, 2nd Regiment of the 173rd Airborne. He, Annie, and Hal would survive this. He knew that because Henry Two Crow said they would be taking her home at the next new moon. It was just a matter of facing the "tough things" in between.

In his peripheral vision he saw the lights of a vehicle come on to his left, about 40 yards down the street. It was a white van. So, he had been watched for a few minutes. That was the kind of people they were dealing with. Well, so be it, he thought. They don't know what kind of people they're dealing with.

The van pulled up parallel to his position and a man in a black jacket stepped out of the passenger side and immediately opened the sliding door and glanced his way. William walked deliberately forward. Hal had described the black jacket man to him as well as the man who would likely be driving.

At six feet four inches, William was a head taller than the man in the black jacket, who had to look up to get his attention. The man was slightly built, younger than 40, and wound as tight as a spring, William guessed.

"The middle seat," the man said, pointing.

As William ducked low to climb in, he noticed a third man in the last seat, small, like the one in the black jacket. William slid to the far end next to the other door. The first man followed him in and sat at the end of the seat, closing the door behind him. Glancing down at the door, he wasn't surprised to see that the handle had been removed.

No one spoke during the drive. After a left and a right, they were on a main thoroughfare. A few minutes later they turned north onto the highway he had come in on. Not long after that they slowed and turned and stopped at a turnoff with double iron gates. Once through the gates, the gravel road went up a rise and then down through a few miles of tall grass on either side. A house came into view on the left, with a large barn to the right. The van came to a stop in front of the barn's double doors. A man stepped out of the shadows to push a button and the doors opened. The van entered and stopped at the other end of a corridor filled with stalls on either side.

Barely had the van stopped when the door was opened and the man stepped out, motioning for William to move towards a wall. The driver exited quickly, as did the third man in the far back seat. All three took positions in front of William.

"Arms out from your side," the driver said.

William lifted his arms and the other two men patted him down thoroughly and expertly. The one in the black jacket reached into William's inside jacket pocket and took his satellite phone, and then knelt to feel his hiking boots. He stood and stepped back.

"Empty your pockets," he said.

William reached in and took out some coins and his pocketknife, which the man took. He nodded at the driver, who opened a door to reveal an office like room.

"Inside," he said.

A woman was sitting in a tall leather chair. William immediately recognized her as the one at the farmhouse the day Annie was taken. A flicker of recognition flashed in her eyes as she pointed to the leather sofa.

"Please, have a seat, William," she said. Her voice was low and authoritative.

Two of the men remained standing, keeping a wary eye on William. The driver went to a desk in a corner.

"I'm Bernadette Covena," she told him. "My maiden name is McGiven."

William nodded.

"You are Annie's other grandfather," she said.

William nodded again.

Bernadette tilted her toward a flat screen television on the wall. "Have a look," she said. The driver pointed a remote and clicked the screen on.

Annie appeared, sitting at a table and eating. William kept emotion from his face as he watched. After a couple of minutes, the screen faded to black, and then was shut off.

"Your granddaughter is safe and well," the woman told him.

"I'm sure she's safe," William replied. "But she's not well."

"Really?"

"Yes, really," he said, evenly. "Annie was diagnosed with a form of childhood leukemia. She needs to begin treatment for it as soon as possible."

"So I've heard. Since I do care about her health and welfare, I've scheduled an appointment for her with a pediatrician who specializes in that area."

William held the woman's gaze, studying her face and her posture. She seemed self-assured. "Good," he said.

"Now there is the issue of her two grandfathers," she pointed out. "I'm surprised that you're here, frankly, and your presence concerns me."

"We've not contacted law enforcement authorities here or at home," he told her. "I'm sure you have ways of verifying that."

She smiled.

"Where is Hal?" he asked.

"You'll join him in a few minutes. Tell me, what did you hope to gain by coming here?"

"Our granddaughter. To take her home to her parents, her grandmothers, and to the care of a doctor."

"Commendable."

"I'm sure you understand about family loyalty," he said.

She stood, keeping her eyes on William. "Tomorrow is another day. My men will show you to your accommodations for the night."

Bernadette stood and left the room.

The man in the black jacket motioned for William to go to the door and went out ahead. "Out the door and to your left," the driver said. "To the end past the stalls."

At the end of the corridor the man in the black jacket unlocked a large padlock on the gravity hasp on the front of a stall door. As it opened,

William saw a wooden door behind it. The man turned the large handle and pushed the wooden door open.

"Señor Lamar," he spoke loudly into the room. "Stay where you are and do not come near the door."

"I hear you," came Hal's sleepy voice.

A push from behind prodded William into the room. As quickly as he stepped inside, the doors were shut behind him and he heard the padlock being locked on the metal stall door. Glancing left he saw Hal sitting on a narrow cot.

"Are you okay?" he asked.

William nodded. "You?"

Hal nodded. "Don't take this the wrong way, but why are you here?"

"You called me."

Hal shook his head. "No, I didn't. They took my phone. But it sounded like me I'll bet."

William took a quick look around the room and sat on the floor against the far wall.

"What do you mean?"

"Hollister *is* dead, and the person I've been talking to is a chubby white guy who can imitate him to a T."

William nodded. "Yeah? Well, he imitated you to a T."

"Shit!"

"My thought exactly."

Hal took one of the blankets and tossed it to William, who was looking around at the walls.

"I already checked the place out. No way out, not without a sledge-hammer or a stick of dynamite."

TWENTY-FIVE

William glanced around at the room. It was clearly a horse stall that been converted, his guess was expressly for the purpose it was fulfilling at the moment. William shook his head slowly. "I saw horses in some of the stalls," he said, "but those three men who brought me here are definitely not gauchos, or vaqueros, or whatever ranch hands are called here."

Hal nodded grimly. "Yeah. She said she doesn't want more money because she has enough of her own. I mean, anyone who has a place like this and people working for her has something else going on. So why the hell did she kidnap Annie? Was there a guard or someone outside the barn?"

"Yeah, someone opened the door."

"Did you notice the guy in the black jacket has a pistol, a semi-automatic?"

"Yeah, he acted like someone who has experience pushing people around."

"So, what are we up against?"

"I have a feeling we'll find out in the morning."

"What do you think we should do?"

William held up a hand, cautioning Hal to stay quiet, as he glanced around the room. "Meet me in the middle of the floor," he said. He stood and went to the middle of the room and motioned for Hal to join him. When he did, he leaned in close and whispered softly. "Can you hear me?"

Hal nodded, a quizzical expression on his face.

"Good. Let's not take a chance they have a way to hear what we're saying."

"Okay," Hal whispered back.

"For sure, the lady has a plan. I was not part of it, but I am now," William said. "It's possible they might separate us. If they do, you need to know that a friend of mine gave me medicine that Annie needs. It's in a safe at the hotel in my name. It's in a leather bag inside a wooden vial. It's a medicinal tea, made from a plant. It has to be steeped in boiling water. She needs to take it as soon as possible. Follow me so far?"

"Yeah. What friend?"

"You know him, his name is Henry Two Crow."

"Oh, the medicine man? He gave you medicine for Annie?"

"Yeah."

"Is it good, I mean, will it help her?"

"Yeah, it will. But she still needs to see her doctor."

Hal nodded. "Okay. What else?"

"I gave a heads up to Jarod, so he knows we're here. I told him if he doesn't hear from us in a few days, to use his judgment as far as calling the cops. And if you call him or Jennifer somehow, let it ring three times, disconnect, and call again. That way they'll know it's you. And then tell them it's Half-Pint calling."

"Yeah, okay. Is that because you think Bernadette or someone will try to call them, for whatever reason?"

William nodded. "I wouldn't put it past them."

"Okay. Anything else?"

"Let's try to get some sleep, or rest, at least. We need to be at our best tomorrow."

"All right, all right. But you best sit on the cot, too. That floor's damn hard."

After they settled on the cot, both reclining against the wall with legs over the edge, William pointed at the single overhead light, still on.

"I think we should shut that off," he said.

"It'll be darker than hell in here," Hal pointed out.

"Yeah, but we can relax better without the light."

William stood and walked the four steps to the switch and flipped it off, plunging the room into darkness, though light poured softly through the window.

"Hell," Hal said, "that's from the security light at the end of the building. That's better than a nightlight."

William walked back to the cot and sat down carefully. The light through the window made a small blue square high on the opposite wall, casting enough reflected light to dimly reveal objects. It was a small comfort.

"You know what frustrates the hell out of me?" Hal asked in low voice.

"What?"

"Annie's in that house 50 yards from here," he said. "We're so goddamn close!"

William thought about Henry Two Crow's reassurance that they would be taking their granddaughter home by the next full moon. He decided to say nothing in the event there was a listening device in the room.

"I know how you feel," he said.

They fell silent, sitting nearly shoulder to shoulder as they leaned against the wall. It was not the most comfortable of positions, but much better than being on the concrete floor. They both stared at the square of light on the wall. It was their only connection to the world outside. Each man silently vowed that he would somehow, some way, eliminate whatever obstacles might stand between him and that little girl.

The sharp sound of metal grating on metal woke them both and then the stall gate started to slide open. William threw aside the blanket and sat up and Hal did the same a second or two later. The light in the room was somewhat brighter. Slowly the inner door opened and the man in the black jacket stepped in, with a chilling sign of the day ahead—a black semi-automatic pistol.

He stopped in the middle of the room as the man behind him snapped on the light, forcing William and Hal to squint at the sudden attack of brightness. It was the chubby white guy.

"Gentlemen," he said, "you have 15 minutes to get ready. I suggest you use the facilities." He pointed to the composting toilet. "You have a long day ahead of you."

The two men left as quickly as they had entered, punctuated by the jarring sound of the stall door being slammed and closed.

William and Hal moved stiffly off the cot. "That doesn't sound encouraging at all," Hal said.

"Nope," William agreed.

"Any guesses?" Hal asked.

"The man said, 'long day,' so I think we may not be sleeping here tonight."

"Shit!"

"Anything is possible with this woman. Don't forget, she attacked Jarod and Jennifer. We have to deal with whatever happens."

They each used the toilet and, at William's urging, stuffed bottles of water in their jacket pockets. Fifteen minutes on the dot later, the doors opened. The man in the black jacket walked in, gun drawn, but pointing down.

"Follow him," he said, pointing to the chubby one standing outside the door.

William moved first and then Hal. They walked down the corridor to the office at the end of the barn. Chubby pointed to the sofa.

"Sit," he said.

A minute later Bernadette arrived, dressed in running sweats and a handbag with a long strap hanging off her shoulder.

"Mr. Hal Lamar and Mr. William Black Spotted Horse," she said. "Today is the beginning of the rest of your lives and it will be measured in seconds, minutes, and days, and no more. Days, gentlemen, days!"

She paused for effect. Hal glanced at William who shook his head slowly to caution him to remain quiet. Then he looked up at Bernadette.

"We're listening," he said.

"Good. Now, first let me reassure you that Annie is doing well. On the chance that you are both telling the truth about the leukemia, I am taking her to see some doctors."

"Thank you," Hal said.

"Oh, I'm not doing it for you, Mr. Hal Lamar," Bernadette shot back. "I'm doing it for Annie. Now, as for you two, you have a long day ahead of you, several long days, I would imagine."

She turned to look directly at William. "I overlooked you, simply because I had no issue with you. I'm sorry to have to do this to you, too, but you chose to involve yourself."

She then turned to Hal. "Not only are you going to suffer, but you will cause Mr. Black Spotted Horse to suffer as well. All this is on you. You did not treat my father fairly, to say the least. He put all his savings, a bit of money he borrowed, and his hopes into the partnership with you. And because he made a small error in judgment, you took away both his livelihood and self-respect. For me, this is about payback.

"I've spent a lot of time thinking about how to do that. The first thing I thought of was this." She reached into her bag and drew out a Glock 9MM. Stepping forward, she held the muzzle six inches from Hal's forehead. He gasped.

"No, don't do it!" William pleaded.

Her finger pulled the trigger and a loud metallic CLICK filled the room. Hal jerked and fell against the back of the couch, his gasps exploding in short puffs. William closed his eyes in relief.

She put the gun back into her bag, a taunting smile on her face. Hal's face had gone completely white.

"That would have been too easy for you," Bernadette went on. "I want you to suffer the way my dad did, so I'm going to put you in a situation where your money will do you no good. Do you know why, Mr. Hal Lamar? Because I believe you are nothing without your money."

As Hal and William stared at Bernadette and saw the searing hate in her eyes directed at Hal, they heard the sound of a heavy truck driving into the barn.

Bernadette kept her eyes on Hal. "There's your ride, Mr. Hal Lamar. It will take you straight to hell."

She glanced at the two men in the room and nodded. Without another word or a look back, she strode from the room.

After a door slammed somewhere, the chubby white guy spoke to them. "Stand up and follow me."

A two and a half ton military-type snub-nosed truck filled the corridor, its cargo box covered with a camouflage tarp. Two more men stood next to the cab, dressed in woodlands camouflage battle dress uniforms. William noted that their footwear was ordinary hiking canvas top hiking boots. But there was nothing ordinary about the AR-15 rifles they carried.

The chubby guy stopped at the back of the truck and pulled the tailgate down. "Get up there and sit, legs out," he told William and Hal.

They had to jump and hoist themselves up. At the chubby one's nod, the man in the black jacket lifted his pistol and pointed it at them and the two other men came to the back, setting their weapons against the wall. From a canvas bag they pulled out large plastic zip ties. They bound Hal first, starting with his ankles and then his wrists, and then moved over to William. Then, with little effort, one of the men stepped on the end of the truck's bumper and jumped into the bed. He grabbed Hal under the arms and pulled him and then William farther into the truck bed. Chubby tossed two large plastic jugs into the truck.

"So, you won't have to piss in your pants," he said, without emotion. "Get those water bottles out of their pockets," he said to the man in the truck.

The man took the water bottles from William and Hal's pockets and tossed them to Chubby, and then jumped down.

"Now," Chubby said, "here's the deal. I'm going to say this only once." He pointed at the men in camouflage. "My friends here have orders to shoot you if you try anything, anything at all. Enjoy the ride."

As Chubby stepped back, the two men rolled down the back canvas covering and zipped it shut, and then closed and locked the tailgate.

Inside the light became dusky. William shook his head as Hal started to say something, holding a finger to his lips. "Wait," he whispered. They listened to the noises outside: movements, the truck doors opening, an outdoor building door sliding open, and then an extended conversation in Spanish.

Deke Smith handed a map and a large manila envelope to the driver as the two men stepped up into the cab. He spoke in Spanish.

"I've marked on the map where Señora wants you to take these two," he said. "This is an old fire road that ends at a cliff, seven kilometers north of this road." Smith touched the map. "It's wild and uninhabited. Leave them there with the two jugs of whiskey in the back. Take their boots and socks. Then as soon as you regain cell phone coverage, call me. Take the truck to a village called Redondo, to a man named Bautista. He lives in a house with a blue front door at the north end. He'll trade you the truck for a pickup. Report to me as soon as you're back here."

"Si," they both responded, nodding.

"One last detail," Smith said, producing two handguns in plastic holsters. "I'll take the ARs, and you take these."

Though a bit puzzled, the men did as Smith indicated. They were, after all, just the hired help who were getting a substantial amount of money for this one job, more money than either of them had ever earned in one year.

Smith stepped away from the cab and gave the go ahead signal. The double barn doors slid open as the truck fired up. Soon it was past the barn and rolling down the road from the ranch to the main highway, looking like nothing more than a military vehicle with two soldiers dressed in camouflaged battle dress in the cab.

In the back, William and Hal swayed and bounced with the movement of the stiff suspension. In a few minutes they rolled onto a smooth highway surface and then took a right turn. Here they heard the sound of other traffic, a lot of it.

"South," William said, "we're going south right now. Keep track of the turns. A left turn is west and a right turn is east."

Hal nodded. "I have a feeling we're in for a long ride." He nodded toward a cardboard box ahead of the left wheel well. "You don't suppose that's food or water, do you?"

William slid the box to him and tore open the lid, and grinned. "Well, water is one of the ingredients," he said cynically. He tipped the box to show Hal.

"Whiskey?"

"Looks like it." He pointed to another box in the forward right corner. "Slide that over, but don't make large movements."

Hal slid the other box carefully and looked in. "No whiskey here," he announced. "Just two quarts of oil, I think."

William looked around the interior. By now their eyes had adjusted. "This is really buttoned up tight," he observed. "We can't peek out, unless we poke a hole." He glanced to the rear, at the spare tire and hydraulic jack bolted to the inside of the truck box.

"That won't do us any good," Hal said.

"No, but that lug wrench might. Makes for a good club."

"What do you think we should do?"

"Make a break for it the first chance we get," William replied.

"You mean tied up like this?" Hal held up his bound wrists.

William pondered for several seconds. "I'm guessing these jokers will stop now and then and eyeball us, so if we break out of these ties—and I think we can—they'll notice right away."

"Okay, I got it. We break them, but make it look like we're still tied up, somehow."

"Yeah, that's our task for the immediate future. And we got nothing but a wrench."

Hal grinned wryly and stared at the plastic ties around his wrists. "They're pretty tight," he muttered, pulling a bit.

"How tight is the one around your ankles?"

Hal wriggled his ankles. "Tight, but a bit of play, I think."

"Try pulling your foot out of your boot," William suggested, scooting a bit until he was directly in front of Hal, grabbing the heel and toe of his left boot. "Okay, now pull, but be careful, don't jerk or fall over. Those guys might feel something."

"Right." Hal pulled hard, the exertion contorting his mouth. "Hey! I think my heel moved up."

"Good! Keep pulling."

Hal took a deep breath and pulled again. "It's sliding, it's sliding!" He nearly fell back as his left foot slid out of the boot. "Damn! It worked!"

The empty boot loosened the tie around the right boot. William slipped off the tie and studied it closely. After a few seconds he twisted the flat tie in the triangular slot and slipped it out completely.

"Now that's a victory I didn't expect," he declared. "Okay, put your boot back on and I'll put the tie on loosely, but it'll look like you're still bound."

"Yeah, if I have to, I can run like hell now. What about yours?"

"Well," he said in a low voice, looking at his boots, "it's the same as yours. I'm sure I can get it off." He looked around at the covering over the truck box. "Our jailers don't seem all that smart. First, there's no window, so they can't see us. And if they want to check on us, they'll have to stop to do it. Second, they put the ties just below the tops of my hiking boots. I'll bet if I just work them up, they'll slip over the edge."

He was right. After a minute of wiggling and pulling at the tie, he worked it over the top edge of the left boot. That, of course, put enough slack in the tie to turn it and slip it out of its slot. Then he slid the tie down loosely around his ankles with enough slack remaining to undo the tie when the time came.

"Now," he said, looking at his wrist ties. "The beauty of this design is also its flaw."

"The tiny slots on the side are the locks when the tie is tightened. They grab the bottom sides of the triangular opening. If I grip it hard enough, I can twist the tie sideways and up into the opening. Then it slips off. Let me try yours."

Hal held up his wrists as William looked closely and then worked the tip of his thumb and forefinger into the V between Hal's hands, and pinched. The trick was to twist without losing the grip.

"My kingdom for a pair of needle nose pliers," William said, through clenched teeth.

Twice his fingers slipped, losing the grip. It was one thing to wrestle a calf down using brute strength, or heft a 30-pound post, but quite another to apply strength through the tip of one's fingers. After losing his grip the fourth time, William shook his fingers and tried again. The fifth time was the charm. He twisted the tie in one direction just enough for the slots to slide through the triangular opening.

"Okay," he said, "now your turn. Nothing to it."

"Right!"

"Wait!" William cautioned as the truck slowed, gearing down, and then made a slight turn to the right and then gradually resumed highway speed.

"That was not a full right turn," Hal said.

"Yeah. I think we're still heading south, more or less."

They waited a couple of minutes and then resumed the task at hand. Hal bent to it, grunting slightly as he gripped the tie as close to the triangular lock as he could. It was a simple matter of having enough room to twist the tie up at an angle. Hal's thick fingers were a slight drawback, but years of hard, physical labor gave him a grip of iron. He succeeded after the second attempt.

"Thanks," William said. "Things are looking up."

They adjusted the ties so that they appeared to be in place but were loose enough to remove easily, and then scooted carefully to the front end of the box to lean against the side. The ride was tolerable on a smooth highway.

"I think the canvas or whatever that tarp material is has to be pretty damn tough," Hal said, in a low voice. "I don't think it's a simple matter of untying or unzipping it."

"You're right. I watched them close it. The bottom edge fits in a channel at the top of the tailgate. We might be able to push it out, but it looks pretty tight. It's not flapping at all."

"We need a sharp edge, a pocketknife."

William pointed to the lug wrench. "That's got a point on it. Don't know how sharp it is but it should work. There's enough sway and road noise; it'll be hard to hear anything from the cab if we poke a hole and tear it and they only have side mirrors. They can't see the tailgate."

"Okay, and once we do that we have to get out, because if they come back and see a friggin' hole, they'll damn sure tie us up really good."

"Good point," William agreed. "And it'll be dangerous to jump out at highway speed. We'll have to wait until they stop long enough."

"Or slow down enough."

"Right now, we're still on a paved road and I'm guessing we're going about 60 miles an hour. This deuce and half can't do much more than that.

We don't know how far we're going, but maybe they'll stop for gas or food. That's our chance if they do."

William pointed to the lug wrench. It was held in place by a large wing nut on a long bolt through a circular plate, all of which kept the spare tire in place. "It won't be hard to get that off," he said. "A few seconds at the most."

Hal indicated the box with the whiskey. "What the hell is that about?"

William shrugged. "Maybe a delivery to someone."

They were quiet for several minutes, jostled slightly by the sway and bounce of the truck, listening to the sounds of cars. The traffic on this road was not as heavy, though vehicles did pass by on a regular basis. It was easy enough to tell the difference between a truck and a smaller vehicle. Now and then, there were hills, but not often. It was a dull, monotonous ride.

"I was thinking about something," Hal said. "About that damn pistol in my face, and what Bernadette said to me, and it made me wonder where they're taking us."

"What do you mean?"

"She said she would put me where money won't help."

"Oh, yeah. Obviously somewhere you can't buy your way out of trouble."

Hal nodded grimly. "Yeah, but where is that?"

"Well, given what's happening at the moment, I think I know where that is."

"Yeah?"

William nodded slowly. "I think we're headed for the wilds, the wilderness. And they have a doozy down here."

"Patagonia?"

"Yeah. I think that's where they'll take us and leave us with what we have right now. No food, no water. Sure as hell nowhere to spend money to buy food or shelter."

They fell silent again, this time for nearly half an hour. By then they had been on the road for nearly two hours. They could only guess because their watches had been taken. Slowing gradually, the truck made a sharp right turn, and then accelerated slightly for a few seconds before stopping. Noises indicated vehicles and people.

"Potty break, food, or fuel," William surmised. They heard both cab doors opening. On the driver's side, after several seconds, the gas cap was removed and a fuel nozzle inserted, then the sound of fuel flowing. On the other side came footsteps toward the tailgate. The end flap of the tarp wavered as it was unlatched and then unzipped. The bottom swung out and up, revealing a brown face peering in; dark eyes studied them for several long seconds.

With a grunt, the man dropped the flap, zippered, and latched it shut. They heard his footsteps fading away into the myriad of other sounds. Several minutes later the fuel nozzle stopped and the gas cap was screwed back on. The driver climbed into the cab and drove the truck and parked again, presumably away from the pump and traffic. Then he got down and walked away.

"Damn, this would be a good chance to get the hell out of here," Hal said.

"Hell, yeah, I'm willing to chance it," William declared. He scooted toward the spare tire and began to take off the large wing nut holding the L-shaped lug wrench in place. Rust had built up a bit on the long bolt, making the nut hard to turn. It was slow going. By the time he got it close to the end of the bolt, they heard footsteps and voices. He froze.

The truck doors opened and the two men climbed in. In the next second the engine started and the transmission clicked into gear, and they were moving. William hurried to finish. By the time he did the truck was back on the highway and gaining speed.

"Damn it!" he spat disgustedly. "Shit!"

"Hey, it's okay. We'll be ready the next time," Hal declared.

William bolted the round plate back on to hold the tire in place. He put the lug wrench on the truck bed. "And that might be when they stop for gas again," William said. "Maybe in another 200 miles, four hours, more or less."

"How far is Patagonia?" Hal asked. "And how big is it?"

"Near the end of the continent," William told him. "At the bottom of the world. I'd say it's about as big as the state of South Dakota."

"Damn!" was all Hal could say.

TWENTY-SIX

Deke Smith nodded at the server as she brought him a steak with oven roasted potatoes. In the northeast part of Santa Rosa, there was a small house that had become Café Estella some three decades ago. It was never filled to capacity, but always had a steady flow of diners throughout the day, many of whom were regular customers. Smith always sat in the same booth whether alone, as he was now, or with others. He sipped Dos Equus from a tall, chilled glass and looked at his watch. It was time to place his call.

There were no numbers on the contacts list on this flip phone, which he kept to call only one number. He dialed from memory on the keypad almost too small for his fingers.

"Hello," said a male voice.

"American major league baseball bats are made of ash and maple," Smith said, which was the code to confirm to his contact that it was indeed Smith that was calling.

"Indeed," the male voice replied in English, with a definite trace of a Hispanic accent. "What news?"

"There are two Americans," Smith said. "Both of the girl's grandfathers."

"Two? This is an unexpected twist."

"Yes. The one who showed up unexpectedly is Native American—William Black Spotted Horse. He worked for the U.S. government and is now retired."

"Interesting. What else do you know about him?"

"He's 61, married, his son is the girl's father. Well-educated, has two master's degrees. Served in the U.S. Army Airborne, saw combat in Vietnam. Of the two, he is more competent."

"What are her plans for them?"

Smith glanced around to be sure no one was within earshot before he spoke again.

"At the moment, they are being taken by truck to a northern region of Patagonia. As per instructions, the escorts think their job is to dump them in the middle of nowhere."

"Excellent. What is their route?"

"South of the Chubut River is the town of Paso de Indios. There is a road west, the only road, which goes into the mountains."

"That is good. And what of plans for the girl?"

"That has not been indicated to me. But I think she plans on adopting."

"Ah, how motherly. There has been a serious breach of trust here. American authorities could still be brought in, perhaps by the girl's family. I gave the Señora an opportunity to tell me the details about her trip out of country. She did not. She has put us in jeopardy because our federal authorities have had their eye on her. This issue with the white American rancher could not have come at a worse time."

Smith shook his head silently. He hated being caught in the middle. "What's to be done, sir?"

"She will have one more chance. There will be an invitation to a small gathering in a few days. If she does not attend or if she again does not disclose details of her trip, there is no choice. She must be eliminated."

Smith rubbed his face. "I understand."

"And the old men as well. Thank you for the information."

"Of course."

Deke Smith closed the phone and rubbed his eyes. Almost from the moment Bernadette had hired him as a runner, Esteban Palomino got his hooks in him. He knew Smith was not his real name, and that he was AWOL from the U.S. Navy and hiding out. That was his leverage, even now. Of course, the cash deposits in an offshore account were powerful inducements as well.

Smith was scared. Palomino was efficient and ruthless and not fond of loose ends. If he eliminated Bernadette, the only other person who would know was Deke Smith and he would become a loose end. He picked at his food and downed his beer in a few gulps. The two foolish Americans were definitely loose ends. They had no idea what they were dealing with, thinking it was a matter of writing a check and following instructions. They had seen too many movies. Reality was not as clean and was much crueler. Cowboy Lamar and Indian Black Spotted Horse would be dead and buried before the day was out.

"Señor," said the server who was suddenly standing over him. "Is your steak not done to your satisfaction?" She looked concerned.

"It's very good, as always," he assured her. "I'm just not as hungry as I thought."

"Is there something else you would like?"

"Another beer. Thanks."

After he finished the beer, he laid money on the table and left. Instead of going to his car, he walked a few blocks to a little shop that specialized in coffee and rented out time on computers to get on the internet. There was an email he had to send to soothe his conscience.

As Smith sat at the computer composing his email, Esteban Palomino walked out to the still unfinished patio in his new house by the ocean, north of the coastal village of Carnarones. The view to the west was beyond spectacular, the boundless and moody southern Atlantic Ocean. His eyes lingered on the tempestuous waters for a few seconds before he joined a man at the teak patio table. A second later, a serving girl appeared with a tray of tea and coffee.

The man nodded his thanks to the lovely girl and lifted his cup of tea to salute his host. "Wonderful to see you again, Señor," he said, with a German accent. Schrader was in his mid-40s and fit as a fiddle. He was the epitome of Hitler's dream of Aryan manhood with bright blue eyes and close-cropped blond hair.

"Thank you for responding so quickly," Palomino replied, returning the salute.

"It seemed urgent."

"It is, requiring your specific skills."

"Urgent, as in days or weeks?"

"Days, perhaps even hours. I will provide whatever you will need…"

Schrader nodded, sipping his tea. Except for an occasional glass of red wine, he was a teetotaler. "I see. What are the details?"

"At first, there was one target, now there are two. Your fee will be adjusted accordingly, Two Americans, are being transported by truck. The destination is the mountains west of here, approximately 300 kilometers. I will see to it you have a map."

"Americans? Do you have photographs?"

"Unfortunately, no. But they are hard to miss.—Both are tall, over six feet from what I am told; one is white and the other is Native American."

"Native American? Ah, I spot him and I know it is the correct pair."

"Yes. The truck will turn west on the only road out of Paso de Indios in that direction. They should arrive there in approximately five hours. There is time to make preparations. A Land Rover Defender four-wheel-drive is at your disposal."

"Thank you and I also have a list of equipment and supplies I will need."

"Yes, I'm sure we can supply everything." Palomino pointed to a building lower on a slope. "It should all be there."

"Ah, very efficient, as always. I thank you. And payment?"

"Half will be wired to your account today." Palomino pulled a satellite phone encased in plastic, along with a spare battery, from his pocket and laid it on the table between them. "You'll get the remaining half when you call and tell me the task has been completed. My number is already programmed in. This should be one of your easier assignments. These are two unfortunate souls who have simply gotten in over their heads. Nothing is ever exactly as it seems."

Virginia finished setting the table for lunch. She and Marie had been staying at Jarod and Jennifer's house in Cold River since Jarod was set up to instantly communicate with Hal and William in Argentina. They hadn't heard from them in several hours and she was beginning to worry, despite what she had seen and heard last night.

The biggest reason, however, for staying with Jarod and Jennifer was being near Annie's room, their only tangible connection to their granddaughter. Virginia had hung a crucifix on one wall and Marie a Lakota medicine wheel on the other and they prayed there each morning and evening.

Virginia looked over at Marie who was slicing tomatoes for the salad. Jarod and Jennifer had gone to walk on the high school track to take the edge off their nervousness.

"Can I ask you something, about the ceremony last night?" she said to Marie.

"Sure," Marie responded.

"I've always believed that faith was based on acceptance, you know, you just accept and believe in what a pastor or minister tells you. So, I just believed since I was young and I didn't need signs. So, at the ceremony last night when I felt something on my face after Mr. Two Crow said the eagle people were there with us, I was shocked."

"You felt the air moving, like a soft breeze?"

"Yes, yes! That was exactly it. You felt it, too?"

Marie turned and smiled gently. "We all did. When an eagle flaps its wings, the air moves. That's what we felt."

"So, you're telling me that an eagle was there with us, in some form?"

"Yes. But, as you say, it depends on what you take on faith. Some say seeing is believing, but I think believing is seeing."

"Well, maybe you're right. And you know what else surprised me a bit? Jennifer and I were the only white people there last night, yet I didn't sense any resentment from anyone. I mean, given the realties around here, mainly, non-Indian attitudes toward you all. And there were over 20 people. Were they all praying for Annie to regain her health?"

Marie nodded as she brought a large bowl of salad to the table. "Well, I don't know what you were expecting, but Jennifer's been going to ceremonies for years. All those people know you're her mom. And, yes, they were all there to pray for Annie. I'm glad you decided to join us. I know you had some misgivings."

Virginia shrugged. "I guess I did. But as you said, it wasn't about me, it was about Annie. And the ceremony was called a *lowanpi?*"

"Yes, a *lowanpi*, which means 'to sing.' There are songs to invite the Spirits, songs to honor them, and songs to thank them for helping us."

"The lights, the pinpoints of light I saw, they were the Spirits?"

"And the Spirits were rattling the gourds and blowing the eagle bone whistles."

Virginia nodded, recalling all she had seen and heard, especially the prayers said on behalf of Annie. Many non-Indian people regarded "Indian religion" as witchcraft and paganism, some even going as far as calling it devil worship. And one of the severest critics was a part Lakota Pentecostal pastor who routinely called Lakota medicine men necromancers. Such venom from one of their own. Yet last night, Virginia felt welcomed, and the presence of a power, or powers, she couldn't describe. In the end, she was grateful because each person in that room prayed unselfishly for her granddaughter.

Virginia contemplated for several seconds. "I just wonder how many of those people would have been welcome if they showed up for Sunday service in my church. Anyway, I'm thankful for what Mr. Two Crow told us, you and me, after the ceremony—that our little girl will be safe with her grandfathers by the new moon. I hope that's the case."

Marie poured tea for them and joined Virginia at the table. "I know it will be. But he also said they—Hal and William—have some difficult things ahead of them."

Virginia nodded thoughtfully. "I'm reassured by the certainty of your resolve. I'm still worried though, scared actually. Our husbands are not the same as they were in their prime physically. And, for heaven's sakes, they don't even like each other. Sometimes I don't know whether they deserve a hug or a kick in the nuts."

Marie laughed. "My thoughts exactly."

Virginia pointed to a picture on a nearby wall of a young William in uniform, next to one of Jarod in uniform. "That's quite a statement there," she said. "How old was William when that picture was taken?"

"Eighteen, right after he finished jump school at Fort Campbell. A few weeks later he was with the 173rd Airborne in Vietnam. You know, he was part of the only mass unit combat jump to happen in Vietnam."

"Oh, my."

"Yeah, and some years ago he went to an Airborne reunion in Denver and he said he saw your father there."

Virginia looked for a moment longer at the photographs. "Yes, Dad was in the 101st, the Screaming Eagles. He jumped in Normandy. He hardly talked about it."

Both women were quiet for a couple of minutes, until Virginia spoke again.

"I was listening to the news this morning," she said. "Lots of things going on in the world. Terror attacks, that crazy dictator in North Korea, all the debate over global warming, and our dipstick of a president. But all of that isn't important to me, at least not at the moment. All I care about is Annie being back safe with us. When we come down to it, the world doesn't care about us and our problems. We send in armies to protect oil interests, under the guise of something noble. But no one's going to send an airborne brigade to Argentina to rescue our little girl, so I'm glad her grandpas are there, because I know they'd die for her, if it came to that."

She reached up to wipe away the tears sliding down her face, as did Marie.

"I know," she said, "so here's to devoted and pissed off grandpas. Every child should be so lucky."

Virginia lifted her glass. "Here, here."

TWENTY-SEVEN

They came to a town and stopped. From the sounds and noises outside, it was another fuel stop. Once again, the driver filled the tank and the shotgun rider opened the tarp and looked in, gazing at them for at least a minute. Dark eyes in a round face flicked from one man to the other. Satisfied they were still bound securely, the man closed the tarp and walked over to speak to the driver.

"My butt is sore," Hal complained in a loud whisper. "And I have a feeling this may be close to the end of the line. It looked like a small village out there, what I could see of it. I thought I saw mountains, or at least foothills."

William nodded. "I think you're right. Once we get going, I think we should get ready to make a move."

At the end of the narrow street, a man peered intently at the two-ton truck painted in military camouflage. He was sitting in a late model Land Rover Defender, a two-door model civilian version of the rugged four-wheel-drive used by the British Army. A slight smile played on his rugged features and a pair of wrap-around sunglasses hid his bright blue eyes. In the passenger seat was a gray and white military style backpack and on the narrow backseat was a ten-inch wide, two-foot long Kevlar case. He was dressed in dark gray outdoor camouflage clothing, the type that blended in with just about any landscape.

Schrader knew the truck would take the only road west out of Paso de Indios. He started his vehicle and slowly drove past the small fuel station. Beyond the end of town, he watched in his rearview mirror as the camouflaged truck pulled onto the road. He accelerated a bit until he topped a rise, then slowed down. He wanted to keep the truck in sight for a little while longer. According to his topographic map, there was some steep terrain ahead, so once in that segment of the road the truck would slow down, giving him plenty of time to find a spot for his ambush.

From the sound of the wheels on the road and the slower speed, William and Hal knew the truck had been on a gravel road since the last fuel stop two hours ago, but it was still moving too fast to jump safely, not without incurring a sprain or a broken bone. They would need to be sound and in one piece if they were to have any hope of escape.

"We're on a back road," Hal observed. "We must be in the mountains."

William nodded. "If there's a steep uphill slope or a long one, we'll slow down. That may be our best chance. The road's a bit bumpy so they won't be able to feel our movements back here. Let's get close to the tailgate."

They scooted slowly to the end of the bed. William looked at the box of whiskey and the folded tarp. "We should take those with us," he said.

"What good's whiskey going to do us out here?" Hal asked.

"Not the booze, the glass bottles. We can carry water."

"Right."

William slid the box against the tailgate and grabbed the tire iron and looked at Hal. "Once I tear open the tarp, we're committed to doing something. Start praying for a steep hill."

"Got it. Go for it!"

William nodded and pushed the flat tip of the lug wrench against the bottom tarp where it met the top of the tailgate. The tarp stretched and he had to push hard, but in a minute or so he poked a hole. After that it was a matter of widening it. He worked at that going upward, first a hard-earned inch and then two. In a few minutes, he had torn an opening to the top. For the first time in hours, they had an unobstructed view of the landscape. They were definitely in the mountains with forest on either side of the narrow gravel road under a partly cloudy sky.

William started a tear sideways just above the tailgate and worked it first to the left, until it was halfway to the end. They felt the swirling wind from the truck's movement.

"Hang on to the loose end," he said. "We don't want it flapping where they can hear it or see it in the rearview mirror."

Hal tossed aside the zip strip and grabbed the torn edge of the tarp being pulled by the wind. With his other hand he pulled off the strip around his ankles. William meanwhile tore the tarp to the right until there was an opening nearly four feet wide. He looked down from the top of the tailgate.

"There's a bumper," he said. "It's just below the bottom of the tailgate. When the truck slows, we can step over and find a foothold on the bumper."

Hal looked out and down and nodded.

Twenty minutes passed as they were buffeted by the mild turbulence while hanging on to the ends of the torn tarp. As the landscape passed, it was easy to see they were moving up an incline, with the truck laboring just a bit. Several long minutes later they heard the transmission downshift and felt and saw a decrease in speed. An idea struck William.

"Hey," he said, "I'm going to have a quick look over the top. I don't think their side mirrors can see up that far."

Hal nodded. "Don't lose your balance."

William grabbed the top of the tailgate from a kneeling position and steadied himself. Rising slowly, he raised his head over the top of the bar like a prairie dog peeking out of his burrow, just enough to see.

He nodded in relief. First because he couldn't see the side mirrors, which meant the two men in the cab couldn't see him, and second because they were approaching a steep uphill grade. Lowering himself carefully, he raised a thumb to Hal.

"Get ready," he said. "There's a steep climb ahead. When the truck slows down, we go."

"Right."

"You grab the tarp, I'll take the box, somehow," William said. He slid the lug wrench into his belt at the small of his back and pushed the box with the whiskey bottles up against the tailgate. There was nothing to do but wait.

"What do we do after we jump down?" Hal asked.

William thought for a moment. "Lay flat on the road until they get to the top. As long as we don't move, they probably won't see us."

The truck downshifted again and the speed declined. It was now or never. William swung a leg over the tailgate and found the narrow tubular bumper, and then swung his other leg over, all the while hanging on to the torn flap. He ended up in a squatting position with his feet on the bumper, facing frontward and hanging on to the top of the tailgate with his right hand. He nodded to Hal.

Hal did exactly as William did.

The end of the torn tarp suddenly slipped out of Hal's grasp and popped in the wind, causing momentary panic. Luckily, though it flapped in the wind, it didn't extend over the top or past the side. William let go of his flap and reached up and over into the box of whiskey and pulled out a bottle. Hal followed his lead and grabbed the tarp, fitting it between his knees. William handed the bottle to Hal and reached and grabbed the other. The truck slowed yet again.

He lowered the bottle as far as he could toward the road and dropped it. They couldn't see but didn't hear glass breaking. Hal did the same.

"Okay," William said. "At the count of three, drop and go belly down, and don't move!"

"Okay, I'm ready."

"One-two-three!"

They both pushed off and somehow landed on hands and knees, though it was a hard jolt. In the next instant they were prone on the road-bed, watching the truck slowly laboring up the hill. There was a slight curve to the left below a steep bank a hundred yards or so farther up the road. Once around that bend, the truck would be out of sight. It seemed to take forever to reach that bend.

William looked right and left. Left was south, as far as he could determine, and that meant right was north. They needed to go north.

"We go that way," he said, nodding toward the thick forest off to their right. "You grab the tarp and run and hide. I'm going after the bottles and then I'll join you."

The truck slipped from their view behind the bend. Hal jumped up and grabbed the tarp and ran toward the trees. William had to run nearly 40 yards back down the road to retrieve the bottles and then trotted into the trees where he had seen Hal disappear. He found him next to a large, rotted stump, panting from the exertion and stress.

"Well," Hal said, his eyes wide, "we got the world by the tail now, huh?"

"Yeah," William said, panting as well. "Considering those fellows probably had orders to blow our brains out, I'd say so."

"Right. Maybe we should move as far into the trees as we can. When they see that we're not there, they'll come back, for damn sure."

"Yeah." William broke the seal on the first bottle and poured out the amber liquid into the grass.

"A waste of good whiskey," William lamented. He saved a little, took a sip and passed it to Hal, who downed what remained.

William opened the other bottle, took a sip and then offered it to Hal, who did the same again. "Well," William said when he took the bottle back, "here's to fair skies and warm winds. May our enemies be blinded by our courage."

William stood. "Let's get a couple hundred yards farther in and take a moment to make a plan."

They crossed two narrow clearings, keeping to the rocky ground in order not to leave an obvious trail. The air was cool but not chilly and walking steadily kept them warm. The forest was old growth with tall, thick pines, patches of deciduous trees, and thick undergrowth. They were surrounded by warbles, chirps, and squawks from birds, and at one point heard the hunting cry of a high-flying hawk, though they couldn't spot him because the forest was too thick.

They paused to rest on a giant fallen pine log devoid of bark and branches and well into the last phase of its existence on earth.

Hal stared down at his Luchese boots. "Well," he said, somberly, "these things are made for smooth sidewalks and swanky dance floors, not for mountains and forests, that's for damn sure."

William chuckled. "On the other hand, you've got a defense against rattlesnakes."

"Yeah, hadn't thought of that. You saying they got rattlers here?"

William shrugged. "Probably."

"What other critters are in these deep woods, do you suppose?"

"Well, a couple of species of deer, peccaries, bear, and mountain lions, I think."

Hal glanced around. "And me without even a slingshot." He fell quiet and watched as William untied his right hiking boot and extracted a narrow, soft plastic case. a small compass with a magnifying glass on the end.

"Well, shit," Hal declared. "That might come in handy."

William held the compass flat and watched the needle swing around until it settled, then turned it until he lined the S up with the needle. "I've never used a compass in the southern hemisphere, so I'm hoping it works the same way down here. According to this, I think that's north," he said, pointing in the direction they had been traveling.

"Hell, I hope you're right. What else do you have there?"

"A magnifying glass, to read maps and start fires," William explained. "As long as we have a bright sunny day, we can make a fire."

William loosened the laces on his left boot and another small plastic case appeared, this time with eight wooden matches.

"Any other surprises?" Hal wondered.

"No," William said.

"Well, at the very least we'll know where we're going. Speaking of that, maybe we should think about heading back to that last town," Hal said.

"Well, that's a good 30 miles, I'm guessing. But we're in for a hike no matter what. What do we gain by going back there?"

"Ah, a car maybe, of some kind."

"Yeah? We have to have transportation. Remember, though, they took everything. We have no money, no phone cards, no identification. We're obviously not from these parts, so we'll be spotted right away. If any cops catch us, I've heard horror stories of Americans languishing in South American jails for months, even years, for no other reason than being American. I don't think they like us much down here."

"But we still need a car."

"Yeah, we do," William agreed. "Well, you know, when I was leaving for Vietnam, my grandpa gave me a bit of advice. He said when I was in a crappy fix, I should just face every shitty thing that came along, and eventually I would get through it or solve the problem. That's what we have to do, what we've been doing. So, if we're going to get our hands on a car, we have to steal it."

"I'm up for it," Hal asserted.

"Hell, we don't know what those two jokers will do when they know we're gone. They're going to backtrack for damn sure and might assume we'll be heading back to that town. We have to stay hidden. If we're going to steal a ride, better if we do it at night under cover of darkness."

William looked around at the tall trees and thick underbrush all around them. "That means about 10 to 15 hours of walking, based on an average walking foot speed of three miles an hour, but that's over unobstructed terrain. This forest will slow us down, so that means we camp tonight and get to that town tomorrow."

"All right. We might have to take a chance and build a fire to keep warm," Hal said. He pointed to the folded tarp. "We have shelter."

William grinned. "There you go. A veritable 'Forest Hilton.'"

They sat for another minute, looking around at the dark forest. Shadows were beginning to lengthen, indicating late afternoon.

"I think we got a couple of hours before sunset. Night falls fast in mountains," Hal said.

"My thoughts exactly. Time to move out," said William as he took another reading on the compass and pointed east. "That's where civilization is," he said. "And all roads and trails lead to Annie."

"Damn straight," Hal declared.

TWENTY-EIGHT

At that moment Schrader adjusted the driver side rear view mirror, framing the long gravel road that led up to the crest of the ridge where he was parked. After a few minutes, he saw a small dark spot on the road growing gradually larger. The truck was moving slowly but steadily up the steep grade. A couple of minutes later he could discern the front profile.

He grabbed the Sig Sauer 9mm from the passenger seat and stepped out of the vehicle. At the front of the truck, he opened the hood, propping it on its long support arm. From his jacket pocket he pulled out a suppressor and attached it to the pistol's muzzle, then slid the weapon in the waistband above his buttocks. He could hear the whine of the truck's engine now as it came closer and closer. Leaning out from behind the raised hood, he could clearly see the two men in the cab. When the truck was at 30 meters, he stepped away from his own vehicle, waving and smiling. The truck slowed and stopped.

Schrader walked to the driver side of the cab, wearing his most affable smile. "Good afternoon," he said cheerily. "I seem to have run out of petrol. You wouldn't by some chance have a spare liter or two?"

The two men exchanged puzzled glances. The driver finally answered. "Lo siento, no hablamos ingles."

Schrader put on a disappointed expression, then threw up his hands.

"Lo siento," the driver repeated.

Schrader shrugged. He stood dejectedly, and in a flash, he reached back and had the 9mm in his right hand and got off two shots. The driver's head snapped sideways, followed by the second man's head. Blood spattered the back window of the cab and their bodies slumped.

Schrader glanced down the road and stepped toward the rear of the truck. Anger flared as he rounded the corner and saw the torn ends of the tarp. He pulled down the tailgate and stared into an empty cargo bed. He stood for a moment, contemplating his next move.

Putting away his weapon he stepped to the cab, opened the door and climbed in, unceremoniously shoving the driver's body over. Putting the transmission in gear he drove up the road and turned where the terrain was rock strewn on either side. He turned right and bounced over the stony ground until he was several meters into the edge of the forest, and out of sight from the road. Cutting off part of the sleeve of the driver's shirt with a knife, he carefully wiped his prints off the gearshift handle, the steering wheel, and the inner and outside driver's side door handles.

Staying on rocky ground, he followed a different route back to his car, considering what to do. A call to Palomino could wait until he confirmed what had happened, that the two Americans had jumped from the truck, probably when it had slowed on the steep grade.

Schrader made a U-turn and drove slowly down the hill, staying in the middle of the narrow road and looking for any sign at all. He stopped periodically and walked ahead to study the gravel surface. The Americans had obviously jumped from the truck while it was moving, so there would be signs of some kind where they landed. He wanted to find them before any other traffic showed up.

Near the bottom of the grade, he found what he was looking for. There were scrapes and indentations clearly showing where they had landed. Strangely, one set of footprints went back down the road some 40 meters, and then north toward the edge of the forest. Schrader had tracked men more than once, but each situation was different. Most people were careless in the wilderness, overwhelmed by the setting and the circumstance. However, according to Palomino, one of these men was a Native American and a former soldier at that. Still, they were unarmed and in an environment new and unknown to them. He was prepared to track and follow them until he could do what he had been hired to do. Back in his car, he made the call to Palomino. and reported the situation, ending the short conversation with the assurance that he would find his prey.

First, he had to hide his vehicle, and then use the remaining daylight to determine the Americans' direction of travel.

Nearly four miles to the east, William and Hal were slogging steadily through thick underbrush. The forest was cut by ravines and gullies, most of which had to be skirted. Anyone who might happen to spot them would likely conclude they were a strange pair, because one was carrying two empty glass bottles and a tire iron hooked in his belt and the other a folded tarp and little else. They both had light jackets tied around their waists. They had no backpacks, which most wilderness hikers had, or any type of firearm for big game season. Nonetheless, they were moving steadily, constantly on the lookout. At the edge of a narrow and steep-sided gully, William paused and raised a hand.

"Hear that?" he said softly.

Hal listened for several seconds and nodded. "Yeah, running water, somewhere."

The shadows were darker now, but the sound of a trickle of water was very near. "I think it's below us. Maybe a natural spring," William said. "I'm going to climb part way down and have a look. Wait here."

Hal found a rock to sit on and watched William slowly working his way down, holding onto rocks and shrubs. In a minute he was gone from view. In another minute he called out.

"I found it," he said. "It's a spring."

Fifteen minutes later he emerged from the shadows, carefully maneuvering his way back up the slope while holding the two full bottles. He found a spot near Hal's rock and sat, handing a bottle to him.

"I had a drink," he said. "It's cold and sweet."

Hal took the bottle and unscrewed the cap and took a long drink. It was good. "You didn't happen to see a tray of doughnuts down there, did you?"

William grinned. "I'll look again." He looked around at the forest hemming in the gully. "I think we should make camp here," he said.

"Yeah, okay by me. I'm kind of tired."

"I'll gather kindling if you get firewood," William offered.

"I'll get on it."

After he gathered a large pile of kindling, William made one more trip down to the spring to refill a bottle. By sundown the fire was burning. Thanks to William's creative arrangement of light kindling, only one match was needed. They fashioned a shelter from the tarp, which turned out to be larger than they anticipated. Beneath it they cleared away brush and rocks, practically to the bare ground.

"It'll be cold tonight," Hal declared. "A nice down-filled sleeping bag would do nicely."

"Sure would. Maybe a heat reflector will keep us comfortable."

William had used the tire iron to dig the fire pit and now he dug a narrow trench just behind the pit. In it he placed dead, dry branches upright and side-by-side to reflect the heat from the fire toward the shelter. It was an effective tool used by experienced wilderness campers.

"You know, the light from this fire can be seen for miles, probably," Hal observed. "But I think it's a chance we have to take. I don't want to freeze."

"I don't think those two guys who were hauling us are going to go to any trouble looking for us. They didn't seem the type. I'm sure they've reported us missing to Bernadette by now. She'll try to find us, but not before tomorrow. By then we'll have reached that little town."

"Speaking of which," Hal muttered, scooting closer to the fire, "don't you think Bernadette will think of that, and have someone waiting for us? I mean, I would, if I were her. She's smart; she'll anticipate that."

"Good point," William admitted. "That will be a huge problem for us. There's no way we can blend in, not in a small town where everyone knows everyone else. If we spoke the language, we might have a chance. But none of that precludes the fact that we need transportation, as quickly as we can get our hands on something."

"We can hot wire a car. But we probably traveled 600 to 700 miles today and that's a lot of gas for which we don't have any money," Hal pointed out. "And that little bit of walking we did today damn well played me out. I'm not as young as I used to be, and I'm feeling it."

William sighed and nodded. "I know what you mean. I'm aching in places I forgot I had. I think first we get our hands on a vehicle of some kind, and then worry about how to fill the tank."

"All of this was the farthest thing from my mind. It doesn't seem real, you know?" Hal said.

William nodded again. "It may not seem real, but it is just as real as fighting over 640 acres of pasture, which you thought was so important a few days ago."

"Yeah, well, that suddenly seems like small potatoes," Hal asserted

A distant sound interrupted them—something between a screech and a woman's scream.

"Hey," Hal whispered. "That sounded like a mountain lion."

"I think you're right. But not close, I hope."

Hal added wood to the fire. "I'd rather take my chances with a two-legged enemy than that thing," he decided. "I vote we keep the fire going all night."

"Right."

Minutes passed as the fire crackled, sometimes kicking sparks out. Other night sounds were all around. An owl cried somewhere to the east and a wolf-like howl floated on the breeze.

William looked up into the tall trees surrounding them.

"You think something's up there?" Hal wanted to know.

William shook his head. "I hope not," he replied. "I think I'm going to try climbing up and getting a look around."

"It's dark, Will."

"Yeah and lights of towns and outlying ranches should be easy to see."

He picked out a pine with a wide trunk and solid branches, just within the reach of the fire's light. Moving slowly and carefully, sometimes contorting himself to get past a tight spot, he pulled himself up from one branch to another. It was dark inside the outer cover of pine needles, although patches of stars and night sky could be seen between openings.

Several times he paused to rest until the pounding in his chest subsided before he resumed the climb. Both palms and the bases of his thumbs were sore from gripping the rough bark. The shorter branches near the top of the pine, which he estimated to be at least 100 feet tall, seemed to have fewer needles. Up high he could feel the tree swaying.

Near the top, William finally caught a glimpse of a pinpoint of light to the west. After climbing another 10 feet, he saw a line of lights emerge that could only be the village. Not wanting to push his luck, he stopped and tried to estimate the distance to the lights. He recalled that on clear nights the lights of the closest town north of Cold River were easy to see, at just over 20 miles. He could only guess in this instance, but it had to be more than 20 miles.

The breeze was chillier in the treetops as he started back down. Now he had to be extra careful, picking his footholds with care. Gravity had a way of altering judgment. It had been decades since he had been this high in a tree, if ever, and the trail back to Annie started at the base of this tree. He needed to be in one piece to begin that journey.

His quadriceps had borne the brunt of the climb and his hamstring and calf muscles began to burn well before he was near the base. Once back on the ground, he moved carefully through the dark brush and back to the camp. It was several minutes before his heart rate began to subside and he had to take deep breaths to recover his wind once more.

"What did you see?" Hal asked.

"Lights of a town to the east. No outlying rural places."

"Any traffic on that road?"

"Didn't see any moving lights or hear an engine or anything like that."

Nearly a mile away another man was high in the branches of a tall pine. He had the benefit of binoculars and a night vision scope. A pinpoint of light in the forest to the east of his position brought a smile. A flickering light. It had to be a fire. It was a minor miracle that he had been able to see any light in the dense forest. Of course, if it was a campfire, it could very well be hunters since it was red stag season. But the tracks he found had led north into the forest from the road, so chances were good he had found the Americans.

Schrader started back down the tree, turning on the compact flashlight strapped around his head. He adjusted the beam and descended carefully. Tomorrow he would have them. They were old men and likely would not be traveling fast, especially through the dense forest. As he climbed down, he debated whether to hike back four miles in the dark to where he had hidden the Land Rover. He thought not. He had what he needed to make camp. In fact, he could stay in the wilderness for days if need be. He had MREs (meals-ready-to-eat), a waterproof tarp for shelter, and an arctic grade sleeping bag, not to mention a camelback water flask that held two liters. No, he would camp and make coffee and have a good night's rest.

Night passed fitfully for William and Hal. They slept in snatches, awakened twice by the chilly air when the fire went down. They used the last of their wood just as the darkness began to turn to light.

Quickly gathering armloads of dry wood, they revived the fire and got it burning high and hot. Pouring water on their hands they washed off their faces, though the shock of cold water did more to wake them up than to clean them.

"That sun's going to feel good when it's up," Hal commented, "if it can get to us in these trees."

"We'll find a clearing later and get warm," William said. "As soon as there's a bit more light, I'm going down to get more water. So have a drink, a big one. I think we're at a high elevation, so we're going to need lots of water."

When there was enough light, William started down the slope to the spring. Hal folded the tarp and added the last of the wood to the fire. When William returned with the fresh supply of water, they saw the first rays of sunlight skimming the tops of the trees.

With no further preparations to be made, William took a reading on the compass and pointed east.

"That way leads to Annie," he said.

TWENTY-NINE

Like many Lakota elders, Henry Two Crow was an early riser. But this morning it was more than habit that took him from his bed. In the predawn darkness he dressed in his usual morning apparel of the past 10 years—black running sweats and beaded moccasins—and slipped through the silent stillness of his house with a large, beaded bag in hand. He started his coffee, then went quietly out the back door to the fire pit in the backyard.

Though 82 he still had the brisk, loose-limbed walk of a much younger man. It would be a warm day, he felt, as he put the bag down on a bench near the pit and prepared to make a fire. With the practiced motions of one who had built thousands of outdoor fires since childhood, he struck a wooden match to the kindling, which was soon crackling.

The old medicine man stared at the fire, going into a quiet and meditative frame of mind, shutting out everything but the reason for his early morning prayer. He opened the beaded bag and took out a smaller bag, pouring dried, flat, cedar needles into the palm of his hand. With his other hand, he reached down into the pit to the base of the fire and grabbed a burning twig. He placed this on a flat rock at his feet and then sprinkled the cedar needles on the burning ember of the twig. The needles crackled and emitted a sweet scent. The old man suddenly felt the presence of a helping Spirit and then another and another. He spoke to them in Lakota.

"It is good that you are here," he told them. "There are two men in a faraway land that need your help and your strength to guide and protect them."

Jarod kept his eyes closed against the pounding in his head before he pushed the bed covers aside and sat up slowly.

"What time is it?" the sleepy voice beside him asked.

"Almost six, I think," he said. "I didn't mean to wake you."

"You didn't. Are you okay?"

"Yeah, hon. I'm going to take one of those damn pills and maybe put on some coffee. It seems to help my headache."

"Which? The pills or the coffee?"

"Both. Then let's have a talk."

Jennifer rolled to her side and reached out for him. "Something wrong?"

"I'm not sure. It's something Dad and I talked about a couple nights ago."

Twenty minutes later Jennifer joined her husband at their round dining table in the corner of the large kitchen. Their house was small and didn't have a separate dining room. She had just finished her shower. Their moms were still asleep in the spare bedroom and Annie's room.

"What's up?" she asked, sliding her chair forward, reaching for the container of half-and-half for her coffee.

Jarod allowed himself a moment of distraction, grinning at his wife with her hair wrapped in the large towel atop her head before his expression turned somber.

"It's been over 24 hours since we heard from our dads," he pointed out.

She nodded and sipped her coffee.

"We knew this situation was iffy and unpredictable," he went on. "But the last conversation with Dad has been on my mind."

"What did he say? Wasn't that before he was waiting to go to Bernadette's ranch?"

"Yeah. I mean, I told you all that he said. He obviously wasn't sure what would happen. Which is understandable."

"Right, and now we haven't heard from them in over 24 hours. So, what are we going to do?"

Jarod glanced down the hallway toward the bedrooms. "Have a talk when our moms are up."

Nearly 45 minutes later all four of them were sitting down to breakfast, at Virginia's insistence. "We have to eat to keep body and soul together," she said.

Jarod glanced at them all in turn. "We're all worried about the lack of contact with Hal and Dad. We can wait or I can go there by myself. Another option is for us to call the FBI. There are pros and cons in each case."

Marie looked at her son, somewhat surprised. "Calling the FBI is not an option for me. What about the four of us going down there?"

Jarod stared at his mother. "You're serious?"

"Of course I am."

"I like the idea, but one thing worries me," Jennifer pointed out. "If we leave, we give up our ability to be a resource to them."

Marie looked at her son and daughter-in-law. "Okay, let's think this through," she said.

Virginia nodded. "What are the facts we should consider?"

Jarod sighed with raised eyebrows. "I called both their phones last night. I think they're off or the batteries are drained. What worries me is that both phones have an extra battery. So, either all four batteries are used up or the phones have been switched off. Or disabled."

"Why would they do that?" Virginia wondered. "Why would Hal and William turn both the phones off?"

Jarod shook his head. "Hal went to Bernadette's place first. Dad called me and he was clearly anticipating the possibility of something going sideways. That's why he gave those instructions for letting the phone ring, and so on, when he was waiting for his ride to Bernadette's."

"Something probably went wrong," Virginia said.

"What if two of us go ahead and two of us stay behind and then catch up," Marie suggested.

"That's a great idea," Jarod interjected. "We're their back-up, their informational resource. We can't drop that ball. So, for instance, Mom and I would go first," he said, turning to Jennifer, "and as soon as we are in Buenos Aires, you two follow. That way, you're here if and when they call."

"How would they know where to contact us?" Marie asked.

"There's only one slight drawback," said Jarod. Tickets are going to be really expensive, especially booking flights at the last minute."

"You let me worry about that," Virginia said. "This will be on our dime, Hal and me."

Silence descended on the table as they all contemplated the alternatives at hand. "But I'm wondering, son," said Marie, "what about your injury? Will it be aggravated if you fly?"

"I don't know. I do know we need to go there."

"So, if we go through with it, what are the specifics?" Virginia pressed, after a moment.

"Mom and I go first and set up at the hotel Hal stayed in, the Conquistador." Jarod turned to Jennifer. "Once we're there, you and Jennifer leave. That way, two of us are available at all times."

The two mothers nodded. "Once we're there, will you still be able to have access to information, like you do here," Virginia asked.

"Absolutely, as long as there's internet," Jennifer pointed out. "We'll take laptops and whatever else we need or we can probably purchase equipment once we're there."

"Okay, when do we leave?" asked Marie.

"As soon as we can get tickets," Jarod replied. "But I would like to go see Grandpa Henry first, sometime today, and tell him our plans. And maybe we should talk to Sheriff Triplett as well. We need a contingency plan, just in case."

"You're right," Virginia agreed. "And I should have a talk with Adrian, our ranch hand."

Jarod reached for his wife's hand and looked at his mother and mother-in-law. "So, we're all in favor of going?"

They all nodded.

"Okay, then we need to dust off our passports and buy some tickets. Both Dad and Hal went from Sioux Falls to Miami and then Buenos Aires."

Henry Two Crow listened politely to Jarod and agreed that he and Marie should be close to whatever was happening with Hal, William, and Annie. "Pray for us," Jarod said.

"I do and I will. Make tobacco bundles, seven blue and seven green for each of you," he instructed. "When you get there, put them in your left pockets."

Jarod stood. "We will, Grandpa. *Lila pilaunyayapi* (Thank you, from all of us)."

"*To* (Yes). *Tokaktesniyelo* (It will be alright). Your dad has been in life and death situations before, so have you. He knows about the Shadow Man."

Jarod nodded. "You think this is that kind of situation, Grandpa?"

"It could be, but as long as your dad calls on the Shadow Man, it will be okay. It's what Lakota warriors, some of them even women warriors, would do. They would paint their faces and bring out that part of themselves that can do the tough things, that shadowy part of themselves that hardens the heart to overcome the fear and doubt."

Jarod drove back to town, strengthened by Henry's words of encouragement, but disturbed by the continuing silence of the cell phone in his shirt pocket.

THIRTY

One hour and two miles into the day's trek, William and Hal locked eyes with the penetrating gaze of a mountain lion, standing 20 yards away from them. At the same instant, they saw the dead animal in its jaws.

"I think that's a peccary it has," William whispered. "Didn't you say they were good to eat? Maybe that's our chance for a meal."

That chance hovered between slim and none, considering the long, low, warning growl gurgling from the depths of the large cat's wide chest. It was definitely a fresh kill, perhaps only in the past few minutes.

They had turned a bit to the north into a wide east-west valley, mainly to get out of the thick underbrush of the forest because it was slowing their progress. They had found another stream, clear, fast moving, and cold. Though it meandered a bit, its floodplain was not as thick with brush as the forest above, enabling them to increase their pace a bit. They had spotted the mountain lion while crossing a clearing.

It stood in a thicket of amber colored plumes of tall grass, so effectively concealed only a flick of its long, thick tail gave away its presence. There was fresh blood on its jaws.

They stared at the unexpected scene. It wasn't quite the same as choosing between a T-bone or a rib eye steak in the fresh meat section of the grocery store, but considering the circumstances, it was just as appealing. But the big cat with the wild pig in its jaws was easily over 100 pounds, in its prime, and not pleased with the sudden appearance of two interlopers.

"What are we going to do?" Hal whispered.

"Well, that is fresh meat right there," William said.

"And a goddamn big cat! He ain't giving it up."

"Not without some persuasion."

William glanced down. There were stones and broken rocks of all sizes in the dry creek bed they were standing in. "At the very least we need to protect ourselves, somehow. I think we bend down, slowly, and pick up rocks to throw at him."

They heard another long, low menacing growl. The lion was not backing down or leaving.

Hal looked down. "Okay. I'll go first, you keep an eye on that son-of-a-bitch."

"Right."

Hal slowly dropped the folded tarp, then squatted and reached out to gather egg size stones within his reach, filling his coat pockets, and rising carefully. He had two stones in each hand.

William squatted, putting aside the water bottles, carefully collected stones, and then slowly rose.

"Okay," he whispered. "Let's move apart a step or two and at the count of three we start throwing. Chances are he'll just take off. Maybe we can scare him enough to drop that pig. Ready?"

"Yeah, as I'll ever be."

They stepped apart slowly, the lion watching them intently, its dead prey still firmly in its jaws.

William turned sideways and brought his arm back, ready to throw. Hal did the same. "Once you start, just keep throwing. One, two, three!"

The first stones missed widely and the lion only flinched slightly and didn't move. Throwing rocks or baseballs was a perishable skill and years had passed since either man had thrown anything. In the absence of precision, persistence did the trick. Two or three of the heavy stones thudded into the cat's side, startling it with a painful sensation it had never known in its life. A split second of surprise and confusion was just enough to cause it to loosen its hold on the carcass in his mouth. When another stone cracked it behind the ear, it yelped in pain and retreated into the grass and tall brush.

They stood, panting, fully expecting the animal to regroup and come charging out of the grass. When they finally decided the cat was gone, William moved cautiously forward and pushed the carcass with his foot. Satisfied that it was dead he grabbed it by a hind leg and moved away from the tall grass.

"It's heavy," he told Hal, glancing back cautiously into the tall grass. "Feels like almost 20 pounds."

"Yeah, and how are we going to butcher it?"

"I'm sure we'll figure it out," William ventured. "That problem is not as life threatening as the one we just faced."

Bernadette had known for some time that there was a mole inside her inner circle because she had allowed it. One did not earn Palomino's trust once and for all. One had to keep earning it. He had unexpectedly offered his help with Annie's adoption, which she had shared with only two other people—Marta Manzanares and Deke Smith. She had knowingly shared the information with them because she had long suspected Marta was Palomino's spy.

As if all that that wasn't enough to raise her blood pressure, there had been no word for two days about Harold Lamar and William Black Spotted Horse. The two men who had been assigned to leave them in a remote canyon with nothing but two bottles of whisky had not reported to their contact in Paso de Indios. The contact should have called late last night, but the call never came. She was forced to put Deke Smith on the trail.

Two other issues were of more concern. An email had showed up yesterday with a clear warning that Palomino was about to make a move, and that she—Bernadette—would be invited to his seaside villa for a gathering. "*Patron* knows," had been the last ominous words in the email, blunt and to the point. Then there was the attitude of the doctor who had ordered the tests for Annie yesterday. He was more suspicious of how and why Bernadette suspected Annie had childhood leukemia. Conclusive results would take at least two weeks, he had told her.

Having the test done strengthened Bernadette's maternal instincts. She would protect Annie in any way she could and give her a good life— the life she would have given her own daughter.

All of this weighed heavily as she drove toward Palomino's villa. Her options were few and her very survival—physically and business-wise— was on the line. And now she also had Annie's welfare to consider. There was only one viable option: eliminate Palomino before he eliminated her.

She had, at most, a day to finalize her plan and put it into play. The plan had been in the back of her mind for years and she constantly updated and improved it as the business factors outside her control ebbed and flowed and changed. The plan was all about mitigating the very circumstances that were now facing her. The greatest of her fears was Esteban Palomino. He was the only person in the world she was afraid of.

Bernadette glanced at Annie who was in the passenger seat staring at the passing landscape. "Annie, have you ever ridden in a helicopter?" she asked.

The girl shook her head, indicating "no" without taking her eyes off the passing sea of grass.

"Well," Bernadette went on, "in a few days you'll be doing just that."

Annie glanced briefly toward Bernadette and nodded and turned back to staring out the window.

A fire burned in a hastily dug pit near the stream the men had found. The skinned and gutted carcass of the peccary hung over the flames on a make-shift spit. Already the smell of cooking meat was enticing.

William made good use of the lessons from the workshop he had taken on making stone projectile points; flintknapping. Using the tire iron as a hammer of sorts, he split some river rocks until he produced a couple with edges sharp enough to slice through the pig's tough hide and cut off its head. With Hal's help he had managed to split the carcass in two. After washing it in the creek, they built a cooking fire.

"I hunted these things in New Mexico," Hal recalled. "I did get one, though I didn't eat it, but a friend of mine did. Of course, he had the luxury of getting it processed by a butcher. He said the meat was damn good."

"Sure smells good," William said. "We got food and water. All the basics we need."

Hal pointed to the larger stream, about 20 yards away. "You think that goes near that little town?"

"It likely passes north of it," William replied. "We would be better off to stay in this valley. That river meanders a bit, but there are fewer trees and less underbrush. We might not get there any faster, but it'll be easier going."

"Yeah, let's do that."

"All right. The meat's almost done, so we can cut it up, eat what we can and take some with us. But we might as well be warm when we can."

Hal turned the meat as it roasted over the fire, pausing to listen for any sudden or unusual sound. He had been secretly fretting that the lion might circle back around to reclaim its food. For now, the fire negated that possibility, he hoped. He looked around at the campsite which was situated in a small clearing against the river's old bank, now root-bound and worn but still high enough to provide a windbreak. If it wasn't still morning, this would be a good shelter for the night. The fire was at the base of the bank. No more than 10 yards away were two mature pine trees, tall, sturdy, and majestic.

William emerged from among the clumps of tall grass balancing a high armload of dry wood. Hal saw a stick fall from the top of the load. As William paused to carefully squat to retrieve it, Hal felt a sting and a tug on his cheek below his left ear at the same time he saw an eruption of something bright red from the base of William's neck, inches below his right ear. Then, strangely, William rolled forward in a somersault, the load of wood falling and scattering.

THIRTY-ONE

Schrader kept his scope trained as he watched the long-haired Native man dragging his companion away from the fire and out of sight into a thicket of trees. The white man was either dead or seriously wounded. The Native man was using only his left arm.

"Verdammt!" He kept the scope on the spot where they had disappeared into the trees. His original intention was to take two fast shots, the Native man first since Palomino had indicated he was the more dangerous of the two. But the situation had unexpectedly turned into a sniper's dream when they inadvertently lined up, one behind the other.

They were somewhere in that thicket 120 meters from his position on the lip of a rise among bunches of tall grass. He was in a sitting position and had used the bipod on the barrel to steady the shot. Schrader was impressed, and bothered, that the Native man had reacted so quickly because he had put a muzzle damper on to silence the blast. It was at best a loud pop, but it wouldn't have been heard at that distance. Apparently, the man had instantly known what was happening. Now Schrader had no choice but to get to the thicket and finish them off.

Taking a last look, he gathered up his backpack, folded the bipod back against the barrel, and headed toward the thicket by the creek. He slung the rifle over his shoulder, and then did a slow visual sweep around to make sure no other people were in the area. He would have been surprised if there were, but caution was an ingrained habit. After a few seconds, he turned and walked down a short slope, breaking into a trot toward the thicket by the creek.

Schrader had been in countless wilderness and backwater places. Most were tolerable and some outright pristine, such as here in Patagonia. He hated the jungle, any jungle, anywhere, especially those with dense growth and canopies that blocked out the sun. The snakes that lived in such places put the fear of God in him. They were some of the biggest and most poisonous anywhere. It was late autumn here, so the likelihood of snakes was small, or at least he hoped that was the case.

He decided to flank the thicket where the men had disappeared and turned farther north. Realistically, they could be anywhere in the trees and thickets along that creek. They were probably hiding and trying to have a look. Or, if they were both alive, they could be in panic mode and moving as fast as they could. But the fact of the matter was, he was armed to the teeth and they weren't, so he had the edge. Still, any kind of cornered prey was dangerous.

Schrader ducked behind a low rise of tall grass and increased his pace. Staying behind cover he pushed into a clump of some type of berry bushes, pausing to scan the ground for snakes. He kept still and listened but heard nothing other than a flutter of small wings and a bird warbling somewhere. A slight breeze was moving small branches and tall grasses. Reasoning that the cowboy and Indian couldn't have moved this far, he crawled through the bushes and stayed prone, taking out his binoculars. There were too many intervening clumps of grass, shrubbery, and low branches at this level. He needed to get higher for a better perspective, a risk worth taking since his quarry weren't armed.

Leaving his backpack in the grass, he climbed slowly and carefully up a sturdy tree. At about 10 feet high, he tried the binoculars again. After a minute of careful panning and adjusting the focus, he spotted something that looked out of place—something dark and small. Resting the glasses on a small, thick branch, he zoomed in as much he could. It was a boot.

Schrader's first thought was that the boot was left behind in the haste to get away. It was a logical assessment given that his bullet had hit at least one of its intended targets, perhaps both. On the ground he stayed low, unclipping his semi-automatic pistol from the holster on his belt. He estimated the distance to the boot to be about 40 meters. He moved south from grass clumps to thick shrubbery and trees with wide trunks. Nothing else seemed to be moving in the thicket. After several minutes he knelt behind a tree to listen. A slow breeze rustled dry brush, and there were birdcalls.

Coming to a dry watercourse, he waited before crossing it in a low crouch and pausing against a large tree once he regained cover. Moving his head out carefully from behind the tree, he saw the boot. It was in the middle of the dry watercourse he had just crossed, farther downstream. A minute of scanning the area with the binoculars showed nothing but open ground, tufts of grass, twigs, and other forest debris. For a second, he was tempted to let it go, but there might be tracks on the sandy, dry creek bed. Staying in the shrubs and trees, he rose and carefully moved ahead.

Satisfied that he was the only human in the immediate area, he meandered through intervening shrubbery and clumps of grass until he was even with the boot. It looked new and expensive. He snickered involuntarily. Leave it to an American cowboy to wear an expensive boot in the outback, but there were telltale tracks near it. Someone had been dragged across the dry creek bed and into the opposite thicket. The tracks indicated the person who had been dragged was not ambulatory and showed the mobile person digging his feet into the sand in order to move the other man, maybe a dead man.

Putting the semi-automatic back into the belt clip, he stepped toward the boot, careful not to disturb the tracks. Heal and toe marks indicated the one dragging was moving sideways. Schrader glanced at his watch. Nearly 50 minutes had passed since he had taken the shot. They couldn't be that far away, likely hiding in the trees to the west. Looking at the furrows in the sand, he spotted the first drop of blood.

Schrader squatted for a closer look at the boot. And then a sledgehammer hit him in the back of the neck. He felt a split second of heavy pain before the darkness.

William used some of the cord he found in the man's backpack to tie his hands, each arm backward around a tree. The man was slumped against the trunk, chin drooping on his chest. While Hal went through the man's shirt and trouser pockets, William removed his hiking boots, socks, and belt.

"Put all that stuff in the backpack," he suggested to Hal. "We'll check it out later." He held up the small first aid kit. "This guy was ready for anything. There's probably antiseptic in here to clean out that gash on your face."

"What about the hole in your shoulder?" Hal pointed to the blood soaked into the right shoulder of William's shirt.

"Yeah, that, too."

"There's no ID anywhere," Hal pointed out. "How'd you know he was shooting at us?"

"The hum," William replied. "The round made a low hum after it passed though me, and I saw it hit behind you. I thought he got you in the head."

"Is that why you dragged me for 20 yards?"

"Yeah, and to get behind cover."

"You heard a hum?

"Yeah, sort of like a—a bumblebee. When a round comes close, really close, it sort of hums."

"I'm trying to get my mind around this. Why—I mean, did Bernadette send him? Is he even after us? Maybe he mistook us for someone else," Hal panted, his adrenaline still spiking. "After what's happened the past couple of days, I'm betting Bernadette sent him to finish us off."

Hal shuddered. "Hell, you're probably right. Hey, that must be quite a hole in the top of your shoulder. It's still oozing."

"Yeah? Well, I'm glad I'm here to talk about it. If there's adhesive tape in that kit, I'll tape some gauze over it. What else does he have in that backpack?"

Hal did another visual inventory and tossed two boxes of pistol ammunition to William. "More rounds for the rifle, too, some food, several bottles of water, a compass, a satellite phone, matches, a roll of money, and keys for a car. He had a folding knife in his pocket, and the 12-inch belt knife, a map, and all that cord." He pointed to the camelback water pouch. "And that."

"Well, it's all ours now, the spoils of war."

"What are we going to do with him when he comes around, if he comes around?"

"I want to know who sent him, but I doubt if he'll tell us. He looks like one tough son-of- a-bitch. Probably a pro."

"You mean he kills people for a living? That kind of pro?"

William nodded. "That's my guess."

"Sure glad your trap worked. You must have hit him awful damn hard when you dropped from that branch up there." Hal pointed up to two sturdy branches jutting out over the creek bed at about 10 feet high. The tree was large and resembled a weeping willow, a perfect place to hide. "I mean, he didn't look up once, too busy checking out the boot and the tracks."

"Lucky for us."

"Yeah! I mean, that shot, one or two inches to the left and we'd both be dead."

"Fortunes of war. Now we have weapons, food, a map, and a compass. All we need is a ride."

Hal held up the keys. "What about this? Has to be a truck of some kind, maybe a four-wheel-drive."

"Yeah, but where is it? Miles from here, you can bet."

A moan came from their attacker still slumped forward from the tree.

William sat cross-legged about six feet in front of him and signaled Hal to be quiet. Nearly a minute passed with no further sound. But William guessed that the man had regained unconsciousness and was trying to grasp the unexpected circumstances he found himself in. When he did lift his head, his eyes were clear and focused. After another few seconds he tugged mightily at his bonds, to no avail. He lifted his eyes toward William.

Schrader saw the large, dark-skinned, long-haired man beyond his own bootless, sockless feet. Then he realized that his pockets were empty, his belt was gone, as well as the water pack. All of it was piled near his backpack, which was near the other man, a white man. His last concrete memory was reaching for the lone leather boot in the sand. Suddenly the dull ache at the back of his neck intensified. This was not how he had seen it all ending.

The dark-skinned man's gaze was cool and inscrutable whereas his white companion's expression seemed uncertain. He had never seen a North American Native in person, and there was something about the fact the first one he did see had his—Schrader's—9mm semi-automatic pistol clipped to his belt.

He cleared his throat. "What happens now?" he asked.

The dark-skinned man's expression didn't change, and the voice was low. "That depends on your answers to my questions."

THIRTY-TWO

Schrader had a sense that his charmed life was over. He didn't know anything about this man who held the key to his future, but he did know cold, hard resolve when he saw it. And it was unmistakably in the eyes of the dark-skinned man. Although Schrader had 26 confirmed kills to his name and had eluded retaliation a few times, he had long felt that the chances of dying an old man in his own bed were likely nonexistent. Strangely enough though, the end would not come at the hands of someone like himself—which he had totally expected—but at the whim of this dark-skinned man. It was evident he was capable of it.

"I have to know," Schrader rasped. "Who are you?"

A hint of cold disdain flickered in William's eyes, and then disappeared. He nodded toward Hal. "That is Harold Lamar. My name is William Black Spotted Horse. He's from the State of South Dakota. I'm from the Smokey River Reservation. Who the hell are you?"

"Schrader. Dedrik Schrader, from Dusseldorf, Germany."

"Who sent you?"

Schrader shook his head. "I cannot tell you that."

William glanced at Hal and then back at their prisoner. "No? You mean you won't tell us. Well, okay, here are your options. If you tell us who

271

sent you, we'll leave you here alive, in the exact condition you are in right now. I'm sure eventually you'll work yourself free somehow."

"And if I don't tell you?"

"There's only one way to learn what happens in that situation."

Schrader snickered. "I will tell you this, you're in way over your heads. You're up against powerful people."

William shrugged. "We got you, didn't we?"

"Owing to unexpected luck and a momentary lapse on my part. That can't be the case every time."

"Who sent you?"

"Go to hell."

"You know what, we're there already. Our granddaughter was kidnapped and taken half a world away from her home and family." He nodded toward Hal again. "His family and mine have been sick with worry. Don't threaten hell to someone whose people have been living it for generations, because of people like you. I'm not impressed. Who sent you?"

"Fuck you!"

Schrader fully expected what transpired next to happen, maybe not in this exact sequence, but something like it. He watched the dark-skinned man get to his feet and take the pistol from its holster and extract the clip to count the rounds to see if one was in the chamber. There was. The man reinserted the clip.

"Hey!" said Hal, getting to his feet. "What are you going to do?"

"Get answers," William told him, keeping his eyes on Schrader. "Now, Dedrik Schrader from Dusseldorf, who sent you?"

"Fuck you!"

William looked toward Hal. "Hey," he said, "toss me that black canvas case, the one you took out of the backpack."

After a moment of puzzled hesitation, Hal reached down and tossed the triangular shaped case to William, who unzipped it open. From inside it, he took a four-inch tube and attached it to the muzzle of the pistol.

"Is that a suppressor?" Hal asked.

"That's what it is," William told him.

"What are you going to do?"

"Remember what you said a few minutes ago, Hal? 'Another inch to the left and we'd be dead?' Well, get your mind around one thing: this son-of-a-bitch came here to kill us."

Hal nodded, uncertainty masking his face.

William turned his attention to Schrader. "Last chance. Who sent you?"

Stubbornly, Schrader shook his head, even as he saw the dark-skinned man pointing the pistol at his bare feet.

The sound of the shot was not unlike someone pounding a tabletop, but the scream of agony that came from Schrader was full-throated. He jerked his right leg back involuntarily, intensifying the pain. His breath came out in gasps between clenched teeth. Looking down, he saw splinters of bone where his ankle had been and blood pumping out with each heartbeat.

"What did you do?" Hal took a step forward, totally shocked.

"Stay back!" William waved his arm to enforce his command. His eyes were fixed on the man writhing in pain. He waited until the man's breathing became steadier and a semblance of clarity and focus came back into his eyes. Meanwhile, he knelt and pointed the pistol at the other ankle.

"Is this how you want your life to end, by seeing how much pain you can stand?" William asked. "You have one good ankle left, and two kneecaps still in one piece. Consider them as last chances to answer my questions."

Schrader nodded; his eyes still glazed with pain.

"Who sent you?"

Schrader nodded. "A man by the name of Esteban Palomino." His breathing was ragged as he set himself against the pain. His shattered ankle was twitching involuntarily.

"Esteban Palomino. Who is he? What does he have to do with Bernadette Covena?"

Schrader steadied himself. "Palomino is Covena's boss. He is the headman of a drug cartel, the Black River Cartel, a powerful man."

William glanced at Hal and turned back to Schrader. "Bernadette Covena is in the drug business?"

Schrader nodded. "She is number two, behind Palomino. They've run the cartel for years."

William looked toward Hal, who was still in shock, staring blankly at the wounded man.

"What else do you know?" William prodded.

"There's going to be a meeting in four days at Palomino's hacienda near the coast. Covena will be there. There's trouble between them. Palomino plans to kill her."

"What do you know about our granddaughter? Covena has her."

Schrader shook his head. "Nothing. I know nothing about your granddaughter."

"Why were you sent after us?"

"Because you're connected to Covena, somehow. That's all I was told."

"Okay. Where's your car, and what is it?"

"Six kilometers west, a Land Rover Defender, covered under a camouflage netting, not far from the truck you were in. They are both in the trees north of the road, about two kilometers from where you got off."

Hal knelt on one knee in the sand near William. He was astonished. "Do you believe all that? I mean, Bernadette is part of a drug ring, or something?"

William nodded. "That explains a lot. But here's the thing. If this Palomino is out to get Bernadette, Annie is in danger."

"What are we going to do?"

"We're going to find his car, find where this place is and get there as fast as we can."

"It's near a village called Carnarones," Schrader volunteered, "a few miles from the coast. It's a gated property and it's well-guarded."

"Oh, I'm sure it is," William replied.

"What about him?" Hal asked, nodding toward Schrader.

"What about him? He was sent to kill us. What are we supposed to do, drop him off at the nearest hospital?"

"Are we going to leave him here, like that?" Hal's voice was strident.

"Yeah, we are." William pointed to the man's shattered ankle. "He can't walk on that and he's lost a lot of blood. If he tries to walk, he'll bleed out before he gets 100 yards."

"A nice fire would be good," Schrader said. He knew the score. His life was now measured in hours, if not minutes. The shock of the injury was wearing off and the pain was down to a hot throbbing, as long as he didn't move the ankle. And it was still bleeding. "And if you could untie my hands?"

William turned to Hal. "We have to hurry. First let's gather up some dry wood and make a fire here." He pointed to the dry creek bed in front of the wounded man.

"Really?" Hal was a bit surprised.

William nodded. "He's not going anywhere."

Twenty minutes later the beginnings of a fire sputtered in a deep fire pit. A pile of dry wood was at hand. Hal shouldered the backpack and the sniper rifle. On an impulse he tried on the wounded man's boots. They fit. He waited as William cut the cords that held the man to the tree.

There was nothing more to be said or done. With only an occasional glance back, William and Hal followed the dry creek to their original campfire. From there they gathered the water jugs and sliced the peccary meat into chunks and strips. After taking a compass reading, they headed back toward the southwest.

Schrader stared at the pile of wood and wondered if he would use it all before he—. Something rustled in the leaves on the opposite bank of the old creek. Lifting his eyes toward the shrubbery on the other side, he immediately saw the yellow eyes. They were staring at him from behind a swatch of grass. He knew what was sizing him up. It was the first time he had ever seen a mountain lion in the wild and it would also be the last. The scent of fresh blood had attracted the beast and only the fire was keeping it at bay.

He wondered what would go out first, the fire or him. In either case, the lion would be waiting.

THIRTY-THREE

Retracing their route, and literally their own footprints now and then, they soon came to the spot where they had encountered the mountain lion and passed it without comment. According to Schrader's watch, it was past noon. Silence was their companion as they moved as fast as the terrain, grass, shrubs, and trees would allow. They had roughly six hours until the light would begin to fade, so they obviously needed to make the most of it.

Hal, however, had an additional reason for his reticence. The image of William shattering that man's ankle with a bullet played over and over in his head. He didn't know how to broach the subject and was not really sure if he should. He had seen a new side to William. William was a big man, and a combat veteran, and now he had a 9mm strapped to his belt and an obvious willingness to use it. It was all for the good, Hal understood that. But it was still a scary episode, nonetheless. He kept his silence until he noticed William was limping slightly. It was the opening he was hoping for.

"Did you hurt yourself jumping from that tree? You're limping just a bit," he pointed out.

William glanced back for a second. "Yeah, I think so," he said. "I think I twisted my right ankle. At least that's what it feels like. Nothing to worry about though."

"Well," Hal replied, "as soon as we find that Land Rover, we won't have to walk after that. Trouble might be finding it."

William pointed up to the top of the slope they were climbing. "Hey, let's stop up there and rest for just a bit and make a plan."

"I'm for that," Hal came back quickly, panting a bit.

A group of small boulders at the edge of the narrow plateau provided places to sit. The sun was warm, but not hot. Still, they were sweating slightly from the exertion of walking at a fast pace. William indicated the sniper rifle after Hal carefully leaned it against a rock.

"That's quite a weapon," he said. "My guess is it fires a NATO round, seven point six two, very fast. Doesn't pack the wallop of an M-14, but still effective. Put a nice hole in my shoulder and plowed your cheek good."

Hal reached up to touch the line on his left check that was beginning to scab over. He had cleaned it with the antiseptic in the first aid kit. "Guess I'm going to have a scar to brag about," he muttered. After a deep sigh, he nodded toward the little valley where they had left the wounded man. "Hell of thing, back there," he said. "Sure didn't expect that when I woke up this morning."

"Anything can and does happen," William said, unfolding Schrader's map.

"He is going to die, isn't he?"

William looked up at Hal and nodded. "Yeah. He won't last the day."

Hal shook his head. "What makes a guy do that for a living? I mean, how do you live with killing people?" He paused to shake his head again. "That sounds kind of strange."

"Some people can do that, live with killing people," William pointed out. "They have no remorse. Some do it because it pays a hell of lot of money. Maybe the money soothes their conscience. It's not an easy thing, knowing you've killed another human being. At least not for most people."

Hal saw the haunted look in William's eyes. He wondered if that episode had reawakened some old crap from Vietnam, but he wasn't about to ask.

"Scares the hell out of me that he was out here to kill us. That guy, Palomino or whatever, must really have a burr up his butt."

William looked up from the map. "That town Schrader mentioned is close to the ocean. It's a long drive from here, but I've got a thought."

"Okay. What are you thinking?"

"A couple of things. First, his phone. We can use it to try to connect with the kids and let them know we're okay. But I'm wondering if it might have some kind of tracking device on it. If it does and we use it now, we won't be moving very fast so it would be easy for our location to be identified. I say we turn it on after we find his car and then try to call. If anyone pinpoints where we are, we'll be out of there fast in the car."

Hal nodded. "Right, you're right. What's the other thing?"

"Our rental truck is in Santa Rosa. But more importantly, I left Annie's medicine at the hotel. I stored it. Not to mention our cards and my cell phone."

"You thinking we should go get the truck and the medicine?"

"The medicine at least. Listen, Schrader had the phone for a reason, maybe to check in periodically or to let Palomino know the job is done. It's a stretch, but maybe we can get close to that hacienda in Schrader's car. They might think it's him."

Hal sighed. "We got a few hours of hiking to think about it. Can we do that?"

William nodded as he folded the map. "Yeah, yeah, we can." He looked at the watch. "How about we push hard for two hours and stop to rest."

Hal nodded and stood. "Let's go."

And push hard they did, despite William's limp. Once away from the valley and into the forest proper, their progress slowed a bit, but they kept as fast a pace as they could, with no conversation at all, each man wading through his own thoughts and feelings and sweating profusely. After two hours William pointed to a fallen log.

"Rest and water," he said. "How are them boots working for you?"

"Beats slipping and sliding in the Lucheses," Hal said. He reached into the backpack and handed a bottle of water to William, taking the other for himself. Each of them drained nearly half.

William checked the compass again. "I remember this part of the forest," he said. "I'm guessing we have another two to three hour hike to the area where we came into the trees. He said the car is near there."

Hal was taking deep breaths as his panting slowly subsided. "I haven't walked this far in a hell of a long time," he admitted. "It's starting to wear me down."

"Yeah, I'm feeling it, too," William said.

Hal took another long drink and leaned forward, elbows on his knees and head hanging. "Hey," he said. "If I can't keep up, you might think of going on without me."

William slowly turned his eyes toward Hal and shook his head. "Ain't going to happen. We have to stick together. We can't give up, not even in our own minds—especially in our own minds."

"I was just thinking of Annie. I don't want to turn into a liability, you know? Spoil her chances."

"I'm thinking of her, too. Us sticking together is her best chance."

After a minute Hal finished off the water. "You know, two days ago when Bernadette locked me up in that stall, it scared me. But, I have to tell you," he paused and looked back down the slope they climbed, "what happened back there was a whole different level of real."

William nodded slowly. "Yeah, almost getting killed does things to a guy. But here's the thing, Hal. Forty some odd years ago I got shot at for the first time in my life. I saw guys get hit. One took a round through his gut and suddenly part of his intestine was poking out. The funny thing was—I didn't think about dying, I wondered if I could keep my nerve and not turn and run. I think I was more afraid of measuring up than dying."

"That's kind of weird."

"Well, war is hell but combat's a motherfucker. It gets really personal."

"Guess it just did."

William finished his water and crushed the plastic bottle with his hands. "You know, I hear a phrase now and then. I usually laugh it off because it's not who I am. 'Cowboy up.' You know it. And if it means to be a man and measure up and push past the doubts and fears, then I get it. That's what we got to do, Hal. This ain't a big game hunt or an issue over tribal land. It's about our granddaughter. That world out there doesn't give a shit about our problems. It doesn't give a shit about our granddaughter. And it doesn't matter because that's our responsibility. There ain't much good between us, you and me. I've wanted to knock you on your ass since we were in high school, and I know you felt the same about me. The only good thing we have in common is Annie. The other shit can wait, it'll all still be there, and we can fight and squabble all we want afterwards, but for Annie we've got to man up, and right now, Hal. We go until we get her back or until we use up the last shred of will or strength."

Hal nodded, reaching up after a moment to wipe away the moisture in his eyes. For several moments they sat in silence and only the breeze whispered through red cedars.

Hal looked toward the trees. "Yeah, then let's get to it. We have to find that car."

Two hours later they reached a giant fallen pine log, where they had stopped to rest the day before. Hal noticed that William's limp was more pronounced. He pointed to the west.

"That truck kept going after we jumped out," he recalled. "If we keep heading west at the edge of the tree line, we might see something."

Half an hour later they spotted a shadow at an odd angle to the others cast by the tall trees. It was green camouflage netting. Within a few yards from it they saw the square shape beneath it.

"He had it all figured out, didn't he?" Hal asked rhetorically. "That son-of-a-bitch. He hid it because he was coming back here."

Reasoning they might need it later, they folded the netting and put it in the cargo area. It also covered the backpack and weapons. The car looked relatively new. Next to the spare tire on the back were two rectangular plastic containers. Hal opened the cap to one and took a whiff.

"Gasoline," he announced. "About six extra gallons, I'd guess."

They loaded their gear in it and jumped in. It started with the first turn of the key. William looked down at the instrument panel.

"It has three quarters of a tank of gas," he announced. "But I think these things are notorious gas hogs."

"Well, there's an extra six gallons or so and we got his money."

"So, what's your sense about our next move?" William backed the car around and turned it to face the road.

Hal stared at the landscape for some moments, thinking. "You know," he said, "maybe having two vehicles will give us some kind of an edge. And as far as that satellite phone, I'm a little nervous about turning it on. It damn well could have some kind of tracker on it. We could stop somewhere and find a calling card, maybe."

William nodded. "Yeah, two vehicles might be an advantage and I like your idea about the calling card. Besides, my credit cards and yours are back in Santa Rosa. I say we check out this map and find the quickest way back to Santa Rosa." He glanced at the digital clock on the dash. "We'll get there in the middle of the night, perhaps early morning, but that's okay."

They looked at the map and William pointed to the line drawn, showing the route from Carnarones to Paso de Indios, and from there west into the mountains. He indicated Paso de Indios. "From there we go back north," he said.

"Shit, that's a stretch from Santa Rosa to Carnarones," he said, exhaling sharply. "But we got to do it."

"Right, no time like the present."

Reaching down to the console he put the gearshift into Drive and eased the vehicle forward over the uneven ground. Its heavy-duty suspension was stiff, designed for rough terrain, making for a swaying ride. William steered between large grass clumps and what he assumed was sagebrush and an occasional slab of rock. Progress was slow.

"There's something in the trees," Hal said, pointing north. "Maybe a cabin."

They both stared at the horizontal line of a structure of some type visible between the openings in the trees.

"It's not a pitched roof," Hal commented, as William turned his attention back to finding the road. "The cabin they stuck me in had a pitched roof,

I imagine because of the snow." He shifted in his seat and stared at what had to be a manmade object. "Hey!" he called out. "Wait a minute. Stop!"

"What is it?"

Hal reached into the pack and yanked out the binoculars. It took him a few seconds of adjusting the focus. "Shit! You know what that is?"

William peered past Hal into the trees. "What the hell is it?"

"I think it's that truck they hauled us in. I can see the torn tarp."

"You're kidding."

Hal handed him the binoculars. After a few seconds, it was his turn to be astonished.

"It damn sure looks like it. But what's it doing there?"

Glancing toward the road, William drove into a grove of pine and stopped. "Come on," he said. "Grab the rifle, I'll get the pistol. We need to have a look."

Two minutes later, after a careful approach, there was no doubt. It was the camouflaged painted truck with the torn tarp. It was parked in the middle of a thicket. Circling the shrubbery, they slowly and carefully worked their way to the cab. An odor like rotten eggs grew stronger. Then they saw the shattered passenger side window and then the bodies.

They were speechless, staring at the two dead men, each with a hole in the left temple, eyes staring blankly. Both had golf-ball sized exit holes on the opposite temples, congealed and then dried, almost black. Spatters of black also clung to the back window.

Hal lowered the rifle. "Schrader did this, didn't he?"

William nodded. "Yeah. I'm guessing he stopped the truck somehow, probably on the road, and shot them. Someone told him we were in the back, but we were lucky. We got out and spoiled his plan."

Hal finally turned away. "Goddamn it! I'll bet these poor bastards didn't know what hit them."

"Yeah. He took them by surprise. Come on. We have a long way to go."

Halfway to the car Hal glanced back for a second. "These are some bad people we're dealing with, Will." He jerked a thumb toward the truck. "I'm going to see that for the rest of my life.

THIRTY-FOUR

After driving east for 45 or so kilometers on the mountain road, they came to a small town where the truck had last stopped for gas. They recognized the small station with two pump islands and pulled up to one.

"How do they do it here?" Hal wondered. "Do they prepay, like at home?"

"Damn, I never thought of that," William admitted, looking at the pumps. "I don't see a card reader on the pump. Maybe we pump and then pay and the price is in pesos."

"What shall we do?"

"Well, we need to top off this tank, so I will get out and hope my brown skin blends in. You sit tight. This looks like the older pumps at home, you lift the lever and start pumping the gas. I guess if I do it wrong, someone will come."

"Okay. Good luck."

William stepped out of the Land Rover, glad that the mud on the side of the vehicle more or less matched his dirty and wrinkled clothes. Pulling the nozzle from the pump, he lifted the lever and saw the tumblers in the window zero out, then start spinning as he started the flow of gas.

A mild panic gripped him when he saw the numbers 680 and 16 on the tumblers, until he realized he was looking at 16 liters and 680 pesos. Returning the nozzle, he reached into his pocket for Schrader's money. Pausing, he found the 50 and 100 peso bills and counted out the rounded amount. Affecting a slow walk he hoped was nonchalant, William headed for the front of the station. Inside he was thankful there was a counter and behind it a young man. Stopping at it, he pointed out toward the pump and handed the clerk 700 pesos. With a nod and a hint of curiosity in his eyes, the young man took the money and rang up the sale, although his eyes went to William's bloody shirt. After putting the currency in the drawer, he returned a 20 peso bill. William nodded his thanks and turned, trying again to appear as nonchalant as possible, though his heart was beating heavily.

He got back into the vehicle, realizing that his legs were rubbery. "That was nerve wracking, but easier than I thought it would be," he said to Hal.

"Good. Let's get the hell out of this one-horse town."

"Right. The clerk knew I wasn't from these parts."

Hal waved Schrader's highway map. "According to this, the road north to Santa Rosa is a few kilometers east. I think we stop at that junction and call home. And if there is a tracking thing on this here phone, they won't know which direction we're heading. After we call, we get rid of the phone, maybe throw it in the ditch or something."

"Great idea."

The junction came up sooner than they expected. Pulling off onto a wide shoulder as far as they could, Hal powered up the phone and handed it to William. "Here, you're better at handling these things than I am," he said.

William grinned and took the phone and immediately punched in Jarod's cell phone number and was disappointed when it went to voice mail. "Hey, Son," he said. "This is Dad using a borrowed satellite phone. We're okay, got a lot to tell you. Call this number back as soon as you can. I'll call Jennifer's cell. Bye, for now."

Ignoring Hal's questioning look, he dialed Jennifer's number, immensely relieved when she answered after the second ring."

"Hello?"

"Jennifer, this is William. I'm here with your dad."

"Dad! Oh, my god, you're okay!"

"Yeah, we're okay, hon. How's everyone there?"

The relief in her voice was obvious. "We're good. We were worried when we didn't hear from you and couldn't get you on the phone. Are you sure you're okay?"

"We are, hon, we are," he reassured his daughter-in-law. "A lot has happened though."

"Well, we have news, too."

"Okay, tell us."

"Yeah, yeah. Jarod and Marie are on an airplane from Miami to Buenos Aires."

William paused and glanced at Hal. "They are?"

"Yeah, and after they arrive Mom and I will take off from Sioux Falls. That's where we are now."

"Okay, ah, just a second. Hold on, I'll tell your dad. Just hold on."

"Jarod and Marie are on their way to Buenos Aires. Jennifer and Virginia are in Sioux Falls, about to leave."

Hal's eyes were wide. "The hell! They must have got tired of sittin' on their hands. What else?"

"Jenny? What's the plan?"

"Well, after we didn't hear from you, we decided the wisest thing to do was go there. Is that okay, I hope?"

"Yeah, yeah, I think so."

"Listen, Dad. Is there a speaker button on the phone you're using?"

"Ah, maybe, let me check, hold on."

William looked at the keypad and saw the button with SPK and touched it. "Can you hear me, hon?"

"Yeah, I can hear you. Hey, Dad, how are you?"

Hal quickly wiped away the moisture in his eyes. "I'm good, my girl. Sure glad to hear your voice," he said.

"Okay, Dad. Mom's listening, too."

"Hey, you, two," Virginia chimed in. "We're really glad to hear from you. We were worried."

"Oh, just a little setback is all," Hal said. "So, you two are about to get on an airplane?"

"Yeah," Jennifer replied. "Jarod and Marie are landing in Buenos Aries in a little less than two hours. So, we timed our flight accordingly. That way, if you did call, someone would be available."

"We're sure glad," Hal said.

"So, what's the situation there?" Virginia asked, the worry evident in her voice.

Hal looked at William, nodding at him to explain.

"Well, as Hal said, we had a bit of a setback, but we have things under control. We know where Annie is and we're working up a plan to get her. At the moment, we're starting back to Santa Rosa."

"And then what?" Jennifer asked.

William glanced at Hal. "Well, we're not sure, but since you two will be in the air soon and out of touch, let us talk to Jarod and Marie after they land. Then we'll take it from there."

"Okay," the two women both said. "Where's Annie?"

William glanced at Hal. "She's with Bernadette, but we saw a video of her a couple days ago. She's okay."

They both could hear the anxiety in voices on the other end. "How did she look?"

"She was eating," Hal said. "She's not being mistreated."

During the long pause, they could hear soft murmurs and waited for Jennifer and Virginia to speak. "So, okay, that's good news," Jennifer finally said, her voice choked with emotion. "Jarod is worried, and so is Marie. So, call them in about three hours and talk to them. They'll turn their phones on as soon as they land."

"Right. we won't be able to call them until later tonight. When do you get to Buenos Aires?"

"Tomorrow afternoon, I think around two o'clock."

"Okay," William said, "Once you're all in country, we'll have a conference call. Do us a favor and text Jarod, tell him we talked and to expect a call late tonight, maybe after midnight. It'll be my cell phone or a local number in Santa Rosa."

"I can do that," Jennifer assured him.

William had been watching the roads and checking the rearview mirror. He spotted a vehicle approaching from behind. He tapped Hal and motioned to the rear. "We have to go," he mouthed.

"Okay, honey," Hal said to Jennifer. "We have to head out. Talk to you later."

William kept an eye on the approaching vehicle. "Hey," he said, "put that phone on this center console." Hal laid the phone on the center armrest. With the butt of Schrader's combat knife, William smashed the phone until it was in pieces. He picked out the battery. "Throw the rest into the ditch." After Hal picked up the pieces of the phone, William put the battery down and smashed it as well, then tossed the pieces out the door.

A few seconds later they made the left turn and headed north. William watched the intersection but the vehicle he saw kept going.

"I'll take the first two hours," he volunteered. "You probably should get some sleep. I'm sure that seat leans back. We stay on this highway, right?"

"Yeah, according to the map." Hal found the lever and reclined the seat.

William glanced over and saw Hal staring out the window. He'd seen that look before, somewhere between shock and disbelief, along with a vacant detachment. He'd seen it on teenage soldiers after surviving their first firefight.

"Get some sleep," he said again.

THIRTY-FIVE

Nearly three hours later Hal finally stirred, rubbed his face and brought the seat back forward. "Where are we?" he asked.

"About 180 miles down range," William told him.

Hal pointed to the sun about to set, slipping orange rays through a bank of long narrow clouds. "Sunsets are beautiful anywhere" he pointed out. "No matter if things are bad or good." He noticed that William was steering with his left hand and glanced up at the dried blood below the right collar of his shirt. "I bet that hole is still bleeding," he said.

William nodded. "Feels like it."

"I'm ready to drive. You're probably beat."

"I think there's a town about 10 miles or so up ahead." William glanced down at the instrument panel. "We're down to about half on the gas so I think we find a place and fill up and make a pit stop."

When they came to the town, they saw what looked like a store with gas pumps out front. While William filled the tank, Hal found the bathrooms behind the building. William went inside and paid for the gas and felt bold enough to buy bottled water and what he hoped was some form of beef jerky before getting back on the road.

Dusk turned to darkness as William turned on the dome light to study the map and looked at Schrader's watch. "We'll probably get there after midnight," he estimated. "I think we get the truck and find a different hotel."

As it turned out, his estimate was accurate. At nearly 12:30 they reached the southeastern outskirts of Santa Rosa. There was very little traffic as William awoke and sat up. Some 10 minutes later they were turning into the parking lot behind the hotel. Hal parked and turned off the lights and engine.

"I'll go in and get our stuff and Annie's medicine," he said. "I lost the receipt, so I hope someone remembers. You just hang here."

Thankfully, the night clerk did recognize William, though she cast puzzled glances at his bloody shirt collar. A couple of minutes later he exited the lobby with Hal's credit cards, and passport, and the container with Annie's medicine. He retrieved the truck keys from the trailer hitch and opened the cab.

From the backpack William took his cell phone and the leftover cash. With him leading the way, they found an unobtrusive little inn with a turquoise sign that said *Posada de Carlotta* and took a chance. They paid for two rooms for three nights.

In a small cozy room, William lay on his left side, staring into the semi-darkness, unable to sleep mainly because of the throbbing wound. A welcome hot shower felt good. It cleaned the wound, but also aggravated it. He sat up and turned on the lamp near his bed. According to what they had learned from Schrader, Bernadette might not be at her ranch. Perhaps she was already near the coast in the area of the town Schrader had mentioned, Carnarones. Or perhaps she was still at her ranch, with Annie. Turning on his cell phone, he saw the battery level was at just over 60 percent. He decided to call Jarod and use the signal he had prearranged.

Hanging up after the first ring, he waited. In less than 20 seconds a call came back.

"Jarod, it's Dad. Hope I didn't wake you."

"No matter, how are you? Where are you?"

"Hal and I are back in Santa Rosa. I'm guessing you've heard from Jennifer?"

"She told me to expect your call. It's really good to hear from you, Dad. What's the situation?"

William filled him in from their capture by Bernadette's men to overpowering Schrader and taking his vehicle, although he left out the grisly details, including the fact that both he and Hal were wounded.

"So," Jarod concluded. "Annie could be at Bernadette's ranch."

"That's my thought and I'm forming a plan, although I haven't talked to Hal about it yet. Now that Hal and I know the layout of her place, I'm thinking it might be a good idea to sneak in. Given what Schrader told us, they certainly won't be expecting us and this time we're armed to the teeth."

"Well, that sounds fairly risky, Dad. On the other hand, if Bernadette is there, she might think all that other guy's men are with him and might have her guard down. And if she isn't there, then you would know that."

William sighed. "Yeah, it is risky, but if Bernadette is there, we might have a chance to rescue Annie."

"Right," Jarod agreed. "But if I can suggest one thing, Dad?"

"Oh, sure."

"Get close enough to observe for a bit, before you make a move."

"Good idea, Son. But first I have to talk to Hal. If he's okay with it, we'll go. Whatever we decide I'll call you in a bit. How's Mom doing?"

"She's good. She and Jennifer and Virginia are tougher than I am, I'll tell you that."

William chuckled knowingly. "Yeah. Whoever the hell thought women were the weaker sex was a dumb shit. After I talk to Hal, I'll give your mom a call."

Ten minutes later, William had finished outlining a general plan for sneaking onto Bernadette's ranch and his rationale.

"Let's get on it," Hal said. "But let's take Schrader's car and go up the road a bit, and leave it on the side of the road, make it look like it ran off into the ditch or something. It can't be traced to us if anyone sees it. We can cross the fence and hoof it to the ranch from there. Worst that can happen is that we have to walk back into town afterwards. If Annie is there and we get her, we can steal a car."

After that there was simply nothing to be done but get ready. Everything they would need was already in Schrader's Defender. Fifteen minutes later they passed the main gate to Dancing Horse Ranch and proceeded east for a mile. Pulling off into the ditch, they gathered their gear. William took a few minutes to wipe their prints off the surfaces they had touched inside and outside the car, took the keys and locked the car. A minute later they were under the wire fence. At this hour there was no traffic. Overhead there was a starry sky. A slight breeze pulled the grass in a slow dance.

After setting a steady pace through the tall grass, they came to a rise southeast of the ranch. Hunkering out of sight in the grass they glassed the buildings and the area with the binoculars and rifle scope. They saw no vehicles outside or any kind of movement.

William pointed to another rise across the road to the ranch. "Let's go there next and take another look. If we see nothing, we'll figure out a way to move in."

Five minutes later they were hidden in the tall grass again when they heard the sound of tires on gravel. Seconds later white shafts of light cut across the wide meadow. They recognized the white van immediately.

"Well, well," murmured William. "Chubby and Black Jacket. Two of our favorite people."

The van drove to the barn and stopped in front of the main door. A man stepped down from the driver's side and walked to the door switch on the outside wall of the barn. As the van drove in, the interior lights automatically came on and only the driver stepped out of the van. The door stayed open.

"That's Smith," William said. "He's alone. I say we high tail it down there and see who else is inside."

"Let's go!"

Winded after a fast trot, they ducked to the right of the open door and cautiously peeked in. "It's parked in front of that office room," William said. "The door is still open, so I think Smith won't be here long. I say we go have a talk with him."

Moving carefully against the side of the middle aisle, they went past the stall room where they had spent the night. Halfway into the building William paused and indicated the stalls. "No horses," he whispered.

"I noticed," Hal said, nodding. "Wonder what that means."

They arrived at the office door, which was slightly ajar, and heard music playing. William nodded at Hal and they stepped in to see Smith at the file cabinets in the corner. His casual glance turned into shock and horror.

"You look like you just saw a ghost, Mr. Smith," William said. He turned to Hal. "Keep a watch for anyone else."

Hal nodded.

William motioned to Smith with Schrader's Sig Sauer in hand. "Put your hands on your head and take a seat on the couch."

A wide-eyed Smith complied immediately.

"Last time we saw you, you were forcing us into that deuce and a half truck. I'm guessing you were sure you'd never see us again. I'll bet you also know about one Dedrik Schrader, that blue-eyed German." William waved the pistol. "This is his pistol. I'm guessing Mr. Schrader is a corpse by now."

If the look on his face was any indication, Smith was expecting the worst.

"Who's in the house?" William asked.

"No one."

"Where is Bernadette and our granddaughter?"

"Along the coast west of Carnarones."

"What are you doing here?"

"Getting documents."

William's gaze held no mercy. "For who, Palomino?"

Smith couldn't hide his shock and surprise. He shook his head. "No, for Bernadette. Part of her plan."

"Really? Where are you supposed to take those documents?"

Smith swallowed nervously. "To Palomino's men, at his place."

"Where are the horses?"

"Mrs. Covena sold them."

"Why?"

"She's leaving the country."

"Where is she going?"

Smith shook his head, his eyes fixed on the pistol in William's hands. "Spain."

"When is she leaving?"

"Tomorrow, at three in the afternoon."

"How?"

"By chopper—helicopter to a ship waiting off the coast."

"So, you're to grab documents and then what?"

Smith took a deep breath. "Take them to Palomino's place tonight."

William shot a quick glance at Hal before returning his attention to Smith. "Hal, something tells me we should ride along."

"Works for me," Hal said.

THIRTY-SIX

A thorough search of Smith yielded a wallet, a large wad of money, and two cell phones, one of which was obviously a burner phone. Smith readily admitted the burner was his direct line to Esteban Palomino. William was skeptical that Bernadette's house was empty.

"I'm sure you know how to get into the house," he said to Smith.

"Yeah. There's a hidden keypad and a pass code."

After they pilfered the tack room of zip ties, cords, and ropes, they left the barn and parked at the house. William forced Smith to remove his shoes and socks and took him to the main entrance. Smith had been telling the truth. The place was empty and eerily quiet.

"Where was my granddaughter kept?" William asked.

Smith led the way to a second story corner room, with bars on the outside of the windows. It was tastefully furnished.

"Mrs. Covena, she really likes your granddaughter," Smith volunteered.

A few minutes later they were back in the van and William bound Smith's wrists with zip ties, the same kind used on him and Hal.

"What's our plan?" Hal asked as they drove back toward Santa Rosa.

"Well, Smith's buddies are expecting him to show up driving this van. It's our way to get inside, a surprise attack as it were. But that means we drive through the night."

Hal nodded back at Smith, lying on the middle seat with a gag in his mouth. "We can do it. We just hog tie that bastard and take turns driving. We know the way to that junction and after that he can show us the way."

After they gathered the rest of their gear at the hotel, they tied Smith to the passenger seat in the van and put his phones in the tray atop the dash, in the event someone called him, then hit the long road ahead. William took the first leg. It was, William admitted to himself, a complicated gamble. Anything could go wrong at anywhere along the way.

William glanced back at Hal who was already asleep, curled on the middle seat. Smith sat staring ahead, filled with dread. Somewhere, several hundred miles to the south was Annie. At three o'clock tomorrow afternoon a helicopter was scheduled to arrive at Palomino's estate to fly her and Bernadette to a ship offshore. That would certainly happen if he and Hal didn't overcome all the obstacles ahead of them. William flexed his left shoulder and sighed. First things first; they had to get there. First the long road, and then whatever waited at the end of it.

Ninety minutes later, William pulled off the road for a pee break but they were back on the road in less than 10 minutes. Two hours later they stopped again, to switch drivers. Since leaving Santa Rosa, Smith had not spoken a word and had slept off and on. The sun rose during Hal's shift and at the end of his three-hour stint they arrived at the crossroads they had started from about 14 hours earlier. Waking Smith, they unfolded the map and had him mark out the route to Palomino's estate, which was another four hours according to him.

In order for them be as rested as possible, William suggested that he would drive two hours while Hal slept and then Hal would drive the last two hours while William slept. Four hours later, Hal pulled off onto a narrow dirt road and woke William.

Putting a pen in Smith's hand, William instructed him to draw the layout of Palomino's property. The main house was a hundred yards southeast of the barn and above it on a slope. The barn itself was living quarters for the security detail provided a place to guard the main entrance to the road leading up to the house.

"How far are we from the barn?" William asked.

"Twenty minutes," Smith replied.

"Who's in the barn and when are they expecting you?"

"Five men and—whenever I show up."

"Is Palomino in the house?"

"No, he's at a resort with his girlfriend. He'll be there at 1:30, ahead of Mrs. Covena."

William glanced at the watch. It was just past nine.

"What about Bernadette? When will she arrive?"

"I'm guessing just before the meeting. She'll call for the gate code. It's automatic. When she pulls up to the gate, the gate monitor calls the phone in the barn and whoever sees her on the screen answers and gives her the code. It's changed every day."

William thought for a moment. "That could be tricky. Can she see whoever gives her the code? Is there a screen outside?"

"No. It's audio."

"Who decides the code?"

"The computer. It's a five-digit code."

"Okay. When does the computer pick the code?"

"Anytime after midnight."

"Where's the computer?"

"In the kitchen and dayroom. It's where everyone hangs out, unless they're in the workout room, the bathroom, or their own room."

"Do you need a code to get into the building?"

"No. I just call the dayroom phone and whoever answers opens the garage door. Sometimes it's already open."

"Are there visitors? Do people just show up?"

Smith shook his head. "No. I mean, there are deliveries, but they're scheduled.

"Palomino doesn't want unannounced visitors."

Hal looked at William. "I'm guessing you don't want us to show up too early."

William nodded. "Right. On the other hand, we will need time to neutralize the security detail, somehow, after we take them by surprise."

"How we going to do that?"

"Well, first we're going to find a place to hide until about 12:30. That gives us about three and a half hours to come up with a fool-proof plan."

"I tell you what," Hal said. "I'm ready, at least mentally, and I'll go as far as this tired old body will go."

William looked at Smith and pointed to the narrow road they were on. "Does this lead to someone's property?"

"No. It's all Palomino's land from here. This is just a dirt road that leads nowhere."

"There aren't any tracks," Hal affirmed.

"Okay," William said. "Let's go over that rise ahead and beyond it and turn the vehicle around. We'll hunker down out of sight."

Nearly half an hour later Hal and William were sitting on the ground behind the van in the shade, using part of the map to write out a plan.

"Getting inside the barn will be the easy part," Hal pointed out, "if Smith is telling the truth. Getting the drop on those five guys is the sticky part. We have to get them out of the way before we can do anything else."

"Right. Well, we got him," William said, jerking his thumb back toward Smith who was still tied to the passenger seat. "We use him, somehow, to get all those guys in one area, maybe the garage. If they know it's him, they won't be meeting the van with guns drawn."

"Great idea. Let's tie him to the driver's seat and he can drive us in. We'll hide in the back. This vehicle has sliding doors on both sides. The trick is to get all the men into the garage."

William thought for a moment and nodded. "Yeah. You know, the van's sliding door windows on back have dark tint. They can't see in. maybe Smith can tell them he has something to unload, boxes, maybe. When they open the door, we get the drop. But, if we're going to hide back there, we have to get rid of that middle seat."

"And once we have the drop on them, then what?"

"Disable them, tie them up."

"Right. Okay, important and tough question here, Will. What if one or more of them goes for their gun?"

"We have no choice then. Shoot. Remember, we're here to rescue Annie."

"Right, you're right."

"I don't know if those guys wear bulletproof vests. We can ask Smith, but just in case we do have to shoot, aim for their upper legs. I don't care how tough or well-trained anyone is, they will react to getting shot. And once we start shooting, we keep shooting."

Hal nodded, beads of sweat on his forehead.

After a moment, William looked at the notes on the map. "So," he said, "our plan is simple. Get in, get the drop on those guys, and neutralize them. Now, I suppose we should see if there are tools in this vehicle so we can try to remove that middle seat."

William fixed a cold, threatening stare at Smith. "You drive this a lot. Any tools?"

"Yeah, in the spare tire well," the man said.

Twenty minutes later, they finished removing the bolts that held the seat to the floor and dragged it out, unceremoniously dumping it in the ditch.

Hal wiped his brow. "I could use a big breakfast right about now," he said. "But I'll settle for good luck."

William looked up at the sun. "Yeah, we've been lucky so far. I think as long as we keep taking the initiative, being decisive, our luck will hold."

Hal nodded and reached back into the van for a bottle of water. "This is way beyond the usual things in life," he said. "You know, before the chance goes by I want to apologize to you."

William shot a quizzical look at Hal. "For what?"

Hal shrugged. "For all of this, for where we are at this moment, for what we have to do, or try to do. None of this would be happening if it hadn't been for me forcing Hollister McGiven out of our partnership. None of this would be happening if I hadn't got my nose out of joint over a few thousand dollars. Hell, all he was trying to do was take care of his little boy."

William was surprised. He never thought he would have to find words of solace for a man he had despised all his life.

"Well," he said, after a long moment of silence. "Are you trying to tell me you'd rather be back home where you and I would be at each other's throats, full of piss and vinegar and making our families uncomfortable?"

Hal chuckled. "Damn, all that seems so stupid."

"Let's look at it this way, then. Those issues back home, between you and me, we've sort of put them on hold. If we get through this mess alive, both of us, then we'll see where we stand on that shit at home."

Hal glanced over at William. "Yeah, that's a good idea."

"Okay. Then, let's go over our plan and work ourselves into a kick-ass frame of mind."

THIRTY-SEVEN

By noon they were ready to go. Smith was securely tied to the driver's seat with ropes across his hips and under his arms. As he started the car, the burner phone rang. William leaned over from behind the passenger seat and placed the muzzle of his pistol in Smith's crotch, causing him to gasp.

"Answer it, and no matter what, speak only in English, and put it on speaker."

Smith nodded and reached for the phone, flipping it open. "Hello."

William leaned in close to pick up the conversation.

"Major league baseball bats are made from ash and red maple," said the voice other end.

"Indeed," replied Smith.

"Slight change of plans," the voice said. "I postponed my meeting with Señora Coven until tomorrow. However, unless I'm mistaken, she will still arrive in time to meet the helicopter she chartered to pick her up."

"I see. What would you like me to do?"

"Stand by for further instructions, just in case I might need you."

"Understood."

"Where are you now?"

Smith glanced at William. "I am about to arrive at the ranch," he said. "Sir, may I ask, are you allowing her to leave on the chopper?"

"No, of course not. I will be flying the chopper, and I will arrive at three precisely. By that time, Gomez should have taken her out. I have positioned him on the mountain, and he is in place now, near the summit. He will help me load the bodies of the woman and the girl and I will dump them into the ocean, miles from the shore."

"I understand."

"Good. I want you to tell the guards to sit tight. If I need their help, or yours, I will call you."

"Understood."

The call clicked off as beads of perspiration popped out on Smith's face. William sat down on the floor behind the passenger seat, much to Smith's relief.

"I heard," William said to Smith, "but tell me what you heard."

"That was Palomino," Smith said, licking his lips. "He will be flying the chopper and landing at three on the summit. But he's got Gomez already on the mountain, waiting for Señora Covena. He has orders to take her out—and your granddaughter, too."

"Oh, good God!" Hal said. "What do we do now?"

"Ah, well, either Bernadette will show up for her ride, or she won't," William surmised. "In case she does, we have to be in place, somehow, somewhere."

"Right. But what about Gomez?"

William thought for a moment and then looked at Smith. "How big is that summit, in terms of acres?"

"It's about two acres but it's narrow and long."

"What's the terrain and vegetation?"

"The top is flat, graded smooth. The slopes are rough," Smith said, "and deep gullies. Bushes and shrubs."

"Where is the landing pad?"

"At the south end, above the parking area. A gravel road leads up there and ends at a parking area. From there it's a 50-yard slope up."

"Okay. There's a road to the parking area. What about from the north?"

"There is, yeah, a maintenance road, I think. It circles around from the north and then up the east side."

William glanced at his watch and turned to Hal. "Those guys don't know we're coming," he said. "Let's get into that garage, neutralize those guards, and then figure it out from there."

Hal nodded grimly. "Okay. Let's do it."

William stared at Smith. "Get going. Do those guards speak English?"

Smith nodded. "Yeah, they all do."

"Okay, when we get close, if the door isn't open, you will call them and have them open it. Every word in English."

Smith nodded, his hands trembling on the steering wheel.

"Let's go."

After 15 minutes they turned right off the main highway onto a new wide gravel road. The garage and the large Mediterranean style house were visible from there. William estimated it would take them less than two minutes to reach the garage.

"Stop," he told Smith. "Call them and tell them to open the door and that you need help unloading boxes for Palomino."

Smith complied, stopping in the entrance and dialing his own phone.

"Hey," he said, when a voice answered. "This is Deke Smith. I'm on my way down and I need the garage door open. I have boxes for Señor Palomino to be unloaded immediately. Everyone meet me in the garage."

"Si, Señor," said a deep voice. "We be here."

Soon after they started down the gradual slope the wide garage door opened. At about 40 yards they saw four men standing inside the wide bay, watching as the van approached. At the far end of the bay was a vehicle, a dark blue SUV. William noted with relief that none of them had weapons in their hands.

"Pull in close to them before you stop," he whispered to Smith. "Between now and then if you do anything but drive and park, or if you say a word, I'll put a bullet in your brain."

Smith nodded, keeping his eyes straight ahead.

Without taking his eyes off the interior of the garage, William whispered to Hal, "They'll all be on the left side of the van. As soon as we stop, I'll unlatch the handle, you pull open the door. Then we jump out, you to the left and me to the right. Keep your gun on them. If anyone so much as moves an arm or a hand, shoot."

Hal took a deep breath and nodded.

Tires crunched on the gravel. They could see the four guards standing against the south wall of the garage, talking among themselves. They were all about the same height and appeared solidly built. Only one seemed to be wearing a pistol clipped to his belt.

"I see only one weapon," William whispered to Hal. "But we don't take any chances."

"Gotcha."

William ducked down as the van entered the garage. "Stop," he said to Smith.

Smith applied the brakes and the van rolled to a slow stop behind the SUV.

William nodded at Hal and reached for the door latch and pulled it down, clicking it open. Hal pulled on the vertical door handle and yanked the door open, putting them in full view of the four guards. In the split second after that William jumped out of the door with his pistol raised, followed by Hal with the sniper rifle.

"ON THE FLOOR!" William shouted. "NOW!"

Surprise and shock delayed the men's response, but once the alarming reality of the moment hit, they all went down to the concrete floor.

"HANDS ON YOUR HEADS! HANDS ON YOUR HEADS!" William shouted. Again, the men complied.

He turned to Hal. "Keep your gun on them," he said. "I'm going to get his gun and search all of them."

Hal stepped sideways and nodded as William stepped to the second man and quickly yanked the pistol of the man's clip holster, then did a quick pat down. In less than a minute he finished searching them all, finding nothing more than money and two cell phones. He threw the cell phones on the concrete and smashed them.

"Keep your eyes down!" William said in warning. "If anyone moves, we shoot all of you!" He stepped to the van and opened the driver's door. "Where's the switch to close the garage door?"

Smith nodded toward the far wall. "Over there. Near the door."

William pointed at the prisoners with his pistol and the captured weapon and spoke to Hal. "Close the door, and then we need rope and zip ties."

Shortly after that Hal finished binding their prisoners' wrists behind them with two zip ties each and tied their ankles together with rope. Only after that did he and William momentarily let down their guard. Double-checking the ropes and the zip ties, Hal took a seat on a chair against the south wall. William reached into the van and took the key out of the ignition as Smith sat staring ahead, scared shitless. The bound prisoners had not made a sound, obviously shocked by how they had been so quickly overwhelmed. Each of them cast quick, furtive glances at the tall, brown-skinned man with the long braid. He was obviously a *Norte Americano*, but the likes of which none of them had ever seen before.

"I'm going to have a quick look around," William told Hal.

In a room behind the wall at the end of the two-car stall, he found two all-terrain vehicles and garden and yard tools and several work coveralls. A wide sliding door with two porthole windows was on the east wall. The front area nearest the garage was a day room and kitchen area with sofas, chairs, lamps, a dining area, and two computer stations. On the south wall hung a vertical rifle rack with five AK-47 assault rifles in six holders and below them were six slots containing four holstered pistols. On the east wall, above the computers, was a small closed-circuit television screen with an overhead shot of the security gate adjacent to the north wall of the barn. Also on the wall was a large map of the 50 acres of the estate proper.

William paused to study the map. There was a road leading from the garage south to the parking area below the helicopter pad, exactly as Smith had described. What he hadn't mentioned was the two narrow roads, both labeled *Mantenimiento*, which he guessed meant Maintenance. One basically paralleled the road to the parking lot and the other went north of the main house and then curved south on the other side of the mountain. The maintenance roads gave him an idea.

He rejoined Hal and their prisoners in the garage. "I think I have a plan. I'll run it by you, but first I want to make sure these guys don't get loose."

Hal watched in fascination as William fashioned a slip loop and put it around the neck of the first man, then ran the rope under his bound wrists and tied the end around his ankles with the man's legs bent sharply at the knees. Trussed up in this manner, if the man tried to straighten his legs, he choked himself. William repeated the setup with the three other men.

"One more step," he said. Removing their shoes and socks, he stuffed half a sock into each man's mouth, then tied the other sock around the man's head to keep the gag in place.

"Where the heck did you learn all that?" Hal asked.

"You don't want to know," William replied wryly. "Even if they yell, it won't be loud and no one will understand a word they say. Anyway, let's take Mr. Smith into the kitchen. He can man the computer and watch for Bernadette."

After letting Smith use the toilet, they tied his ankles to the legs of the small office chair in front of one of the computers. "Listen," William said, leaning down into Smith's face. "Your job is to keep an eye on that monitor. When Bernadette shows up and asks for the gate code you give it to her in your best Hispanic accent."

William took Smith's phones out of his own pocket and put them on the computer desk. "What are the odds Palomino will call you again?"

Smith shook his head. "He probably won't, until he takes out Señora Covena."

"What about Bernadette? Think she'll call?"

Smith shrugged. "It's possible."

"If it rings, don't answer unless it's Bernadette."

William turned to Hal. "I'm going to have a quick look in the back."

Hal pulled a chair close to Smith. "Right. I'll be here."

There were six dormitory style rooms in the back and a central bathroom with an open shower area, also urinals and four stalls with toilets. William was looking for weapons and ammunition or anything that may be of use. He gathered up all the cell phones he found and dropped them into the toilets. Rejoining Hal in the day room, he looked at the hanging rack holding the AK-47 assault rifles on the south wall, and the slots containing the semi-automatic pistols. Three slots were empty, one for a rifle and two for the pistols.

William stepped over to Smith and spun his chair around and pointed at the weapons rack. "Where's the missing rifle and pistol?" he asked.

"Gomez must have them up on the summit, waiting for Bernadette. Palomino's stacking the deck. That's why there are only four men here."

"Right." William glanced at Hal. "You know, our best chance to rescue Annie is when Bernadette pulls up at the gate. The problem is, after we take Annie and neutralize Bernadette, Palomino is going to wonder why she didn't show, and he has a helicopter."

Hal pondered for a few seconds. "Yeah, I see your point. We got to do something about Palomino."

William nodded, gathering his thoughts. "Okay, we take Bernadette, tie her up, and I'll take her truck up to the summit along with the sniper rifle."

"Don't forget the guy that's already up there," Hal pointed out. "You're going to have to take him out, too. First, probably."

William nodded. "Yeah. There's no choice."

"Okay, but what do we do about Bernadette? How do we take her out of the equation?" After a few seconds, Hal spoke again. "Or maybe we don't. Maybe we go up to the summit, take out Gomez and Palomino, and then deal with Bernadette."

William nodded as a phone rang. It was Smith's.

"Who is it?" demanded William.

"Señora Covena," Smith told him after glancing at the screen.

"Answer it, put it on speaker."

Smith complied nervously. "This is Deke."

"Right." Bernadette sounded angry. "Plan B. I just got a call from Carbana Air Service. My ride's been hijacked. Esteban is on his way, flying the chopper himself. He'll be there at or around three, according to the flight plan. Meet me at the second pickup point at 19:30."

"Will do."

"Good. This is our last contact until I see you at the pickup."

"Understood."

The call disconnected. William spun Smith's chair around and pulled him face to face.

"What's Plan B?"

"Pickup on the coast."

"You obviously know where it is. How long will it take us to get there?"

Smith swallowed nervously, his eyes darting from William to Hal. "About two hours, maybe three, and then it's a hike for about half a mile and it's pretty rough. That's what will take time."

"Did you inform Palomino about Plan B?"

Smith emphatically shook his head. "No, no!"

William's icy stare bore into Smith's nervously blinking eyes. He pulled out Schrader's combat knife and held the tip under Smith's chin. The man sucked in his breath and froze. "This is not the time to lie to us," William warned.

"I'm not lying," Smith croaked.

William stared at Smith, the tip of the knife drawing a bead of blood. "So, you're saying Palomino doesn't know about Plan B?"

"Right."

William stared into Smith's fear filled eyes for another second before he put the knife away and turned to Hal. "That means we have to deal with a two-headed monster: Palomino and Bernadette. Or maybe we just focus all of our efforts on getting to Bernadette."

"Bad idea," Smith blurted.

"Why?" William asked.

"My guess is Palomino hasn't heard from Schrader. He has to assume you're not dead. That's too much of a loose end. He always eliminates loose ends."

Hal shook his head, leveling a perplexed look at Smith. "Damn. Whose side are you on?"

Smith's eyes flicked back and forth between his two captors. "Mine. I'm on my side. I want to get out of this alive. Seriously, Palomino will send someone to the States if he thinks you survived. He's not sure right now, but he won't stop until he knows. He's a son-of-a-bitch."

William stared at Smith for a few seconds before he turned to Hal. "What this shithead just told us is the truth. Palomino will come after us. We have to take him out."

Hal nodded. "I know, goddamnit. How do we do it?"

"Well," William said, sighing and glancing at his watch, "it's not a 'we' thing. I go up the mountain, hide and wait for the chopper. As soon as I leave, you and Mr. Smith hightail it toward the coast in his car. He can show us the pickup location on our map."

"And you'll follow?" Hal asked.

"Yeah, if I'm successful. You get away from here and find a place to stop and hide, about an hour from here. Again, Mr. Smith can show us where. If I'm successful—."

"If?"

"Yeah. If I'm successful I'll take that Range Rover in the garage and follow you."

"And if you're not successful?"

"Then it's up to you to rescue our granddaughter."

Hal rubbed his face. "Oh shit. That's not how it played out in my mind. Okay. Let's do it."

William glanced at the weapons on the wall. "Yeah. Ah, know anything about an AK-47?"

Hal nodded. "As a matter of fact, I do. A couple of years ago I shot one at a range in Wyoming, just 'cause I was curious."

"Good. I'm going to need the sniper rifle. That means you'll have to take one of those rifles and a few clips and one of those pistols, too. The rest we'll toss in the nearest hole or ditch."

"Okay," Hal said. "That takes care of the weapons. What about the tactics?"

"I'm open for any ideas."

"I was afraid you'd say that. Ah, maybe you go up there now, find a place to hide and dig in. If you see that hidden shooter, take him out. If not just wait for the chopper. Once you take him out, you've cut the head off the snake."

William nodded. "Works for me." He glanced at the clock on the wall. "We've got about two hours before Palomino gets here. I'll get ready and go up there. How about you wait an hour and go down the road to find a place to wait. We'll stay in touch by phone as much as we can."

"Along the coast there is no cell phone reception," Smith said.

Twenty minutes later Smith marked out the route to the coast on the map. "You might have to stop for gas," William said.

"There's a 500 gallon underground tank on the east side of this building," Smith volunteered. "There's a switch in the garage to turn on the pump."

"Okay," William said, looking at Hal. "Mr. Smith knows the way, so tie him in the driver's seat. He can drive you there. An hour out you let me know where you are. Leave the pump on in case I need to top off that Range Rover."

"Tell you what," Hal said. "I think we should fill both vehicles and position both for a fast exit, just inside the garage door. And maybe you can help me get him situated in the van before you go."

"Gentlemen," Smith said. "You won't have any trouble from me. Like I said, I want to get out of this alive and I'm one of those loose ends Palomino doesn't like."

William nodded. "We get it, but we're going to err on the side of caution."

The Range Rover's tank showed full and after filling the van, they parked both vehicles just inside the door, facing out. William counted the rounds he had for the sniper rifle and came up with 14. He slipped two extra 16-shot clips for the Sig Sauer pistol into the slots on the ammunition belt he found. After checking the zips ties and ropes on their prisoners, William helped tie Smith to the driver's seat of the van.

"I'm going to take one of those ATVs up the maintenance road. It's a long uphill slope and I don't want to walk and get there winded and tired," William told Hal. He reached into his pocket and put the satellite phone on vibrate. "I'll let you know when it's over. After I leave, wait an hour and get on the road."

Hal nodded. "Good luck. I'll see you down the road."

"Count on it." With a nod William turned and crossed the garage into the back storage room. Taking a key off a board on the wall, he opened the double doors on the east wall. The key fit into the first ATV.

THIRTY-EIGHT

According to the map in the day room, the maintenance road eventually hooked up with the main gravel road just before the parking area. William decided he would take the vehicle as far as he could as long as he had cover. That turned out to be about 10 yards from the gravel road. He had practically idled the ATV up the road to keep the engine noise low. Stopping next to a ledge along the maintenance road, he shut it down and set the brake. Peeking over the rocky ledge he surveyed what he could see of the south-facing slope. There was not much brush, but the slope was strewn with boulders.

William didn't expect to see anything of the shooter, he simply wanted to survey the terrain and find a spot near him where he could hide and still see the slope. Clumps of closely bunched low-growing grass to his left looked promising. Keeping his head still, he studied everything he could see by moving only his eyes. Nothing was moving, suggesting that an intruder had frightened away anything that had been there.

Getting to the clumps of grass meant about a 15-yard belly crawl. Looking through the binoculars, he studied every shape and shadow scrupulously for several long minutes. His patient scrutiny was rewarded with a slight movement. Something resembling the front part of a hiking boot appeared to the side of a large boulder, as if someone had stretched out a leg. The boulder was, he estimated, five yards from the top of the summit. From there anyone would have an unobstructed view of the parking area, which William couldn't see from his position. No matter, no one would be coming up the road and apparently the hidden ambusher didn't know that, otherwise he would have abandoned his post. Either he didn't have a phone or—no, that wasn't it. William had tossed all the phones he had found down the toilets. So, Gomez, probably the person behind the boulder, was likely wondering why no one was answering his calls.

William looked at the watch—90 minutes until the chopper arrived.

One reality could not be overlooked; nothing ever turned out the way it was supposed to. William was reasonably certain that Palomino would arrive in the chopper, but would he land and be an easy target? Bernadette's truck would not be in the parking area and that might cause some suspicion. Perhaps Palomino would not land and would decide to do an aerial observation and leave. However, given that his objective was to eliminate Bernadette, William was guessing that Palomino wouldn't leave until he knew where she was. The instant he realized she had countered his move and perhaps escaped, he would react.

But what would he do?

William ducked down behind the ledge, pulled out the satellite phone, and dialed his own cell phone, which he had left with Hal.

"What's happenin', Will?"

"Nothing, though I located the shooter," William said, keeping his voice low. "I have a question that needs answering. Ask our friend Smith if he knows what kind of helicopter Palomino is flying."

"Okay, will do."

William listened to the conversation on the other end, and clearly heard Smith's reply. "She's chartered from that company before, and it was always a French helicopter, a civilian version of a military chopper called the Gazelle. It's a four place and is painted bright yellow. That's all I know."

"You sure about that?" Hal asked, a warning in his tone.

"Yeah, yeah," Smith assured him. "She's friends with the guy who owns the charter company. He's the one, I'm guessing, who told her that Palomino took the chopper."

Hal got back on the phone to William. "Smith says it's a bright yellow French model."

"Yeah, I heard. I wouldn't know a French chopper from an American one, but I can recognize the color yellow. How about you head out now. Don't wait."

"Yeah, we could. Something you know that I don't?"

"No, just a feeling. Let me know when and where you stop."

"Right. We'll head out. You stay safe."

"Yeah. Talk to you later."

William disconnected the call and peeked over the ledge, planning his route to the clumps of grass. Any kind of camouflage clothing would have been helpful, but he was fortunate the sniper rifle was painted in a woodlands camouflage pattern with non-reflective paint in shades of gray, including the scope. He was also glad it was semi-automatic.

The clumps of low-growing grass would hide him from anyone looking down from the summit. But if that helicopter stayed at altitude or took a pass over the area, there was no hiding from it, even if he'd had camouflage clothing.

There was one possibility. He could take out the sniper and then take his place. Palomino knew his man would be on the slope, so a man hiding among the boulders would be expected. There were two immediate obstacles to that idea; the shooter was armed, and William had less than 90 minutes before Palomino arrived.

There was one other factor that was basically favorable. Gomez was not expecting anyone or anything but that helicopter.

To hide in plain sight was the answer to the problem, and that meant taking out the shooter. William knew how that had to be done. Go back down the maintenance road until he was out of sight from the summit and the shooter's position, then move up the eastern slope of the mountain, and after that approach the shooter from the north, across open ground. It was not without risk, but it was not impossible.

William tightened the rifle sling to keep the weapon from jostling about as he climbed. Keeping low, he started back down the slope on foot. When an intervening bend hid him from the shooter's vantage point, he shifted his direction to the east and up the slope.

Keeping a crouched position put a strain on his legs and he could feel his heart thudding. In a few minutes he was panting. The slope wasn't steep, but footing on the gravelly surface wasn't always solid. He paused several times until his heart rate slowed and then moved again. Just over 20 minutes after he started the climb, which was mostly a crawl, he gained the summit, guessing he was a little less than 100 yards from the shooter's position. He considered his next moves as he used his sleeves to wipe the sweat from his face and rested his shaky legs.

The sound of a gunshot wouldn't be a problem, but as he stood and moved across the mostly flat and occasionally undulating ground, he didn't like the crunching his hiking boots made. Sitting, he loosened the laces and slipped them off, taking off his socks as well and stuffing them into the boots. Tying the laces together, he draped the boots around his neck. Now as he moved ahead, he was in total silent mode. Emboldened, he walked toward the southern end of the summit, soon coming to a circular landing area marked with long red plastic streamers attached to short round poles embedded in the ground. On top of the poles were lights for night landings. The streamers emitted a soft rustling noise that masked his approach.

Beyond the marked landing area, which he estimated to have a diameter of 30 yards, was the edge and five yards or so below that was the shooter.

Drawing his pistol, he moved ahead one step at a time. The shooter was behind a boulder and obscured from view to anyone looking up the slope. Unless he had his back against another boulder, he should be visible from the top.

A few feet from the summit's edge, William noted the angle of the sun relative to where his shadow pointed. He was not casting a long shadow, which was one less worry. Boulders and sparse shrubbery came into view little by little as he inched forward. A quick glance at his watch indicated he had just over an hour before the chopper came.

More rocks and boulders and the gravelly surface of the down slope came into view as he eased forward, then a military style desert camouflaged boot. Another few inches forward and he saw an extended right leg and the left drawn up at the knee. The man was reclining against a low rock, a boonie hat on his head. A slow, careful move to the right brought a rifle into view, an AK-47. Then William saw the holstered pistol on the man's belt. The shooter was dressed in desert camouflaged battle dress utilities.

William took a deep breath and exhaled ever so slowly. There was enough of the man's torso in view that a killing shot was possible. Or he could shoot him in the leg and then try to disarm him. The latter was preferable, morally speaking. But nothing ever turns out the way it is supposed to.

Taking careful aim at the upper fleshy area of the man's right leg, William took in a breath and held it, and pulled the trigger.

BOOM! The sound of the pistol surprised him as he saw the man's leg jerk and a hand immediately grab for the wounded area. William jumped down the slope, landing 10 feet from the disoriented man. To his dismay, William saw the man's hand reaching for the holstered pistol on his belt.

"NO!" he yelled. "NO!"

For a second, he saw the man's confused and pain-glazed eyes as his right hand pulled the pistol from its holster.

BOOM! The second shot went into the center of the man's chest, causing him to jerk violently and then slump to the left.

William stifled a gag reflex. He knew the man was dead, nevertheless he took the pistol from where it had fallen to the ground. The AK-47 was still against a boulder. He avoided looking at the man's face, though in his mind's eye he could suddenly see any number of sightless, dead eyes staring. He looked around at the landscape that suddenly seemed more desolate. For a moment he was at a loss, not knowing what to do.

The dead man's body had to be hidden, somehow. William looked down the slope riddled with narrow gullies and fissures, not from one rain, but from eons of raindrops eroding the ground. There had to be a fissure deep enough to hide a body.

He stifled another gag reflex as he loosened the sling on the rifle and slipped it off over his head and leaned it against the boulder. He sat down to put his socks and boots on. Finished, he took the binoculars and panned the slope and thought he saw what he needed. A minute later he was dragging the body, thankful it was down the slope. About 30 yards later, he pushed the corpse into a deep and narrow cut. The angle of the slope was enough that no one would immediately see it from the summit.

Back at the man's hiding place, he covered the blood near the boulder with loose dirt and gravel-sized stones. Heart still pounding, he sat and reached for the satellite phone. Hal answered in two rings.

"How's it going?"

William cleared his throat. "Shooter is neutralized. Chopper should be here in about 45 minutes."

"Right. Are you okay?"

"Yeah, I'm okay."

"Good. Smith says we're about 40 miles from a little village called Sangria, and south of that is a roadside hostel. Says we can get a room there and we'll be out of sight."

"Okay but keep an eye on him."

"For damn sure."

William disconnected the call and took stock. He reached down and grabbed the boonie hat that had fallen off the dead man's head. This vantage point had a clear view of the graveled parking area below, marked off with a semi-circle of railroad ties. The trail up to the summit, a long series of wooden steps, was off to his left. But from the boulder he had no view of the landing area. For that he needed to be up a little higher. Standing, he looked around to make sure no one else was in the area, then hurried down to the maintenance road and to the ATV. Starting it, he drove it up to the parking area and left it, climbing the steps to the summit. His hope was that it would provide some assurance to Palomino.

If Palomino was coming to kill Bernadette, he would be armed, but with what? A long gun would not be as easy to get out of the chopper. If he had a handgun, it would likely be on his belt or lower on his leg. And was he left- or right-handed? And would he be alone?

If he landed, he would have to take several seconds to feather the blades and put the engine to idle and the gearbox in neutral. His hands would be occupied and so would his attention. That would be the time to rise up from cover, aim, and fire.

At short range it was sometimes tricky to put the crosshairs of a scope on a target, at least for him. The sniper rifle was a semi-automatic, one round each time he squeezed the trigger. His glance flicked to the AK-47; that weapon was a full automatic. Grabbing it he pulled out the clip, which was longer than normal. About 40 rounds, he guessed.

Perhaps the AK-47 was the answer. A long burst into the front of the cockpit should do the trick. Looking closer at the weapon, he found the safety and lifted the gun to his shoulder and aimed down the slope and above the boulders below. A short burst would help to familiarize him. He squeezed the trigger.

POP-POP-POP-POP-POP-POP-POP!

The barrel bucked up and to the left, as he knew it would. Switching on the safety he rose to his feet, thinking that a rehearsal of his movements would also be helpful. He studied the ground up to the summit. There was nothing there that might trip him or cause him to lose his footing unless it was his own nervousness. If he appeared from below the summit and waved while holding the rifle casually in his left hand, Palomino would not be alerted or alarmed. The safety would be off and he would only need to raise the weapon, take aim, and squeeze the trigger. William rehearsed all the movements, from standing, grabbing the rifle, taking three steps up the slope until his head and shoulders were level with the summit, switching off the safety, and then raising the rifle and taking aim. He went through the movements several times and decided on one final step; he would lay the sniper rifle down on the slope near where he would be standing so it would be available if he needed it.

William tried to find a comfortable position to sit against the boulder and relax. Stay loose. For a few moments he toyed with the notion of calling Jarod, and reluctantly decided against it. That might be too much of a distraction. A glance at his watch indicated he had about half an hour to wait. Suddenly he realized that he didn't know from which direction the chopper would be coming. He had been assuming from the north. Of one thing he was certain, the landing area was on the summit and the odds were that the chopper would touch down there. Or maybe it wouldn't land at all. There was simply no way to know, all he could do was react to the circumstances of the moment.

Killing a man at point blank range was not remotely on his mind when he and Hal had left Santa Rosa in the middle of the night. He knew it was all for a noble cause, at least to him and Hal, and that was getting their precious granddaughter back. But that didn't mean that the man at the bottom of the slope was righteously killed. Perhaps it was necessary but there was nothing righteous about it.

Maybe Palomino would not show up. Maybe someone in his organization had learned where Bernadette was going and he would be waiting there.

Doubt was beginning to nibble at the edges of common sense. Maybe he should get the hell off this mountain and follow Hal.

He heard the distant muffled *pop-pop* of a helicopter's blades. It was a sound he knew well, that almost made him physically ill.

Instinctively, William reached for the assault rifle.

THIRTY-NINE

Jarod and Marie waited just beyond the security exit of the customs terminal at Ministro Pistarini International Airport for Jennifer and Virginia. Mother and daughter came through the exit and separated themselves from the crowd, waving as they approached. After a brief reunion and warm hugs, Jarod took his wife's and mother-in-law's roller bags and somehow fit one atop the other.

Marie looked at Virginia. "How are you, dear?"

"Wrinkled and tired, and glad to see you two."

"Let's find a place to sit and catch up," Jarod suggested.

Fifteen minutes later they arrived at the main terminal and got a table in a restaurant with an American menu. Jennifer and Virginia were anxious for news, so Jarod caught them up with a summary of his latest conversation with his dad.

"I say we don't waste any time," Virginia said. "Let's rent a car and head for Santa Rosa. How far is that from here?"

"Several hours," Jarod said. "Are you sure you don't want to sleep a bit?"

Jennifer shook her head. "Mom and I already talked about it. We can sleep in the car."

"Okay," Jarod said. "We took a taxi here and we can take one to the hotel. There's a car rental company a few blocks from there."

"Good plan," Virginia said. "Any recent news from Hal and William?"

"Not in the past few hours. Dad called when they were heading south toward some place called Carnarones. Bernadette may be there or near there with Annie."

"I heard something in Dad's voice I'd never heard before," said Jarod, suddenly serious. "There was an edge, as if that Vietnam warrior was pushing through. And he said that Hal was holding his own. Never in my life did I think I would ever hear anything positive from my dad about Hal. All of that is good, as far as I'm concerned."

Virginia nodded and grabbed her son-in-law's hand. "Thank you. I don't suppose there's any chance of us calling them?"

"I've been thinking about that," Jarod said, glancing at his watch. "It's almost three. How about we grab a bite, either here or back at the hotel. And if we haven't heard from them by the time we have a car and are ready to roll, we give them a call."

Before Virginia could reply, Jarod's phone rang. Glancing at the screen, he nodded and answered.

"Hey, Dad."

"Hey, Jarod, it's Hal. I'm using your dad's phone. How are you?"

Jarod looked up at the expectant faces all staring at him in anticipation. "Good, I'm good. We all are, as a matter of fact. Mom and I just met Jen and Virginia at the airport. What's happening there?"

"Well, I'm about an hour ahead of your dad, driving south toward the coast to intercept Bernadette. I'm in a hostel waiting for your dad to catch up."

"Okay, good. Let me pass the phone to Virginia," Jarod said. "It's Hal."

Virginia took the phone. "Hello, dear. Are you okay?"

"For sure, now that I hear your voice. How's Jen?"

Virginia glanced at her daughter. "She's hanging in, we all are. I'll give her the phone in a minute. Can you tell me what's happening?" She could hear Hal taking a deep breath.

"Yeah, I'm in a hostel near a little town called Sangria, waiting for Will to catch up. He's back up there near Carnarones taking care of something. By sundown we should have some news for you all. We have some inside help and we're a few steps ahead of Bernadette. But listen, I want to save the battery in this phone because the charger doesn't fit down here."

"Okay, dear," Virginia said. "Do be careful. We'll talk to you later."

"Bye, Dad," Jennifer added. "We love you."

"Love you, too, hon."

Virginia looked at Jarod. "What do you suppose he meant by inside help?"

"I don't know, but I'm glad to hear it."

Hal looked over at Deke Smith, who was tied to a tall wooden chair in a corner of the room. He had bound the man's wrists behind the chair and his ankles to the front legs, after making him remove his socks and shoes. For added security, Hal had tied a rope around Smith's thighs and under the seat. If Smith tried to move, he would simply tip over.

A Sig Sauer pistol was in a holster clipped to Hal's belt and an AK-47 assault rifle and extra ammunition clips were hidden under a blanket in the van.

"I appreciate your help," Hal told Smith as he reclined against the wooden headboard of the bed. "That's why I let you use the toilet first. But I don't trust you. I'm in favor of turning you loose once we rescue our granddaughter and William might lean in that direction, too. We'll talk it over. Unless of course, you do something stupid between now and then."

"I'm on your side," Smith said.

"Yeah? Keep putting actions behind that and you just might get out of this alive."

Smith nodded.

Hal had been asleep for nearly half an hour when the cell phone woke him. He jerked to an upright position, pistol in hand. Smith was still in the chair. Hal pulled the phone out of his shirt pocket and looked at the caller ID.

It was William.

FORTY

Once he heard the approaching helicopter, it took about two minutes for William to feel the down wash of the rotors. The aircraft slowed but did not hover or touch down. Instead, it passed over in a southerly direction and then slowed and banked left at a distance of about 200 yards. William immediately lifted the binoculars and brought the bright yellow chopper within focus as it turned. A long, black pod attached to the left strut caught his attention. That pod had to be a light machine gun, probably a 30 caliber.

The chopper finished the turn and headed directly for the summit and William's position. He dropped the binoculars and grabbed Gomez's sunglasses and the boonie hat, putting both on in the next second, as a jumble of thoughts and impulses bounced in his head. Gomez was short and stocky and had short hair, so if William stood Palomino would notice immediately that he was not Gomez. He rose to a squat on one knee, making sure the rifle was within easy reach of his left hand. By then the chopper had come to a hover level with the summit. He estimated the distance at 40 yards, maybe less, but close enough to reveal that Palomino was wearing sunglasses with radio headphones over his ears.

William knew damn well Palomino was assessing the situation, probably suspicious that Bernadette's truck was not in the parking area, and likely with his finger on the button ready to fire that machine gun. He had to do something now while Palomino was still sizing up the situation.

William rose to an upright kneeling position with his left knee still on the ground, and while he waved with his left hand, grabbed the assault rifle with his right hand. Palomino did not wave back and William noticed that the chopper seemed to be rocking slightly, meaning it was not in autopilot hover. It was now or never.

His next move took only a second, but it felt like forever. Bringing the rifle up to his shoulder, he aimed and squeezed the trigger. William consciously pulled down on the rifle to keep it in line as he kept the trigger depressed. Strangely, he heard no muzzle blasts but he did see the chopper's windshield shattering.

He was right, the black tube on the strut was a machine gun and he saw the first muzzle flashes even as the aircraft dipped to the right as its nose bucked upward. The chopper turned on its side vertically with the bottom of its fuselage exposed. William stopped firing as he watched the craft do a slow turn toward the south even as it lost altitude. He heard the sound of crunching metal first and saw blade shards flying through the air, and then the WHOMP of an explosion followed by a bright flash. Three seconds later he felt the blast against his face, but it was no more than a sudden puff of air. Flames appeared and black smoke billowed upward as debris from the helicopter fell earthward. Through the binoculars, William saw that the rotors were gone and there was nothing recognizable as part of the sleek aircraft that had been hovering less than a minute ago, except perhaps the bright yellow paint.

Whatever threat Palomino had represented was gone, as far as William knew, unless the man had left instructions for someone else. He glanced down at his trembling hands and took a deep breath. It was time to go.

He took off the cap and tossed it, reached down for the sniper rifle, and walked toward the steps leading down to the parking area. He left the AK-47 where he had dropped it. He felt more like an observer than a participant as he started the ATV and turned it down the slope, using the gravel road. His mind raced in disbelief. In the space of an hour, he had killed two men. The black smoke in the valley behind him would attract someone's attention sooner or later.

Back at the garage he parked the ATV out of sight and found the keys to the Range Rover where he had left them under the driver's side mat. On the back seat were extra ammunition clips for the Sig Sauer and for a moment he wished he had not left the AK-47 on the mountain. William stood beside the car, mentally going over what he might need to take. Hurrying to the dayroom, he took several bottles of water from the refrigerator and stopped to take a long look at the men still bound and gagged. Walking to the car he tossed the bottles onto the back seat and pushed the button to open the garage door.

As he was about to get into the car, he paused. Taking out the combat knife he walked to the prisoners, noticing their fearful expressions upon seeing the knife in his hand. William leaned down and cut the choke rope between their ankles and throat. When he finished the last man, he knelt to the side where they could all see him.

"Hey," he said, "I know you understand me. I'll make this simple." He pointed to the Range Rover. "That's my car now. Do not follow me. If I see any of your faces anywhere, anytime, I'll kill you. Do you understand?"

They all nodded, still gagged.

"Good. Your boss Palomino is in a valley. His helicopter crashed and it's burning. Looks like you're all out of a job."

He stood and walked away without looking back. It would be awhile before any of them loosened the zip ties and got free. By then he would be long gone. Getting into the SUV he started it, put it in gear, and drove out the door. Away from the building, he felt as though a weight had lifted.

He stopped just short of the highway and pulled out the cell phone and dialed his own cell phone number. Hal answered, sounding sleepy.

"Hey, Will. Good to hear from you. How are things?"

"Looking up," William said. "Palomino is out of the way."

"No shit? That's damn good news! Are you on your way?"

"Yeah, just now."

"Okay, good. Just stay on that highway. There's no towns or nothing 'til you come to the little village called Sangria. There's a sign. Just south of there about two miles is this little hostel to the right by the road, it's painted blue. We're in room three. The van's parked out front. Should take you a little less than an hour."

"Right. See you then."

William disconnected the call and checked for traffic. He found the right button on the dash and zeroed out the trip odometer. He kept his speed low until he saw a blue sign that seemed to indicate that the speed limit was 40 kilometers per hour. Figuring out the cruise control function, he set it at 40 kilometers per hour. The last thing he needed was to be pulled over for speeding. Reaching back, he tucked his long braid under his shirt collar. He suddenly had a yearning to hear some good Lakota drumming and singing.

He kept his eyes on the road and checked the rearview mirrors frequently. Twenty miles into the drive he saw a vehicle that looked suspiciously like a police car with a thick light bar across the roof. He looked in the rearview mirror for its brake lights to come on, but nothing happened. Letting out a sigh of relief, he nonetheless checked the mirror more frequently.

William was getting tired at the 50-mile mark and his wounded shoulder throbbed. Yet he was more emotionally wrung out from the images in his head of a dead Gomez and the burning wreckage of a bright yellow helicopter than he was from his physical wounds. While those images would most certainly conjure up feelings of guilt, they were more than that. They were markers of success along the road on which he and Hal had embarked in their quest to recover Annie and return her to her family.

A village appeared beyond a rise and a sign announced the wide sprawl of low buildings as Sangria. Nothing and no one, except for a black dog, seemed to be moving as he slowed to pass through it. Two minutes later he spotted the hostel and Smith's white van.

Hal was relieved to see William and studied him closely as he sat in the other wooden chair.

"Can you tell me what happened?" he asked cautiously.

William nodded slowly and took a sip of water from one of the bottles he had carried in. "Well," he said, "the chopper showed up a few minutes early. It didn't land and the pilot was the only person in it. It had a machine gun mounted on the left strut. I fired, unloaded an entire clip from the AK. I got lucky. The chopper went down, crashed, and burned. Pilot didn't survive." He said nothing about Gomez.

Hal nodded and glanced at Smith. "Looks like you're out of a job," he commented wryly.

"Okay by me," Smith said.

"How far are we from the coast and that pickup point you were talking about?" William asked Smith.

"Less than an hour."

William looked at the watch. "It's just past 4:30," he pointed out. "You said a boat is coming ashore when?"

"7:30, just before sunset."

"Where do you think Bernadette is now?"

"I don't know, but she's somewhere close to the coast. Knowing her, she probably has another vehicle. There's no road to that part of the coast. There is a trail down to the shore, a crack through the rock formations, actually. It takes a while to walk it. From where it ends it's about 100 yards to the ocean."

"What else? There's something you're not telling us," William prodded.

Smith nodded. "Andujar, one of Bernadette's men."

Hal glanced at Smith and then at William.

"He is conspicuous by his absence," William said, keeping his eyes on Smith. "Where is he?"

"He's waiting for Bernadette," Smith told him. "Palomino's contingency move."

William pulled his chair closer to Smith. Reaching out he pulled the man's chin up, squeezing the sides of his throat. "Where exactly is Mr. Andujar?"

Smith swallowed. "He's somewhere at the end of the ledge trail."

"To kill her?" William's stare was relentless.

"Yeah."

"Why?"

"I'm guessing insurance. Palomino covers all the bases."

Hal slowly shook his head. "You know," he said to William while pointing to Smith. "I told this son-of-a-bitch we might let him live since he helped us. But I can't tell if he's telling the truth now. Could be a trick." He took a step toward Smith causing the man to gasp.

"Well, here's how I see it," William said. "He admitted the truth about Andujar because we hold all the cards now. Palomino is dead." He squeezed Smith's throat even harder, causing him to gag. "Any more surprises, Mr. Smith?"

"No, no," Smith rasped. "That's it." After William released the grip around his throat, Smith took several deep breaths.

"What are we going to do with this fucker?" Hal asked.

"Take him along. Bernadette is expecting him. She'll be looking for his white van." William stared again at Smith. "Where will she be waiting?"

"On the beach," Smith replied. "If Andujar doesn't take her out."

"Aw, shit!" Hal exploded. "That means Annie's in danger. I don't give a damn about Bernadette. How are we going to stop Andujar?"

"Well, maybe we don't. Maybe we catch up with Bernadette and stop her before she and Annie get to the beach."

Hal thought for a few seconds. "Yeah, yeah, that might work."

"What's at the trailhead?" William asked Smith.

"Just a parking area, an open area."

William looked at Hal. "Maybe if we get there before she does, we'll use him as bait," he said, pointing at Smith. "We'll hide and get the drop on her."

"There you go," Hal agreed. "That's how we'll do it."

William glanced at his watch again. "No time like the present. Let's get ready and go."

They reprised the same tactic that had successfully gotten them into Palomino's garage and surprised the security detail. Smith was securely tied in the driver's seat, still barefoot, while Hal and William sat in the back on the floor.

"What you do in the next few hours determines whether you get out of this situation with your balls still attached to your body," Hal said to Smith. "Any little screw-up and you're a eunuch. And believe me, I've cut off more than a few balls in my time, a hell of a lot bigger than yours."

"What he said," William added. "Get us there and don't speed."

Smith nodded, the safest response he could make.

Hal looked out the window as Smith pulled onto the highway. If all went well, they would come back for the SUV.

"This would be a damn beautiful place to visit," Hal observed, "if it weren't for this shitty mess."

"Yeah," William agreed. "But something tells me we aren't ever going to set foot in this country again."

"Okay by me, cause we're leaving here with our granddaughter and I don't give a damn how wide a swath we have to cut."

William chuckled. "Well, we've already left some wreckage behind, and it's not over yet."

"We'll get 'er done," Hal said. "We'll get 'er done."

William nodded, seeing again in his mind's eye the inert body of Gomez, and his dull, sightless eyes staring ahead.

FORTY-ONE

Fifty-three minutes later Smith turned off the highway onto a narrow country road that led toward the ocean, which they could see in the distance. The seacoast was an unfamiliar landscape to them and they could only assume that the ocean was farther away than it looked. They could see the watery horizon to the west.

"Damn," Hal said, "we're looking at the curve of the earth. It feels like looking at a hell of a long upward slope."

William pointed to the partly cloudy skies. "Hope that doesn't mean rain."

A few minutes later Smith turned right onto a more obscure road and parked in an open area. Nervously, he glanced at William. "I think Señora Covena is already here," he said, nodding toward the sedan parked 20 feet away.

"Shit," Hal said. "You think that's her?"

"I don't know," William said. "It looks empty, so let's check for footprints and see what we find."

William leaned across and took the key out of the ignition. Leaving Smith in the van they approached the older sedan. "If I wanted to blend in, I would have picked something like this," William commented.

A few feet from the passenger side Hal pointed to the ground. "Damn, look there."

Someone with small feet had gotten down from the passenger side and walked around to the front of the car. They followed and could see plainly where two sets of footprints, one large and one small, merged and headed in a southeasterly direction.

"It's them," Hal said.

William touched the hood of the car. "And not that long ago. This hood is still warm."

"They can't be far ahead of us." Hal pointed toward the van. "What do we do about him?"

"He'll slow us down or get in the way," William said. "Let's get our gear and head out and leave him."

William took the ignition coil connector out of the van and put the device in his pocket for insurance. Ignoring Smith, they took their weapons and followed the tracks. On a slight rise they knelt and glassed the area with binoculars.

"There!" Hal said excitedly. "About a quarter mile ahead. It's them. Annie looks so small." He passed the glass to William.

"Yeah, and they're carrying nothing. I'm thinking Bernadette is expecting Smith to show up, so she might wait somewhere." He pointed to the beginnings of a wide, rocky bench. "I'm guessing that's where the trail that Smith described starts. It's in a crevasse which appears to wind through the rocks. Once they reach there, they probably can't see what's coming behind. As soon as they get there, we need to hotfoot it and close the distance."

"Right."

William kept the binoculars on Bernadette and Annie. "Okay," he said. "They're behind that outcropping. Let's go."

Alternating between a fast walk and a jog, they paused to rest twice. After 15 minutes they gained the outcropping and could see where the long trail to the beach began. The trail wound through the rocky outcroppings like a dry creek.

"I think we sling these rifles across our backs as tight as we can," William advised, "and free up our hands. That crevasse looks really narrow in places and we need to go a little faster."

Several minutes later they had narrowed the gap. William saw them go out of sight around the next bend. A few minutes after they closed to within 30 yards. "I don't think we need to get any closer," William cautioned. "Bernadette might look back and spot us. We'll maintain this separation for now."

"And then what?"

"I think Smith said this trail is about half a mile. We've come about halfway. Let's keep going."

"Sure, but I'm worried that when they get to the beach, Andujar isn't going to waste any time getting off a shot. I'm guessing he'll wait until Bernadette and Annie get out in the open. If we're not close, there's nothing we can do."

William nodded solemnly. "Good point, I'm afraid you're right." He looked up at the side of the rock face. Just behind them was a narrow fissure. "I'll think I'll climb up and have a look."

A minute later William was 10 feet above the crevasse where the slope was less than 30 degrees, he estimated. With the binoculars he studied the outcropping above the crevasse. He thought he could see the end of it. Seconds later he spoke to Hal, keeping his voice low.

"Here's an idea," he said. "We both get up here because I think it's traversable. We might be able to get ahead of them without Bernadette seeing us."

William extended his hand and pulled Hal up the last couple of feet of the incline.

Footing was the main concern, especially where the slope was severe, but thankfully that was only in two areas. A couple of times they had to place their right hands on the slope to keep their balance, but it didn't impede progress. They moved fast when the slope was less severe and nearly level. When they stopped to rest, William crawled to the edge of the crevasse and looked south. They had gained significantly and were roughly 10 yards behind. He reported that to Hal, who was kneeling and catching his breath.

"Tell you what," he said, "when I get home I'm going to walk and exercise a hell of a lot more."

"You and me both," William agreed, as he surveyed the terrain ahead through the binoculars. "The good news is there's a gentle slope ahead, I'm guessing about where the trail ends. The bad news is, I don't know how we stop Annie and Bernadette."

Hal motioned for the glasses and took his turn studying the terrain ahead. "Well," he said, "you're a heck of a lot more agile than I am. So, you stay with them and I'll go on ahead to that flat area up ahead and maybe I can find where Andujar is hiding. If I see him, I'll take a shot.

William nodded. "I'll try to get ahead of them and then figure out what to do."

Hal stood and then turned back to William, reaching out his hand. "We've come this far," he said, "and we can do it. I'm aching all over, but we got to do this, for Annie."

William stood and took Hal's hand. "Me too. I'm hurting, too. But this is for Annie."

Following the undulating rocky rim, he stayed away from the edge, at least beyond the line of sight Bernadette would have if she looked up. In the distance, he could see Hal carefully working his way up a rough slope. Minding his own footing, he kept moving, but stopped when he heard a voice. Words were not discernible, but it was Bernadette's voice. He resumed moving, stepping carefully to avoid loose rocks or anything that would make noise.

William paused after he noticed Hal go from a low crouch to a crawl on hands and knees to on his stomach. With the binoculars he watched Hal unsling the sniper rifle and settle in behind a ledge, using the scope to scan the area ahead and below him. It was time to make some kind of a move.

FORTY-TWO

With the barrel resting on a low finger of rock, Hal slowly probed the rock-strewn beach looking for Andujar, the man in the black jacket. The boulders and rocks below the nearly vertical rock wall, many the size of couches and beds, were good cover for a sniper with a rifle. That led Hal to conclude that Black Jacket was hiding closer to the cliff wall. He guessed the shooter had positioned himself to have a clear view of the end of the ledge trail. The second Bernadette and Annie appeared, he would open fire unless, of course, William could somehow intervene and stop them.

"God," he said under his breath. "I know I'm the last person you'll likely listen to, but please, all we're trying to do is save a precious little girl."

William loosened the rifle sling and slipped it over his head, carefully putting the rifle down; then climbed down through the wide fissure and down onto the trail. The crevasse was not as wide nearer to the beach and the walls were more vertical with fewer fissures. Bernadette and Annie went around a bend directly ahead, no more than five yards away. He paused for a second until they were completely out of sight and then hurried forward. He could hear Bernadette's voice come clearly, saying "Annie, you wait here while I look ahead to make sure the trail is clear. I'll be back shortly."

William didn't hear a reply. This was the turn of luck he had been hoping for. Waiting only a second more, he scooted ahead, sidestepping with his chest against the crevasse wall. Poking his head around a sharp bend, he saw Annie with her back to him—five feet away.

He leaned around the bend and whispered as loudly as he could. "*Takoja* (Granddaughter)!"

Her head turned slightly.

"*Takoja!*" he whispered once again.

Annie turned. Her eyes grew wide. William leaned out more to give her a good view and put a finger up to his lips as he closed the distance, leaned down, and put his strong arm around her shoulders.

"Come on," he whispered, as she started to slump against him like a baby wanting a snuggle. "We have to get out of here."

She nodded, straightening up and suddenly alert. William led her back to the fissure, holding tightly to her hand. Pointing up he lifted her up to the crack. "Climb up, hon," he told her. "There's a flat spot and a rifle."

"Annie!"

Bernadette appeared from behind the bend and called out again. "Annie!"

William looked up. "Lay down," he told Annie. "Lay flat. I'll be right back."

If he scrambled up the fissure, Bernadette would spot him. There was only one choice. Drawing the pistol, he shifted it to his left hand and waited.

"Annie! Where are you?" There was a frantic edge in Bernadette's voice.

William pointed his pistol at Bernadette as she appeared from behind the bend and she froze. After a second or two, recognition filtered into her eyes.

"You! What are you doing here?"

"Pointing a gun at you. Keep your hands where I can see them."

Bernadette's expression indicated she was weighing her options as she stood facing the rock wall. William saw the bulge on her coat at her right hip indicating a weapon on her belt. "What do we do now?" she asked calmly.

"Hal and I are leaving with our granddaughter. You can go to hell."

"I won't stop you," she said. "I need to leave, too."

"So I understand. You have a boat to catch to Spain."

Bernadette's eyes widened. "You have me at a disadvantage."

"No, I have your man Smith. He spilled his guts. Well, I guess he was really Palomino's man."

"What else do you know?"

"I know that your former boss is at the bottom of a ravine in the burning wreckage of a yellow helicopter. I know that another man you trusted is waiting for you somewhere up ahead."

"Who?"

"Andujar."

"Indeed. There's only one thing that concerns me now. I need to leave, so I'm going to the beach. You can shoot me if you like."

"As long as I don't see you going for that gun on your belt, I won't shoot. But I have no idea where Andujar is hiding."

She smiled. "That's not your problem."

In the next instant Bernadette was gone, and she still had her gun. William climbed up through the fissure to join Annie. She jumped up and into his arms with tears in her eyes. He held her to him. It felt like a dream, but he knew it was real because he could smell the freshness of her hair.

Taku skan skan wakan, he said in his mind (All that moves and is holy), *wopila cicu yelo* (I give you thanks).

"You know what?" he said, still hanging on to her. "Grandpa Hal is here too."

"He is?"

"Yeah. Let's go find him."

Then they heard the gunfire from beyond the end of the trail, two shots that sounded like one.

BOOMBOOM!

FORTY-THREE

As soon as she ducked away from William, Bernadette worked her way along the trail. She hadn't anticipated that Estancio Andujar was a turncoat. So be it.

She took off her long coat and left it on the rock. Andujar had to be somewhere against the cliff face, behind one of the large boulders. Staying behind a low rock ledge, she called out.

"Estancio! I know you're up there. I know why you are here! I'll give you one chance to talk!"

She waited and watched, looking from one boulder to another. In a moment there was movement.

Andujar waved first and then slowly stood. Bernadette reciprocated and took two steps to exit the cover of the crevasse.

Andujar carried a rifle with a scope in the crook of his left arm. In another moment he started down the slope, walking carefully on the steep grade until he came to a wide, sandy patch. In addition to the rifle, Bernadette saw a holstered pistol on his belt.

"What are you doing here?"

"I have message for you, Señora."

"You could have called me."

"Yes, yes. But I am happy to give you the message in person." Andujar walked slowly until he was within 20 yards. He stared at Bernadette, his expression no longer that of an employee.

The boat was waiting just off-shore to take her to a ship, and then to Spain. First, she had to remove this obstacle. Bernadette affected an affable expression as she moved to her left.

Andujar had the tactical advantage because he was up slope, about five feet above her in elevation. She would need to lift her pistol higher and that would take a split second longer.

"What's the message, Estancio?"

"Just one word, Señora. *Adios.* Good-bye."

Bernadette smiled to hide her nervousness while staying aware of where Andujar's right hand was, resting on the stock of the AR-15.

"I see. And who is the message from?"

"I think you know, Señora."

"Yes, yes, I do. But I never figured you for a turncoat, Estancio."

"I know where the power is," he replied. "You had it, but no more. It is all different now."

"Then there is nothing to talk about!"

"There is respect," he countered.

"What do you mean?"

"You always treat me fair. You always treat me like a man, and for that I respect you."

"I am glad to hear that. Now I have news for you. The man who asked you to give me that message is dead, tangled up with the wreckage of a helicopter, just north of his new *hacienda.*"

"I do not believe you."

"I don't care. I thought you should know that before you die."

Bernadette's arms were at her side, her right hand below the Sig Sauer in its quick-draw holsters. It would take her a second to draw and take a shot.

"Put down the rifle, Estancio. If you say you respect me, let's make it a fair contest."

"I give you respect now," Andujar said. "I put down rifle and we face each other, like old American West. Fast draw, right?"

"You're crazy," she said.

"It is a crazy world, Señora. We are in a crazy business, no?"

Bernadette watched as he wrapped his left hand around the rifle's grip, and then he slowly lowered it, bending his knees as he did. Smart move on his part, she thought, reducing his target profile by making himself smaller. She figured his right hand was on or near the handle of his pistol.

While he was supporting his body weight on his knees, she drew and snapped off a shot. BOOM!

Andujar's body jerked backward and she heard the BOOM the instant she felt the heavy punch in her abdomen. She had aimed for the base of his throat, assuming that he was wearing body armor. Any sense of victory, relief, or satisfaction was obliterated. She was not wearing body armor.

When William heard the nearly simultaneous shots, he froze, listening hard for other noises.

"Grandpa! What happened?"

"I don't know. Wait here, I'll go see." He climbed down through the crack in the rock and carefully worked his way to the end of crevasse and saw where it ended in the sand off the beach. He saw Bernadette's coat on the ground. Ducking down, he peeked around the outcropping and saw Bernadette on the sand, on her back. He heard a noise behind him, just as he heard a moan from Bernadette.

"Is it her, Grandpa? Is it Bernadette?"

"Yeah. She's hurt."

"We should help her!"

"We have to get away. We need to find Grandpa Hal."

Her eyes were wide with concern. "But she's hurt, we should help her."

William was an instant away from taking her and starting back up the trail but was struck by the pity in her eyes.

"Why do you want to help her?"

Tears filled Annie's eyes. "She was good to me, and she's just a sad lady, Grandpa."

"Okay. I'll go look. You wait here. I'll be right back."

"Okay."

William looked back to make sure she stayed and hurried to the injured woman. Bernadette was clutching at her abdomen, her chest heaving slightly. Yards away he saw Andujar on the ground, either seriously wounded or dead.

Bernadette turned her head.

"Easy! Easy!" he cautioned, noting the blood oozing up between the fingers of her hand. The pain in her eyes was like a veil.

"You!"

"Yeah, it's me."

She nodded, gritting her teeth against the pain.

William heard a scuffling behind him. "You have to help her, Grandpa," Annie pleaded.

He turned and caught her before she could get any closer. "I'm afraid I can't help her, my girl. She's too badly hurt."

Bernadette turned her head toward Annie.

"Annie," she said, her voice weak. "Go with your grandfather. Get away from here. Go, go, and have a good life, Annie." Bernadette's smile faded as the light went out in her eyes.

Annie took a deep breath and hugged her grandfather. "She was nice to me, Grandpa."

"Yes, I understand. But she told us to leave. We have to go."

Hal had been carefully crossing the rocky landscape after he left William. He had spotted the man in a black jacket the moment he emerged from behind a boulder, about 60 yards to the south and below him. He put the red dot in the scope on the man's left shoulder. Strangely, Black Jacket had a rifle in the crook of his arm and seemed to be talking. Then Hal saw a second figure emerge from the edge of the rocky outcropping—Bernadette.

There was no way to hear the conversation that seemed to be going on. After a few moments Andujar slowly put down his rifle. Hal adjusted his position. He knew what he had to do. He had to take Andujar out, eliminate the threat to Annie. He lowered the dot to the man's left hip. *Dear God, please forgive me.*

Movement was a blur in the circle of the scope. Hal saw Andujar convulse and jerk backward as he was pointing his pistol—then he heard the BOOMBOOM of two shots. Andujar was down.

Swinging the scope to the left, Hal saw that Bernadette was down as well, and then William appeared—and then Annie! They were kneeling over Bernadette. It was over. Annie was with William. Hal felt his heart pounding. A split second later he saw movement in the corner of his eye.

He swung the scope to the right and saw Andujar rise to a kneeling position, pistol in hand and pointing at William and Annie. In the next second he put the red dot in the scope on the man's face and squeezed the trigger.

As William stood to pick Annie up, a slight turn of his head showed Andujar pulling himself to a knee, pulling up his pistol, and aiming it at them. He turned and pushed Annie down and shielded her.

CRACK! William knew the shot hadn't come from Andujar. Cautiously he turned his head. Andujar was down and there was only silence and Annie's wide-eyed expression.

"Are you okay?"

She nodded.

"Stay down, don't move," he said.

William rose cautiously and looked toward Andujar's crumpled body. There was a hole in his left temple and both of his hands were empty. The pistol had fallen several feet away. William hurried to the body and saw the exit wound on the right side of his face, about the size of a golf ball.

"Are you guys okay?" he heard Hal call out.

William waved and watched Hal moving slowly down the rocky slope. Hal had taken out Andujar.

William walked over to Annie. "Grandpa Hal is coming. He'll be here in a minute."

Hal stepped onto the sand, stopped for an instant to glance at Andujar, then walked to William and Annie.

"Thanks," William said. "You okay?"

"I am now," Hal said, gazing at Annie. "It's so good to see you, darlin'."

Annie jumped into her grandfather's embrace. William wouldn't have guessed that Hal Lamar was capable of crying, but the tears slid down his face as he clung to his granddaughter. After a minute he lowered her to the sand and knelt to look in her face.

"Are you okay, hon?"

She nodded. "I'm okay, Grandpa."

Hal caressed her face. "Well, the three of us have a lot of catching up to do." He looked up at William. "I think it's time to leave this place."

"The sooner the better, but just one more thing." William stepped over to pick up Bernadette's coat and cover her with it, drawing it over her face, then rejoined Hal and Annie. "We've got a long walk back along that trail. We'll take it slow."

Annie nodded. With tear-filled eyes she looked at her grandfathers. "I knew you would come," she said, looking from one to the other. "I knew you would come."

"Hey, that's what grandpas are for," William said.

"That's for sure," Hal added. "Come on, let's get the heck out of here. It's going to get dark soon."

"Oh, and one more thing," William added. "Your mom and dad and your grandmas are here. When we find cell phone service, how about we give them a call?"

Annie covered her mouth, her eyes brimming with tears, and nodded happily. Her expression changed instantly after she glanced toward Bernadette's covered body. "She was good to me," she said softly. "She took me to the doctor because she was afraid I was sick. Am I sick, Grandpa?" she asked, looking up at William.

He glanced toward Hal who nodded. "She's got a right to know," he said.

William took her small hands in his. "Honey, remember the tests that Dr. Cline did for you, at home?"

She nodded. "Yeah."

"Well, those tests, ah, showed that you have a sickness."

She looked worried but not frightened. "What kind of sickness?"

"It's called childhood leukemia."

"But the good thing is, my girl," Hal said tenderly, "the doctor caught it early so he can treat it and make it go away."

Annie nodded, processing the information.

"And—Grandpa Henry sent along some medicine with us that will help, too," added William. It's in my pocket," he said, patting it.

"It'll be okay," Hal said. "I promise."

Annie nodded. She had never heard either of her grandfathers talk and act like they were about to cry. But if they said it would be okay, then it would be okay.

There were a couple of things that bothered her though. She pointed to the long scab on Hal's face and the dried blood on William's shoulder. "What happened?" she asked.

"Oh, just grandpa scars," Hal said. "We'll tell you later."

FORTY-FOUR

They beat the deep dusk back to the parking area. The van was still there and Smith was still in it. William opened the door and saw the bruises on the man's ankles and wrists. Smith had obviously tried mightily to break free of his bonds. William reached in and retrieved his backpack.

Smith regarded them with an expression of relief mixed with dread and anticipation. The cowboy and the Indian had returned with their granddaughter. Incredibly, two old men had bested both Palomino and Bernadette Covena, not to mention Estancio Andujar. They looked tired but not as angry, a good sign for him, Smith hoped.

Annie stepped to the side and looked dispassionately at Smith as he was thanking his lucky stars he had not mistreated or spoken harshly to the girl. He wondered if that would be in his favor. He gasped when William pulled out the combat knife.

Hal was checking out the small dark sedan.

"Mr. Smith," William said. "This is where we part ways. We can't say it's been a pleasure by any stretch and if we never see you again it will be too soon—if you get my drift."

"You won't ever see me again," he promised. "Where's the Señora?"

William's eyes turned cold. "She and your friend Andujar are on the beach. They shot each other. You're a free man, it looks like."

Nearby they all heard the sedan start and run briefly before Hal shut it down.

Smith froze in fear when William reached in and sliced through the ropes. Hal approached and stood beside the girl. "That car runs just fine," he said, nodding toward the sedan. "I say we take it back to that hostel and then take the SUV from there."

William nodded. "Good idea," he said, reaching into his front trouser pocket and pulling out the van key and the ignition coil connector. "Goodbye, Mr. Smith," he said.

A minute later the van was headed north and was soon out of sight.

"What do you think will happen to him?" Hal wondered.

William shrugged. "Depends on who's left in that cartel, but I'll bet someone will be looking for him."

Night was falling as they arrived at the hostel. William paid the clerk for another night and asked for hot water to steep the medicine for Annie.

"Ah, *por favor*," he said. "*Agua caliente*, ah, for *medicina*. Tea, *te*."

The small elderly woman nodded and smiled. "*Si*," she said. "I bring to room."

"*Gracias*."

"*De nada*."

As he was about to leave, he smelled something delicious and then noticed the handwritten menu tacked to the wall. The only word he recognized was *Tamales*. He pointed. "Ah, Señora," he said, hesitantly. "Can we have six, ah—*seis tamales*?"

"*Si*, I bring."

A pot of hot water, three cups, and three plates of tamales with beans, rice, and corn tortillas as well as utensils on a wooden tray was delivered 20 minutes later. Hal gave the woman a wad of bills in spite of her protest that it was too much. Remembering Uncle Henry's direction, William was about to put half a handful of the dried and crushed leaves into the pot but stopped.

"We have nothing to put it in to take with us," he said, mostly to himself. "Uncle Henry said two cups a day."

"Can you make just one cup?" Hal asked.

"Yeah, good idea. And I'll make one for the morning. We'll be in Santa Rosa by this time tomorrow.

"Speaking of which, shouldn't we call and give them the good news?" Hal asked.

"Go for it," William agreed.

He handed the phone to Annie. "I'm going to put two cups of your medicine tea to steep. In the meantime, call your folks. Your dad's number is in the contacts."

Annie's eyes lit up as she grabbed the phone.

"Hello, Dad?" Jarod answered.

Overcome with emotion at the sound of her father's voice, Annie brought a hand up to her mouth and finally allowed herself to sob.

"Hello, Dad? Are you there?" Jarod said.

"Dad, it's me, Annie," she choked out.

"What? Oh, my god! Annie! Is it really you?"

"It's really me, Dad. I'm with my grandpas."

Annie heard an eruption of sound in the background, an excited and happy mixture of her grandmothers' voices mixing with her mother's voice.

"Honey! Are you okay?" her dad asked.

"I'm okay, Daddy. How are you?"

"I'm happy, really happy to hear your voice. Listen, here's Mom!"

Annie waited, smiling up at her grandfathers. They could all hear the mingling of excited voices through the phone.

"Annie?" Jennifer nearly shouted. "My darling, my darling, baby! Are you okay?"

"I'm okay. I'm here with Grandpa William and Grandpa Hal. Put me on speaker, Mom."

"Okay, you're on, everyone can hear you."

"Honey!" Virginia said. "Where are you guys?"

"Um, in some little town. I don't know what it's called. We're going to sleep here."

"My girl!" Marie chimed in. "It's so good to hear your voice!"

"Hi, Grandma! It's good to hear you, too."

"Check the battery," William said.

Annie nodded. "Just a sec, everyone. I'm checking the phone battery." She looked quickly at the power indicator. "Six percent," she said to William.

William leaned in close. "Hey, guys? We might have to cut this short, the battery's low, and we don't have adaptors for our charger."

"Not to worry," Virginia said. "We're just overjoyed that you're all okay."

"Where are you?" Hal asked, stepping in close.

"At the Three Sisters Hotel in Santa Rosa. The sign is in Spanish, *Tres Hermanas*," Jarod said.

"Okay," William said. "We'll get an early start. I think it's about a 12-hour drive. Our vehicle might have our kind of charging ports in it. But if you don't hear from us, we'll be there."

Happy goodbyes were said as the call was disconnected. William was about to go out to the Range Rover to have a look at the charging ports when a soft knock came at the door. Both men froze instantly, hands going to their pistols.

"Señors," came a soft voice through the door. William recognized it as the woman who had brought their food. He stepped over and opened the door. With the woman was a younger woman and they were carrying a small circular table and another wooden chair.

"My grandma thought you would need these," the younger woman said in flawless English.

"That's very thoughtful," William said, as he and Hal took the furniture and brought them in. "Thank you, again. *Mucho gracias.*"

"*De nada,*" the older woman said, smiling demurely.

"Ah, could you tell us your names?" William asked.

"Yes, this is my grandma, Blanche, and I'm Katie."

"We're pleased to meet you." He pointed to Hal, "This is Hal, I'm William, and this is our granddaughter, Annie. Again, thank you."

"You are most welcome. *Buenas noches.*"

After the women left, they placed the table in the space between the bed and the corner and arranged the chairs around it. William gave Annie a cup of the medicinal tea.

"Grandpa Henry said it would be bitter, so just sip it a little at a time."

Nodding, she took a sip, and wrinkled her nose. "It is bitter," she said, but like the trooper she was, she soon had it all gone.

"I'm going to remember this meal for the rest of my life," Hal said.

"You and me, both," William agreed.

Annie smiled and attacked her food.

They gave Annie the bed and Hal slept on the floor at the foot of it, while William found a space in the corner of the room under the window. Annie slept like a log, although her grandfathers awoke at each creak in the room or sound outside.

They let Annie sleep as they took turns taking sponge baths in the small bathroom, because there was no shower and the bathtub was tiny. Annie did take a bath after she awoke. As they were gathering their gear, they saw Katie through the window and then heard a knock at the door. William opened the door.

The young woman was carrying another wooden tray, this time with three bowls of oatmeal, a container of honey, and sopapillas. Also on the tray was a paper bag.

"Grandma went to mass this morning," Katie said, "but she left instructions to fix you breakfast. I'll take the other tray."

"Thank you," Hal said, "how much do we owe you?"

"Nothing," Katie replied. "It's a gift from us, my grandma and me. We don't have many travelers like you stop here." She passed the tray to William and picked up the other, pointing to the paper bag. "There are taquitos in there, for the road."

"That's very kind, young lady. We'll never forget you or your grandma." Hal said.

"Thank you," she said, pausing in the doorway. "*Vaya con Dios.*"

"And to you and your grandma as well," Hal said, so emotional his voice almost quivered. After all they had been through, he was grateful to be treated so kindly by strangers.

"Thank you," Annie said, waving at the young woman, who turned away with a smile.

They sat down to their breakfast and Annie drank her morning cup of medicinal tea. "You know," Hal said, reaching into his pocket. "We have some cash left over. However much it is, I think we leave it here for Katie and her grandma. We'll be okay, we have our credit cards."

"Let's do it," William agreed, and wedged about $500 worth of pesos into an empty glass.

Taking a last look at the small room, they closed the door gently and walked to the Range Rover.

FORTY-FIVE

Dark thoughts and harsh images whirled in William's head as he drove. Annie was asleep, her seatback reclined. He heard stirrings in the back as Hal pushed himself up to a sitting position after sleeping for the last three hours.

"How's our girl?" he asked in a raspy voice.

"She's been sleeping, too."

"Good, good. Where are we?"

"Just stopped in a town for gas. We're still near the coast and we've gone at least 200 miles, so that's about 320-something kilometers, I think."

"Damn, that's good. How far from Santa Rosa?"

William handed the bag of taquitos to Hal. "They're delicious. I had a couple. I have some water up here, too. I think we've got about eight hours to go."

"Thanks. Feeling okay? Want me to take over?"

"Oh, I think I'm good for another hour, about the time we all need a pee break."

"How's your shoulder?" Hal asked.

"Down to a dull throb."

Forty-five minutes later William pulled off at a roadside rest stop. They both waited outside the one that said *Bano de Mujeres* until Annie came out, and she waited with Hal until William used the men's room, and then with William when Hal went in. None of them were letting each other out of their sight.

While in the toilet William had unbuttoned his shirt and checked his bandages, surprised and pleased that very little blood had soaked through, which belied the persistent hot throbbing.

Hal insisted on driving and William laid down in the back seat. "Just remember, speed limit is 90 kilometers an hour," he advised.

"Got it. Your turn to get some sleep," he said over his shoulder as they got back on the road. He winked at Annie. "We got this, don't we, my girl?"

"We do," she replied cheerfully.

An overcast sky caught up with them while William was asleep and two hours later Hal pulled over at a row of roadside vendors near another rest stop. After a bathroom break, they bought beef shish kabobs from one of the vendors, along with a small loaf of bread. Hal insisted he had another good hour in him and they resumed their journey toward the closest thing to home—their wives and children, and Annie's grandmothers and parents.

William was driving while Hal and Annie slept, when he recognized the southern outskirts of Santa Rosa. It was nearly seven in the evening.

Hal awoke as they pulled into the hotel parking lot. "Are we there yet?" he asked.

"We made it." William parked and touched Annie's shoulder and pointed to the hotel. "Your momma and daddy and your grandmas are in there."

She looked, her eyes bright and glistening.

"We can't forget to make your medicine. We'll do that inside. Twice a day, according to Grandpa Henry. We might forget once the excitement starts."

Seconds after Hal tapped on the door to room 23, it flew open with a frenzy of joyful noise and activity. As Annie sat with her parents on the couch, cradled between them, William and Hal rested at the counter in the galley kitchen, tired but happy.

"What happened to your face?" Virginia gently asked Hal.

"Just a scratch," he said, in a low voice.

"Right. I think there's more to it than just a scratch." She glanced at William. "And you, that's more than a scratch on your shoulder."

William nodded.

Marie joined Virginia at the counter. "What happened?" she said to William. "Are you okay?"

"Yeah, just a little tired."

Virginia and Marie turned to the two men.

"Okay," Virginia said, firmly. "Fess up. What happened?"

Hal and William glanced at one another.

"First of all," Hal said, "we're okay, hurting bit, but we'll live, and we probably should see a doctor."

"Yeah," William added. "We're good. There was sort of a dust up with a bad guy."

"A dust up? What does that mean? That doesn't tell us anything," Virginia insisted.

Hal and William exchanged looks again. William nodded.

"Ah, there was a sniper, but he missed, mostly. We were lucky. The important thing is our granddaughter's back with us. I think there's time to talk about it later."

"I think the two of you should have medical attention," Marie said.

"Absolutely," Virginia agreed.

"So, you were both shot?" Jarod asked, walking over.

Hal nodded, glancing cautiously at Annie. "We can talk about that later."

Virginia touched the long scab on Hal's left cheek. It was a quarter inch wide from front to back and three inches long from just below his cheekbone to his ear lobe. "That's the biggest scratch I've ever seen," she said, putting her arms around him.

"Well, I think these two old goats need some rest," said Marie. "How about we find some dinner and then take both of them to a doctor?"

"I'll see where there's a clinic," Jarod said.

Jennifer and Annie joined the crowd. Jennifer tearfully hugged her father and father-in-law. "Thank you," she said, her voice choking with emotion. "We'll never be able to repay you."

"That's not what it's about," her father said. "We're just trying to be good grandpas."

"That's it and that's all," William said.

Virginia and Marie tried to encompass all of their family in a group hug.

"As excited as we all are, Annie and her grandpas have had a long haul. They need food, and then some rest."

"There's just one more thing," William said, taking the bag of medicine out of his pocket, and holding it out to Jennifer. "This is the medicine from Uncle Henry. Boil water and steep half a handful, once in the morning and once in the evening. She had a cup this morning."

After more hugs, the grandpas and grandmas left the room to Annie and her parents.

In their own room, Marie turned into a drill sergeant. "Okay, mister, take that shirt off," she directed William. A bit more blood had seeped onto the makeshift bandages and through the t-shirt from both wounds. William winced as he pulled off the undershirt and again when Marie peeled off the bandages. She pointed to the bed, pulling over two pillows for him to put under his head. "There," she said, "on your side. I want to take a close look."

A few seconds later as she leaned in close to look at the wounds. "The hole in your back is smaller and the one in front is larger. I'm guessing the bigger one is the exit wound. My God, what the heck happened?"

He decided this was not the time to be flippant. "It's from three days ago," he said. "Like we said, a sniper, but he wasn't exactly on target."

"The shoulder was scabbing over until I pulled off the bandage and now it's bleeding a little," she said. "Sorry."

"No worries," he said, "a little bleeding is okay."

"There are so many thoughts in my head. Part of me is angry, part of me is in disbelief."

"We have our girl back. That's the main thing," he said.

"Of course, but I see a look in your eyes I haven't seen in, oh, 50-some years. Should we worry about that?"

William looked up at Marie. "You helped me through it the first time. I think it'll be okay."

A warm and loving smile spread over her face. "No worries, we'll do it again if we have to."

He reached up and caressed her cheek. "Annie's across the hall with her momma and daddy. That's really good medicine. We'll get her home and get her started on her treatment. It will be okay."

Marie wiped her eyes. "It's like she was born again," she said, and returned her attention to the slightly bleeding wound. "Well, I'm going to clean that and put real bandages on. I know your tetanus shot is up to date, but you need antibiotics. I'm surprised you don't have a fever."

"No time for that," said William, allowing her to tend to him.

In Room 21, Hal willingly endured his wife's scrutiny as she looked closely again at the "scratch" on his face. "Someday I hope you'll tell me exactly what happened."

"I got shot by a sniper. He missed his mark by two inches," he said.

"Really? Doesn't look like it to me."

"Well, two or three inches to the right…"

Her worried eyes studied his face. "Thank God he was off target."

"Exactly. But, you know, it might be good if we can get together with William and Marie, and he and I can tell you what happened together. I only want to tell the story once," he said, "and then move on."

"I've been with you for many years," Virginia said. "I know how to wait til you're ready to tell me something."

In Room 23, Annie was dressed in new pajamas and lay between her parents. She had just had a shower and her hair was still wrapped in a bath towel. Neither parent could take their eyes off her.

"This is exactly like the first time we brought you home," Jennifer told her. "You were in between us on the bed all wrapped up."

They had agreed that the talk they would have with her about her illness would wait for a day or two, not knowing that her grandfathers had told her. Jennifer noticed with a sense of relief that Annie's color was good. Her cheeks were actually rosy.

"Can we take Grandpa Hal and Grandpa William to the doctor tomorrow?" she asked.

"Yeah," Jarod said, "whether they want to go or not.

"Good," she said, a serious expression on her face. "Now I have a question."

"Sure," her mom said. "What is it?"

"Why did Bernadette do what she did?"

Jennifer and Jarod exchanged a glance. Jarod said, "None of us know that exactly, but I think it's something we should talk about later."

"Okay," Annie said. "She was nice to me and she had a nice house, but—"

"But what?" Jennifer said.

"It didn't feel happy, like a happy place. It didn't feel like our house. I think she was a sad lady."

"Is there a reason you think that she was sad?" Jarod asked her.

"The graves," Annie replied. "I saw three graves on a hill, from the window of the room I was in. Then I saw pictures in her office—a little girl and two men. One was on a horse and one had black hair, like you, Daddy. I think they were the people in the graves."

"Well, maybe there were reasons for her to be sad," Jarod said.

Annie nodded. "I saw her when she died," she said, almost whispering.

Jennifer took her hand. "Oh, honey, I'm sorry you had to see that." She leaned down and kissed her daughter's forehead.

Annie nodded again. "She shot a gun at a man, but the man shot her, too, and she fell. Grandpa William and me, we tried to help her. But she died." She reached up and wiped away tears.

"We're proud of you, honey," Jennifer said, stroking her face. "We're proud of you for trying to help her, and for being so very brave."

"Like Grandpa William and Grandpa Hal," she said.

"Yes, they are brave," Jennifer said. "And we're all so lucky you have grandpas that love you so much."

"I knew they would come," she said.

FORTY-SIX

After a leisurely breakfast, Virginia and Marie took their husbands to a clinic where Jarod had made an appointment. Fortunately, the waiting area was deserted but the physician who examined and treated them was obviously suspicious of the explanation of "a hunting accident" for the injuries. The situation was exacerbated by the doctor's limited English-speaking ability, though thankfully a nurse was able to translate. In the end he did not need to stitch William's shoulder and gave each patient antibiotics.

Back at the hotel Hal had a question. "How hard would it be for us to contact the American Embassy, wherever there's one?"

"Shouldn't be too difficult," Jarod guessed. "Why do you ask?"

"Well, that doctor's attitude bothered me a bit," Hal admitted. "I don't think he'll do it, but what if he calls the cops?"

"What does that have to do with the American Embassy?" Virginia wanted to know.

Hal shrugged. "I just think we should tell someone, who's sympathetic. I think we should tell them what happened."

William nodded. "You know, that's a good idea."

"Because…" Marie said.

"Well, we ran up against one of the largest drug cartels in South America, and now their main players are gone. Who knows what kind of safeguards they had in place. And we don't know how many people they employed. It's possible that someone we don't know about saw us or made videos or took photos of us. We might be on somebody's radar and don't know it."

"Good point, Dad," Jarod agreed. "I think we should make hotel reservations in Buenos Aries and go. There has to be an American Embassy there; it's the country's capital. We can get some phone numbers and make some calls, Jennifer and I."

While driving to Buenos Aires, Jarod had a change of heart after a series of frustrating conversations with people answering the U.S. Embassy phones. At a lunch stop he presented an alternate plan.

"We do need to tell someone about Annie's abduction and the events that followed," he said. "But what if someone at the embassy in Buenos Aires decides to turn you over to the Argentine federal authorities?"

"I never thought of that," Hal admitted. "Is that possible?"

"I don't think we should consider it impossible," Jennifer cautioned.

"So, what shall we do?" Virginia asked, concerned.

"Well, I think we should go back on three separate flights," Jarod said to his mother-in-law. "Mom and Dad, you and Hal, and then Annie, Jennifer, and me."

"Why?" Hal asked.

"I don't think anyone has issued an all-points-bulletin for you two," he said to his father and Hal. "And the only people who would do that is someone from Palomino's organization, if they know who took him and Bernadette out. So, if we schedule flights for tomorrow—and we would just be changing our return flights—we'd be okay."

"What about telling the authorities?" Virginia asked.

"We could do that back in the states, probably Sioux Falls or Pierre. I think Dad and Hal could just walk into an FBI office, with an attorney in tow, and tell the story."

Hal nodded emphatically. "That makes the most sense. There's just one thing. You young folks can take care of doing all that booking and rescheduling stuff, but we're all going to upgrade to first class, on our dime," he said, nodding toward Virginia. "It's the least we can do."

"Oh, absolutely," Virginia quickly agreed.

They reserved rooms in an American hotel chain that night and Jennifer and Jarod took care of rescheduling the return flights. Jennifer, Jarod, and Annie would fly at midmorning, Hal and Virginia in the early afternoon, and Marie and William would be on the airline's last flight of the day to Miami in the early evening. They would figure out transportation home from Sioux Falls once they were all there.

Virginia and Hal rode to the airport in the same hotel courtesy van as Jennifer, Annie, and Jarod. William and Marie left the hotel just after checkout. Jennifer and Jarod kept in touch with everyone by text. By five in the afternoon William and Marie were in the international terminal. William didn't breathe a sigh of relief until the airplane lifted off the runway an hour later.

Marie clasped his hand. "How's your shoulder?" she asked.

"Down to a dull ache."

"I think in William-speak that means it's probably throbbing like hell."

He smiled. "This is the first time I've ever flown first class."

"Me, too," she admitted.

"I can think of a few other things we've done the first time together," he said, raising his eyebrows.

She shook her head in mock exasperation. "You know," she said, "I was thinking this morning of that day Hal stormed into Dora's Café, madder than hell."

William chuckled. "Yeah, hard to forget."

"And now he bought us first class seats. A lot has happened in between."

He nodded. "Yeah, something happens to you, to your perspective about life, when you almost get killed."

Marie squeezed his hand. "Is that what happened?"

He nodded. "Yeah. First it was the sniper in the mountains. He almost took us out with one bullet. An inch or two and we wouldn't be having this conversation."

She squeezed his hand. "I'm glad you had Uncle Henry's protection."

"Me, too."

"So, what's going to happen to us now?"

"I don't know," he said. "All I know is I'm glad our little girl is safe. I'm going to savor each sunrise and sunset, and everything in between."

"Why?" Marie asked. "Why did this happen?"

William shook his head, taking a second to recall his moment with Bernadette in the office of the horse barn. "Retribution. Bernadette was avenging her father for what Hal did to him."

"She must have hated Hal, or what he did."

"Both."

"According to Jarod, she had it all planned. What was she going to do, just kill Hal?"

"Yeah. She was going to turn him loose in the wilderness, with nothing, and make sure he died out there. Then I turned up, so she dumped us both in the wilds. But what she didn't figure on was the cartel boss finding out. Palomino had a spy in her organization and he sent a man out to kill us."

"So, she abducted Annie to get even with Hal. She had no inkling what she set in motion when she did that."

William nodded. "Hate is powerful. I saw it on her face when she was talking to Hal in her barn. Sometimes I wonder if hate isn't more powerful than love. I guess when it comes down to it, I'm more afraid of hate than guns, knives, and bombs. Everything that Bernadette did was fueled and driven by hate. Except for one thing."

"And what was that?"

"She didn't feel that way about Annie. She cared about Annie."

"Thank goodness for that."

"Well, Annie had her own assessment, and I think she's right. She said Bernadette was 'a sad lady.' She had a lot of losses in her life: her dad and her husband and daughter. Annie said there were three graves on a hill."

Hal was clearly nervous at customs in Miami, especially after the agent took a long look at the scab on his face. After they collected their luggage and made it to the domestic terminal, he finally relaxed. Virginia checked the flight itineraries she had printed out. "The kids are still in the air," she said. "They'll land in Sioux Falls in two hours."

"Good," Hal said. "How about some good coffee? We've got a long layover."

After they found a table in a familiar chain restaurant, he reached across the table and took Virginia's hand. "I lost those Luchese boots you gave me for Christmas," he said. "I'm sorry."

"That's the least of our worries. We'll just get you another pair," she said.

"Ah, that won't be necessary," Hal said quickly. "They're not really made for walking and I'm going to be doing a lot more walking and exercise. My God, I didn't know how out of shape I was til I was scrambling around to save my life and Annie's in that country I hope to never see again."

"You know," Hal said, hanging his head down, "I brought all this down on us."

"I was wondering when guilt would rear its ugly head," Virginia said.

"I put that hate in Bernadette McGiven's eyes and heart."

"Bernadette could have chosen to live her life without blaming you," said Virginia. "Hate is a poison you put out for your enemy that ends up poisoning yourself. It destroys your soul. It's probably a good bet that there were other issues in her life, beyond her father. No one forced her, as far as we know, to become a drug lord."

"Yeah, maybe," he said, raising his eyebrows. "But there's something else that happened while we were over there. If it weren't for her kidnapping Annie, I would have kept on thinking that William Black Spotted Horse was an arrogant son-of-a-bitch who I wanted to punch in the face every time I saw him."

"Really? And now what do you think?"

"He's a good man, capable. Tough, very tough, and smart."

Virginia smiled. "Did you know that William was a hand-to-hand combat instructor in the Army?"

"Oh, shit. No, I didn't know that. How do you know?"

"Marie told me. And his airborne unit in Vietnam was the only one to make a mass combat jump in that war. He was still a teenager when he took part."

Hal nodded. "That explains a lot. After that sniper almost took us out with one shot, William put it into another gear. He didn't panic. I didn't know what the hell was happening. He knew in an instant and saved my life."

"For which I'm grateful."

"Ironic, isn't it? We fought in high school, knock-down drag-out fights. He joins the Army, learns how to fight, and after that he could have kicked my ass anytime, but didn't. And eight days ago he saved my life."

"Says something about his character, I think."

"Yeah, and his whole focus in Argentina was doing whatever it took to get Annie back. He set aside his ego and let me pay for a rental truck and he asked for my opinion on every decision we had to make. He also set aside our political differences. But it's over now, so I don't know what's going to happen."

Virginia checked her watch. "Well, I thought the two of you were going to talk to the FBI. That's going to require that you're in it together or it might not be good. More so for William."

"What do you mean?"

"Look, a lot of people in South Dakota are racists and most FBI agents are white. You can't guarantee me that a white FBI agent is going to be totally objective listening to a brown-skinned man."

"Yeah, I see your point."

"I think we all have to have a talk you, me, William, Marie, Jennifer, and Jarod. We have two important topics—Annie's treatment and whether or not you and William talk to the FBI."

"Right. But let's start with finding a waiter."

FORTY-SEVEN

Good news came as Hal and William sat in a waiting area in the Billings, Montana, lawyer's office waiting room. Annie's white blood cell count was down and Dr. Cline was extremely pleased with her overall condition. Buoyed by that information, they walked confidently into Max Westfield's office when the receptionist ushered them in.

Westfield had agreed to take the meeting on the recommendation of a client who knew Hal from Cold River, South Dakota. A check into his and William Black Spotted Horse's backgrounds raised a question in Westfield's mind. Why were two men who were as different as night and day here together?

Westfield rose from behind an old wooden desk and stepped up to greet them. "Gentlemen, pleased to meet you," he told them. After shaking their hands, he pointed to a corner of the office where four high back leather chairs stood around a coffee table with refreshments. "Please, have a seat."

William noted with some satisfaction that the room was not overly decorated as many prominent lawyers' offices often were. There were only a few photographs on the walls and the obligatory undergrad and law school diplomas. The furniture was tasteful and the desk looked like a 1960s era schoolteacher's desk. Maxwell Westfield himself was just as unpretentious, despite a flamboyant reputation and a 40-plus year career. Among his clients were a few movie stars and U.S. senators. His full head of white hair, piercing blue eyes, and thin frame hinted at a kindly old teacher rather than a nationally known attorney. He was dressed in blue jeans, cowboy boots, and a dark blue flannel shirt.

Westfield noted that his guests were both calm and at ease, but still wondered what a very wealthy white rancher and a Lakota career bureaucrat had in common.

"Gentlemen," he said, "I know you traveled a long way for this meeting and I know you want representation for whatever brought you here, so allow me to open by assuring you that anything that is herein discussed is subject to attorney client privilege, whether I decide to represent you or not, or if you should decide that I am not your choice."

"Thank you," Hal said, nodding and shooting a glance at William. "I've asked William to start off for us."

William nodded and softly cleared his throat. "Mr. Westfield, a few weeks ago our granddaughter Annie was kidnapped and taken to Argentina by her abductor, who threatened physical harm or worse if we contacted law enforcement authorities. Our families decided to take that threat seriously. While we did not contact law enforcement, Hal and I—with our families' blessing—traveled to Argentina in an attempt to recover our granddaughter. We were successful, we're happy to report, but certain events occurred in the process, and that is why we are here."

Westfield nodded. "I see. Please continue."

Twenty-three minutes later, Westfield leaned forward, poured a glass of water, and looked thoughtfully at each man.

"Gentlemen," he said, "I do not for a second doubt the veracity of your story. And I'm sure you heard the same news on CNN that I did yesterday about the mysterious deaths of the top two people in the Black River Cartel, the second biggest South American drug cartel. Officials are speculating that those two people, whom they didn't identify, died hours and 100 miles apart. Your story has been corroborated." After a pause and another sip of water, he looked again to his guests. "I take it, however, that it is not in your plans to turn yourself in to Argentine authorities."

Both men shook their heads. "No," Hal replied. "Not if we can avoid it."

"Indeed. How can I help?"

"Advice," William replied, "and hopefully we won't need you for anything beyond that. Our question is this: do you think we should speak to the FBI?"

"Off the top of my head, my answer is 'no,'" Westfield said. "The United States does have an extradition treaty with Argentina, however, given who and what you were involved with, I doubt if Argentine law enforcement's primary objective will be to solve the murder of two reprehensible individuals engaged in an activity that is one of the great scourges against humanity. I'm guessing their primary focus will be to use this opportunity to put the Black River Cartel out of business permanently."

"Okay, I'm happy to hear that," Hal said. "So, what should we do?"

"Well, we'll take the information you provided and transcribe it and then make it a sealed file, accessible only to me," Westfield asserted. "From what you've indicated, it would seem that only a few people connected to Black River could identify you: the man named Deke Smith and the four security guards at Palomino's estate. I doubt they would have anything to gain by identifying you. Besides, I'm sure they've gone deep underground by now.

"If, on the off chance, this situation does lead to your doorstep, we'll then talk to the FBI. To mitigate that if it happens, we—my investigators, with your permission—will launch our own investigation with the intent to compile information to support your facts."

"Thank you," Hal and William said in unison.

"Therefore, if you don't mind, I have some follow-up questions, mainly about the man Smith and Bernadette's mother."

After the meeting, the men stopped for lunch at a steak house recommended by Westfield in downtown Billings. "I agree with Westfield," Hal said. "I don't think we have to worry about Smith. As Bernadette's right-hand man and a mole for Palomino, I'm sure he has plenty of enemies. I'm guessing he left the country and is hiding out somewhere and jumping at shadows."

"I'm inclined to agree, but I also know that Deke Smith will do anything to save his own skin."

"Does that worry you?"

William sighed. "Not really, just a thought. But I am wondering how much Mary Lee Cronin really knows about her daughter."

"Well, I'm sure Westfield's investigators will talk to her," Hal surmised. "But Virginia and I were talking about her a couple days ago. Virginia wants to talk to her."

"Virginia wants to talk to Mary Lee Cronin?"

"Yeah. Damn adamant about it, as a matter of fact. She wants us to make things right with her."

"I see. How do you feel about that if you don't mind me asking?"

Hal nodded. "She's got a point, I think. After all, as Virginia pointed out, McGiven didn't actually steal any money."

William was surprised that Hal didn't seem to object to his wife's thinking, although he did have a concern. "I have a thought," he said. "Maybe you should let Westfield know your intentions."

"Right. I'll give him a call." Hal reached for his cell phone. "Maybe right now."

A minute later he was surprised when Westfield actually answered his own phone. After he briefly explained the plan regarding Mary Lee Cronin, Hal listened, nodding occasionally, and ended the call with a "Thank you."

With a sigh he glanced at William. "Well," he said, with a sigh of resignation. "I guess Virginia will have her chance. Westfield says he'll hold off his people until after we talk to Mary Lee."

William nodded, concentrating on finishing his buffalo steak.

Hal put away his phone and did the same. After a few bites he wiped his mouth with a napkin and set aside his silverware.

"There's something that's been bothering me," he said hoarsely. After a sip from his water glass and a quick glance out a window, he leaned his elbows on the table.

"Andujar?" William ventured.

"Yeah. When I talked about it this morning, a lot of stuff came up in my head."

"Guilt?"

"Big time. Virginia has been asking me what happened. I haven't told her everything and I sure haven't told her about Andujar. I can't help but think about that. All I see is his head in the crosshairs of the scope before I pulled the trigger." He paused and stared at his half empty water glass. "I never killed a man before this." He looked across the table, his expression pleading. "What do I do?"

"There's no good answer, Hal. But there is one thing: don't deny it. It happened and it will always be with you. I know society says it's wrong to kill another human being in any circumstance, but I have a different slant on that."

"What do you mean?"

"Well, look at it this way. If you were to walk down Main Street at home with a gun in your hand and blow away the first person you saw, just because you have a gun in your hand, that is totally wrong in every way. As far as I'm concerned, Hal, we humans don't have any more right to life than any other living thing. That's one thing. The other is to consider the circumstances. If you hadn't pulled the trigger, Andujar might have shot Annie, or me, or maybe both of us, and you would be feeling guilty about that."

Hal dropped his eyes to the glass again and stared. "So, let me ask you this. What did you do after Vietnam?"

"I tried denial and that does not work. And when the bad dreams and dead faces almost pushed me into the whiskey glass, I got counseling—two years of it. And, of course, I had Marie in my corner. You have Virginia, so don't ignore that. You're afraid she'll think less of you if you tell her everything that happened. Let me tell you something, Hal. Women are tougher than we are. Give your wife a chance to help you."

Hal pursed his lips. "Yeah, well, I'm not the smartest man in the world, but I do know this; everything comes at a price. And if the bad shit in my head is the price for Annie being home safe, I'll gladly pay it."

William nodded. "It's our job to take care of our families, to protect them. That's what we did, Hal. On one end of the spectrum, it might be just driving Annie to school, and on the other end, it's taking her back from bad people who took her. That's our job, and we did it. We didn't go waltzing into Patagonia and say, 'let's hurt some people for the hell of it.' And remember, they started it. Bernadette wanted us to die in those mountains, and so did Palomino."

Hal nodded again. "Yeah, I know. You're right."

"Won't make the bad memories and images go away, so all we can do is keep things in perspective. *Bernadette* attacked us. *She* abducted Annie. *We* did what we had to."

Forty minutes later they lifted off from the airport in the twin engine Cessna Sky Courier Hal had chartered from Pierre. Three hours later they headed home from Pierre in separate vehicles, each man wrestling with the thoughts and images bombarding them.

Among the thoughts for William were a few regarding Deke Smith. He wondered if it had been wise to let him go free.

FORTY-EIGHT

As he followed Marie into Hal's den, William noticed that the mounted game animal heads were gone, as were all the photographs of Hal posing with his kills. The walls were bare. Virginia and Jarod were already in the room

Hal pointed at the leather sofa and motioned for Jarod to sit there with his mother and mother-in-law. He and William pulled two small leather armchairs closer to the long coffee table in front of the sofa. Coffee, tea, water, and snacks were laid out on the table. The two men had decided on the charter flight back from Billings that they needed to tell their families together everything that had transpired in Argentina, sooner rather than later. Annie and Jennifer were in the entertainment room on the other end of the house, well out of earshot. Jarod would relay the information to his wife. The last person to join them was Sheriff Mel Triplett.

After Virginia graciously made sure everyone had refreshments, Hal began. "Will and I are glad you all agreed to this, because we only want to do it once."

"It's not an easy story to tell, parts of it anyway," said William glancing at his wife, son, and Virginia. "The good thing is you know the story up to the point that Hal and I met in Buenos Aires. For Sheriff Triplett, most of this is new."

Mel Triplett leaned back in his chair, hands folded over his chest.

An hour later, Marie and Virginia were dabbing at their eyes, not so much because of the details of the story their husbands told, but because they saw how difficult it was for them to describe some of the things that had occurred.

Jarod had seen the same kind of difficulty for several of his fellow Iraq combat veterans. He knew his father was not new to the experience, but he also knew that old wounds could be reopened. It was apparent that for his father-in-law, it was still a shock.

After several moments, Virginia ventured a question. "So, you will follow Mr. Westfield's recommendation and not talk to the FBI?"

"Right," Hal affirmed. "He was confident that any investigation that Argentine authorities conducted would not go beyond their borders. Is that your feeling as well, Will?"

William nodded. "It is. Just before we left his office, he told us that his general notes of our meeting were date stamped and notarized. That way, if there is any inquiry, the date of our statement is on record. That way if someone comes asking, our response won't be a knee jerk reaction."

Triplett finally offered a comment. "I think your attorney is right. I don't think anyone from the Argentine police or that drug cartel will come here looking for you."

Virginia sighed deeply. "I know I speak for all of us," she said, glancing at both men, "when I say I am so thankful both of you and Annie are home and safe. I'm so, so sorry that you had to do these difficult things. And I, for one, will always admire both of you for that. If I haven't said it already, thank you."

"Amen to that," Marie said.

"Absolutely," Jarod followed up, his voice full of emotion. "Jennifer and I will never be able to thank you enough or repay you for what you did."

"Oh, I don't know," William said, glancing at Hal for a second, "I won't ever turn down a 'Thank you' and a hug, but repayment isn't necessary. There are a couple of things you could do for us, however. One is never ever take family for granted, and the other is that we all do our part to take care of that precious little girl of ours."

"Works for me," Hal agreed.

Mel Triplett cleared his throat and rose to his feet. "Folks, I really appreciate you including me." He turned to Hal and William who had stood as well. "The two of you, you did the right thing, as it turned out. Now do whatever it is necessary to take care of yourselves." He reached out to shake their hands.

When Hal returned to the den after walking the sheriff to the front door, Marie decided to broach a sensitive topic that was on her mind. "Virginia and Hal," she said, "there's something I'd like to bring up, and you can take it or leave it."

"What is it?" Virginia said.

"Counseling," Marie replied. "Over forty some years ago it's what helped William immensely and saved our marriage. I insisted that Jarod do it as well. There is a tragic reality I read about, an article that talked about the untold numbers of World War I, World War II, Korean, and Vietnam veterans who fell into alcohol and drug abuse, or worse, because they didn't talk about their trauma. In the 1940s and 50s, the prevailing attitude among family and caregivers was to advise vets to 'suck it up,' to bury it. That was also the mindset of many vets and it failed miserably. And we can't forget about Annie. I'm sure she'll need counseling as well."

Virginia and Hal both nodded.

"Thank you," Jarod said. "We all should enjoy the gift of going on with our lives, and for Annie being back in our lives." He looked thoughtfully at his father and Hal. "Our lives are almost back to being the same, but there are also different circumstances because of what the two of you and Annie went through. I say we take those variables into account, adjust or mitigate where we can, and go on."

Hal smiled at his son-in-law and nodded. "Wise words," he said. "Adjust and mitigate. Well, Virginia and I are about to do that. We decided to go to North Dakota to meet with Mary Lee Cronin, if she'll talk to me."

"When?" Marie asked.

"As soon as we can be sure that she still lives in that small town. Garrison, I think," Hal said.

"We can ask Mel Triplett or Chief Avery to verify that," William suggested. "Maybe Avery because he has contacts with the BIA police on the Fort Berthold Reservation. They found Mary Lee."

Hal nodded. "Right, and that's where the nearest airstrip is. I don't relish the thought of driving six to eight hours one way."

When Jarod described the meeting to Jennifer, she said "I know these kind of things happen; that people are capable of abducting children and hurting other people. But I've led a sheltered life. I thought that small town America was far removed from most of humankind's ills. I was wrong. I can't imagine what our fathers are going through. I know you know, but I don't."

Jarod glanced in the direction of the closed door to Annie's room. They had waited until she had gone to sleep. "I debated with myself about not telling you everything," he said, "but you have just as much right to know."

She raised an eyebrow. "I'm glad you did tell me everything," she said. "It could have been worse, much worse and I shudder to think what that would have been like. She's back with us now, but she and her grandpas paid a price. And for what? Because Bernadette McGiven wanted to punish my dad for something that happened 20-some years ago?"

"Well, I know one thing. I think your dad is feeling guilty about that. He and your mom are going to North Dakota to see Mary Lee Cronin. Do you remember her?"

"Yeah, vaguely. She worked at the school, a teacher, I think."

"What about Bernadette's little brother who was sick? Do you remember that?"

"Not really. I think there were two boys, but I'm not sure."

"So, whatever it was that Bernadette was taking issue with, you don't remember that either?"

Jennifer thought for a few seconds and then shook her head. "I don't remember," she said. "But apparently it was something deadly serious to Bernadette. I do sort of remember her. She came to work with her dad now and then."

"I guess your dad dissolving the partnership with Hollister McGiven was enough for her to plot revenge."

"Revenge that meant inflicting pain and death," Jennifer said. "Her actions forced our dads to do some really, really difficult things. I wouldn't have, in a million years, thought that they would be that strong."

Jarod sighed. "My dad told me something after he couldn't talk me out of joining the army. He told me about the Shadow Man."

"The Shadow Man?"

"Yeah. There's a part of each of us that is capable of doing dark deeds when the need arises. When our Lakota warrior ancestors prepared for battle, they would paint their faces and bodies to bring out that shadowy part of themselves, that part that was capable of unyielding strength. And when the battle was done, the trick was to put the Shadow Man away. It was that part of him that helped my dad in Vietnam, and it helped me, too, in Iraq. And it helped them—my dad and yours—to do what they had to in order to rescue Annie."

"I will always be grateful to my dad and yours because of what they did," Jennifer vowed, "and I refuse to ever think less of them for what they had to do. Human beings have done far worse for far less justification."

They heard the sound of tires crunching on their driveway. "It's probably Dad," Jennifer said as she stood to answer the door.

"Come in, Dad," she said, hugging him warmly and bringing him to join them at their kitchen table.

"Thanks," he said, "I know it's late."

"It's okay, Dad. So, you and Mom are going to North Dakota?"

"Yeah. Maybe it's a fool's errand, but I have to try."

"Try what, Dad?"

Hal gazed lovingly at his daughter and then glanced at his son-in-law. "To apologize," he said, "starting now."

"What do you mean?"

"The first person I want to apologize to is your husband, my son-in-law."

It was Jarod's turn to be puzzled. "For what?"

Hal chuckled. "Take your pick. My attitude toward you, or how I treated you. But especially for something I said to your dad, the day after Annie was taken."

Jarod was still puzzled. "What did you say?"

"I told your dad you were a coward, and he knocked me on my ass. I'm sorry I said that because you're not a coward. Anyone who spends a year in a combat zone getting shot at is not a coward. And anyone who faced all the shit I dished out while you were courting my daughter is no coward." Hal reached a hand across the table.

Jarod nodded, obviously touched by the gesture, and grasped his father-in-law's hand. "Apology accepted," he said.

"Thank you," Hal said, nodding.

"Thank you, Daddy," Jennifer whispered, wiping her eyes.

Hal nodded, his eyes brimming too. "Now," he said, "Mom will be here in a few minutes to pick me up. I'm leaving my truck with you. I know you have your old sedan while you're waiting for your SUV to be repaired, but Mom and I thought you would be more comfortable in the truck for your trip to Sioux Falls for Annie's appointment."

"Oh, thanks, Dad," Jennifer said.

"You're welcome to use it as long as you need to. We're driving to Pierre in the morning and chartering a plane from there. Hard telling when we'll be home."

Jarod turned to Jennifer after Hal left and said, "I knew there was another side to your dad, a softer side. I saw it each time he was around Annie, or you. Same for my dad, too. They sat together earlier today and told us what happened in Patagonia with no anger and resentment between them."

Jennifer walked over to embrace her husband. "They shared something out of the ordinary, to say the least. I may be selfish, but I hope all they went through will move the powers that be—whoever and whatever they may be—to heal their granddaughter. In a perfect world, that kind of sacrifice should mean something."

Four miles from home Hal's phone buzzed. "It's Henry Brinkman," he said to Virginia, "with the Northern Plains Cattlemen's Association."

"Good evening, Hal. How ya doing?"

"I'm good, Henry. How 'bout you?"

"Oh, can't complain," rasped the old rancher from Gillette, Wyoming. "I'm calling about the upcoming testimony in D.C., about that darn reparations bill for Indian lands."

"What about it?"

"I'm lining up who's going. You said earlier that you'd like to be part of it, so I was thinkin' that you could give our testimony to that senate committee. Jerome Kleiber and a couple others suggested you to do that."

Hal glanced at Virginia. "Well, Henry, I guess now's a good a time as any to tell you. I won't be making the trip."

"Sorry to hear that. Any particular reason?"

Hal looked out the passenger window at the stars in the night sky. "To be honest, Henry, my heart's just not in it."

"Really? Ah, that's kind of a sudden about face, my friend."

"Yeah, yeah, it is. I've been thinking about it for a couple of weeks, and while I'm at it, I'm going to withdraw my membership in the Association. I'll give Esther Krelling a call, since she's the treasurer, but if you would alert her that I'll be wanting my membership dues refunded."

"Damn, Hal. I can't believe what I'm hearing. Are you sure about this? I mean, you're one of our most prominent members. What's going on, Hal?"

"Well, you've been a good friend, Henry, and I appreciate that, but things change. You know? Just time for a change, to get to know my family better. That's where I'm at."

After a momentary silence, Brinkman spoke again. "Damn, Hal. Maybe I'll come on down and we'll talk about it over a steak dinner."

"You could, Henry, and I would enjoy the dinner and talking, but it won't change my mind."

"I still consider you a friend, Hal. I'll see you down the road somewhere."

"Right, and you can make good on that steak dinner."

"I'm proud of you, dear," Virginia said, softly.

Hal nodded and rubbed the new scar on his left cheek. The scab was gone and in its place was a three-inch long, shallow, quarter inch wide pale red gouge. It itched now and then and each time it reminded him of the moment he felt the bullet burn into his face.

"Thanks," he said. "I hope you can say that when the sun sets tomorrow. I don't know how this thing with Mary Lee will turn out."

"However it does, I'm proud of you for trying."

FORTY-NINE

At about the time the small twin-engine Beechcraft touched down at the Garrison, North Dakota, airstrip with Virginia and Hal in it, Dr. Dennis Cline returned to his office in the Kramer Medical Building in Sioux Falls and smiled at the three people who were waiting for him—Annie Black Spotted Horse and her parents, Jennifer and Jarod. He was amazed at how much the 12-year-old was a perfect cross between her Lakota father and her mother, who was of Swedish and Norwegian descent. Annie's hair was auburn instead of blond and her eyes hazel instead of blue, and her facial structure and build were definitely from her father.

He smiled to ease the anxiety he saw in the parents' eyes. "I saw some of the preliminary results," he told them, "especially the white blood cell count, and it's very encouraging. The count has gone down, and that is great."

"Oh, thank you, Doctor," Jennifer said.

"Don't thank me, thank Annie. Her immune system is strong." He looked directly at the girl. "And you look so good, especially your color, and all your basic vitals are normal. Whatever you're doing, keep it up."

Annie nodded, smiling.

"I know what is likely contributing to her well-being," Jennifer said, tentatively.

"Oh?"

"Yes, we went to a traditional healer."

Dr. Cline paused, his hands over the keyboard of his desktop computer. "A traditional healer?"

"Yes, a medicine man, and he gave us dried herbs to make into a tea, and Annie's been drinking two cups a day for over a week now."

Dr. Cline nodded, turned and entered his password into the computer, and then swiveled his chair to look at Annie. "Seems like you have a lot of people in your corner," he said. He looked up at Jennifer and then Jarod. "Did the medicine man say how long Annie was to drink the tea?"

"Three new moons, three months," Jarod said, cautiously.

"Good," the doctor said, nodding. "I will arrange another appointment in two weeks, and we'll run more tests. If the drop in white blood cell count continues, then we'll rethink our course of treatment. And when the final results of today's tests come back, I'll email them to you." He leaned toward Annie. "In the meantime, good healthy foods, nothing fried, no sugar or sodas, plenty of water, and lots of good rest and exercise."

Annie nodded again.

"Of course," Jennifer replied.

"Good. Well, I'll see you all in two weeks."

Jennifer texted her mother the good news half an hour later after they sat down to lunch. Jarod looked at his watch. "Your folks are probably about to land in Garrison," he guessed.

Jennifer nodded her agreement. "You know, I was frankly surprised at Dr. Cline's reaction to the news of the medicinal tea. Doctors usually frown on traditional Native medicine."

"Me, too," Jarod admitted. "We've been through a rough patch, to say the least, but somehow I think circumstances have turned in our favor." He smiled at Annie. "And, since I don't have to go play soldier this summer, maybe we can go camping again, before I have to go back to work."

Annie nodded, smiling broadly. "And can we put up the *tipi* this time?"

Jarod nodded. "I think so. I'm sure your Grandpa Hal will let us use his truck, that way we can haul the lodge poles."

Sergeant NoHand Hillenbrand was waiting at the only building at the end of the airstrip as the twin-engine Beechcraft taxied to the end of the asphalt tarmac and cut its engines. His captain had acquiesced to the Smokey River tribal police chief's request for a favor. Hillenbrand was to be an escort for a couple—Harold and Virginia Lamar. He guessed they wouldn't be Native, and he was right. In fact, they were quite the opposite. Mr. Lamar was tall and dressed in western cowboy clothes and Mrs. Lamar was a petite blond in a light green dress. Hillenbrand stepped from his unmarked police SUV and walked to meet them. He opted to dress in civilian clothes, given the circumstances. "Good afternoon," he said. "I'm Sergeant Hillenbrand, your ride."

"Thank you," Hal said, extending his hand. "Very kind of you to do this for us. I'm Hal, this is my wife, Virginia."

Hillenbrand took them to the northwest part of town and parked on the street in front of a small frame house. A midsize blue sedan was in the driveway next to the house.

"Mary Lee is expecting you," Hillenbrand told the Lamars. "I stopped by about an hour ago." He handed his card to Hal. "My cell phone number. Call me when you're finished."

Hillenbrand waited until he saw the door open and the couple stepped through into the house before he drove away, heading for the only restaurant in town.

Mary Lee Cronin opened the door and pointed toward the sofa at one end of the small living room. "Please," she said, a bit timidly, "have a seat."

After they sat, she offered coffee or water.

"I think water for me," Virginia replied, smiling politely at the thin, white-haired woman dressed in a simple, light blue dress. Despite the wariness in her blue eyes, she was still lovely.

Hal nodded.

Mary Lee returned with three glasses with ice and three bottles of water.

"Thank you," Virginia said, pouring for herself. "And thank you for seeing us."

Mary Lee nodded as she took a seat. Her glances at the couple were quick and furtive. "Truthfully, I wasn't sure what to do when Mr. Hillenbrand stopped by. But you did come a long way, so… What is it you want?"

"Actually, I, don't know where to start," Hal said nervously. "I'm here to apologize, and—well, that's what I'm doing, apologizing for what I did, for ending the partnership with Hollister. I shouldn't have done that, and I know what it did to your family. I'm sorry."

Virginia reached and grabbed her husband's hand.

"That was a long time ago," Mary Lee said, "almost 25 years. Why now? Why are you here now, after all this time? Hollister died, did you know that?"

Hal nodded. "I know."

"I had to divorce him. He wouldn't stop drinking and when he left, Bernadette went with him. And right after that her brother Gary joined the Navy, and he's been gone, too."

Virginia looked over at Mary Lee. "So, you've been alone since then?"

"Well, Gary came home a couple of times, but, yeah, I've been alone, except when I was working. I taught school until I retired last year." She paused and looked at her hands, her glance lifting briefly again to Hal. "So, I still want to know—why now?"

"Because it took me this long to realize that what I did was wrong, and because something happened recently where I learned what happened to Hollister."

"Really? How?"

"From your daughter, Bernadette," Hal said.

Mary Lee opened the bottle and poured water into her glass, her hand shaking slightly. "What about her?"

"There's some bad news, I'm afraid."

"She's dead," Mary Lee said, almost in a whisper.

Hal was surprised. "How did you know?"

"How do you know, Hal?" Mary Lee asked. "How do you know Bernadette is dead?"

Hal sighed. "Because I was there when it happened, when she died."

"How did she die?"

"She was shot."

For the first time since the couple walked into her house, Mary Lee looked directly into Hal's eyes. "Was that in Argentina?"

It was Hal's turn to be confused. "Yeah, it was. But how do you know?"

Mary Lee's eyes lingered on Hal's face before she turned to look toward a door at the end of the living room.

"Gary," she called out. "Come in here."

A man walked into the room. Hal gasped when he recognized the face—it was Deke Smith.

FIFTY

Hal jumped to his feet, which stopped the man in his tracks. Except for a fresh buzzed haircut and different clothes, Hal was looking at Deke Smith, or according to Mary Lee Cronin, Gary McGiven—younger brother of Bernadette.

Virginia leaned forward to look at the man. He was young, and obviously afraid of Hal.

"I'm not here to cause trouble," McGiven said carefully. "I came home to see my mother."

Hal stared at the man for a second before he turned to Mary Lee. "So, he told you what happened in Argentina?" he asked.

Mary Lee nodded.

"He wasn't there when Bernadette was shot," he said.

"So, if you don't mind, maybe you can tell me."

Hal looked back at Gary, or Deke. "I'd feel better if you'd sit down, and I have to ask, are you armed, are you carrying a gun?"

McGiven shook his head. "No. You can search me if you want. Like I said, I'm not here to cause trouble. I'm in enough trouble as it is."

"Not with me," Hal said.

"I didn't mean that. I'm a deserter from the U.S. Navy."

"Still in all, I would feel better if you sat down there," Hal said, pointing to a chair.

McGiven nodded and sat. "I told Mom that you and William let me go and that you didn't have to do that. You had every right to get even if you wanted."

Hal sighed and sat down. "Well, you did help us, and now I'm guessing it was because you were trying to save your sister."

McGiven nodded and glanced at his mother. "Yeah."

"Hal," Mary Lee said. "Bernadette and I parted ways a long time ago. She chose to go with her father. But she was my daughter and I would like to know what happened at the end."

Hal nodded. "Of course."

For the second time in two days Hal Lamar described the showdown between Andujar and Bernadette. "I'm sorry we had to leave her there. We didn't know who else might be after us. We wanted to get our granddaughter to a safe place."

Mary Lee Cronin pulled a handkerchief out of a pocket in her dress and wiped her eyes.

After a moment of awkward silence, Hal turned to McGiven. "Listen, there's something I have to know," he said. "Is it possible that someone from Palomino's cartel will be coming after William and me?"

McGiven shook his head. "I doubt it. Palomino was plotting for years to get rid of Bernadette, looking for ways so it couldn't be connected to him. When she took your granddaughter, it gave him the excuse he needed. He wanted total control and he picked people, all men, who were blindly loyal but not too smart. My sister was smart, so he was afraid of her. What I'm saying is there is no one in the cartel who knows what to do. I sure as hell don't think they know about you and William. Besides, Black River is done, the *federalis* are moving in and tearing it apart."

"How did Schrader figure in? Why was he after us?"

McGiven cleared his throat "His job was to eliminate you so Palomino could backtrack you and remove all traces that you were ever in country. Get rid of all the loose ends."

"Including you?"

McGiven nodded grimly. "Yeah, including me."

"So how did you get out?"

"I always had a contingency plan. Had money and passports and stuff stashed away. After my sister was in Spain for a while, I was going to join her. But all that went to hell, so I decided to come home." McGiven looked at his mother. "We're all we got. Maybe we can be a family again."

"What happened after you left Sangria?"

"I went back and recovered my sister's body. I took her to Santa Rosa and buried her next to her family: her husband, her daughter, and Dad."

"You took a hell of chance doing that."

McGiven shrugged. "I couldn't save her, so it was the least I could do."

"What about the Navy?"

"Well, I'm going to turn myself in and hope they go easy on me. I don't think they want me back, so maybe a dishonorable discharge. I went AWOL in Brazil years ago. I know that's nothing to be proud of, but right now, a dishonorable, rather than years in the brig, looks awful good to me. Especially because I could be dead."

Hal turned his attention to Mary Lee. "Well, I guess the last thing on your mind is my need for forgiveness. You've got a lot on your plate, so Virginia and I will get out of your hair."

Mary Lee stood. "It took a lot for you to come here," she said. "Thanks for saving Gary's life."

"Oh, I think he did that for himself."

McGiven stood. "No, I owe you and William. By the way, I never caught his last name."

"Black Spotted Horse."

"Cool name for a bad ass dude. You both are."

Hal allowed himself a smile. "I've never been called that before. And, oh, this is my wife, Virginia."

McGiven stepped forward and reached out a hand. "Pleased to meet you, ma'am."

"Likewise. You take care of your mom."

"Yes, ma'am."

Five minutes later they were on the curb waiting for Sergeant Hillenbrand. "That man showing up was the last thing you expected, wasn't it?"

"That's an understatement."

"How do you feel about him now?"

"I don't know. I don't think I'll ever trust him, but I don't have to live with him. And, as he said, they're still family, or can be."

Virginia put an arm around her husband's waist. "Family is where it's at. In any case, Mr. 'Bad Ass Dude,' I'm hungry. I'm sure there's a restaurant in town."

"I'm sure there is. Heard from the kids?"

"Don't know, let me check. I shut my phone off."

"Hey, listen to this," she said. "Waiting to hear from Dr. Cline on Annie's final test results, but the important news is her white cell count is down. Dr. Cline was very pleased. We're heading to the mall.'"

"Outstanding. That calls for a celebration."

"I'll settle for lunch."

Sergeant Hillenbrand accepted the invitation they offered him for lunch.

"May I ask you a question, Sergeant?" Virginia said.

"Of course."

"A personal question, actually."

"Sure."

"Are you Native?"

Hillenbrand smiled. "Yes, ma'am. My mother is Hidatsa and my father is German. Well, was, he passed a few years ago."

"Our granddaughter is half Lakota and half Swedish/Norwegian. She resembles both her parents."

"Well, I've been told I resemble my mom more."

"We appreciate you taking time to help us," she said.

"My pleasure."

"What is your job when you're not driving crazy white folks around?" Hal asked.

"I'm a Special Investigator for the BIA police on the Fort Berthold Reservation. Been a police officer going on 16 years."

"Of course," Hal said. "You located Mary Lee several weeks ago, initially. As far as you know, how long has she lived here?"

"I think over 20 years. She taught school. How do you folks know her if I may ask?"

Hal waited as the server brought their food to the table. "Her husband Hollister and I were business partners years ago," he said, somberly.

Hillenbrand remembered that name. "I see."

"Mr. Hillenbrand, you may find this a bit unusual," Hal said, hesitantly, "but I need to ask a favor of you."

"Well, tell me what it is and I'll see if I can help."

"Thanks. I would like to know Mary Lee's financial situation, not to pry into her personal affairs. My wife and I are concerned about her situation. She told us she retired from teaching, and I'm wondering, well, for example if she owns her house or if she is renting. Does she have health insurance? Those kinds of concerns. I didn't want to embarrass her by asking her directly. Is there any way you can find out for us?"

Hillenbrand gazed thoughtfully at the well-dressed couple. As a cop he depended a lot on his initial reaction to people, that first impression. He liked them, especially Mrs. Lamar, who seemed genuinely kind.

"I'll see what I can do," he said. "I'm guessing this is a right-away issue."

"Right," Hal said. "I can give you my phone number. I'm not much into the email thing."

"Sure. My phone number is on the card I gave you." Hillenbrand reached into his jacket pocket and pulled out a small notebook and a pen and wrote a list. "Financials, health insurance, house," he said as he wrote. "Anything else?

"Let's start with that. If we think of anything else, I'll call you. I know this is way out of your usual duties, so we're more than happy to pay you for your time."

Hillenbrand shook his head. "That's not necessary, since I assume you're buying the lunch," he said, chuckling. "Besides, I like Mary Lee. She's a sweet lady, though she strikes me as having had a tough life."

"You're very observant," Virginia said. "She *has* had a hard life."

"Goes with the territory, for being a cop, I mean."

"One more thing," Hal said. "Mary Lee had three children, a daughter and two sons. Only one son is still alive and he just came home. His name is Gary McGiven. He might pop up when you're checking into things."

"Right. What do we do about him?"

"Nothing, just thought you should know."

An hour later Sergeant NoHand Hillenbrand sat in his SUV and watched the pilot do a visual check of the Beechcraft. Mrs. Lamar waited with her husband while he made a call on his cell phone. Ten minutes later Hillenbrand watched the twin-engine plane lift off from the runway and waited until it was nothing more than a dot in the sky before he drove away. In his line of work he learned that everyone had stories, and most of those stories were on the tough side. But there was a common thread in all the stories—change. Things were always changing, brought on by good as well as bad. Hillenbrand didn't consider himself a wise man, far from it because he was still a young man. But he was an observer, a watcher, and always had been. And the one reality he saw was that there were consequences for how well or how badly people reacted to change.

Be like the river, his Hidatsa mother had said more than once. *The river changes its course when it has to in order to keep flowing. Change doesn't keep it from being a river. Change is what makes it a river.*

FIFTY-ONE

William stepped out the back door onto the covered back deck attached to their house. Marie was with Uncle Henry and Auntie Ollie, reading a text message on her phone. He refilled the coffee cups and set the carafe to the side.

"Good news, I hope," he said.

"It is." Marie looked up smiling. "Annie's white blood cell count is down and Dr. Cline is pleased with her overall physical condition."

"That is good news," William said, taking a seat. "I have a feeling it was the medicine you gave her," he told Henry.

Henry nodded, a smile in his eyes. "*Takoja* (Granddaughter) will be well again. We all prayed for her. You and her other grandfather were willing to sacrifice yourselves. All of that does not go unnoticed by the Spirits. They heard us; they watched what you did."

"In that case, when the time comes, we will have a Thanksgiving ceremony," William said.

"Good!" the medicine man said.

"Anyway, what brings you and Auntie to our house, Uncle?"

"Just felt like visiting," Henry replied, and pointed to the small cloth-wrapped bundle he had laid on the patio table. "And to give you that. It's a poultice for your wound. It will stop the blood from oozing." He nodded toward Marie. "Maybe my niece can put it on for you in the mornings."

"I can do that, Uncle," Marie said. "What do I need to do?"

"Take a small handful, soak it in warm water for a little bit, squeeze out some of the water and then put it over each wound, front and back. Keep it in place for, oh, 20 minutes." Henry turned his gaze briefly toward William. "How's your knee? I see you're still limping."

William nodded. "It's getting better."

"What about what's in your head? What about that?"

William looked off to the south, toward the line of trees and thickets on either side of the river. In the small pasture west of the barn he saw the Spanish Barb stallion standing at the fence. "A few bad dreams," he said.

"Old wounds are sometimes reopened," Henry said. "Some that are not completely healed. That comes with being a *wica*, a warrior."

"Our granddaughter is home where she belongs," William said. "She is safe. Whatever the cost is for that, I'm glad to pay it."

Henry nodded, studying William's face. Then he glanced at Ollie and Marie before he returned his attention to William. "I remember when you left for Vietnam," he said. "Your folks, your family, put on a feast for you because they were so proud of you. You wore a parachute and silver wings on your uniform. You were a sky soldier, shining with confidence. You were only 18, yet you were taking on the world.

"I remember when you came home, skinny and angry and ready to take on the world for a different reason. Your mom came to me, crying because you couldn't sleep at night. I remember what she said to me. 'My son has lost his smile.' She wondered if you would ever smile again. We did a ceremony before you went back to finish your enlistment."

"I'm telling you this because we don't want you to lose your smile again because of what you went through, you and your in-law. I know you're older and wiser now, but sometimes when something happens, we can go back to the times when we were weak, or angry. So, we're going to do a cleansing for you."

"*Wopila, Leksi* (Thank you, Uncle). When?"

"Tomorrow. We'll do the *Inipi* (the rebirth) at sundown and then the cleansing after that. It's good that you left behind the weapons you used. But what you had to do is still clinging to you. We did this for you when you came back from Vietnam. It's the same ceremony. I invited all your relatives. Since your mom and grandma aren't here anymore, your Auntie Ollie will stand in for them. She'll do the cleansing for all the women in your family."

William turned to Ollie. "*Wopila, Tunwin* (Thank you, Auntie)."

"*Tokasni ye, Tunska* (It's alright, Nephew). I helped your mom and grandma all those years ago, so you could get your smile back."

"I remember," William said.

Marie wiped her eyes and stood to hug Ollie and then Henry. "Thank you," she said. "I want to fix some lunch for us. And, Auntie, I'll be glad to help you prepare the meal for tomorrow night."

Ollie nodded, her old eyes twinkling. "Good."

Henry turned to look at William again. "Something else I been wondering about," he said. "How do you feel about your in-law now—Lamar?"

William watched the stallion trot to the end of the fence, yielding to pent up energy, his tail arched and nose high and testing the air. "Well, I don't feel like beating the crap out of him anymore," he said.

"So did he change or did you?"

"Oh, I don't think either of us changed all that much. We're still the same. We just found common ground—our granddaughter. What we thought about each other didn't matter. We didn't say it in so many words, but we both knew there was something more important."

Henry sipped his coffee and nodded slowly. "Now you're back to hating each other?"

William shook his head slowly. "After what we went through, I can't hate Hal Lamar, not anymore. I depended on him, and he depended on me. He saved my life. I don't know if I'm going to have Sunday coffee with him at Dora's, but things are a bit different now."

"Does that mean he's not a racist anymore?"

"I don't know. I saw a side to him I didn't know was there, but that doesn't mean he changed across the board. I haven't. I still don't trust white people as a group, you know, the prejudiced cops and judges, the people who yell racial slurs at our Native athletes when they beat the white teams. So, I'm sure his basic attitudes are the same. He'll probably still glare at the street people in Cold River."

" I'm wondering, *Tunksa*, when you and he were down there trying to save your granddaughter, was he trying to save only her *wasicu* half? Were you trying to save only her *Lakota* half?"

After a moment of mild surprise at what he assumed was teasing, William glanced at Henry. The old man wasn't teasing.

"I can only speak for myself, *Leksi*," he said. "I didn't look at it that way."

"If your in-law felt the same way you did, that means there's hope for all of us," Henry concluded.

"Yeah, I hope so. But there's something I've been thinking about," William sighed. "No one back here, white or Indian, knows what happened, what my family and the Lamars went through, except for Ben Avery,

Clayton Lone Hawk, and Sheriff Triplett. But it's not public knowledge, not that I want anyone to know. It's not that, it's that despite what we went through, what we did, nothing here—on this rez—has changed. Meth, booze, and drugs still have us by the shorthairs. There's still homelessness, still over 80 percent unemployment for Indians, there's still diabetes, racism. There's still Lakota trying to live like whites."

Henry nodded, tossing a probing glance at William. "Well, you didn't go to Argentina to solve the rez's problems. You went looking for your granddaughter, and somehow you learned to stop hating your in-law. So, like I said, if Lamar feels the same way, that's two good results, and maybe there *is* some hope."

William's cell phone buzzed and a quick glance at the screen told him it was Hal. "Hey, Hal. Are you in North Dakota?"

"Yeah, we sure are. We're about to take off back to Pierre. I just wanted to let you in on a bit of a surprise."

"About Mary Lee?"

"You could say that. Bernadette had two younger brothers. The youngest one died when he was still a boy, I think I told you about that. The other brother, Gary, joined the Navy after high school, I guess, and I met him a couple hours ago."

"I see. Was he living with his mother?"

"Well, yes and no. You know him."

"I don't think so. I never met Hollister McGiven or any of his family, at least I don't recall."

"Yeah, you did and just recently, but you know him as Deke Smith."

William was stunned. "I hope you're joking."

"No, I'm afraid not. I'll fill you in more in a day or so. However, the good part of it all was that he is certain no one from the Black River Cartel would be looking for us. Palomino and Bernadette were the two top dogs. And since they're gone there's no one else. Plus, the law is swooping in."

"Still in all, it makes me a bit nervous. He's a bit of a snake. If what you say is true, he turned on his sister."

"Well, the way he explained it, he said he was trying to save her. He was Palomino's mole, but he did it to help her. Palomino didn't know they were related."

William shook his head in astonishment. "That sort of makes sense. Is this something that Max Westfield should know?"

"For sure. I'll call him tomorrow. Did you and Marie get the good news about Annie?"

"We sure did."

"Great. We're about to take off. See you down the road somewhere."

FIFTY-TWO

Two weeks later more good news came regarding Annie. Her white blood cell count had diminished significantly again. William and Marie were reveling in the news when Elijah and Edna White Bear knocked on the front door. The news they brought was astounding and puzzling.

William stared at the cashier's check that had been delivered in person to Elijah only this morning by a realty officer from the Smokey River Bureau of Indian Affairs Agency. It was for $58,000.

"He said it was for the quarter section that my grandpa Amos sold, back in 1928," Elijah told him. "And the guy who wrote that check is your in-law, Harold Lamar."

William nodded. The remitter of the check was indeed Harold Lamar. He looked at Elijah as Marie brought everyone coffee. "*Tahansi* (Cousin), do you know the situation connected to the sale of your grandpa's land?"

"Not really," Elijah admitted.

"Okay. Here's what I know," William said. "Your grandpa did not know his land was sold, not right away. It was done illegally. The Indian Agent at the time allowed the sale and the buyer was Harold Lamar's grandfather, Alfred. When your grandpa found out, it was too late."

Elijah simply shook his head. "Okay. So, what's going on here? Why did your in-law do that?" he said, pointing at the check in William's hand.

"I think I know," William said, "but let me make a call."

Three minutes later, after a conversation with Julie Sacroix at the Smokey River Agency, William's assumption was confirmed. Harold Lamar had insisted on seeing the record of sale regarding Amos White Bear's land. The next day he had returned with the cashier's check and requested that it be delivered to Elijah.

"It's all good, *Tahansi*," William assured Elijah. "Hal Lamar wanted to set things right, according to what he told the BIA realty people." He handed the check back.

"Yeah, okay." Elijah waved the check. "But this is a hell of lot more than the land was worth in 1928."

"Yeah, I think it's what it's worth now. And, you know, maybe Lamar is trying to make up for running into you with his car, back in 1962. Like I said, it's all okay and I know you'll put it to good use. If you want, I'll go to the bank with you."

That same afternoon a few hundred miles to the northwest, Mary Lee Cronin walked into the Prairie State Bank in Garrison, North Dakota and asked to see the loan department manager. She reread the letter in her hand while she waited, still puzzled.

"Hello, Mary Lee. It's really good to see you," Sofia Moorhead said. "Come on in."

Mary Lee unfolded the letter and put it on the loan manager's desk. "Sofia," she said, genuinely mystified, "I don't quite understand what this is about."

Sofia smiled, not bothering to look at the letter she had written to Mary Lee. "It's very simple. The mortgage on your house has been paid off."

"But why, who?"

"Well, the person who paid it off wanted to help you, and to remain anonymous."

Mary Lee nodded. "Well, okay. That's very kind and generous. You obviously know who that person is. Who am I to look a gift horse in the mouth? Can you tell him or her 'Thank you' from me? It seems so inadequate, but if you can do that, I'd really appreciate it."

"I certainly will, Mary Lee. In a few days, you will be getting the deed to your house in the mail."

Mary Lee nodded. "Thank you." After slipping the letter back into her purse, she walked slowly out of the bank.

Earlier that day, she had gotten a call from Gary. After turning himself in to military authorities, Gary had been taken to the Great Lakes Naval Base in Lake County, Illinois. Although he was sentenced to a year in the brig, it was suspended; and three years of good behavior would wipe it off his record. He was coming home.

FIFTY-THREE

William walked into Dora's realizing he was about to eat his own words. The usual Sunday afternoon crowd—if seven people could be called a crowd—were still ensconced at their usual tables. A couple of them nodded at William as he picked one of the smaller tables toward the back. In a moment Dora came with a cup and a coffee carafe.

"Just brewed it," she announced. "Are you alone today?"

"No, someone's joining me," he said.

"Menus?"

"I'll take a slice of apple or peach pie."

Dora and everyone else heard boots on the floor as Hal Lamar walked in, immediately removing his hat and hanging it on the rack next to the door. Then headed straight for William's table.

Dora looked worried, and everyone paused to see what was about to transpire.

"It's okay, Dora," William said.

"Hey, Dora, how are you?" Hal said, pulling out a chair and joining William.

"I'm good," she said, clearly confused. "And you?" Her eyes were drawn to the scar on Hal's left cheek but she looked away quickly.

"Couldn't be better. I'll take some of that," he said, pointing at the coffee. "And maybe whatever pie you got,"

"Okay," Dora said, hesitantly, as she filled William's cup. "We have apple, peach, rhubarb, and chocolate cream today."

"A slice of peach."

"I just dropped Virginia at the kids' place," Hal said to William. "You probably know that the ladies, including Annie, are painting her room."

"Yeah, I was told, politely, that my help was not required," William chuckled. "Far be it from me to contradict that."

"I hear ya. Where's Jarod?"

"National Guard, monthly drills up in Pierre. He'll be back sometime this evening."

Dora returned with their pie and coffee. "Gentlemen," she said, "anything else I can get for you?"

"I think we're good," William said. "Thanks."

Dora smiled and walked away, shaking her head. Glancing back over her shoulder she saw William pouring coffee for Lamar. "Will wonders never cease?" she said to herself.

"I been meaning to tell you," Hal said. "I won't be going to D.C. with the cattlemen's association. You know, for that testimony."

William nodded as he dug into his pie.

"I imagine you'll be going," Hal went on.

"Yeah. I have to."

"Sure, sure. Well, don't take any shit from Senator Grant."

"I won't."

"So, what's on your mind?" Hal asked. "Besides pie."

"Well, before I get to that, I was thinking, this morning, how damn lucky we were for things to turn out the way they did. Anything could have gone to hell on us, at any time. One wrong move here, one minute one way or another."

Hal sipped his coffee and briefly glanced around the room. "Yeah, damn amazing, isn't it? I guess it was just meant to be."

"Yeah, maybe you're right. Anyway, I wanted to thank you for what you did for Elijah White Bear."

Hal stared down into his coffee, memories playing behind his pensive expression. "It just seemed like the thing to do."

"Well, we didn't change the world doing what we did," William observed. "But we did change things for our families. You did the same for Elijah White Bear. Life here is still what it is, for all of us. There are still problems, some of them downright shitty. But things changed a bit for Elijah. Some good, even a little, is better than nothing good."

"Yeah. I guess we take it where we can. The good moments, I mean."

William wiped his mouth with a napkin, suddenly aware that the restaurant was strangely quiet and that everyone was staring at them. He chuckled to himself, mainly to lighten the mood. "Well, before we went to Argentina I had a line on a couple Spanish Barb mares, but I didn't get back to the owner in time, so he sold them."

"Sorry to hear that"

"No, no, it's all right. But the thing is, it will be awhile before I have anything to put in that section. So, it'd be okay if you kept your cows there. I mean, that way you won't have to move them until next spring."

Hal sipped his coffee and nodded. "Yeah, that would help a lot, and we can work out some type of sublease."

William shook his head. "No, no, that's—."

"Yeah, yeah. It's okay. This is business."

"Okay, sure. I'll put it in Annie's college fund."

"Even better!"

They ate in silence for a few seconds, the only noise the clink of their forks on the saucers.

"Yesterday I got a call from Max Westfield," Hal announced. "His investigators dug up a lot of stuff about the Black River Cartel."

"Yeah? Hopefully they're done for."

"The Argentinian police are milking it for all it's worth, making it look like it was their takedown."

William nodded. "That's okay by me."

"Oh, hell, yeah. But you and I will always know the truth." Hal grinned as he refilled their coffee cups. "And the truth is it took a cowboy and an Indian to bring them down."

William raised his cup for a toast. "Damn straight."

EPILOGUE

The appearance of the crow and his family after the hunts did not go unnoticed by the wolves, and they were annoyed. One day the mated pair of the wolf family hid and watched the crow family eating a carcass they had left after an especially long and arduous hunt.

Emerging from a thicket they called out to the crows. Of course the crows were startled, and the younger ones flew away to the safety of a nearby tree. The older male and female stayed to face the wolves.

"Brother Crow," the male wolf said. "I see you are eating well."

"We are, Brother Wolf," the crow replied. "We eat what you leave. We thank you."

"I am glad to hear that," said the wolf. "Since you eat well because we hunt, I have a proposition. A way for you to help us hunt."

"How can we, slow and weak crows, help the greatest hunters among us?" The crow humbled himself.

"You fly. I have seen you high in the sky. From there you can see far across the prairies and the forests."

"That is true," the crow affirmed.

"You are able to see where the deer and elk are hiding," the wolf said.

"Yes, we can."

"Then, perhaps, when you see them you can tell us, and we can find them easier and save our strength for the chase. In that way you can repay us, and we would leave more for you to eat."

And so the bargain was struck. The crows would fly high when they heard the wolves were preparing for the hunt and locate the elk or the deer and tell the wolves where to find their prey. It was an arrangement that served the wolves and the crows well, and one honored generation after generation.

There came a time, sadly, when the creatures of Turtle Island lost the ability to speak each other's languages. But that did not end the bargain struck by the wolves and the crows. They honor it, even to this day.

ABOUT THE AUTHOR

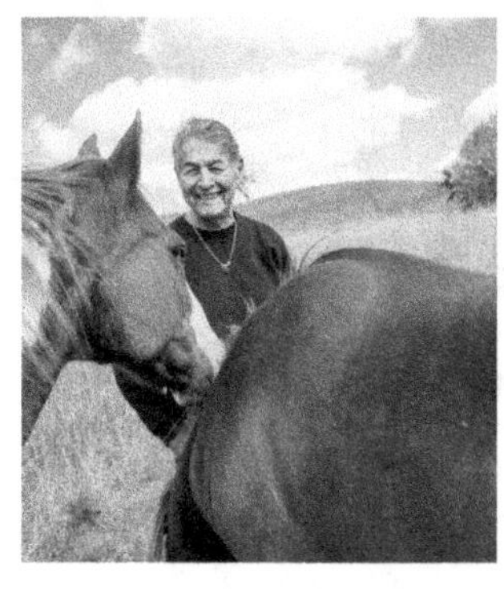

Joseph M. Marshall III

Award-winning Sicangu Oglala Lakota author and historian, Joseph M. Marshall III, PhD, is one of the most prolific Native writers in the United States. Raised by his maternal grandparents in a traditional Native household on the Rosebud Indian Reservation in South Dakota, he has written eighteen historical fiction and nonfiction books and narrated his own audio books. He is best known for award-winners *The Lakota Way*, *The Journey of Crazy Horse*, and *The Day the World Ended at Little Bighorn*. His work is informed by his background as a Lakota craftsman, who makes his own Native Lakota bows and arrows; a skilled archer; and specialist in wilderness survival. The accounts of real historical figures along with the events that he experienced on the reservation and heard as a child from his grandparents and their generation of oral storytellers figure prominently in his books. His Native name, given to him at age five is *Ohitiya Otanin*, which means "his courage is known."

Marshall's accomplishments include co-founding Sinte Gleska University on the Rosebud Reservation; teaching; public speaking; mentoring of indigenous youth; and serving on the Board of Directors of Lakota Youth Development, Inc. He has been a teacher at the high school level and a professor at several colleges and universities, where he taught Native culture, Lakota language and history. He often lectures and speaks on Native issues and topics. In 2022 he received the Crazy Horse Memorial®

Foundation Educator of the Year Award for his lifelong leadership in education and the impact that he continues to make on Indigenous youth and communities.

Marshall has served as a cultural and historical consultant and technical advisor on films, television series and documentaries. He has also appeared as an actor in two television mini-series *Return to Lonesome Dove* and *Into the West* as well in documentaries and film. In 2023, Marshall was inducted into the Western Writers Hall of Fame, and he received the Owen Wister Award by Western Writers of America for lifetime contributions to Western literature. Previous honorees include Pulitzer Prize winners N. Scott Momaday and Louise Erdrich.

Marshall's "Smokey River Suspense Series" represents his first contemporary fiction. His latest novels are based on current issues facing Lakota people, including crime and the interface between tribal government, the Bureau of Indian Affairs, and the FBI, and the ongoing epidemic of Missing and Murdered Indigenous Women that has largely been ignored by the American public and media. After spending many years in Santa Fe, New Mexico, Marshall has once again returned home.

www.ingramcontent.com/pod-product-compliance
Lightning Source LLC
Chambersburg PA
CBHW070232200726
48293CB00005B/1585